RIVER
THIEVES

RIVER THIEVES

Michael Crummey

Houghton Mifflin Company

BOSTON • NEW YORK

2002

For information about permission to reproduce
selections from this book, write to Permissions,
Houghton Mifflin Company, 215 Park Avenue South,
New York, New York 10003.

Visit our Web site: www.houghtonmifflinbooks.com.

Library of Congress Cataloging-in-Publication Data is available.
ISBN 0-618-14531-1

Printed in the United States of America

QUM 10 9 8 7 6 5 4 3 2 1

Various versions of this event have appeared from time to time in our histories and other publications, but as numerous discrepancies characterize these accounts, I prefer to give the story as I had it from the lips of the late John Peyton, J.P. of Twillingate, himself the actual captor of the Beothuk woman.

— James P. Howley,
The Beothuks or Red Indians,
published 1915

Before all of this happened the country was known by different names. The coves and stark headlands, the sprawling stands of spruce so deeply green they are almost black. The mountain alder, the tuckamore and deer moss. The lakes and ponds of the interior as delicately interconnected as the organs of an animal's body, the rivers bleeding from their old wounds along the coast into the sea.

A few have survived in the notebooks and journals of the curious, of the scientifically minded who collated skinny vocabularies in the days before the language died altogether. Annoo-ee *for tree or woods or forest.* Gidyeathuc *for the wind,* Adenishit *for the stars.* Mammasheek *for each of the ten thousand smaller islands that halo the coastline,* Kadimishuite *for the countless narrow tickles that run among them. Each word has the odd shape of the ancient, the curiously disturbing heft of a museum artifact. They are like tools centuries old, hewn for specific functions, some of which can only be guessed at now.* Kewis *to name both the sun and the moon, the full face of pocket watches stolen from European settlers.*

Whashwitt, *bear;* Kosweet, *caribou;* Dogajavick, *fox.* Shabathoobet, *trap. The vocabularies a kind of taxidermy, words that were once muscle and sinew preserved in these single wooden postures. Three hundred nouns, a handful of unconjugated verbs, to kiss, to run, to fall, to kill. At the edge of a story that circles and circles their own death, they stand dumbly pointing.*

Only the land is still there.

The Lake

March month, 1819

The infant woke her crying to be fed and she lay him naked against her breast in the shadowed river-bottom light of early morning. No one else in the shelter stirred and she almost fell back to sleep herself in the stillness. She could smell a clear winter's day in the air, an edge of sunlight and frost cutting the scent of leather and spruce.

A crow called from the trees outside. The gnarled voice of the forest's appetite. She sang crow's song under her breath while her son's mouth tugged at the nipple.

When he was done nursing, she lay the child beside her husband and pulled on her leather cassock, tying the belt at her waist. She stepped to the entrance, pushing aside the caribou covering. Outside, the glare of sunlight off the ice made her eyes ache and she stood still for a moment as she adjusted to the brightness. The cold in her lungs pricking like a thorn. Thickly wooded hills on the far shore, a moon just visible in the pale blue sky above them. The crow called again, the brindled sound in the clear air like a shadow cast on snow.

She had turned and begun walking towards the trees when the stranger's voice carried across the clearing. He was standing on a finger of land behind her, a single figure in a long black coat, one arm raised in the air. A current of blood rushed to her head, the roar of it in her ears, and she screamed a warning then, running for the entrance of the mamateek. Inside she gathered her child in her arms as the others startled up from their berths around the firepit. A tangled maze of shouting and a panic for the light, adults carrying children outside, heading for the forest behind the shelters.

She followed a small group led by her husband, running down onto the ice and making toward a distant point of land. Over her shoulder she saw the one who had called to her and the others who had lain in ambush, eight or ten of them moving on the camp, carrying their long rifles.

The baby had come only three weeks before and the tearing pain below her belly burned into her legs and up the length of her back as she ran. The weight of her son like a beach-rock in her arms. She called to her husband and he came back to take the boy, still she fell further behind them. She heard the voice of the white man she had seen on the finger of land again and when she looked over her shoulder he was nearly upon her. She ran another hundred yards before she fell to the ice and knelt there, choking on the cold air and crying.

She turned without getting to her feet and undid the belt at her waist, lifting the cassock over her head to reveal her breasts. The white man had taken off his long coat to chase her, his hair was the colour of dead grass. He set his rifle on the ice and kicked it away, then the smaller gun as well. The rest of the black-coated men were straggling up behind him. He spoke and came towards her with his hands held away from his body. He was terrified, she could see, although she could not imagine the source of his fear. He slapped his chest and repeated several of his words. She looked over her shoulder a last time to the point where her people had disappeared. She turned back to the man approaching her then and she covered herself and stood to meet him.

This was before her husband came down from the distant point to speak to them, before her face was pressed into the grain of a coat as pliant and coarse as deer moss, before the first muffled gunshot was fired. But even as she spoke her own name and reached to take the white man's proffered hand she knew what was lost to her. Her child and husband. The lake. The last good place.

The white man nodded and smiled and then he turned towards the others of his party as they came up to them on the ice.

Part 1

Hag n cp *OED* ~ 1 c obs (1632, 1696) for sense 1...

1 The nightmare; freq in form **old hag**....1896 *J A Folklore* ix, 222 A man...told me he had been ridden to death by an old hag....1937 *Bk of Nfld* i, 230 Nightmare is called by fishermen the "Old Hag."

— *Dictionary of Newfoundland English*

The Face of a Robber's Horse

1810

have the face of a robber's horse: to be brazen, without shame or pity.

— *Dictionary of Newfoundland English*

O N E

It was the sound of his father's voice that woke John Peyton, a half-strangled shouting across the narrow hall that separated the upstairs bedrooms in the winter house. They had moved over from the summer house near the cod fishing grounds on Burnt Island only two weeks before and it took him a moment to register where he was lying, the bed and the room made strange by the dark and the disorientation of broken sleep. He lay listening to the silence that always followed his father's nightmares, neither of the men shifting in their beds or making any other sound, both pretending they weren't awake.

Peyton turned his head to the window where moonlight made the frost on the pane glow a pale, frigid white. In the morning he was leaving for the backcountry to spend the season on a trapline west of the River Exploits, for the first time running traps without his father. He'd been up half the night with the thought of going out on his own and there was no chance of getting back to sleep now. He was already planning his lines, counting sets in his head, projecting the season's take and its worth on the market. And underneath all of these calculations he was considering how he might approach Cassie when he came back to the house in the spring, borne down with furs like a branch ripe with fruit. A man in his own right finally.

When he heard Cassie up and about downstairs in the kitchen, he pushed himself out of bed and broke the thin layer of ice that had formed over his bathing water and poured the basin full. His head ached from lack of sleep and from his mind having run in circles for hours. When he splashed his face and neck the cold seemed to narrow the blurry pulse of it and he bent at the waist to dip his head directly into the water, keeping it there as long as he could hold his breath.

The kettle was already steaming when he made his way down to the kitchen. Cassie was scorching a panful of breakfast fish, the air dense with the sweet smoky drift of fried capelin. He sat at the table and stared across at her where she leaned over the fire, her face moving in and out of shadow like a leaf turning under sunlight. She didn't look up when he said good morning.

"Get a good breakfast into you today," she said. "You'll need it."

He nodded, but didn't answer her.

She said, "Any sign of John Senior?"

"I heard him moving about," he said, which was a lie, but he didn't want her calling him down just yet. It was the last morning he would see her for months and he wanted a few moments more alone in her company. "Father was on the run again last night," he said. "What do you think makes him so heatable in his sleep like that?"

"*O unseen shame, invisible disgrace!*" Cassie said. She was still staring into the pan of capelin. "*O unfelt sore, crest-wounding, private scar!*"

Some nonsense from her books. "Don't be speaking high-learned to me this time of the day," he said.

She smiled across at him.

He said, "You don't know no more than me, do you."

"It's just the Old Hag, John Peyton. Some things don't bear investigating." She turned from the fire with the pan of capelin, carrying it across to the table. She shouted up at the ceiling for John Senior to come down to his breakfast.

By the second hour of daylight, Peyton was packing the last of his provisions on the sledge outside the winter house while John Senior set about harnessing the dog. He was going to travel with Peyton as far as Ship Cove, a full day's walk into the mouth of the river, but both men were already uncomfortable with the thought of parting company. They were careful not to be caught looking at one another, kept their attention on the details of the job at hand. Peyton stole quick glimpses of his father as he worked over the dog. He was past sixty and grey-haired but there was an air of lumbering vitality to the man, a deliberate granite stubbornness. Lines across the forehead like runnels in a dry riverbed. The closely shaven face looked hard enough to stop an axe. Peyton had heard stories enough from other men on the shore to think his father had earned that look. It made him afraid for himself to dwell on what it was that shook John Senior out of sleep, set him screaming into the dark.

His father said, "Mind you keep your powder dry."

"All right," Peyton said.

"Joseph Reilly's tilt is three or four miles south of your lines."

"I know where Joseph Reilly is."

"You run into trouble, you look in on him."

"All right," he said again. There was still a sharp ache in his head, but it was spare and focused, like a single strand of heated wire running from one temple to the other. It added to the sense of urgency and purpose he felt. He'd come across to Newfoundland ten years before to learn the trades and to run the family enterprise when John Senior was ready to relinquish it. His father electing not to work the trapline this year was the first dim indication of an impending retirement. Peyton said, "I won't be coming out over Christmas."

John Senior had set the dog on her side in the snow and was carefully examining her paws. "January then," he said, without raising his head.

Peyton nodded.

His father took a silver pocket watch from the folds of his greatcoat. He was working in the open air with bare hands and his fingers were bright with blood in the morning chill. "Half eight," he said. "You'd best say your good-byes to Cassie. And don't tarry."

The floor of the kitchen was strewn with damp sand and Cassie was on her knees, scrubbing the boards with a long, hard brush. She had tied her dress in a knot about her thighs. She sat back on her heels when he came in and looked up at him where he stood in the doorway.

Peyton's mouth was dry and his breath stuttered in shallow gasps. The strength of his emotion surprised him. He'd been concealing his feelings for so long he managed to underestimate them himself, and they surfaced so sharply now his chest hurt. He coughed into his fist to try to clear the unex-pected tightness. "We'll be off," he said. He thought Cassie might be able to hear his heart drumming under the layers of his clothing and he folded his arms firmly across his chest.

She raised a forearm to wipe her forehead and cheeks, the brush still in her hand. She said, "Mind yourself out there, John Peyton."

"Don't worry your head," he said and he looked down at his boots, disap-pointed. Even her most soothing, affectionate words had an edge to them, as if she was trying to hold down another's panic. She was like a person lead-ing a skittish horse that could bolt at the least provocation. Something dogged and steady in her, like a hand gripping the bit.

It occurred to him Cassie might not even stand to see him off and the thought of this made the months in the woods ahead of him suddenly repel-lent. She had always been oddly disposed to him, her manner a mixture of aloofness and concern. As if she was waiting for him to prove himself some-how. She was six full years his senior. For the first two years they knew one another she was taller than Peyton, and for several more after he finally surpassed her in height she remained, officially, his tutor. It was taking much longer than he hoped to overcome the distance those things had set between them. His one comfort was the distance she maintained between herself and everyone else around her. There were few women on the northeast shore and every year Cassie received proposals from men who could not spell their own names, who had lived by themselves all their adult lives and spent no more than an hour alone in the company of women since leaving their mothers. It was clear in Peyton's mind that Cassie was saving herself for something that promised more than these men could offer.

The dog barked outside, harnessed and anxious to set out.

"I should make a start," Peyton said, already moving through the door.

Cassie dropped the brush then and he turned back to see her get to her feet and unknot the dress, the layers falling around her stockings. "Hold on," she said. She went out through the hallway to her room off the kitchen and came back with six candles tied up in a strip of paper.

Peyton lifted the candles to his face to smell the beeswax. Cassie made them herself and used them to read by in the evenings. The wax threw a cleaner light, she said, and lasted hours longer than tallow. John Senior thought it was a ridiculous undertaking and even Peyton felt the labour involved in collecting the wax and turning the candles was out of all order with the rewards. He had been brought up to think of reading as a leisure activity, but it was clear that in Cassie's mind it was something else altogether. She read and reread Goldsmith and Fielding and Milton, fat novels by Fanny Burney all named for the main character: *Camilla* and *Cecelia* and *Evelina*. She knew many of Shakespeare's sonnets by heart and sometimes had Peyton listen as she quoted a few lines aloud. He wanted to acknowledge her enthusiasm, to share in it with her, but the most he could offer in response was to say, "That's pretty, I guess." She shook her head. "You're hopeless, John Peyton," she told him. And there was an admission of helplessness in the statement that he was sorry to continually drag her back to.

He held the candles out to her. They were an extravagant gift and would be wasted on him. "I never packed any reading," he said.

Cassie smiled at him and shrugged. She said, "The light is good for close work, if you're mending your rackets or sewing a rent in your clothes."

Peyton nodded. A quiver nearly buckled his legs. His feet felt heavy, as if he had just overtopped his boots in water. He looked at her steady and said, "You look after John Senior while I'm away."

Cassie turned away from him, retying her dress around her thighs. "I always do," she said. She knelt on the floor, leaning all her weight on the brush to scrub at the boards as he pulled the door closed behind him.

Cassie stood at the window to watch the two men move down to the land-wash and away along the water. She followed their progress until they disappeared around the line of the beach and then turned back to scrubbing the kitchen floor. The boards were already spotless, but there was a knot of anxiety she was working against with the weight of her torso on the brush, the motion of her arms repeated and repeated until they burned. Sand grating against the bare grain of the wood.

She thought of John Peyton in the doorway, watching her. The naked emotion on his face that made her pity him and wish him away. He was a man who always and only wanted the best for everyone around him, which in Cassie's mind meant he was fated to be disappointed. And likely to hurt a share of the people he cared for besides. It was a mistake to have given him the candles, she knew, there was that to worry about. And there were the weeks ahead of her, alone with John Senior.

Cassie was accustomed to having two months and more on her own in the winter house during the trapping season, the darkest time of the year. By December there were barely seven hours of light to the day to see her through the chores about the property, feeding the animals not slaughtered for meat in the fall and cleaning their stalls, carrying in her supply of wood, fetching water. Long evenings of pitch black outside the circle of her reading light and the fire tormented by wind in the chimney. Not a soul on the shore within a day's hard travel. It was something she anticipated with equal measures of exhilaration and dread, the loneliness of relying on no one but herself.

When she first heard John Senior wouldn't be trapping this year she was relieved at the thought of having his company through the winter, but now the idea distressed her. As if she was being cheated somehow.

After she had scrubbed every inch of the floor she swept it clear of sand. She packed bread and cheese into a pouch and collected a pair of Indian rackets, a rifle, powder horn and shot. She pulled on a heavy overcoat and followed the track of the sled down to the landwash. She turned in the direction opposite the one taken by the men, walking along the beach a mile and a half, then following a brook inland to where the country opened into a clearing of bogland studded with clusters of bare alder. There was plenty of snow down to cover the ground, but it wasn't cold enough yet to have frozen the hidden pockets of bog-water solid and Cassie skirted the clearing, keeping close to the treeline to avoid stumbling into them.

Half an hour into the bush she came upon the tracks of partridge in the snow, the distinct prints overlapping in wide arcs, as if the birds were incapable of walking in a straight line. She took off her heavy leather mittens and moved slowly forward with the rifle at the ready. The birds would have moulted their summer camouflage for the coat of white feathers that made them nearly invisible against the snow. It was movement she looked for, white against the dark background of spruce, white in motion on a field of white.

She came upon a cluster of three or four ahead of her. She aimed just above them, the birds bursting off the snow when the gun fired, a dull explosion of down in the blue air. One of the partridge fell back to the ground gracelessly, like a bag of sand, then scrambled into the undergrowth trailing a useless wing and a string of feathers spotted with blood. Cassie removed her rackets and laid aside the bag of food and the powder horn to push her way into the spruce. The bush was thick and heavy going, the ground under the canopy of branches almost bare of snow. When she came upon the partridge it was lying at the base of a tree, as if it had run blindly into the trunk and dropped there unconscious.

There was always a pinch of sympathy she had to set her teeth against, seeing the creature this close. She took a breath through her nostrils and reached for the bird, but it jumped again, thrashing wildly under the branches. Cassie fell backwards, then struck at the partridge with the rifle butt until it lay still. She placed a boot on the bird's broken wing to hold it against the ground and then twisted the neck backwards.

She laid a fire just above the beach, in a washed-out alcove of peat and tree roots that kept her clear of the wind. The sun was warm enough that she could take off her coat. She plucked the bird clean and singed off the pin feathers in the fire, then gutted the naked carcass and propped it over the coals on a stick.

When she was left on her own during the winter, she came down to this spot once or twice a month to hunt or just to sit by a fire for an afternoon. There was something stripped and pitiless about the land that she envied. The wind in the spruce trees, the surf muttering on the beach were hypnotic, so empty of meaning they could be mistaken for silence. A scatter of islands teetering on the ocean's horizon. The sea a blue just this side of darkness, the colour of the sky when the first evening star appears. Out of sight of the winter house she could imagine the entire coastline was uninhabited but for her, and she found some comfort in that notion.

She reached for that feeling now, but couldn't move past the anxiety she'd been trying to ignore since starting out. She turned away from it and away from it, like the partridge moving in wide overlapping arcs, and each time came back to that sullen heaviness. She leaned closer to the heat and turned the bird on its stick. Fat dripped into the fire, the smell of it darkening the air like a bruise.

All that day, the two men travelled along the bank of the River Exploits without speaking of more than the conditions of the snow or the temperature.

Peyton stood to the back of the sled and worked it over bald patches of rock, holding it upright over angled layers of beach ice. He was happy for the physical labour of it, the steady immersion into fatigue that released some of the tension in his body, but it wasn't enough to keep him from going over his conversation with Cassie in his head. The candles like an afterthought or was she playing her feelings as close as he was? The light good for needlework and whether that meant anything like he hoped. How quickly she turned away then and her saying, "I always do," when he spoke of his father. It seemed to Peyton there was a note almost of defiance in her voice as she said it.

John Senior stayed beside the bitch most of the day, using a hand in the harness to help haul or steady the animal when needed. Where the path or stretch of beach was too narrow to allow them to walk abreast, he travelled ahead and the dog adjusted her pace to keep close to his heels. She nearly bowled him over as they came into sight of Ship Cove, John Senior stopping suddenly in the dusk of late afternoon. The dog sat on her haunches behind him and whined.

Peyton said, "What is it, now?"

John Senior pointed with his mittened hand. "There she is," he said.

The HMS *Adonis* was a bulk of shadow in the distance. They couldn't see the chains about her waist that secured the vessel to the shoreline, but it was clear the sails and all the rigging had been taken down for the winter, the bare masts rising over the ship like a row of crucifixes atop the spires of a church.

"Never been a navy man on the shore this late in the season," John Senior said. "Not in all my years."

Peyton couldn't discern the drift of those words, whether they were wistful or angry or fearful. All that summer they had heard stories of the commander of the *Adonis*, a Lieutenant Buchan, travelling across the northeast shore in a cutter. Mapping the coastline was the explanation that had come to them, a notion John Senior was suspicious of almost out of habit. When word reached the Peytons that the vessel was going to winter-over, it was like a confirmation of the worst, though nothing said between them acknowledged any specific concern.

"What is it this Buchan is after?" Peyton asked.

John Senior shook his head. He was squinting into the light of the sun as it fell into the forest. "Leave me worry about the navy man. You worry about keeping your powder dry. And minding the ice."

Peyton nodded and they pushed on towards Ship Cove as the darkness seemed to rise out of the countryside around them, the sky turning black overhead by imperceptible degrees. They didn't speak of the *Adonis* or Lieutenant Buchan again, although in his head Peyton was already running through the possibilities. He had another full day's travel to face in the morning. And he could see, exhausted as he was, he had little chance of sleeping through the night again.

For much of July and August and through the month of September, Lieutenant David Buchan had been commanding a cutter from the HMS *Adonis,* searching the harbours and coves of Notre Dame Bay for the small bands of Red Indians reported to frequent the area during the summer months. He and his crew of marines had covered almost two hundred miles of coastline, steering up dozens of rivers and narrow gullies, marching for hours through bush and across marshes when a mooring stake was discovered near a trail. The blackflies and mosquitoes over the water were so thick that a used handkerchief came away blackened. The insects crawled into the mouths and ears of the marines and necklaced them with blood. When his men complained about the useless effort and the choking flies, Buchan ordered them to ship their oars and sat the boat still on the water so long they begged him to set to rowing for the relief that only the breeze of movement offered.

There was no lack of evidence of a Beothuk presence — abandoned mamateeks, recently used firepits, well-marked trails. Twice Buchan and his men approached camps in which fires were burning and birds on wooden skewers were angled over the coals, but the occupants had seen or heard them approach and disappeared into the woods. The marines spoke of it among themselves as otherworldly, the work of fairies or the Old Man himself, their enthusiasm for the search waning as their fear and distrust increased. To Buchan, it seemed almost a deliberate seduction, a teasing game that strengthened his determination to carry on.

It was Governor John Duckworth, newly appointed to the office in Newfoundland, who first offered the undertaking to Buchan. They had met on an April evening at the London Tavern in St. John's. It was cold and miserable outside and heavy sleet tattooed the windows with each gust of wind. There was one double-burner Argand lamp to light the entire room and the near dark and foreboding weather gave a clandestine air to their discussion. They sat beside the flagstone fireplace over plates of mutton and peas. "Marie is well, I trust," Duckworth said.

"Fine, yes."

"And the girl?"

"Thank you, yes. By the latest news I have."

"Good," Duckworth said without enthusiasm. "Good." He looked at his plate of food and sighed heavily. "In my experience," he told the officer, "public service is submission to discomfort." He ticked off his ailments on the fingers of his right hand. The dull pall of headaches, attacks of the night sweats, nausea or constipation or the trots. It was a physical expression of the sense of impotence that arose from one's inability to please everyone. He was only a fortnight into his appointment to the position of governor and the Society of Merchants in St. John's was agitating for the removal of the chief justice, Thomas Tremlett. Illegal building on the waterfront had, according to a long-established custom, gone on through the winter in the absence of the governor and would now have to be dealt with. And there was, closest to his heart, for no reason of consequence to his office or the Crown, the matter of the Red Indians.

In preparation for his posting to Newfoundland, Duckworth had done a meticulous review of the literature. He burrowed through letters, reports and ledgers, correspondence from previous governors to the Privy Council and the Board of Trade, the short and invariably disastrous histories of plantations established in the colony during the seventeenth century. As he read through the paperwork, he began taking note of the infrequent asides regarding the natives of the island, christened *Red* Indians for their practice of covering skin and clothing, shelters, canoes and tools in a pigment of red ochre. The Indians were a shadowy presence in the colonial literature as they were on the island itself. They surfaced as a minor category in descriptions of the landscape, weather, animals and fishing conditions of the country. They once occupied the entire coast of Newfoundland and there were infrequent but promising contacts with Europeans in the early 1600s, some symbolic acts of trade, ritual exchanges of gifts. Then several pivotal misunderstandings. There were incidents of pilfering from English establishments prompting acts of violence in retaliation. Bloodshed. The Beothuk began to withdraw from those areas overrun by strangers, surrendering the Avalon Peninsula, then Conception and Trinity bays to the rapidly expanding English shore fishery. The French Shore was abandoned to the itinerant presence of the French and their Mi'kmaq allies who migrated from Cape Breton Island. The Mi'kmaq also moved inland to hunt and trap around Grand Lake and the countryside as far north as White Bay.

Duckworth stared across at Buchan. He said, "I hope I'm not boring you, Lieutenant."

According to the evidence of the literature Duckworth had read, the displacement of the Beothuk took place with a curious lack of concerted resistance. The Red Indians seemed almost to dissipate, like a dream that resists articulation, becoming increasingly elusive as the Europeans occupied and renamed the bays and points and islands that once belonged to them alone.

The scattered references to them fascinated, then obsessed Duckworth, like an unfamiliar word that begins to recur in a way that seems loaded with import. He had written letters and attended informal meetings with members of the Privy Council in London before beginning his appointment. He wanted some action taken to protect the Indians, to establish a formal relationship. He argued, quoted statistics (manufactured out of the air to lend weight to his opinions), bullied and harangued to the point that people began avoiding him, coming down with sudden illnesses that made it impossible to keep their appointments. He was gaining a reputation, he was told by friends, as a quack. Each month his appetite decreased. The crick in his neck tightened like a body on the rack.

Duckworth sat back from his meal. The Privy Council, he told Buchan, had been made aware of the dire situation of the local natives by most of the colony's governors in recent memory. A series of ineffectual proclamations had been issued in response to reports that attacks of inhuman barbarity were being perpetrated against the Indians by settlers. The decrees placed the natives under the protection of the Crown and exhorted settlers to "live in amity and brotherly kindness" with the Red Indians. There was a report from an officer of the navy in 1792, the state of the tribe was discussed at a commission of inquiry, there were official recommendations. There was talk of a reservation in Notre Dame Bay, of making an example of some of the worst offenders in the Bay of Exploits. All of these suggestions the Privy Council took under advisement and proceeded to ignore, unwilling to risk alienating the growing population of settlers by appearing to side with local natives. The English cod fishery on the Grand Banks was the richest in the world, Duckworth reminded Buchan, and the revolt in America had not been without its lessons.

They washed their food down with tankards of a dark molasses beer brewed on the premises and Duckworth lifted a hand to signal for more. Despite the chill in the air, the effort of eating raised beads of perspiration on the governor's forehead. As far as he could determine from his own inquiries, he continued, no one had ever succeeded in building a sustained relationship of trust with the Red Indians. The remnants of the tribe had retreated to the northeast shore, wintering seventy miles inland on the Red Indian's lake. During the warmer months they scavenged a living among the sparsely populated maze of islands in the Bay of Exploits. From May to September they hunted for eggs on the bird islands and harvested seals and took salmon from the rivers not yet occupied and dammed by English settlers. They dug for clams and mussels on the shoreline and pilfered ironwork and nets from the settlers' tilts and they sometimes cut the English boats from their moorings in the dark of night in a useless display of bravado or protest.

The settlers responded to their constant stealing and vandalism by shooting at them on sight or raiding and looting their camps in retaliation. An old man named Rogers living on Twillingate Great Island had boasted of killing upwards of sixty of them. Several people Duckworth knew personally — he leaned dangerously low over his plate of food — had seen Red Indian hands displayed as trophies by furriers in the Bay of Exploits.

Buchan was vaguely familiar with much of the information Duckworth was relating, but he saw the governor's need for a naive audience, his desire to find a convert. He shook his head in disbelief. He nodded, he made small disgusted noises in his throat, he offered pained expressions where appropriate.

Duckworth had tucked a linen napkin into his waistcoat to protect the white silk. He leaned his bulk back from the table and methodically wiped his hands clean with the napkin before removing a folded sheaf of letters from the waist pocket of his frock coat.

"One of my predecessors," he said, wiping at the corners of his mouth with his thumb, "consulted a magistrate by the name of Bland for advice on this issue." He flipped through the pages for a particular passage and turned a letter up to the poor light of the lamp when he found it. "'Before the lapse of another century,'" he read, "'the English nation, like the Spanish, may have affixed to its character the indelible reproach of having extirpated a whole race of people.'" There was a noticeable tick in the pale jowls of his face. He folded the papers and laid them on the table at the officer's elbow. "My dear Buchan," he said.

Duckworth rested his chin on the starched muslin folds of his cravat as the lieutenant leafed slowly through the letters. Buchan was a Scotsman who had signed on as a cabin boy in the Royal Navy at the age of ten. By the time of the most recent war with the French he was master of the HMS *Nettby* and was instrumental in sinking and capturing several French ships in the conflict. He'd served intermittently on the Newfoundland station for several years and had mapped much of the island's south coast. The two men had crossed paths in official capacities for nearly a decade and they recognized in one another an instinctual devotion to duty and Empire. They both felt the same confirmation of their natural inclinations in service to the ways and laws of Britannia.

"I'm speaking to you now," Duckworth said with a conspiratorial air, "as a gentleman and a friend."

Duckworth wrote Buchan a letter of orders to spend the late summer months navigating and mapping the coastal waters of the northeast shore to justify the expense of assigning the *Adonis*. He sent the officer away with a proclamation issued on the first day of August, 1810, which promised a reward of one hundred pounds to any person who could bring about and establish on a firm and settled footing a friendly intercourse with the native Indians. "Of course, I have no authorization to propose a reward," Duckworth admitted, "but the brutes will simply laugh at you if you come without one."

By the end of September, Buchan had conceded the failure of his summer mission and wrote to the governor to inform him the *Adonis* would winter over in Notre Dame Bay and undertake a trek to the Red Indian's lake after the freeze-up. The Indians' winter camps were reputed to be much larger and less mobile and Buchan was certain a dialogue could be forced if he was able to reach them. Duckworth offered his consent with the understanding that Buchan would act as a floating surrogate while he was stationed there, hearing civil cases across the district. The *Adonis* was anchored in Ship Cove by chaining the schooner to trees on the shoreline and the chain links were studded with brass nails to keep them from chafing through the trunks.

Buchan consulted with local fishermen and made a list of the most prominent settlers on the shore, then set about visiting those he had yet to meet. He presented the governor's proclamation, outlined his plans for the winter, and, where it seemed likely he might receive some, he requested advice and assistance. About the middle of October, shortly after John Peyton had left the coast for the traplines in the interior, Buchan and a small party of marines from the *Adonis* arrived at John Senior's winter house.

TWO

"I was just now across in Ship Cove," John Senior said. "Not a week past. Your man Bouthland offered me a little tour of the *Adonis*."

"He told me." Buchan pushed his empty plate towards the centre of the table. "I'm sorry to have been away," he said. "Though I would have lost the excuse to impose on your hospitality." He smiled across at his host, but John Senior made no effort to return it and Buchan looked quickly around at the kitchen. The house was well appointed for this part of the world. It was the first two-storey building Buchan had encountered outside the village of Twillingate. He said, "This is quite a property, Mr. Peyton."

"This is where we spend the winter. Come the spring, we move across to our place on Burnt Island. We're after the cod from April or May. My son works out there with me." He nodded towards Cassie who was moving about the table. "Cassie is with us. And there's three or four hired men come out around the capelin scull to help with the busy times."

They had long ago finished their meal and Buchan had given Corporal Bouthland a nod to take the marines off to the hired men's quarters for the evening. "You have salmon rivers as well, Mr. Peyton?" he asked.

"My father come across with his partner one season before he died and I took on his share of the fishery afterwards. There was hardly a Christian in the Bay of Exploits in those days. Harry Miller and me weired up a new river every couple of years, set them up with hired men. A dozen and more rivers now between Gander and Badger bays. Plus the cod, and traplines through the backcountry come the snow."

"Your son is working out here with you, did you say?" There had been no mention of a wife and Buchan kept clear of the subject.

John Senior nodded. "He's off on a trapline. Third generation on the shore," he said.

"The Peyton dynasty," Buchan offered amiably.

"I wouldn't want to overstate the case, sir. John Peyton have yet to marry, let alone sire a child. But a man has hopes."

"You don't winter-over in England?"

"Not since John Peyton came out from Poole, sir. It don't appeal as it once did. I'm happier where I'm situated."

"A livyere, then. You've gone native."

"In a manner of speaking."

Buchan nodded. "This area," he said. "The last bastion of the Red Indians, I understand."

John Senior looked at the officer. To his mind, there was something of the dandy in his appearance, in the spotless spats over the polished half-boots, in the buffskin-coloured kid gloves tucked into his tunic. His prematurely greying hair was oiled back from the high forehead, his face was narrow, well proportioned. He was prettier than a man was intended to be, John Senior thought. "There's enough Indians to warrant taking precautions," he said.

Buchan nodded. "You have much dealing with them?"

He laughed, a single half-choked barking sound. "You could say I have had dealings with the Reds, yes. That lot have got the face of a robber's horse."

Buchan stared across at his host. "Pardon me?"

"They're brazen, sir. They'll make off with anything not stood over with a musket. They are a shameless lot of thieves altogether."

Buchan said, "I came across some signs of them on the coast this past summer, but had no luck meeting with a soul."

John Senior picked at the remnants of food on his plate. *Luck*, this man was thinking of. He wasn't the first naval officer to come nosing around, asking questions about the Reds. "From what I hear talk of," John Senior said, "you're meant to be drawing maps of our coastline, is that right?"

Buchan smiled at him and nodded. He had made efforts towards mapping much of the northeast shore as they'd travelled through it. The tightly packed offshore islands were an impossible puzzle, they hid and mirrored and nearly overran one another. The granite coastline was so deeply abraded with harbours and bays his drawings resembled a ragged saw-blade. He thought of the countryside first as untidy and wild, then as something less than that, devoid of any suggestion of design, of intent. In the Bay of Exploits the only English habitations they'd encountered were half-hearted little clearings at the edge of forest, or a collection of flimsy outbuildings on promontories of bald stone. The fishermen lived in single-room tilts roofed with bark, as if the land was already in the process of reclaiming them. It was as if the country existed somewhere beyond the influence of human industry, of human desire. He had moments when he thought a map was somehow beside the point.

"Mapping the coast is part of my undertaking," Buchan said, "Word gets around, I see."

"I think you'll find it's nigh impossible to hold any story close on the shore," John Senior told him.

They stared at one another for a moment then, the silence between them for all the world like a struggle of some kind.

"I suspect then," Buchan said, "you already have some notion of the expedition I am planning to undertake this winter. To the Red Indian's lake."

John Senior shrugged. "Corporal Bouthland made some mention of it. The Reds is not to be trusted," he said. "Mind I didn't warn you."

Buchan leaned away from his plate and brushed at his breeches. "What

I'm proposing, Mr. Peyton, is the only way to end the thieving and vandalism you complain of."

"With respect, sir, it's not the only way."

"Yes well," Buchan continued, "if I read you correctly, may I suggest that what I propose is the only humane way to end the thieving. Christian charity, Mr. Peyton —"

"You may read me any way you like," John Senior interrupted. "The Red Indians are not like the Canadians. The Micmac are Christians of a sort and they'll listen to reason if you mind to speak to them. Our lot haven't got but a civil bone in their bodies and there's no amount of charity will teach them any manners."

John Senior lifted his empty tumbler and Cassie refilled it from the bottle provided by their guest, then proffered the rum across the table. The smell of salt beef and boiled greens permeated the kitchen and made the heat of the fire feel close and stifling. Buchan was already feeling somewhat unpleasantly drunk. He shook his head almost imperceptibly and Cassie set the bottle down.

Buchan leaned forward and spoke into his folded hands. "I am well aware," he said, "that those who have lived amongst the Red Indians have had to take extraordinary steps to protect themselves and their property."

John Senior made a small disgusted sound in his throat. "What you are aware of amounts to a piece of dun fish. You didn't have to bury what they'd left of Harry Miller belly down in the woods. Waited for him in the bush behind his tilt and pierced him in the back like a crowd of cowards. And then run off with his head."

Buchan considered the man across the table. There was a passage from one of the letters the governor had passed to him at the London Tavern he recalled now. *Perhaps to expel Mr. Peyton from the Bay of Exploits*, Bland had written, *would be an essential point gained in the desired end*. He said, "There was an act of retribution, I assume."

John Senior passed his empty plate to Cassie and she gathered up Buchan's as well, carrying both to the pantry. "We had a right to spill some blood as I saw it," John Senior said quietly, as if he was afraid of being overheard. "I mounted a party the following winter and we made our way up the river, swearing to kill big and small for the hurt they had done Harry Miller." They'd walked in all hours of daylight and, when an early moon allowed it, in several hours of darkness besides. The ice was flat and clear and they made as good as twenty miles a day. They ate only hard tack and bits of boiled salt pork and seemed to subsist on fury and talk of revenge. A day beyond the second waterfall on the river they came upon a camp of Beothuk nestled in a copse of trees and the men pulled up to load their weapons and shrug out of their packs.

Having come within hailing distance of the Indians, the mood among the men shifted suddenly to one of unease and uncertainty. "Some of the men overtopped their conscience and said they would not kill women and children," John Senior explained. "And I could not argue with them on that point, so I says to the gang, 'We'll give them fair play.'" He was talking directly to the light of the candles on the table now, as if the officer wasn't present. "We moved in at the ready then, prepared to take our pick of their materials if they run off. If they chose to stand, we swore to kill one and all and no quarter given."

He told the officer how, at the first sight of them approaching, the occupants of the camp scattered to the woods. A few shots were fired to chase them off and they echoed back and forth across the river as the shouting of the Beothuk died away in the trees. They stood alone in the clearing then and looked at one another. A crow scolded them from a treetop. John Senior raised his rifle and fired at it and the bird sailed out above the river before circling back over the camp, then disappearing into the woods. They spent a night in one of the mamateeks with two men at a time on watch and in the morning they set fire to the shelters and left for the coast with all they could carry of furs on sledges and fresh caribou meat in their packs.

There was a silence in the room when John Senior finished speaking and Buchan sat back in his chair, sighing quietly. Without some concession from this man, he knew, nothing would come of the governor's undertaking. At the moment, it looked rather hopeless.

Cassie came back into the kitchen and he turned to look at her. It was odd that a woman of her age should have remained in service for so long and to be unmarried still. Her face was beginning to darken and line with weather and age, but there was a peculiar quality about it that he found compelling. Something of the whole was slightly off-centre, her nose or her close-lipped smile. She had one lazy eye that winked nearly shut as she went about her work. She had barely spoken a word all evening and it occurred to him suddenly that she might be an idiot. "Miss Jure," he said, "I am curious as to your opinion on these matters."

She said, "I have a position, Lieutenant. Not opinions."

Buchan smiled up at her. "I see," he said. The barely perceptible imbalance he saw in her face niggled at him and he turned away, scanning quickly around the room as if something else might come to his assistance. "Would you excuse us for a moment?" he asked her finally.

Cassie looked to John Senior and he nodded his head without taking his eyes from the lieutenant. "Gentlemen," she said.

"I would like to apologize," Buchan said. "Perhaps I have misrepresented my meaning. If you think I have come here this evening with a threat, you misunderstand me. It is true that things can no longer be done as they once were. There is a court established in St. John's. The Red Indians are under the protection of the Crown," he said.

John Senior turned his tumbler in his hands and took a generous mouthful of rum and held the slow burn of the liquor there for a moment before swallowing. He reached for the bottle to refill his glass and without asking topped up Buchan's glass as well.

"You and your men have been a law unto yourselves for many years, out of necessity perhaps. It is not my place at this time to judge. But I have become familiar with many of the depredations carried out by both sides in these conflicts and as a magistrate I am duty bound to bring them to Governor Duckworth's attention."

John Senior pushed slowly away from the table and crossed the room to stand with his backside towards the fire, as if he had suddenly caught a draught.

"The governor," Buchan continued, "would look quite favourably upon those who are willing to assist in our endeavour, Mr. Peyton." He removed Duckworth's proclamation from his coat and shook it open on the table. "I know you have no interest in financial reward. But you may wish to know that, as well as the money, the governor has promised that any man who exerts himself towards the successful outcome of our project 'shall be honourably mentioned to His Majesty and shall find such countenance from the governor and such further encouragement as it may be in his power to give.'" He looked up from the parchment and folded it carefully before returning it to his pocket. "May we count on you in this regard, Mr. Peyton?"

John Senior took the silver pocket watch from his waistcoat and opened it. He stared a while at the face without paying any attention to the time. He said, "I have my doubts about what good it'll do us to trek into that lake in the middle of hard weather."

"Leave the good or bad to me, Mr. Peyton. All I am asking is that you help me try."

John Senior looked at his boots and nodded his head distractedly. He said, "I expect a word to the good with the governor."

Buchan nearly smiled but thought better of it. "If a good word is ever necessary," he said, "you shall have it."

The two men carried on drinking through the evening. John Senior threw back shots of rum with the heartsick determination of a man trying to drown an animal he can no longer afford to feed. Buchan worked to keep up with him, as if everything he had accomplished that evening was tenuous and dependent on his ability to match the older man's enormous capacity for alcohol.

He managed to make his way to bed without assistance and removed enough clothes to satisfy himself he wasn't hopelessly drunk, but he fell into a stupor as soon as he lay on top of the sheets in the cold and didn't stir until the gathering squall of nausea woke him. He stuttered downstairs as quietly as he could manage and pushed out the door into a gale of wind, running around the side of the building to vomit into the snow. He held his stomach and stamped his feet as the convulsions passed through him.

Cassie was kneeling beside the fireplace when he came back into the kitchen. She was stoking the small pyramid of coals that had been covered in ash and preserved beneath an overturned pot to start a new fire. The timid light moved across her features as she stared into it. She held a woollen shawl about her shoulders.

"I was hoping not to disturb anyone," he said.

"I was lying awake anyway," she lied. "You set yourself there —" she nodded towards the daybed with her chin. "I'll get you a cup of something that'll settle your guts."

Buchan shook his head, the motion exaggerated and vehement. "I won't have Mr. Peyton awake as well."

"Naught but the Old Hag can shake John Senior out of the state he gets into when he's sleeping. And we'd hear him over any racket we might be making, I can tell you. Sit," she said. "It'll only be a few minutes to boil the kettle."

He sat on the narrow bed, holding a forearm across his stomach as if he'd been stabbed. "I've not been feeling well these last number of days."

"There's not many can keep up with John Senior on the bottle. It's nothing to be ashamed of."

He looked up at her quickly and she smiled at him with her lips pressed firmly together. A crooked smile, he thought. He shivered violently. He was wearing only his undershirt and a pair of long underwear, and he'd pulled his half-boots on over his bare feet. Cassie removed her shawl and wrapped it around his shoulders.

"Please," Buchan said. He held a hand out to fend her off.

"Oh now," Cassie scolded. "I've heard you retching outside in your small clothes in the middle of winter weather. You've no pride to protect around me."

He nodded uncertainly. She showed an easy forwardness with him that belied her position in the household. Her lazy eye winked at him. "I'm somewhat partial to invalids, Lieutenant," she admitted. "I should have been a nurse."

When the kettle boiled she made tea and sweetened it with dark molasses. Buchan sat cradling the mug in his lap and she pulled a chair close to the fire to sit across from him. His face was chalky white, his eyes swollen to slits. He raised the mug towards her in thanks and then sipped at the hot liquid.

"The secret to drinking with John Senior," she advised him, "is to be the one refilling the glasses. Less attention gets paid to how far behind you are."

"I'd like to ask you something," Buchan said suddenly.

Cassie waited for his question. He seemed to be struggling with the proper words, or to have forgotten himself completely. "Lieutenant?" she said.

He smiled but wouldn't look at her. He said, "I'm afraid it may be somewhat indelicate."

She shrugged. "There hardly seems a point to standing on ceremony from here."

"That being the case, then," he said. He looked unsteadily across at her. "I'd like to know why you are not yet married."

"You make it sound inevitable, Lieutenant. Like death."

"There are some that see it that way." He closed his eyes. "And that's not an answer to my question besides."

She said nothing.

"Forgive my forwardness," he said. And after a moment more of silence he said, "You've had proposals."

"A number, yes."

"And no one has suited you?"

"Every one of them has talked of taking me away from here," she said. She looked about the kitchen.

Buchan followed her eyes. "From Mr. Peyton, you mean."

She shrugged again, but she didn't dispute the statement.

"Are you in love with him?"

"The thing I most appreciate about John Senior," she told him, "is that he's never talked to me about love."

"I'm sure I don't understand why that would endear him to yourself."

"No," she said. "I'm sure you don't."

Buchan sat a while, drunkenly considering the woman across from him and what he knew of her station. It seemed a lonely life for a woman too young to be a spinster to be leading and he said as much to her.

She tipped her head side to side, as if she wanted to dispute the assertion but in all honesty could not. "There are worse things in life," she said, "than loneliness." And before Buchan could respond to this, she stood and placed the chair back in its place beside the table. "Can you make the stairs on your own?"

He raised the mug again, as if to demonstrate the extent of his sobriety.

"Just leave the shawl there when you go."

She turned to leave the room, but he stopped her. "Miss Jure," he said. "I would be in your debt if you didn't make a story of this." He motioned helplessly about himself.

Cassie folded her arms beneath her breasts and smiled. "Why is it that men are more afraid of being seen as a fool than they are of behaving like one?"

Buchan nodded. "I can see," he said, "why so many men have talked of taking you away from here."

The heavy weather continued through the next day, which kept Buchan and his men from leaving for Ship Cove as he'd planned. He was still feeling rough from the previous evening's exercises and was happy enough to stay put. John Senior occupied himself with the officer as long as he could stand to sit about idly and then dressed to look in on the animals. Buchan offered to accompany him but John Senior motioned him back into his seat. "Pay no mind," he said. "Cassie," he shouted into the pantry. "Make the lieutenant some tea."

Buchan watched her with a shy, apologetic look as she set out the mugs at the kitchen table.

"Are you feeling yourself today?" she asked him. There was no sympathy in her voice, but she wasn't simply making fun of him either.

"Better," he said. "Thank you."

They spoke for a while about the violence of the weather and what it promised for the winter ahead. When they had exhausted the topic there was an awkward silence between them. Finally Cassie said, "How long will you be with us, Lieutenant?"

"We'll be leaving for Ship Cove as soon as the weather moderates, I expect."

She shook her head, but didn't look at him. "I mean on the northeast shore."

"Oh. Of course. Just until the spring breakup. We'll make for St. John's as soon as we're clear of the ice."

Cassie nodded. "You'll be coming back this way again? This is your station?"

"No," he said. "This trip was a special assignment only. Barring any unforeseen events, I doubt I'll be back."

Cassie continued nodding her head but said nothing, and they fell back into silence. Buchan slapped his knees with his hands. He said, "Did you say yesternight that John Senior is hag-ridden?"

"Aren't we all on occasion, Lieutenant?"

"You said we would hear him if it happened."

"I've heard him come to himself upstairs in the middle of the night, shouting at something or other. My father had the Old Hag a time or two."

There was a defensive tone to her voice he wasn't willing to test and he said, "I couldn't help noticing your library." He lifted a book that was sitting on the table. There were books scattered throughout the rooms of the house. "I have rarely seen a private library as large."

"Most of them were procured by my mother," she said. Her mother was the daughter of a clergyman and a woman of some learning. She was hired by St. John's merchants, in the absence of schools in the community, to tutor their children in reading and writing and she was paid with books imported from England on the merchant ships.

"I understand from John Senior that you are a woman of unusual learning as well, Miss Jure."

"This surprises you, Lieutenant?"

"You do strike me as being somewhat" — he shifted in his chair slightly — "somewhat unlikely, shall we say. How did you come to live here?" He held his arms wide, as if to say she could interpret the word "here" as broadly as she liked.

"The short answer to your question is that John Senior hired me to tutor John Peyton when he first came across from England, and to act as housekeeper."

"And the long answer?" He let the pause go on a moment and then said, "There hardly seems a point to standing on ceremony from here, Miss Jure."

She smiled and cleared her throat. She grew up, she told him, in St. John's. Her mother was born and raised in Nova Scotia, but she married against her parents' wishes and then moved to Newfoundland with her husband to live beyond the constant light of their disapproval. Cassie looked about the room and then at her hands. "I'm not usually given to telling stories," she said.

He nodded. "I am quite discreet," he said. He gestured with his hand.

Her father owned a public house above the waterfront in St. John's with a large portly man from Devon named Harrow. Harrow was a single man in his early forties who had served for years in the navy and lived in half a dozen countries around the world before settling in St. John's. There was no time of the day or night when he couldn't be found pouring drinks at the public house, suffering the drunken harassment of customers with a fierce good humour, clearing the chairs of those who had passed out at their tables to make room for others coming in the door. He had lost an eye in the navy and wore a patch over the dark hole in his face. He slept only three or four hours a night in a tiny room at the back of the tavern and seemed to have no interests or ambition beyond the walls of his desolate little dominion. His immersion in the place gave Cassie's father more leeway than he would otherwise have had to wander the countryside during the summer, to read as much as he pleased, to drink freely and often. She said, "Mostly to drink, is the honest truth."

As a result of her father's habits, the family became an object of speculation and a kind of pre-emptive disdain within the town. Her mother had once enjoyed a modicum of respect as an educated woman, but her work as a tutor and the recognition it garnered her slowly disappeared. People began to avoid them in the way lepers were avoided in biblical stories, as if any physical contact might infect those who touched them. Their only visitors were men her father dragged home from the public house.

Buchan said, "Is this where John Senior comes into it?"

She nodded. This was in the fall, she told him, when the season's catch was brought to market. John Senior and Harry Miller came to the house with her father in the course of a night of drinking in various taverns above the waterfront. After a round of stilted introductions the two women removed themselves to a room upstairs but they could hear Miller singing bawdy songs and inserting her mother's name or Cassie's wherever he could make them fit. He made lewd propositions to the two women, shouting to them through the ceiling.

She saw Buchan's look of incredulity. It wasn't an unusual occurrence in their lives at the time, she told him.

John Senior came by the following day while her father was out. She was reading *The Rape of Lucrece* to her mother. Cassie closed the book and stood from her chair to face him. He smiled awkwardly, like a man confronted with evidence of someone he once was, someone he was now ashamed of. He asked what it was she was reading and how Cassie had come to learn to read and whether she had taken it upon herself to teach others. He nodded as she spoke and couldn't seem to remove the smirk from his face.

"My husband," her mother said finally, "is not at home."

John Senior shook his head. He said, "I come to say my best to both of you and to apologize for Mr. Miller."

"An apology from Mr. Miller would be more in order," her mother told him.

He said, "When it comes to apologies, Mrs. Jure, it is sometimes a case of taking them where they can be got."

Cassie paused in her story there to pour the steeped tea into Buchan's mug and then into her own. It had been sitting so long it was black and barky. She went to the pantry for sugar and fresh cream. Her movements were slow and slightly distracted, as if she was the stranger in this house and was unsure where things were kept. Buchan was surprised he hadn't noticed the limp before, the buckle in her step.

"What happened to your leg?" he said when she'd taken her seat, already sure it was connected somehow to the story she was telling.

She watched the officer a moment, then leaned forward, lifting the heavy layers of the skirts to her knee. She slipped her knee-length stocking to her ankle and traced a finger the length of the purple scar on her shin. When she was twelve, she said, she tried to separate her father from the bottle he was working his way through. He had thrown her down the stairs of their house.

Buchan's stomach came up into his throat. The fall. The impact. He could see in this revelation the same unexpected forwardness she had shown the night before, wrapping her shawl around his shoulders. There was something childlike about the intimacy she assumed, the disregard for markers of class and station. He felt a sudden flush of embarrassment, as if he had blundered into a room while she was dressing.

She pulled her stocking up her leg and ruffled the skirts back into place. She had brown eyes so dark they seemed to be all pupil.

The tibia had snapped and come through the skin. Where it protruded the bone was tinged a pale green and flecked with blood. Her mother sat crying at her head, holding Cassie's clenched hands while her father knelt over her to examine the wound. "What have you done?" her mother said. "What have you done to our child?" She went on repeating the question, her voice escalating with each repetition until she was nearly hysterical with rage and her father began shouting back. "Shut up, Myra. Shut up." Even after she had stopped he pointed a finger and repeated himself one more time. Both her parents were visibly shaking. "Shut up," he said. He poured a glassful of rum then and handed it to Cassie. "Drink as much of that as you can," he said. Then he topped up the glass and drank it straight off himself. "You hold her good," he told his wife.

Her mother mixed a paste of egg and flour to cover the wound after the bone was set and two straight sticks were wrapped tight to either side of the leg with cloth. The scar and the limp were not as severe as they might have been, she said, given the circumstances.

"On the weight of your witness alone," Buchan said quietly, "your father sounds like a beast."

Cassie stared at him with a bald look that was almost accusatory. "A man should be what he seems," she said and then shrugged helplessly. "I knew him a different person when I was a girl. Before the drink got the better of him."

He had to turn away from her for a moment, staring down into his mug. She said, "My mother gave up everything for him, you understand."

Buchan nodded. "Are they still in St. John's?" he asked.

"My father," Cassie said. "My mother died before I left, after an illness that kept her bedridden for the better part of a year. She had a head of black hair when she went to that bed and it was grey before the year was through." Her arms and legs atrophied, the muscles beneath the skin slack and toneless as the flesh of a cod tongue. Her heels turned black against the mattress with blood blisters. Cassie said, "I never thought a bed could do so much damage to a person."

Buchan set his mug down on the table and folded his hands in his lap.

"Near the end she wanted me with her through the night, she was afraid of dying alone in the dark, I imagine. If I fell asleep in the chair, she'd wake me, ask me to light a candle, to read to her."

Buchan uncrossed his legs and crossed them in the other direction. "I know what it is to lose a mother," he said.

Cassie tipped her head side to side. "It didn't seem real, honestly. The stories I read to her seemed more real than her dying." She seemed embarrassed by this notion and went on quickly. "I was at a loss as to what to do afterwards. I thought of moving to Nova Scotia, I thought of America. But I hadn't the means."

"And John Senior arrived at this time? The white knight?"

"It doesn't suit you to scoff," Cassie said, but she managed a smile. She said, "He'd heard news of Mother's death on his way through St. John's in October. He offered to take me to the northeast shore to teach his son and keep house when he returned in the spring. He told me Harry Miller was five years dead. He said I could take the winter to consider the offer. But I'd already made up my mind. I packed Mother's books into a trunk and had it carried to the postmaster's above the harbour. Then I wrote to John Senior in Poole."

"You've never returned to visit?"

Cassie shrugged. "I have my memories of my mother. The rest of the life I lived in St. John's is not worth revisiting."

"So," Buchan said quietly, "is this a penance of some kind?" He motioned around the kitchen with his arm.

"A very Catholic sentiment, Lieutenant." She smiled across at him again.

"Perhaps," he agreed and nodded. "Perhaps I have spent too much time among the Irish." It was her entire face, he decided. The lines from her temples to the tip of the chin. By the tiniest of margins they were asymmetrical. As if a traumatic birth had skewed the shape of her face and it had nearly but not quite recovered itself.

Cassie said, "I have everything here I want." She said it slowly, and it seemed to Buchan she was warning him not to question or contradict her.

"Your books," Buchan said, lifting one from the table. "Your poetry."

She shrugged and looked away from him. "A good book will never disappoint you," she said.

John Senior came through the door then, stamping snow from his boots, slapping at his sleeves. Cassie turned her head and let out a little breath of air, relieved to have the conversation interrupted. She rose from her chair and went to the pantry to fetch another mug.

Three times in the following six weeks Buchan visited John Senior's house, outlining his plans and seeking the old man's advice on every aspect of the expedition as if the planter was his senior officer. He agreed to include more men in the expedition than he originally envisioned. He changed the departure date to ensure the river would be frozen sufficiently to allow sledges to pass safely and then again to wait for John Senior's most experienced furriers to come in off the traplines to accompany the party.

Although salmon stations and traplines had moved further up the River Exploits each year, William Cull had been the first Englishman to trek as far into the interior as the Red Indian's lake in forty years. "Only man on the shore near as long as me," John Senior said. "Not a young pup, you can imagine. But he won't cry crack till a job is done." In late November, after the first furious storm of the season that kept them housebound for several days, John Senior and Buchan took dogs and sleds across to White Bay where he helped the officer recruit Cull to the expedition.

THREE

Fall in the backcountry had been fresh with early snow and the cold weather made the land animals a little more careless than they might otherwise have been. Peyton did well in his early take of marten and weasel and otter. But his beaver line was a disappointment. At the beginning of November he shifted his traps to a line of brooks and ponds running within two miles of Reilly's tilt on the River Exploits. Three weeks later, at the end of a round of fresh-tailing this line, he walked the extra distance to look in on Reilly and his wife, Annie Boss.

Reilly held the door wide to the cold, staring at him. He was a tall, stick-thin Irishman, with a narrow face that tapered like the blade of an axe. "Is it you?" he said. "Annie," he shouted over his shoulder, "the little maneen has got himself lost now, what did I warn you?"

Peyton said, "Shut up Reilly."

Reilly stepped back from the door to let the younger man in out of the weather, slapping his back to welcome him in.

The two men hadn't seen one another since the August haying on Charles Brook. For years Peyton and Cassie had travelled to Reilly's station at the end of the summer to spend several days in the large meadows of wild grass on the hills behind Reilly's tilt. It was there that Peyton first heard he would be running the trapline alone this season. He and Reilly were sitting on the newly shorn grass, sharing a heel of bread. Reilly pointed at him. There was a confusion of scars like an angry child's drawing across the back of the hand he pointed with. He said, "John Senior talk to you about running the line this season?"

Peyton looked across at the Irishman. "He haven't said anything to me different from other years."

Reilly made a face. "Well I'm not meant to be saying anything about it maybe. But he's not trapping, he tells me. You're to have a go at it alone."

"Since when did he say this?" He tried to keep the smile from his mouth, in case Reilly was simply making a joke.

"When he come over in June, checking the cure. I tried to talk him free of it is the truth. Sure you haven't been but John Senior's kedger these years, you'll be getting yourself lost back there."

"Shut up Reilly."

"What are you, twenty-six years old now? And haven't skinned but a buck-toothed rat without your Da to hold your hand." He was grinning at Peyton with just the tip of his tongue showing between his lips.

"Shut up," Peyton said again. But he was too pleased at the thought of running his own line to feel honestly angry. "We'll see who sets the most hats on the heads in London this winter," he said.

"The little bedlamer with his own line," Reilly had said then, shaking his head. "Next thing you'll want to be getting married."

Peyton carried a halo of frost into the Irishman's tilt as he stepped inside, as if his frozen clothes were emanating their own cold light after hours in the outdoors. "Get that coat off you now," Reilly said. "Close the door behind you." Peyton was propped near the fire with a glass of rum where he presented his frustrations with the scarce take of beaver and explained his decision to move his line closer to Reilly's own. Through the conversation the Irishman helped Annie prepare the food, nodding and asking questions and throwing out good-natured insults at every opportunity. Reilly's constant teasing was a kind of flattery, as ritualized and intimate in its way as dancing. Unlike John Senior's rough silence, which Peyton couldn't help thinking of as an implicit condemnation of his abilities, his aptitude, his judgement. He felt vaguely guilty about his affection for Reilly, as if he was being unfaithful to his father somehow.

They sat to a huge meal of salt pork and potatoes and afterwards the two men filled their glasses and their pipes while Annie Boss cleared away the dishes. Annie and Joseph had been married eight years, but she was still known to everyone on the shore as Annie Boss. She spoke over her shoulder with Peyton as she worked and bantered with her husband in a mang of English and Mi'kmaq and Gaelic.

Annie's belly, which barely showed when Peyton last saw her during the haying, was now quite obviously pregnant. "She's improving, that one," he said to Reilly.

Annie turned with both hands on her stomach. She said the child was no time too soon, her mother was starting to have doubts about her choice in a husband.

Reilly smiled at her, his ears rising half an inch on the sides of his head.

Later that evening, after Annie Boss had climbed into a bunk at the back of the tilt and the men had coddled several more glasses of rum, Peyton said, "Can I ask you a question, Joseph."

"Suit yourself."

Peyton paused a moment, rolling his glass between the flat of his palms. "What did you," he said and then stopped. He took a sip of rum. "How did you ask Annie Boss to marry you?"

The Irishman laughed. "Well we've all wondered what's been holding you up, John Peyton. Have your sights set on some lass finally, is it?"

Peyton stared into his glass. "Never mind," he said.

"There's not many on the shore to choose from. I bet I could strike the name before the third guess."

"Never mind," Peyton said again, angrily this time.

"Don't mind my guff now," Reilly said. He was surprised by Peyton's seriousness. He leaned forward on his thighs. "It was Annie's doing more than mine is the truth of it. If it had been left me, it might never have come to pass. She sent me off to a have a word with her father."

"I suppose it was different with her." He glanced across at Reilly, but the look on his face made Peyton drop his eyes quickly back to his lap.

"Her being Micmac, is what you mean?" When the younger man didn't answer him, Reilly said, "She's a good Christian woman, John Peyton."

Peyton nodded. He lifted his glass to his mouth and drained it. He said, "Could I get another drop of rum, do you think?"

Reilly cleared the heat from his voice. "Who is this lass now?" he said.

Peyton got up from his seat to fetch the rum. "Never mind," he said over his shoulder.

Reilly asked no more questions and did the favour of not even looking much at him, which Peyton was grateful for. They went on drinking a while longer until Reilly excused himself and climbed into bed as well. Peyton sat up in the dark then, nursing a last finger of rum, upset with himself to have been such a stupid twillick. What he'd intended to say about Annie was altogether different than what he garbled out. And he had never discussed marriage with a living soul before. He wished now he'd had the sense to leave it that way.

Peyton was sixteen the first time he laid eyes on Cassie, shortly after sailing through the Narrows of St. John's harbour, twenty-nine days out from Poole aboard the *John & Thomas*. A fine cold day after a night of heavy rain and the few ships anchored in the still water had raised their sails to dry. Running inland from the east side of the Narrows was Maggoty Cove, a rocky stretch of shoreline built over with wharves and stages, behind them the wide flakes used for drying cod. Each season wet fish fell through the lungers of the flakes and bred maggots on the ground. The dark, bottomless smell of rot rooting the clear sea air.

Peyton and his father made their way to a two-storey building on the east end of Upper Path, which housed the postmaster and the island's first news-paper — a single sheeter folded to four pages that carried government proclamations, mercantile ads, parliamentary proceedings, local news, a poet's corner on the back page. A small harried-looking man with a New England accent came forward from a cluttered desk at the back of the room to greet them. The two men exchanged a few words and John Senior handed across a large leather satchel of mail he'd carried up from the ship, then produced a letter from his own pocket.

The postmaster nodded as he scanned the page. "Got the trunk for you along this way," he said, jerking his head repeatedly to indicate the direction they should follow.

The trunk was large enough to sleep an adult fairly comfortably. Peyton took one end and his father the other. Even John Senior showed the strain of the weight. They huffed it out the door where a crowd had already gathered for the calling of the mail. At the waterfront the trunk was rowed out to the *Jennifer*, a coaster scheduled to leave for Fogo Island in two days' time.

"What's aboard of her?" Peyton asked, watching it being lifted awkwardly over the ship's gunnel. He was soaked in sweat from hauling the weight of it. He took his cap from his head and wiped a forearm across his face.

John Senior shrugged. "Mostly books, I expect."

When they boarded the *Jennifer* two days later, Peyton spotted the trunk set against the back wall of the fo'c'sle. There was a woman seated on the lid in the light drizzle of rain. She wore a dark hat and a long cloak of Bedford cord that showed only black worsted stockings below the knees.

She stood when they approached her and she extended her gloved hand to John Senior. "Master Peyton," she said. Her face was misted with rain, tiny beads clinging to the long lashes of her eyes. Light brown hair pulled back into a ponytail, a small, full mouth. There was a suggestion of misproportion about the features that Peyton couldn't assign to anything particular. He had no idea who the woman was or why she exhibited such a proprietary attitude towards the trunk they'd sent aboard the ship. She seemed to be dressed in a manner meant to bolster a questionable claim to adulthood.

John Senior said, "This is the young one you'll be watching out for. John Peyton," he said. "Miss Cassandra Jure."

She reached out to shake his hand, bending only slightly, but enough to make him draw up to his full five feet five inches. "Are you a reader, John Peyton?" she asked, still holding his bare hand.

He was about to say he was and stopped himself. It occurred to him she was asking something other than whether he knew *how* to read. "I don't know," he said.

"Well," she said. She seemed to wink at him then, giving her words a conspiratorial air. "We'll soon find out."

Through that first summer Peyton worked with his father hand-lining for cod morning and afternoon, and in the early evenings while John Senior cleaned and salted the fish with two hired hands in the cutting room, he did sums at the kitchen table or read to Cassie from *The Canterbury Tales* or Pope's translation of the *Odyssey*. He decided early on that he was not, in fact, a reader. It was something he could easily have given up if he didn't think it would upset Cassie, to whom it seemed to mean so much that he become one. They struggled through Blake's *Songs of Innocence* and *Songs of Experience*, Samuel Richardson's *Clarissa, or the History of a Young Lady*. They read *Paradise Lost*.

She saw much in the poems and stories that he did not. She was sometimes cryptic and high-minded in a way he found off-putting. She could wander into flights of speculation beyond his interest or understanding, and this was usually the case when he was too tired to know what he was reading, the words on the page like beads on a string that he shifted from one side to another.

"What does that mean?" Cassie would ask then. "*To justify the ways of God to man.* What is Milton saying?"

Peyton's eyes were bleary with exhaustion. He had been on the water since five that morning. He did not know what it meant. He stared at her in the hope she would pity him enough to explain it.

"A story is never told for its own sake," she said. "True or false?"

"True," he said. "False," he added quickly.

Cassie sighed and worked her fingers in her lap.

He stared at her. He was the only person in the world she had to talk to about poems, to discuss her peculiar notions about stories. It was a disappointment to them both that he thought of her books as a discomfort, like being forced to walk in shoes full of gravel. She seemed so peculiarly out of place in their house, so lost. Almost as long as he'd known her, Peyton wanted to make that otherwise.

He'd kept his marital aspirations close for years, telling himself he had little to offer yet as a husband. Running his own trapline was a first step towards a station from which he felt he might legitimately declare his intentions, and the thought of this, along with the alcohol, had made him reckless in Reilly's company.

He stepped outside to relieve himself a final time before he went to his own bunk, pissing into a snowbank at the edge of the trees. He said, "*Take note, take note, O world, To be direct and honest is not safe.*" Where was that from again? He lifted his head to stare up at the sky as he shook himself. Stars winking through the moving branches of trees like flankers rising from a distant fire. He was drunker than he realized. He raised his head a notch higher and fell over backwards into the snow, his cock still in his hand.

The morning John Senior and the officer left for White Bay, Cassie pulled a pair of John Senior's leather trousers on beneath her skirt, turning the cuffs up at the bottom for length, and buttoned a sheepskin waistcoat over her bodice. She closed the animals up in their shed with a week's supply of hay and packed herself a bag with provision enough for two days' travel. It was late November and there had been a steady week of snow. She followed the shoreline towards the headwaters of the river until she was in sight of Peter's Arm. Joseph Reilly's trapping tilt was at least five miles more up the Exploits from what she had gathered listening to the men talk among themselves. She decided to make her way to the river through the woods so as not to pass through Ship Cove.

Cassie started into the forest bearing southeast and the large Indian rackets she wore sank a foot into the loose powder with every step forward, coming away with a weight of snow like a shovel. It was heavy work and out of the wind the day was surprisingly warm. She removed her gloves and opened the heavy overcoat to the air and then unbuttoned the waistcoat as well.

Before dark she tramped a piece of ground firm and took off the rackets and sat on her overcoat against a tree. She had no clear notion of how much further a walk was ahead of her. Her right leg ached. She ate a cold meal of blood sausage and bread and closed her eyes long enough to feel the weather begin to steal into her body.

When she pushed herself up to start moving again the pain in her leg throbbed in time to her pulse. It seemed strangely appropriate to feel her heart swelling the hurt that way.

It was a clear night and the constellations watched her through the branches of the trees as she travelled and where she came upon a clearing she stopped to take her bearings by the stars. When she came out of the woods it was near dawn. The River Exploits still ran open but there were runners of ice along the banks. Cassie took off the Indian rackets and strapped them to her pack and headed south, keeping as close to the shoreline as she could, watching all the while for signs of Reilly's traplines or his shelter or rising smoke.

His tilt was built in the bush on the north side of a narrow stretch of river. His dog caught sight or sound of her as she approached and Reilly and his wife came out of the tiny shack to see what had raised the barking. Reilly carried a rifle, thinking it might be a wolf or a bear. Annie Boss was wiping her dark hands in the skirt of her rough calico dress. She whistled for the dog and kicked awkwardly at his shoulders when he refused to quiet down.

Reilly walked down to meet her and shook her hand. Cassie had not until that moment considered what she would say to these people and stood with her mouth open while Reilly smiled at her. He was sure she came with news but was in no rush to hear it.

"Come up," he said, "the kettle is on. We haven't had this much company in all my days on the river."

"Company?" she said.

"Sure the Thames doesn't see as much traffic in a week," he said and motioned up the clearing towards the tilt.

Cassie looked up to where he pointed. John Peyton stood in the tiny doorway in his shirtsleeves, watching her come up the bank.

Annie Boss was born and baptized on Cape Breton Island but she'd moved with her parents to Newfoundland at such a young age that she thought of no other place as home. When she was a child, her family spent winters in the country near White Bay where her father and brother trapped marten, beaver and fox, and each spring they migrated down to St. George's Bay on the west coast for the summer. Her mother was born the seventh of seven daughters, a *puowin*, with a rare gift for healing. Annie accompanied her when she was called to deliver a child or nurse an injury or comfort the dying. She inherited her mother's knowledge of roots and herbs and the position of a child's head in the womb that distinguished a boy from a girl in the same unconscious and predictable way she had taken on her gestures, her habit of hiding her eyes with her hand when she laughed, the way she rubbed the length of her thighs while considering a thorny medical problem.

By the time she married Reilly, Annie had seen all manner of births and their complications and most every form of human injury imaginable. She knew something of how people carried themselves when they had a wound to nurse or hide. And watching Cassie Jure walk up the bank to their tilt, she'd seen something in the woman's gait beyond her customary limp that made her watchful and wary. She stood at the fireplace tending a pan of capelin and leftover brewis but she was eyeing Cassie where she sat with the men. Only something calamitous could have occasioned her visit up the river, but she drank her tea calmly while they discussed the number of animals on the trapline this year and how much snow was down compared to last winter.

Peyton inquired after his father's health, as casually as he could manage. Cassie spoke briefly of Lieutenant Buchan's visit and John Senior's agreeing to assist in the expedition he had planned. She said he had taken the officer across to White Bay to meet with William Cull.

"That's a queer turn of events," Reilly said quietly.

Peyton hid his relief that Cassie hadn't come with bad news of his father by nodding into his mug and wiping his mouth with his sleeve.

Reilly turned to his wife and asked after the food and she waved her hand to shush him up. "Fire don't work no faster 'cause you hungry, Joe Jep," she told him. "Missa Jure not going to starve this minute now, are you, Missa Jure?"

Cassie looked across at her and shook her head no.

When they'd eaten their breakfast and dawdled over more tea and gossip,

Annie shooed the men outside and they dressed themselves and packed food for the day. Peyton looked to Cassie while Reilly checked the works of a trapbed on his lap but she refused to acknowledge him. The men left the shack after guessing they'd be by again around dark and Cassie started in to clear away the dishes. "You walking all night," Annie said, "you got to rest now." But Cassie refused to sit and they worked in silence until they were done. Afterwards Annie boiled the kettle to make more tea and then sat across from Cassie with her legs spread to accommodate the size of her belly. "Must be more than one in there," she said and she laughed and wiped her eyes with the palm of her hand. She said, "Annie Boss not so good at reading your mind, Missa Jure."

Cassie looked towards the one tiny window.

Annie set her mug down and rubbed her hands back and forth along the length of her thighs.

Cassie said, "You're the only person I could ask this of, Annie."

Annie would not make eye contact with her. "Whose baby you got there?"

"Nobody's," she said. "It's not going to be anyone's baby."

Annie nodded. "Make you real sick, Missa Jure, guarantee. Some women up and die with the sick."

The white woman folded her arms and tightened them around herself. Her jaw was set awkwardly askew as if she was gnawing on the inside of her mouth.

"Missa Jure."

"I know what I want," she said.

"Maybe nothing happen but you get ill," Annie said. "You sick and still got that problem."

"I'll take that chance."

Annie nodded to herself and let out a long breath of air. "God decide, not you, not me. Okay?" She crossed herself and got up to gather maidenhair and bog myrtle and skunk currant from the dried bouquets hung from the rafters above the fireplace, talking aloud all the while in her own language as if to someone else in the room.

Cassie said, "Thank you, Annie."

Annie turned towards her, waving her hands in front of her face. "No," she said. "Don't want to hear it." She pointed a finger. "Whatever happen, I got to live with too."

Cassie raised her hand, about to argue, and then thought better of it. She placed her hand back in her lap and simply nodded.

By early afternoon Cassie had begun vomiting and between spells of throwing up she lay on the single bed in the room and held her stomach and keened. The cramps knifed at her stomach and crawled up her spine to her shoulders. Her head throbbed with fever. The dry heaves she fell into were so violent that a blood vessel in her right eye had burst and the dark look she turned on Annie was so forlorn and foreboding that the Mi'kmaq woman crossed herself repeatedly.

There were no resident doctors or clergy on the northeast shore of Newfoundland before the turn of the century and Annie's mother was called to the homes of the French and English settlers as often as those of her own people. At the age of thirteen Annie was sent alone to attend a birth while her mother nursed a boy who had fallen on a fish fork and punctured his abdomen. The pregnant woman's husband had rowed two hours down White Bay to their tilt and Annie's brother walked him an hour more through bush in the dark to the home of the injured boy. He was a tall rickety Englishman of no more than twenty-five with a pinched look of worry and he pleaded with Annie's mother to attend his wife who was in distress when he set out three hours before and might be dead by now for all that he knew. But the boy was bleeding and running a fever so high that Annie's mother was afraid it would kill him. She conferred with Annie quietly and sent her away with the Englishman and he walked Annie back to his boat in a stunned and furious silence. She sat in the stern facing him as he rowed and he watched her carefully in the sparse moonlight. He asked her age and then pulled at the oars so fiercely Annie could see the veins and muscles in his neck straining like anchor chains in a tide.

The pregnant woman was lying in a bunk along the back wall when they came into the one-room shack. Annie told the husband to light a fire and boil as much water as the pot would hold and then she knelt beside the woman. "You keep breathing now," she said, and she used the curt, belligerent tone she'd heard her mother use around whites who were ashamed to be so naked in front of Indian women and to need something from them besides. She put her hand between the woman's legs and felt for the baby's head and asked about the pain and how long it lasted. The husband clanked the pot on the crane and hovered nervously and asked Annie and his wife useless questions until Annie told him to wait outside and leave them to their business.

In an hour the baby was ready and Annie had the woman squat in a corner where the walls gave her some support. She had ripped a bedsheet into towels and boiled them and had a pot of fresh hot water at her side. It was just the end of April but they had struck a solid week of unusually fine weather and the tiny shack was stifling from the heat of the fire. "You got to push when I tell you to push now," she said and the woman nodded and sucked air through her clenched teeth. "Nothing to be scared of but the hurt," Annie said, and when the contractions shook the woman's body again she yelled at her to bear down. The husband shouted through the door as if he thought Annie was doing something to inflict her pain. After the contraction subsided the Englishwoman lifted her chin to take air into her lungs and to tell him things were bad enough without him losing his head and they heard nothing more from him until they were through. Annie wiped the sheen of sweat from her face with a hot cloth and the woman managed a crooked smile until the next contraction ripped through her.

Three days later the Englishman came down the bay to their tilt with a small cask of pickled herring and a kid on a rope. He stooped under the low ceiling of the front room and hemmed his awkward and formal thanks to Annie, who was too embarrassed to look at him. He proffered the barrel of fish and motioned outside to where the goat was tethered.

"You leave the barrel," her mother told him, "but take the animal back home. Annie too young to expect all that, she just a child herself."

The boy her mother stayed to care for was dead by the time Annie returned from delivering her first baby. Birth and death. She could never afterwards think of them as separate things. She saw them both now in the woman she was nursing, Cassie moaning helplessly on the bunk, her arms wrapped tight around her womb. Hours ahead of her and worse still to come, Annie knew. She cleaned the slop bucket and wiped Cassie's forehead and forced her to drink warm water so she would have something in her stomach to throw up.

When Peyton and Reilly returned at dusk, Cassie was bleeding heavily and Annie refused to let the men enter the tilt. She stepped outside the door and told them they would have to set up a camp for the night and refused to answer any of Peyton's questions. She spoke a few words in her own tongue to Reilly and the Irishman took Peyton by the arm and they turned away from the tilt. He looked up towards the sky for a moment and said, "Coarse night," and it was clear to Peyton he wasn't referring to the weather. They found a freshly killed rabbit in one of Reilly's slips on their way towards the river. Reilly skinned and cleaned the animal while Peyton laid the fire. They roasted it on a length of alder, the dark flesh turning black in the heat.

Peyton said, "What's happening up at the house, Joseph?"

Reilly pulled the stick free of the carcass and used his thumbs to break the sternum, then tore the torso along the spine with his bare hands. He offered the piece in his scarred hand to the younger man. "You and that lass are close, John Peyton?"

"Close enough."

"Close enough to —"

"No," Peyton said flatly.

Reilly nodded. "Is she close to anyone else you know of?"

"There's just myself and father," Peyton said and he stopped himself before he took the thought any further.

Reilly leaned away from the fire to rest on an elbow, as if he wanted to step back from the conversation, shift it in some other direction. "I expect the morning will answer what questions you have. No sense making yourself sick with it tonight."

They ate in silence a while then and Reilly put a kettle of snow on to boil water for tea. Peyton chewed his food sullenly. The dry flesh tasted like a mouthful of sand.

After he'd poured them both a mug of tea, Peyton said, "Is it true what I've heard about John Senior?"

Reilly laughed. "I can't begin to guess what you've heard."

"Did he beat that old Indian to death with a trap-bed?"

"I'll bet you two good oars," Reilly said, "you heard that from Dick Richmond."

"What difference does it make where I heard it?"

"Sometimes it makes all the difference in the world."

"Did he do it, Joseph?"

The Irishman gave a long sigh and scratched at the hair over his ear. "That was before my time on the shore," he said.

Peyton stared into the fire. He shook his head slowly.

Reilly said, "John Senior's never told you how he came to take me on, has he?"

Before London hangings were moved to Newgate, the official procession to the gallows at Tyburn ran through Smithfield into the heart of Reilly's neighbourhood, St. Giles, an area of the city densely populated by Irish immigrants. From there it moved through St. Andrews and Holborne and on to the Tyburn road. The City marshall led the parade on horseback. Behind him the under-sheriff headed a group of mounted peace officers and constables armed with staves on foot. Behind these came the carts carrying the condemned men, who sat on their own coffins and were accompanied by a prison chaplain. More constables marched on either side of the carts.

Thousands of people lined the streets and the procession stopped often to allow the condemned men to speak with friends and family, and sometimes to drink mugs of ale and spirits carried out to them from taverns on the route. Women threw flowers and fruit into the carts and ran into the street to touch the hands of the men being conveyed to their deaths. The pace was stately, almost celebratory. It was as if the procession was wending its way to a church for a royal wedding. The condemned men were presented with a pair of spotless white gloves to wear. Some of them spent every shilling they had to their names on their hanging clothes and they were ferried through the streets in linen waistcoats and breeches trimmed with black ferret, in white cloth coats and silver-laced hats, in white stockings, in silk breeches.

Tens of thousands of spectators made their way to Tyburn, arriving on foot and horseback and in coaches. They thronged the cow pastures around the gallows, climbed ladders, sat on the wall enclosing Hyde Park. People fought for places on a scaffold at the bottom of Tower Hill. Entrepreneurs brought carts and sold vantage points above the heads of the crowd.

The condemned were escorted onto the gallows where they were given permission to address the crowd. Some spoke directly, others gave a prepared statement to the prison ordinary who accompanied them. They cursed the law and the country that condemned them or expressed remorse and regret for their profligate ways or commended their souls to the care of their Lord Jesus Christ. Reilly said, "There was one in particular, a tall rawney-boned fellow, he'd a dark scar across his throat like he'd already been hung. He said 'Men, women and children, I come hither to hang like a pendulum to a watch for endeavouring to be rich too soon.'"

A handkerchief was raised and lowered to signal the opening of the trap-door for that sudden drop, the wrenching sickening pop of the rope snapping taut. The body turning slowly on its line, the fine clothes visibly soiled with urine and faeces. They were left hanging there half an hour to ensure the completion of the sentence and after the dead men were cut down the sick were escorted up to touch the corpses for luck and health. A withered limb could be made whole by setting it upon the neck of a hanged man. Women unable to conceive a child would stroke the hand of an executed felon against their bellies to make them fruitful.

Peyton said, "You've seen this?"

"More times than I care to remember." Reilly fed more green wood to the fire.

"Why would anyone want to touch a corpse like that?"

Reilly shrugged. "A dead man is an awful thing to look upon. It's the relic of a thing gone forever from the world. And that's as close as most will ever get to touching something holy."

"I don't see how all this relates to your working for my father."

Reilly looked up, surprised. "You're an impatient pup then." He smiled across at Peyton. "Where are you for now? You've got something pressing to get to?"

Peyton shook his head no.

"Fair enough," Reilly said. "I'll come to your father directly."

But he hesitated then and Peyton could see he was weighing things in his head, that there was a risk involved. The fire gave off a steady hiss, like the sound of a downpour of rain on still water.

He was born in St. Giles, Reilly told him, although his parents were both from Ireland and he was raised Irish, surrounded by Irishmen, and never thought of himself in any other way. Most of the people he knew in the community worked on the waterfront, or in shops along the streets as butchers, apothecaries, wholesalers of cloth, grocers. His father worked as a lumper on the cargo ships on the Thames, but his vocation was stealing from the English. Each night at low tide the river thieves made their way onto the East India ships at anchor. Reilly's father employed his three sons in bailing provisions into the black strip — bags painted black to make them less visible in the darkness — once the casks were pried open. The bags were handed off then to lightermen in flatboats or to mudlarks who waited in the low-tide silt of the river and carried the booty to fences in Alsatia. They could identify the stolen goods just from the smell of it rising through the cloth bags, sugar or indigo, coffee beans, ginger, tea.

Reilly and his brothers also received training from their mother who was an accomplished pickpocket. She went to churches in an elaborate outfit with fake arms sewn to a remarkably large pregnant belly that concealed her hands and she lifted jewellery, pocket watches and money from the people sitting on the pew to either side of her. No one suspected the mother-to-be whose hands were in plain view and had not moved from her belly through the entire service.

She taught her sons to remove rings from a person's fingers as they shook hands, to lift bills or snuffboxes from the pockets of men standing behind them in a crowd. They all became proficient in these sleights of hand but Reilly himself had a talent for it. His mother expressed her delight in his abilities the way other parents fawned over a child's predisposition for drawing or mathematics. Like most gifted children, he was embarrassed by his facility and wished at times to be free of it altogether.

The clandestine nature of his family's enterprises troubled him. He could see that even the Irish in St. Giles harboured ambivalent feelings about them. He wanted to live *differently*, though he never expressed that wish in words. When he wasn't picking pockets at Bartholomew Fair or public hangings, he worked at the Smithfield butcher shop, a job he'd found without consulting his parents. They seemed deeply disappointed in him, as if he had betrayed his country.

Peyton heard an odd note creeping into Reilly's voice, a dimness, a filtered quality. He seemed to have lost the thread of the story and was simply reminiscing.

Hanging days, he said, were the best of times for pickpockets — a large unruly crowd accustomed to jostling and shoving for position, a distant spectacle that held the audience's rapt attention. They talked of it among themselves with careless anticipation: a hanging was to morris, to go west, to be jammed, frumagemmed, collared, noozed, scragged, to be invited to the sheriff's ball, to dance the Paddington frisk, to be nubbed, stretched, trined, crapped, tucked up, turned off. A hanged man, his father used to say, will piss when he cannot whistle.

Reilly shook his head. He could see now there was an odd symmetry to the event, men about to be twisted at the end of a rope for thieving and dozens of others like them moving surreptitiously among the crowd, relieving the spectators of their valuables. A tax on their entertainment. A down payment on future attractions.

"You understand I'm not proud of it now," Reilly said. "I was just a lad."

"My father knew this when he hired you?"

"Same as I'm telling you now."

"What happened, Joseph?"

"Bad luck, I guess," Reilly said. "Bad luck all around."

It was the first hanging of the new year, two men convicted of stealing money and alcohol from a tavern, a young Irish servant who had killed his master in retaliation for a beating. The weather appropriately sombre, a morning of fog and freezing drizzle. No real fall of rain but the threat of it in the air all day. That cold winter smell of wet iron. It was the worst sort of weather for a thief, people bundled under layers, their coats buttoned tight and held at the collar. Reilly managed to lift a silver snuffbox, a handful of shillings, a gold repeater watch.

He found his brothers once the hanging was concluded and people slowly came back to themselves in the fields, setting their hats tight to their heads, pushing their hands into pockets. As they were leaving the grounds, Reilly was taken by the shirt collar and the hair from behind. A large well-dressed man with a round face and surprisingly tiny mouth began bellowing he had caught the thief that had stolen his pocketbook, dragging Reilly towards the gallows where the constables stood. His younger brothers hung off the man's arms and coat, Reilly yelling at them to get away.

"You hadn't stolen a pocketbook," Peyton said.

"No odds in the end. He'd heard me speaking Gaelic, I expect, which is evidence enough in the eyes of some. I managed to sneak the snuffbox and shillings to my brothers before the constables took note of us and they ran off. But I had the watch on my person, which he claimed as his own once it was turned out. There were holes in the lining of my coat that left my hands free when it looked like they were tucked away in my pockets. They'd found a thief, no question. There hardly seemed a point to whether it was him I'd robbed or not."

Peyton listened to Reilly with a growing sense of unease. He could feel the story's dive into calamity, its tragic narrative careening towards his father where John Senior would set it aright as easily as he'd piss out the fire in a tobacco pipe. The thought was profoundly disagreeable to Peyton. He had heard Cassie moaning through the door of Reilly's tilt when Annie Boss came outside to send them away and the memory of that sound came to him again in the darkness.

There were eight men in the docket for sentencing and the sentence was repeated eight times. *The law is that you shalt return from hence, to the place whence thou camest, and from thence to the place of execution, where thou shalt hang by the neck till the body be dead! Dead! Dead!* When his turn was called, Reilly held the wooden rail of the docket to stay on his feet. He broke into tears and wept uncontrollably as the sentence was pronounced and the weeping most likely saved his life.

"Commuted to branding and deportation to the colonies out of consideration for my age and my obvious display of contrition," Reilly said.

"Branding?"

Reilly held his scarred hand up in the light of the fire. "Now we're getting to John Senior," he said. "Patience rewarded."

He was brought to a public square where criminals were punished in the stocks. He was placed face down and constables tied his hands firmly to a wooden post. A small crowd gathered around him in an almost prayerful silence, as if he was about to be baptized. After the charge against him and the sentence were read aloud, the letter *T* was burned into the flesh between the thumb and forefinger of his right hand with a red-hot iron. At first there was a nearly painless shock, like jumping into icy water. Then the ache crawled into the bones of his hand, then his arm, then his entire right side. He felt as if one half of his body was radiating light. Glowing.

He was held in a prison ship on the Thames for seven months. Transportation to the American colonies was suspended after the revolution and a suitable replacement was still being settled on. Some of the men on Reilly's vessel had been aboard four years and more. The ship was filthy with vermin and rats and so overcrowded that prisoners were regularly freed on the condition they would go voluntarily into exile.

Within six weeks of accepting this plea bargain Reilly was in St. John's, penniless, walking from stagehead to warehouse to stagehead, looking for work. He was turned away each time and sometimes chased off by men wielding staves or fish forks if the brand on his hand was noted. Finally he was forced to go from table to table in the grog shops above the waterfront, begging for food, his hand wrapped in a dirty square of cloth to hide his mark. So many men intoxicated to the point of senselessness, he could have robbed them blind. He was tempted over and over and more strongly with each turned head, with each sloppy imprecation to bugger off, with the occasional whispered proposition to suck someone's cock for a shilling.

And that's where he found John Senior sitting alone with a bottle of rum, just in from Poole and waiting for a berth to the northeast shore. He nodded casually as Reilly approached him, almost as if he'd been expecting someone of his description. He didn't say a word when the boy began to tell him how he arrived in St. John's three days past and had eaten only scraps he'd managed to steal from dogs in the street in that time. Reilly took his silence as an invitation to carry on and he did so, impulsively unwrapping his hand to show the stranger his brand. He talked about his life in England until he ran out of things he could think of to say, while John Senior sat listening impassively, as if he'd paid good money for this story and was determined to take in every word. His peculiar stillness Reilly chose to interpret as a show of sympathy and instead of asking for food or spare change he asked for work, cleaning fish or cutting wood or shovelling cow shit from a byre, he didn't care what it was or where. He stood there then while John Senior considered him.

"How old are you, Joseph Reilly?" he asked finally.

"Fourteen, sir."

"You've done some honest work in your time."

"Smithfield's butchers, like I told you, sir. Four years up to this."

John Senior said, "Go on up and get yourself a glass."

They sat drinking a while, without John Senior saying anything to indicate what he intended and Reilly was superstitiously afraid to ask, as if he had now to wait until fate or the saints pointed them left or right.

John Senior reached out then and took Reilly's hand in his own. Two of John Senior's fingers had no nails, only a hard scrabble of callus and scar tissue from some ancient accident. He passed a thumb gently over the raised welt of the brand. He said, "There's no one going to let you live an honest life as long as there's a story that says otherwise."

Reilly nodded. He didn't want this man to let go of his hand.

"Are you willing to do something about that, Joseph Reilly?"

He nodded again, stupidly. He had no idea what was being suggested, what he would endure before the night was out. When John Senior let go of him Reilly turned his hand in the air with a little flourish and held up the man's wedding ring. To show what he was ready to leave behind.

Peyton reached out then and took Reilly's hand, much as his father had done in the grog shop above St. John's harbour. He traced his fingers across the wild copse of scars there. He had never looked at them as anything but a blind injury, an accidental wound of some sort. "Why are you telling me all this, Joseph?"

He let out a long breath of air. "It's just a story is all, John Peyton." After a moment he said, "God bless the mark, but it's a cold night." He refilled their mugs and they sat in silence a long time then. There was a thick cloud cover and no moon or stars showed through.

Reilly said, "If it won't offend you, I'll be saying the rosary a little while."

Peyton lifted his mug in acquiescence and then threw the cold remains of his tea into the snow. His companion took out his black prayer beads and rolled them through his fingers as he muttered those ancient prayers to himself. The dog got up from its place beside the fire, walked a little ways outside the circle of light and began barking wildly into the woods. Reilly interrupted his rosary to quiet the dog but it would not come back to the fire. The hair was ridged along its spine and it stood there growling at the dark. Peyton felt like crawling out beside the animal and joining in himself.

F O U R

Cassie was sitting at the table when Peyton and Reilly came into the tilt the next morning. The skin of her face was pale and translucent and showed the blue of veins beneath it. The bloodshot rim of her damaged eye was as bright as a partridgeberry.

Peyton sat across from her and watched as she fiddled with her fingers, worrying at them with an intensity that suggested she might fall from her chair if she looked away from her hands. There was a thin acrid smell of vomit beneath the aroma of spruce bark that Annie had put on to boil during the night. Reilly stepped across the room to where his wife stood near the fire and they talked quietly together, partly in Gaelic, partly in Mi'kmaq, like parents spelling words to keep them from the ears of children.

Cassie said, "You'll not say a word of this to your father."

Peyton stared at her. The liquid burn of fear that he'd carried all night congealed to something heavier then, something with the heft and solidity of stone.

She looked up to him with her wounded stare. "Promise me," she said.

Annie refused to let Cassie leave for home until the following day and only then when Cassie agreed to allow Peyton to accompany her. Reilly promised to keep an eye on as much of Peyton's lines as he could manage and they set out down the river about mid-morning. Cassie was so weak that they were forced to stop every half-hour or so and when they turned into the bush above Ship Cove the heavy snow sapped the last of her strength. She leaned on the trunk of every third or fourth tree and bowed her head while she sucked at the air. Finally she fell backwards in the snow and could not get herself to her feet again. Peyton cut two thin spruce trees and limbed them out, then lashed the thickest branches between the poles with leather thongs. He harnessed the head of the stretcher to his shoulders and dragged Cassie through the bush. She slept for most of the afternoon and woke only to tell him she felt well enough to walk on her own for a while, then dropped quickly back to sleep.

Near dark he lifted her down into a narrow gully and fashioned a lean-to. He set a pot of snow to boil to make a thin broth for Cassie's supper. She managed to sit up and eat the soup herself, but could only stomach half a bowl before she handed it back to him, then stretched out beneath her blanket and fell immediately asleep.

Peyton laid junks of green wood on the fire and the sap snapped and hissed as the flame took hold. The smoke blew lazily in one direction and then another, and the smell of it in the cold air was clean as laundered clothes just brought in off the line. He looked up to the night sky and even without the vertigo of alcohol he could feel the constellations turning on the axis of the North Star. He filled his pipe and tamped it with his thumb and then lit it with the end of a stick set alight in the coals.

He was twenty-six years old and had never touched a woman or been kissed in any but the most innocent of ways. It seemed a personal failure to him somehow. He looked at the sleeping figure on the opposite side of the fire. His father was still married in the eyes of the Church even if he had not seen his wife in seven years. And Cassie was young enough to be the old man's daughter. But for all the things that said it was impossible, Peyton could not make himself feel surprised and he had to admit now that part of him suspected this for years.

He tried to locate the seed of those suspicions, walking backward through his years on the coast until he came to his first spring in Newfoundland. They'd begun preparing for the return to the summer house on Burnt Island, setting the sloop into the water from her winter dry dock, loading the hold with nets, cordage, sheets, clothing and tools. At that time of year icebergs meandered aimlessly through the maze of tickles, bights and runs among the islands like dazed farmers set adrift in the honeycomb streets of London. But the massive fields of Gulf ice that could cap harbours closed for days or weeks at a time had largely come and gone by then.

John Senior had sent two hired men off to the summer house four days before to prepare for their arrival while he and Peyton and Cassie closed up the winter house. Shortly after the men left a late field of pack ice muscled in, a solid sheet of pans chafing island granite, the white glim of it stretching to the horizon. It was moving steadily on the Labrador current but was so featureless that it seemed completely still.

John Senior sat with his pipe and knitted twine to mend the salmon nets or whittled blindly at sticks of wood, hardly speaking to his son or to Cassie. Seeing that the only option was to wait, a surprising patience and calm came over him. Peyton couldn't believe a man of such grimly relentless energy could give himself over so easily to dawdling. It was more than he could manage himself and he constantly went out the front door to look in on the animals, to see if there was any change in ice conditions. It was on one of these aimless reconnaissance missions that he spotted them, their dark bodies dotting the distant surface of the ice. He burst into the kitchen and grabbed his father by the arm. "Seals," he shouted. "Hundreds of them."

"Seals don't come this far into the bay," John Senior said, but he allowed Peyton to lead him out of the house nonetheless. The barking of the herd carried across the ice to the cape where they stood. Back in the kitchen John Senior turned around several times, like a dog about to lie down, as if the physical motion was a way of settling his mind. He said, "What a time to have those two men stuck on Burnt Island."

Peyton looked at Cassie a moment and then at his father. "Cassie could come out with us."

The older man glanced at Cassie and gave a short heavy sigh. "How do you find your leg, now?" he asked her.

"I'll be fine."

"She's a fierce business on the ice. You won't like it, first along, I can guarantee you that."

"I'll be fine," she said again.

They started out across solid ice near the shore and quickly came into looser floating pans that they copied across in long loping strides, each carrying rope looped across their chests, a short wooden gaff and a sculping knife. Cassie held her long skirt in one hand to keep it clear of her legs. The animals were nearly a mile out on the water. There weren't hundreds, as Peyton first reported, but more than enough to make work for the three of them. The seals stared as they approached, their dark delicate nostrils testing the air.

John Senior said, "The young ones is saucy as the black, they'll come for you if you aren't watchful." He turned to gaffing the seals nearest him, striking down sharply and repeatedly until the animals lay still. "Take them across the bridge of the nose," he instructed as he worked. Many of the older harps were already in motion, undulating towards the open circles of sea water that allowed them access to the ocean. Cassie limped after those closest to escape as she slipped the rope over her head and took off her heavy overcoat. She had surprisingly broad shoulders, Peyton thought, watching her swing the gaff.

"John Peyton," his father shouted between strikes. "Get to work, for the love of man."

The killing went on for more than half an hour. When they knelt exhausted and bent their heads to catch their breath, almost fifty seals lay dead across half a mile of ice. John Senior slowly got to his feet. "We got to get them bled now," he said. "The pelts are worthless if they gets burnt." He smiled across at Cassie and nodded his head, like someone not entirely unhappy to have been proved wrong. Peyton watched her too with the same surprised, conflicted pride.

He and Cassie spent a few minutes observing John Senior as he made a circular cut about the neck of a seal and a second longitudinal cut down the belly to the tail. He gripped the thick layer of fat and fur and sculped it free of the flesh with quick passes of the blade, turning the bloody carcass out of the hide like a sleeper being tipped out of bedsheets. Then they made their own halting, awkward attempts to imitate him. The sleeves of their shirts were soaked in blood and the blood froze solid in the cold air. Blood seeped into the inviolate white of the ice pans. The stripped carcasses were the same dark red as the granite headlands of the coastline, a tightly clustered constellation of ruined stars. The pelts weighed up to fifty pounds apiece and they bulked them in piles of three or four, as many as could be dragged back to shore in one trip. It would take them the rest of that afternoon and all the light of the following day to haul them off the ice.

They hadn't eaten since dawn and had brought only cakes of hard tack with them out onto the ice field. They were all exhausted and freezing and ravenously hungry by the time John Senior worked his knife up the belly of the last seal. He used the heel of his boot to crack the exposed breastbone and then opened the chest cavity to cut the large fist of its heart free. He held it in his hand, the organ still hot to the touch, and he brought it to his mouth, biting into it as he would an apple. He offered it to Cassie and then to Peyton, and they ate the raw flesh together, licking the blood from their lips and wiping their chins with the bloodied sleeves of their shirts. He watched his father and Cassie watching each other. They both seemed immensely pleased with themselves, with the day, with the heat of the dead seal's heart moving in them.

Peyton stared across the fire at Cassie where she now lay sleeping. The shape of her body under the blankets reminded him of those stripped carcasses on the ice, inert, emptied of the energy of the animate. He sat smoking and tending the fire as the stars wheeled overhead. A she-moon rose and set behind them, a shallow crescent on its back. Cassie woke and asked for water and the two of them stared into the dark without speaking until she said, "Tell me a story, John Peyton."

"There's no fun to be found in any of this, Cassie."

"I'm just feeling lonely," she said and lifted herself on her elbows to watch the fire waver and shift in its place. "I can tell you about fire," she said. "I can tell you how we learned the use of fire."

He nodded and stretched a leg and then folded it back underneath himself. "All right," he said.

It was a Greek story, she said, one told to her by her father when she was a girl and too young to understand certain aspects. She said it was an old, old tale about times before our times and the times of the Greeks besides, when fire belonged to the gods alone. Prometheus, she said, and she paused and said the name again. Prometheus was a Titan, and the Titans were a race of giants. He and his brother were entrusted with the creation of the earth's creatures by Zeus, father of the gods. Feathers and claws and talons and shells and fangs were passed out to the animals as they were formed from the clay and when it came time to create people nothing remained to give them. They were left naked, defenceless, scavenging around without a way to cook food or keep warm, it was a sad time to be alive, she said. Prometheus took pity on humanity, and he conspired to steal the secret of fire from Mount Olympus and passed it down to the miserable creatures we were. Cassie stopped for a moment and lay back on the ground. "Are you listening?" she asked.

She said the sad part of the story was this. It was something she couldn't conceive of when she was a youngster. Zeus was a jealous, wretched god, as all the gods of those times were. When he discovered the theft, he punished Prometheus by having him chained to a rock and carrion birds came to him where he lay stretched out and helpless and they pecked his liver from his side and ate it. And every day his liver grew back and the carrion returned and pecked it out and ate it.

Cassie's voice was so slight that Peyton could barely hear her speaking. The fire popped and a large flanker landed on his sleeve. He shook it off into the snow where the cinder winked to ash.

"Terrible," Cassie said.

Peyton didn't know whether she saw herself stretched out in chains and helpless on that rock, or if she intended he should see himself there, or whether it was just a story the fire brought to her mind and nothing more. He swallowed against the ache in his throat and looked up at the blur of stars that were being slowly extinguished by the first light of the morning. "Cassie," he said.

But she had already drifted back to sleep.

He decided to let her rest as long as she needed and even managed to doze off himself as the sun rose. A chill woke him where he sat and he stood to stretch the cold from his legs and then stirred the coals and blew on them while he held a dry branch of pine needles to their billowing heat. He had tea ready for her when she woke and more of the broth she could hardly stomach the night before.

"I can walk today," she told him and he shrugged and said that was fair enough by him, although he doubted how far she might be able to travel. He stripped the leather thongs from the stretcher and they packed their things and started back into the bush. He broke the path, moving as slowly as he could and stopping frequently to adjust the bindings on his rackets or to examine partridge tracks so as not to get too far ahead of her. They came out on the bay five miles down from the winter house and walked the shoreline as the dark of early evening descended. As far as they could see ahead of them there wasn't a single light on the shore.

The air in the building was sharp with three days' frost and Peyton laid a fire and lit candles and then filled the wood box while Cassie sat and leaned her weight onto the table, gathering each breath into her lungs as if she was trying to carry water with her hands. He knelt to pull Cassie's boots from her feet and helped her out of her jacket and waistcoat. He crutched her to the daybed and covered her with flannel quilts. Then he made himself tea, pouring the mug half full with rum, and sat tending the fire and watching her sleep.

His father would be back from White Bay within a few days. He knew she would ask him to leave before then and that she'd go on as if nothing had happened on the river. When he came in off the traplines in January she would act as if they hadn't seen one another since the early fall and he expected he would do the same. He had a long established habit of accommodating the wishes of others even if he couldn't settle in his own mind what was right.

Peyton had just turned sixteen when John Senior announced that his son would leave Poole come April to work in Newfoundland. The family was sitting over the remnants of a boiled leg of pork that had been served with green peas and gravy and there was a moment of dead stillness among them then, as if they were all waiting for a clock to chime the hour. The sound of John Senior's spoon clinked against his cup as he stirred.

His mother pushed her chair back from the table and leaned across to take the spoon from her husband's hand before he'd finished stirring his tea.

"What's that now?" John Senior said.

She was almost too furious to form words. "Not," she said.

"Sit down, would you? What are you saying?"

"You will not," she told him. She placed the spoon carefully on her plate and took it away from the table.

John Senior was astounded by his wife's disapproval of something he regarded as a foregone conclusion. It had been years since he'd thought of the woman as a person with opinions, with influence, and he never recovered sufficiently from his surprise to respond to her objections in any sensible way.

He sat in a restless silence while she spent one evening after the next insisting her son would not leave England before he had finished his schooling and only then if he chose to do so.

Peyton was as disconcerted as his father. He had always assumed he would leave some day for Newfoundland. But he had never in his life done anything against the word or advice of his mother and the strength of her feeling on the matter made him feel strangely fearful.

One evening near the beginning of April, after delivering another variation of the near-monologue harangue that left her feeling exhausted and powerless, Peyton's mother retreated to her bedroom. John Senior stayed on in the parlour, nursing a pipe. Peyton and his sister had spent the time in the kitchen, avoiding the argument as much as was possible in the cramped quarters of the apartment. Susan was three years younger than her brother, but already the more practical and shrewder of the two. Peyton had his mother's light blue eyes and an almost perpetually astonished expression that made him look defenceless. Susan's eyes were grey like her father's. She had a settled, disinterested stare that invested even her most innocuous statement with weight and portent.

"You'll have to choose," she told him.

"Choose what?" He could smell the sweet drift of pipe smoke from the parlour.

"Between them."

"Susan," he said. He had till that moment believed it would somehow be possible to satisfy them both.

After a period of bruised silence John Senior called him into the room. He knocked his pipe into the fireplace and refilled the bowl, tamping the tobacco with his thumb. There was a small coal fire hissing in the grate.

"I'll only ask you the once," he said. "Do you want to come across with me this year?"

"Yes," Peyton whispered.

When they sailed out of Poole there was a steady breeze of wind on the open water and a sea running that rolled the vessel heavily port and starboard, the motion as eerily steady as a metronome. By nine in the morning Peyton was vomiting over the rail. John Senior stood beside him, holding his son upright against the rocking of the ship while he dry-heaved and bawled helplessly.

"You said this was what you wanted," John Senior shouted.

Peyton managed to nod his head. But he knew he would have said just the opposite if his mother had asked him the same question first. He didn't know what to call this tendency of his but cowardice.

The new fire roared in the chimney draught as it took hold, the sound of it steady and subterranean, like a waterfall thrumming in the distance. Peyton poured his mug full this time with rum and drank it straight. Cassie turned on the daybed and spoke meaningless syllables in her sleep and then settled again. He could hardly blame her for the choice she made, wrong-headed and impossible as it was. It was pity he felt for her then though he wished it could be otherwise. Even his willingness to forgive her seemed cowardly and he swallowed a mouthful of rum to choke it back.

The River Exploits

1811

FIVE

Besides himself, John Senior committed Reilly, Tom Taylor and Dick Richmond to Buchan's expedition. John Peyton was to be left to watch over the winter house with Cassie. But shortly before Old Christmas Day a cold that had nagged at him the better part of December deteriorated into something more serious. John Senior slept fitfully through a burning fever and suffered hallucinations while awake. Cassie changed the sweat-soaked sheets and heated beach stones to warm the bed when John Senior was taken with a fit of the shakes. He mumbled and moaned and spoke at length to his dead mother and to Harry Miller who had been killed some fifteen years before. At the height of his fever he thrashed wildly about the bed, swearing and weeping uncontrollably, and Cassie was forced to straddle his stomach and hold his arms to keep him from injuring himself while he carried on urging helplessly against the weight of her and cursing her for his father.

Shortly before John Senior's father died, he had invested all the family's little money in a fledgling cod and salmon fishery on the northeast shore of Newfoundland. His partner, Harry Miller, was a man he'd established a nodding acquaintance with at one of the local brothels in Poole and they occasionally drank together after their *entertainment*. Without intending to, Miller talked the man into joining his enterprise. "Land for the taking," he had said. "Salmon galore and they're fat as a whore's leg." He fingered the crotch of his trousers, making awkward adjustments, as if the thought of the money to be made across the Atlantic stirred up an immediate erection. He said, "I'll have to have another go-round here this afternoon, I can see that." Miller wasn't looking for a partner and considered he was just being sociable.

John Senior's father owned a horse and cart and made a living selling coal from house to house, and he had never considered any other work. But his wife had recently begun sleeping in her daughters' room and barely spoke to him any more, and the thought of living across the Atlantic half the year had an unexpectedly powerful appeal. He sold the animal, the property and business, and handed over almost every cent to Miller.

He only managed to make one trip out to Newfoundland. When John Senior was fifteen his father died of complications arising from a syphilitic infection. For months he suffered lengthening periods of dementia that were exacerbated by steady drinking. He was tormented by uncertainties and constantly demanded to know the time of day, the time of night, never satisfied with the answers given him. He seemed to forget who his family were and treated them as if they were strangers present in the house to steal from him while he slept. He secreted valuables away in cupboards and beneath the mattress. After his death, hidden treasures turned up in the most unlikely places: a brass snuffbox under a loose floorboard, his silver pocket watch buried in a sack of flour.

When the dementia was at its worst he was incomprehensibly abusive towards his children, towards his wife. The violence was completely out of character for the man. He had never said a harsh word to John Senior or his sisters, and never laid a hand on any of them, but for the one time he caught his son stealing sugar from a container in the pantry. It was something John Senior had been doing intermittently for years, a secret pleasure he admitted to no one, holding the rough cubes between his front teeth as he lay in bed, letting them disintegrate slowly as he drifted to sleep. His father made him replace the sugar but didn't speak another word on the matter until weeks later when they attended a public hanging.

A man convicted of robbing a fishing merchant's home of silverware and pewter candelabra stood on a cart, a cord of rope about his neck, the other end tied to a gibbet overhead. John Senior sat on his father's shoulders for a better view of the proceedings. The air smelled of coal smoke and leather. A dark knot of relatives stood with the condemned man, crying and offering words of encouragement, a parson stood behind them whispering prayers. After an allotted time, the cart was cleared of all but the thief and his eyes were covered with a cloth. At a signal from the sheriff the hangman lashed the horses and the cart jerked ahead. There was a murmur from the crowd, an almost imperceptible drift forward. The thief swung and twisted in the air. Two of the men who'd stood beside him on the cart came forward and took hold of his legs, dropping their weight onto the strangling man to bring on the release of death that much sooner. He dangled there a full half an hour then, head lolling heavily over the rough collar of rope, before the hangman cut him down.

They walked back to their home through the streets of Poole in silence. John Senior had come to the hanging at his father's invitation and he sensed there was more than spectacle on the man's mind. There was a cold air of dread about the day that seemed to work against words, that suggested the uselessness of language in the face of the things he had just witnessed.

His father brought him to the pantry, opened the container of sugar and placed it before him on the counter.

"Put your hands up there," he said. "To either side."

He did as he was told. His father took out a long leather strap and proceeded to beat him savagely across the buttocks and shoulders, across the backs of his legs, until the boy could just keep his feet, until his father exhausted himself.

John Senior stood there shaking and crying silently when it was done, hands still on the counter. He could hear his father moving behind him, sucking air heavily through his nostrils to catch his breath. There was the sound of glassware set on the table, a cork loosed from a bottle. "Have some of this now," his father said.

John Senior turned from the counter and took the proffered glass of rum.

His father's thick upper lip was beaded with sweat and his hair frizzed away from his head in all directions, as if he was standing on a charge of static. He said, "You see where thieving will get you."

They never spoke of the incident afterwards. And nothing in his father's demeanour or actions in the years that followed predicted the bouts of blind rage he would descend into once the disease overtook him. When nothing else could appease him or settle his outbursts, John Senior was forced to beat his father senseless, weeping with frustration as he struck the sick man about the shoulders and head.

Through the worst of his fever, fifty years on, John Senior relived those moments, thrashing on his sick bed and shouting. Cassie leaned over him and pinned his arms to the mattress. "I'm not your father," she shouted at him, but he was too delirious to understand her.

The illness was still burning through the old man when Peyton arrived at the house from the traplines and Cassie sent him to Ship Cove to ask after Buchan's surgeon. By the time he returned accompanied by both the surgeon and Buchan himself, the fever had broken. The doctor prescribed a regimen of salts and cod liver oil for strength and told him to put aside any thought of accompanying the expedition that was due to leave in three days' time. Cassie echoed the doctor's orders to the old man and sent the visitors away the next morning with salt fish and bread tied up in a cloth.

Peyton thought she seemed immensely relieved to have settled keeping John Senior at home and to have the navy men out of the way. He studied her look of relief for a moment before going to the door. He called out and motioned them back up the path and volunteered to take John Senior's place on the expedition. He told the lieutenant he would come down to the *Adonis* on the twelfth. Buchan shook his hand and thanked him and nodded another goodbye to Cassie who stood behind Peyton in the kitchen. "Miss Jure," he said.

John Senior was as furious as his weakened state allowed. "It's a goddamn fool's errand," he said.

"You were fool enough to sign on. And to send Taylor and Richmond and Reilly along."

John Senior began to speak but fell into a fit of coughing that purpled his face. Peyton called for Cassie who came running from the kitchen and lifted the sick man forward and pounded his back with the open palm of her hand until he had coughed up a mouthful of green-and-black phlegm into a handkerchief.

"I had my reasons," John Senior managed as she helped him back against the pillows. His lungs clawed at the air.

"Out," Cassie said to Peyton. A lock of her hair had fallen out of the bun at the back of her head and she turned it behind her ear with a distracted motion that made Peyton's stomach knot. "Go on now," she said when he made no move to leave. "I mean it, John Peyton," she said.

Cassie was already up and had lit the fire and boiled the kettle for tea by the time he made his way down to the kitchen. The dark play of light from the fireplace sent her shadow up the opposite wall like a vine. There was a single candle burning on the table where she'd put out a plate of brewis in pork fat for his breakfast.

"What way is he this morning?" Peyton asked after he sat down.

She set an earthenware mug in front of him. "Well enough to be contrary," she said. "He'd be down here now if I hadn't threatened to start the fire with his boots." She pushed the sugar towards him and he ladled a teaspoonful into his mug. "Are you going to look in on him before you go?"

Peyton shook his head. "He'd just try to talk me out of it, I imagine."

"He's only watching out for you, John Peyton." Cassie turned away from him to add wood to the fire.

"You think this trip is sensible?"

She shook her head. "I'm hardly a judge of what is or isn't sensible now, am I?" She sat across from him and their faces hovered over the stunted light of the candle, an oily stem of smoke curling towards the ceiling. There were half-moons charcoaled beneath her eyes and Peyton knew there was more than just shadow working there. The day he'd come in off the traplines he'd found her scythed over in pain as she stood at the table. Her hands held the edge so fiercely that he had to pry them free to get her to the daybed.

"It's just during my time," she'd told him. "The rest of the month I'm not so bad."

When she was nursing his father she gave no sign of discomfort at all and he could see how it exhausted her to disguise it. As he expected, nothing had been said about the whole affair since he brought her down from the river in November.

Cassie lifted the teapot to refill his mug. "John Senior says Lieutenant Buchan might try to talk you into setting aside the rifles before you come up to the Indians at the lake," she told him. "He wanted me to warn you about that."

Peyton slurped at the scalding tea. "What else did he want you to tell me?"

"He said to say shot is no good to get through those leather cassocks they wear. He said they double them up at the front and shot won't be more than a bee sting through it."

Peyton turned his head towards the window. Two inches of frost framed each pane of glass. The first grey of dawn was just taking root across the frozen bay. "Since we're meant to be heading up there with friendly intentions," he said, "it might not be such a bad thing the old man is down with that fever."

"He just wants you back out of it alive is all."

Peyton looked into his plate. He finished the last morsel of brewis and used his index finger to clean the pork fat from the plate, then he drank the last of his tea. He felt as if someone had dragged his insides through a field of nettles and at that moment he considered saying so. But all he said was, "I better get a move on if I'm to get across to Ship Cove today."

╫

The expedition left Ship Cove at 7 a.m. on Sunday, January 13, 1811. It was a morning of scuddy weather, with low cloud and blowing snow, and it was still not much above light when they started out. In all there were twenty-three men in the group, including among them Peyton, Richmond, Taylor and Reilly; four marines, six Blue Jackets and a boy of the HMS *Adonis*; William Cull and Matthew Hughster, James Carey and several other men in their employ. The volunteers were examined by the ship's surgeon and all but one, a marine who was beginning to show signs of a tuberculosis infection, were pronounced fit for travel.

As well as their packs and firearms the party hauled sledges loaded with 3,600 pounds of provisions and goods — bread, sugar, tea and cocoa, salt pork, salt fish, 60 gallons of spirits, 270 pounds of cartouche boxes and ammunition, 10 axes, 6 cutlasses, and 40 pounds of culinary utensils. The sledges were also packed with a carefully inventoried array of gifts for the Red Indians: blankets, 30; woollen wrappers, 9; flannel shirts, 18; hatchets, 26; tin pots, 10; sundry knickknacks such as beads, thread, knives, fish hooks.

They crossed from the schooner to Little Peter's Point in an onshore gale and drifting snow that needled the eyes of the men. They walked single file and bent into the wind, their heads bowed low to protect the exposed skin of their faces. They wore creepers over their boots to help keep their footing but the ice on the bay was so tightly packed it had cracked and buckled into the air. Long stretches of pressure ridges and pinnacles made hauling the sledges a tricky, exhausting business. The men who carried only their knapsacks followed behind those dragging to keep the heavy sleds from tipping. They had been ordered to stay close to one another but the poor light and the blowing snow made it difficult to see a man ten yards ahead or behind. Buchan scampered back and forth along the line to ensure everyone was accounted for.

Peyton was partnered with Richmond and shouldered the back of the sledge through rough patches and heavy snowdrifts and stepped in with all his weight to keep the sledge from tipping over as it crested a ridge of ice. By the time they rounded a point out of the wind Peyton's shirt and undergarments were soaked through with sweat. The men spelled off the sledges and chewed hard tack and sucked at handfuls of snow. Buchan made his way through the milling group with the air of a busy man who is about to put something down to get to more pressing concerns. There was a relentless, wiry energy about him that struck the furriers and fishermen as incongruous and almost ridiculous in such a short, slight figure. He tugged nervously at the lashings on the sledges to make sure they were secure. "The ice is calm on the Exploits," he told his crew. "We're out of the worst of the wind for now, we'll make good time from here."

"If he's so goddamned hearty," Richmond said to Peyton, "maybe he should take a sledge and we could play sheepdog for a while."

Peyton picked up the harness where Richmond had let it fall. The sweat against his skin was already cold and he wanted to get moving again before the chill settled any deeper. He watched Richmond walk across to Tom Taylor and repeat himself. Taylor turned his face up to the clouds and laughed. The two men continued talking and Peyton could see the nature of the interaction shift in their darkening expressions. They began to argue about something and fell into a shouting match, cursing one another with a practised ease that attracted the attention of the entire party. Buchan made his way across to Peyton. "Should I intervene in this?" he asked.

Peyton shook his head. "It's just their way." He leaned into the harness, resting against the weight of the sledge and staring at his feet. In the ten years Peyton had known them he had never seen Richmond and Taylor carry on a conversation that didn't involve insults and disagreement. The rancour between them was so habitual it was possible to dismiss it as harmless, even affectionate. He found it an embarrassingly intimate thing to watch. "We'd best get started," he said. "If we wait for them to simmer down, we'll be here till dark."

Buchan began issuing orders and as the caravan trudged into motion Richmond turned away from Taylor to catch up with Peyton. His massive shoulders sloped like a barrel stave, his face hidden under a full beard of curly black hair. He was shaking his head and smiling to himself. He looked to Peyton like a man who had just quenched a thirst.

For two miles they travelled well in the lee of a heavy forest of birch and poplar growing right to the waterline of the river. When they reached Wigwam Point, the Exploits veered northwest into the wind and each man shouldered into the weight of it as if the sledges had twice the heft of a moment earlier. A mile further on they passed Hughster's upper salmon station and carried on from there to the remains of a tilt William Cull had used while trapping the previous winter. It was near 3 p.m. with not much more than an hour of light left in the day and Buchan ordered the caravan to a halt. He took Cull and Hughster to reconnoitre the stretch of river ahead while camp was struck.

The tilt's ceiling had caved in and one wall fallen and the snow had drifted six feet deep against the others. Most of the men were engaged digging out the shelter while Richmond and Taylor took the ship's boy to cut fresh spruce for bedding and they gathered several turns of young birch and scrag for firewood. A studding sail was unpacked from the sledges and rigged up across the space left by the downed wall and folded across to form something of a ceiling along one side. Two rifle shots reported in the distance.

"Red Indians?" Corporal Bouthland asked.

"Not likely this far down the river," Peyton said. "If we're lucky, they come upon some fresh craft for our supper."

The party hung their wet stockings on sticks near the fire. Half an hour later the advance party returned, dragging the haunch of a caribou. Buchan announced there was clear ice and fair travel for at least the first two miles in the morning. The sleeves of Cull's coat were laced with blood where he had paunched the animal and severed the back leg from the torso. Large strips of flesh were cut from the haunch and roasted over the fire. The men had not had a proper meal since before dawn and they ate the meat nearly raw.

Buchan made a point of sitting with Peyton. After they had finished eating, both men took out pipes and tobacco, drawing the heat of the smoke into their bodies. "Richmond and Taylor now," Buchan said quietly. "Should I be keeping them apart?"

Peyton said, "You'd have an easier time parting the waters of the Red Sea."

"Is that right then?"

"Like an old married couple," Peyton said, nodding. "Their families fished together on the French Shore, then in Trinity Bay before they came our way."

"They've been with your father how long now?"

"It was Harry Miller hired them. Long before my time," Peyton said. And then he told Buchan the story as he'd heard it from others on the shore.

Richmond first met Miller on a schooner carrying goods and passengers north into Conception and Trinity bays and on to Fogo Island. He was not more than twelve years old. His family and the Taylors were just returned from a winter in England and heading for new fishing rooms in Trinity Bay. The weather blew hard as soon as they sailed into open water and forced the passengers to keep to the shelter of the steerage quarters. Richmond's father fell into conversation with a heavy-set man sprawled on the bunk opposite. He had unruly grey hair and bushy salt-and-pepper eyebrows. "There's land for the taking on the northeast shore," Miller said. "Salmon galore and as fat as a whore's leg. Traplines through the backcountry and not enough people to run them all." He leaned back onto the bunk where he ferreted bed lice out of the straw and nipped them dead between his fingernails. "If you find Trinity not to your liking, you come down to the Bay of Exploits and look for Harry Miller. I'll set you up."

Richmond was sitting beside his father during this exchange. John Senior was on the bunk next to Miller though he never spoke a word through the entire conversation.

When Richmond and Taylor were in their twentieth year, their families suffered through a poor season that ended with a month of almost ceaseless rain from August into September that made it impossible to properly cure the fish. Most of it went green and mouldy with the wet and was fit only to feed their dogs. Even their garden was ruined, the potatoes and turnips rotting in the ground. Richmond's father was barely forty at the time but he looked old enough to have fathered a man nearly his age. He walked with a permanent stoop and a list to one side, as if he was just able to resist letting his body topple over altogether. His mother was convinced that another season like the one they'd just suffered through would be the death of her husband. They had no choice but to look for poor relief in St. John's or to return to England for the winter and she enlisted the support of Mrs. Taylor in lobbying their husbands to abandon the island for good. As the year darkened, the two couples spent their evenings arguing among themselves while they drank glasses of a potent potato alcohol Richmond's father brewed in a still at the back of the tilt. It was clear the women had more stamina and would win out in the end. Both Richmond and Taylor made up their minds to stay behind regardless.

Tom Taylor married Richmond's sister, Siobhan, in St. John's while the rest of their families awaited a passage to England. Richmond's mother pawned a length of fine satin to pay the chaplain who performed the ceremony, and the entire party proceeded to get drunk at one of the dozens of filthy grog shops above the waterfront. Several men were already asleep on the straw lain against the wall when the wedding party arrived. There was an uneven sputter of light from half a dozen tallow candles. Siobhan wore a muslin gown over grey pantaloons tied at the ankle with a black twist. Richmond led the toasts to the new couple and the parents of the bride and groom, and the strangers in the room stood with the families to offer their best and wish the new couple well.

Neither Richmond nor Taylor had ever seen the northeast shore when they left St. John's that week to look for Harry Miller. Richmond spotted John Senior on the wharf when they disembarked in Fogo. He didn't recognize Richmond or remember meeting him. He was about to sail into St. John's enroute to Poole for the winter, but he delayed his trip long enough to carry them across to Miller's winter house.

Miller was already three-parts drunk when he came down to the wharf, his head cocked suspiciously at the three young strangers coming ashore in the company of John Senior. He didn't remember meeting Richmond as a boy either. He didn't recall the harsh weather during the trip out of St. John's or the way his business partner had sat next to him without speaking a word the entire journey. "Although that sounds like the contrary bastard, hey?" he said. He nodded at John Senior where he sat and laughed. He scratched wildly at his hair as if it wasn't untidy enough to suit him. "You didn't just make that bit up now, did you? I promised you work, did I?"

John Peyton had never heard Miller speak but his voice changed when he quoted these words to Buchan, borrowing the tone of contented surliness that those who'd known Miller used when telling the story.

Buchan shook his head. He said, "I'm sorry not to have had the chance to make Mr. Miller's acquaintance. He was quite the character it seems."

"It was Richmond and Taylor that found him. The body," Peyton said. "After the Reds got to him."

Buchan nodded. "And they stayed on with your father."

"Yes sir. And scrapping all the while." Peyton watched the fire. His feet were so close to the heat that steam rose from his boots and still he was shivering with the cold. "As long as they don't turn on any of the rest of us, they can snipe at one another as much as they like, is my opinion."

Buchan tapped the bowl of his pipe against his boot. "All right," he said.

The wind had gone down with the sun and the temperature dropped as the sky cleared overhead. A second fire was kindled and the men huddled between the two under blankets or furs, but the cold was so intense that no one was able to cobble together a proper stretch of sleep. Peyton managed to fall off only a few minutes at a time before the aching woke him and he stamped his feet or slapped his hands to bring the tingle of feeling back into his limbs. Men got up to fuel the fire or simply to pace the length of the camp to ward off the frost.

Some time after midnight Peyton woke with severe stomach cramps from the nearly raw game he'd eaten and he walked a little ways into the woods to relieve himself. He squatted beside a tree facing the sail wall which billowed and snapped in the breeze. The firelight threw the men's distorted shadows on the canvas where they lifted and fell like souls lost in a tide and a sadness that he mistook for fear came over him then. Below the tilt the frozen length of the Exploits was a wide blue scar banked by darkness. The force of the water moving underneath the ice shifted the surface and the forest echoed the hollow crack back and forth across the river. Peyton hunched there and shivered and he thought of Cassie walking alone through these selfsame woods in the fall. The voices of the men still awake in the camp moved in the trees overhead like birds calling against the cold and the darkness.

They broke camp at dawn. The morning was clear with a sharp wind out of the northwest. The men were so tired and in such a frozen state they stumbled and moved drunkenly about, their hands and feet nearly devoid of feeling until the day's exertions returned some warmth to their bodies. They travelled for two miles, past Reilly's trapping tilt nestled back among the trees and on to the Nutt Islands. Half an hour beyond them they reached a small waterfall and stopped to rest and trade off the sledges. Above the waterfall, a long series of rapids had ridged the ice so severely that it was nearly impossible to haul the sledges over them and a small party walked ahead of the main group to map the least treacherous route forward. The leather lashings that held the sledges together worked loose from the constant banging and they were forced to make frequent stops to rebind them.

By late afternoon the expedition had travelled a little less than seven miles. They hauled the sledges into the trees on the north side of the river and cut spruce to fence in the fireplace and cooked a meal of salt pork and meat from the second haunch of caribou that they'd collected on their way past the carcass earlier in the day. The night was no warmer than the one previous but the men were so exhausted that all but the watches slept through until dawn.

Before setting out in the morning, Buchan had a cask packed with two days' worth of bread, salt pork, cocoa and sugar buried at the campsite for use on the way back down the Exploits.

The shelvy ice conditions deteriorated as they moved upriver and the men not employed at hauling worked ahead with axes or cutlasses to level the highest ridges and fill the valleys with ice and snow to keep the sledges from coming to pieces on impact. By afternoon three of the sledges were so badly damaged that the party was forced to stop while repairs were made and the expedition's gear was repacked. Two of Cull's men and the ship's boy were sent a mile ahead to set up camp and start a fire, which the rest of the party reached just after dark.

In the early afternoon of the sixteenth they arrived at the foot of the first great waterfall. Buchan travelled ahead with Cull and Hughster to search for the Indian path used by the Beothuk to portage above the falls and the rest of the party fenced in a fireplace to camp for the night on the north side of the river. Peyton and Reilly strapped on pot-lid rackets and took their firearms up a brook that met the river near the camp and half a mile in came on a beaver dam that backed the brook up into a fair-sized pond. The rattle at the head of the dam kept an area clear of ice and the two men crouched in the woods nearby. Since Cassie's visit to Reilly's tilt, there was a new awkwardness between the two men. Their habitual banter seemed contrived and adolescent and they hadn't managed yet to fashion a language to suit the darkened circumstances of their friendship. They waited for more than an hour in silence until there was little enough light left in the day to see fifty yards ahead and they had almost given up on finding supper. What they shot at was no more than a shadowed movement above the dam.

The beaver's fur was sleek and oily and it stained their gloves as they turned the hump of the animal on its back to paunch it. It lay more than three feet in length from its nose to the tip of the wide, flat paddle of its tail and weighed a good sixty pounds.

"Reminds me of the rats aboard the East India ships on the Thames,"

Reilly said. He tapped the huge buckteeth with his bloody knife. "Fangs the like of that on them."

Back at the camp, they set a large kettle of water to boil and dressed the animal and added the lean fore-haunches to the pot for broth. The back haunches were skewered and cooked undivided until the thick layer of fat was crisply roasted. The night was surprisingly mild and the men ate their fill and talked with more enthusiasm than they had managed since setting out. The Blue Jackets and marines had never tasted beaver and most pronounced it fair eating. After the meat was finished, Reilly fried the tail in pork fat and each of Buchan's men was offered a taste of the rich marrow. The ship's boy chewed meditatively for a moment and asked if it was true as he'd heard it that a beaver, cornered by a predator, will turn on itself and chew off its own testicles.

"True as the tides," Richmond announced solemnly. "Eating for strength, he is. You mind to steep a beaver's pride and drink off the liquid, it does wonders for your nature."

The boy scoffed. "Go away with ye," he said.

"Tom Taylor," Richmond appealed, "am I speaking the God's honest truth or no?"

"Gospel," Taylor said. "Knew a man drank beaver's pride before going out to a bawdy house, didn't he up and die with exhaustion. Licked right out he was. And still hard as the rock of the Church when they laid him out at the dead-house."

"It's all bull you're talking," the boy said.

"Beaver or bull, I could care less about," Corporal Bouthland interrupted. "But who here has seen one of these Red Indians we're after?"

It was the first time since they'd left Peter's Arm that anyone had deliberately pointed in the direction they were heading. Buchan had been sitting with a pipe, making notes in his journal by the light of the fire as he did at the end of each day's travel. He seemed not to be following the conversation, but sat suddenly forward. He tucked the journal into a satchel. "Yes," he said. "How about it?"

Peyton glanced across at Reilly. The Irishman was staring into the fire, but seemed to sense Peyton's look and he shook his head slightly without taking his eyes from the flames. The others fidgeted where they sat.

Buchan said, "John Peyton?"

Peyton cleared his throat. He said that before he came across to Newfoundland he'd seen a young girl put on display in Poole who was said to be a Red Indian. She was outfitted in a dress and shoes and looked nothing much more than an English girl, though someone had painted her face and tied a feather in her hair.

Tom Taylor was stroking his blond beard with both hands and he jumped in then to say that according to what he knew the Reds were a race of giants by and large, and that many of the Indians he'd heard spoken of by others were said to be over seven feet tall.

Reilly said it was only an idiot that believed all he was told, which Richmond took exception to. He said, "A Papist should be one to mock believing what's told us, I'm sure." He and Taylor had worked with Reilly on John Senior's rivers twenty years and more, but there was no love lost between the three. The fact that Reilly was Irish Catholic was enough to make him a target of Richmond's hostility. Reilly's marriage to Annie Boss was more fuel for the steady fire. Richmond stared at Reilly as he spoke now, daring him to contradict or interrupt him. "I have had occasion to come upon old gravesites of the Indians," he said, "and once or twice to satisfy my own curiosity on the matter I have held a shank bone against my own. Now I am no small man by most measures and I was but a lad to the frame of those Indians."

There was a round of murmuring in the camp, a scatter of dismissive laughter. Reilly shook his head but said nothing.

"Mr. Cull," Buchan said. "I understand you carried one into St. John's, didn't you?"

"I did sir, yes. Nigh on ten year ago now, as I recall, it was a young woman out in a canoe by herself and heading for a bird island in Gander Bay." Cull pulled his coat up around his shoulders as if it was about to slip down his back.

He had hardly a tooth left in his mouth and his face had a concave, half-starved look about it. "The governor in those days had offered fifty pound to bring one in friendly-like and it seemed as she was alone there'd be little trouble to do so. Took her up in the fall and they made a bloody great fuss over her, the merchants and their wives tripping over themselves to cultivate her good graces. In all the years I been going into St. John's I was never so much as offered a bare-legged cup of tea by the quality and they brought my savage into the shops on the waterfront and let her walk off with whatever caught her fancy. Mostly ironwork she wanted, pots and kettles and such, I can see her now waddling under the weight of it all in her arms and a bloody great pot on her head to boot. I tried to help her carry some of it, but she seemed to think I wanted to steal it away and wouldn't allow me to touch an item.

"They put on a dance for her one evening and invited all the quality in town to have a view of her. There was music which I remember she seemed fond of but she could not be prevailed upon to dance. She was a modest creature and very sensible to the presence of children as I recall and as long as she was in the company of women she seemed not to mind being where she was. I was the only man she'd permit to hang nearby. I s'pose as I had taken her, she allowed as I would watch out for her or some such thing. The governor paid me my fee and I was told to bring her back with her pots and set her loose."

Corporal Bouthland spoke up again. He was among the oldest marines who had volunteered for the mission, about his middle thirties. The pate of his head was nearly bald but he wore a pigtail stiffened with grease and flour at the back. He had a mole on his right cheekbone that sprouted a cluster of stiff hairs like the feelers of some blind insect. He said, "What did this one look like?"

"She was tolerable fair for an Indian," Cull said, then he looked across at Reilly and said, "No offence now, Joseph. But she was only middle size, this one. She dressed all in deerskins and was covered from head to toe in that red paint they wear and there was no way to persuade her to wash. And eyes as dark as hell's flames."

"What was her name?" Buchan asked.

"We never had a name for her as such, Lieutenant."

"Did anyone manage to speak to her while she was in your care?"

"Not in so many words, sir, no. It was all a dumb show and grunts and such we managed with. There was no sense to be got out of her mouth as far as anyone could tell."

Buchan had refilled and lit his pipe and puffed quietly for a few minutes. "There are some that suggest the Red Indians are of Norwegian extraction and that their language is likewise related," he said.

Cull nodded, a quizzical expression on his face. "Is that right?" he said.

"Private Butler," Buchan went on, pointing out a marine with the end of his pipe, "is fluent in Norwegian and conversant in most of the dialects known to the north of Europe. I'm hoping he can assist us when we reach the lake."

Tom Taylor was incredulous. "Now how did such a young pup manage a feat the likes of that?" he asked.

Butler sat up straight and hugged his knees. "My mother is Norwegian."

"Go on then," Taylor said to the marine. "Give us a listen."

Bouthland prodded the young man in the back. "Get up, laddie," he said.

"Sir?" Butler asked, looking across at Buchan.

"By all means. Perhaps the gentlemen who have heard the Red Indians' language will recognize a similarity."

The marine stood up from his place as if he was about to give a speech or recital. He held his arms ramrod straight at his sides and stared off into the woods as he spoke. He had straight blond hair braided down the length of his back, and an earnestness that made him seem childlike. When he finished his speech or recitation, his shipmates began applauding and slapped his back.

"Well?" Buchan asked.

Cull snuffled his runny nose on the sleeve of his coat. "It's nigh on ten year, as I said, sir. But it's like to be the same gibberish I heard then, as near as I can tell."

++

Peyton lay awake a long time that night. The girl was in his mind for the first time in years, stood up on her tabletop in Poole. An impatient crowd of Englishmen pushed towards the front of the high-ceilinged room. They had all paid their two pence expecting to see a savage child, some mooncalf of the isle, something rich and strange. Not this pale, silent girl in an English dress with strips of white paint or lime daubed on her cheeks. There were shouts, a scatter of boos. The discontent of the crowd frightened her, as if she knew she had disappointed them in a way she was helpless to correct. The English audience pressing in on her must have seemed like the half-wild and savage creatures they had come hoping to see.

It was Richmond who had taken the girl captive, though no one in the party had mentioned this in the company of Lieutenant Buchan for fear of the questions it would raise. Peyton thought of Richmond picking through an Indian grave, holding shanks up to his leg as if he was checking the length of a garment. It was a heartless thing and cold, to Peyton's mind, disturbing a grave that way. Something he wished he could say he'd had no part in himself.

There were Red Indian burial sites all over the Bay of Exploits, though none of those Peyton had seen appeared to be recent. During his first summer on the shore, John Senior had taken him on a tour of the salmon rivers in the bay to meet the men he employed and to show him the country he would some day own a good portion of. They were crossing an open run of water in a scull with sixteen foot of keel. She had a single eight-foot mast and a square sail taking a full sheet of wind. John Senior was in the stern, leaning on the tiller. Peyton was dozing in the bow, lulled by the heavy swell that the boat was riding easily. He was almost asleep when he saw his father lift his head. John Senior stood then, one hand still on the tiller, looking across the bay in the direction of the wind.

"Get the oars in the water," he said. He turned to lash the tiller steady. "John Peyton," he shouted.

Peyton sat up and looked to the horizon where a low bank of dark cloud was blotting light from the water's surface, scudding fast. He was just on his feet when the first knuckle of wind tore in, the boat tilting sideways in the air and slamming back, knocking him onto his backside. John Senior scrambled to the mast and hauled in the strain of the sail as the seas came up around them. "The oars, goddamn it," he shouted. But Peyton couldn't manage to get to his feet at all, and John Senior let the sail flap loose when it came down, crawling to the tawt and setting out the oars.

The seas were running eight and ten feet high suddenly, the bow of the boat lifted nearly perpendicular and then slamming down hard like a maul being used to sink a fence post. The crest of each wave broke over the gunnels, gallons of sea water sloshing around in the bilge. Peyton struggled aft and took hold of a wooden container, scooping and heaving water back over the side. They crested again and he braced himself as the boat hammered down.

"Bail 'er, Johnny," his father yelled. He came back on the oars as they shifted into the face of another ten-footer. "For the love of Christ," he shouted.

Peyton had never heard his father call him Johnny before and as he laced back into bailing he glanced up towards him. He froze in mid-motion, bracing himself with a hand on the gunnel. When John Senior saw his face, he looked over his shoulder towards the bow. Every seam was leaking water.

Swan Island was the nearest point of land and John Senior angled towards it, the seas calming slightly as they veered into the lee. The island's hump of granite hills and sparse patches of black spruce reared into sight at the tip of each swell, then disappeared as the boat pounded into the trough. It seemed a capricious, teasing game, a promise of shelter offered and then withheld, offered and withheld. Peyton stopped looking up at all at the last, bailing furiously, so numb with fear and fatigue he couldn't feel a thing in his arms but the dull levering motion he repeated and repeated. He was scooping and flinging madly when the keel came up solid on the shallows of the beach. They hauled the scull by the anchor line till it was as far clear of the water as they could manage, then dragged the anchor up onto the rocks to hold her there. John Senior picked his way up into the hills until he found a pendant cave that offered some shelter from the wind and rain. They sat there a long time in silence, both men soaking wet and exhausted and breathing heavily.

"You know where you are now?" John Senior asked him finally.

"No sir."

"Indian country, this is." His father's rifle rested across his lap.

Peyton looked at him. He was still shaking.

"Graves all along this shore, in under these cliffs. We're probably sitting on a Indian or two right now."

Peyton had considered his father was making a joke, but it was so unlike him and his manner so matter of fact that he finally accepted the possibility they were sheltering in a burial site. He coughed into his fist to disguise the violent shiver that passed through him.

"Never mind now," John Senior said. "Dead Indians are the least of your worries. It's the quick you got to watch out for."

The wind went down as suddenly as it rose but the rain continued heavy, the steady drift of it stippling the roiling ocean, and water dripped onto their necks from the damp rock cliff above them. Where the dirty quilt of cloud met the sea on the horizon it was nearly impossible to tell one from the other. The noise of the downpour was steady and soothing and eventually Peyton fell to sleep.

His father wasn't beside him when he came to himself. The rain had slowed to a mauzy drizzle. Peyton rolled out into the open and looked up and down the shore.

"Over here," his father shouted to him.

John Senior was crouching near a deep indentation in a cliff face about a hundred yards to the west. As he came up to him Peyton could make out a crumple of reddened material at the back of the cave under a loose pile of stones. They crawled in and knelt beside it.

"Most of them got a winding sheet of birchbark," his father said. He reached to roll away a couple of stones and fingered the rotten canvas. The red-ochre stain came away on his hands. "This one got part of some Christian's sail." He set aside the rifle and began moving the rocks and stones to one side. "Give us a hand," he said.

Once they'd cleared the grave John Senior lifted the shroud away from the bones of the corpse. They'd been picked clean by time and the brine of the salt-sea air. The body had been placed on its side, the knees fixed in the fetal position against the chest. The ribs had collapsed over the spinal cord's shallow crescent. The left hand was missing the bones of three fingers. Only the thumb and fore-finger remained, the digits extended like the stilled hour and minute hands of a timepiece. Everything was covered in a fine red dust. There was a small leather pouch beside the corpse. It was tied at the top with a plaited thong of caribou hide that John Senior cut away with a knife. Inside were several carved antler charms, a piece of iron pyrite and the skulls of two birds. He passed one to Peyton and the boy turned it over in the palm of his hand to examine the deli-cately fluted cavities.

His father gathered the bag's contents back together and carefully retied the brittle leather thong, then held it out to his son. "Here," he'd said. "A keepsake for you."

It struck Peyton as a funny word to use and a peculiar gesture, given how close they'd just come to being lost themselves. It made him distrust his father in a way he was never able to articulate clearly. He disliked remembering the event and was sorry to have it in his head now, lying cold and exhausted and sleepless on the banks of the River Exploits. He shifted restlessly in his blan-kets, tapping his head against the rough mattress of spruce boughs. He turned onto his side then, drawing his legs up to lie in the exact same position as the dead man he'd uncovered years ago, and waited for sleep.

SIX

On the morning of the seventeenth Buchan had a cask of provisions and four gallons of rum buried at the campsite and the party began its ascent around the falls. They hauled the sledges through a winding path among high rocks until the going became too steep to continue. The goods were unloaded and the men carried the casks on their backs to the top of the falls, turning back to make two or three trips before the whole of their provisions and the sledges themselves had been conveyed up the path and across a half-frozen stretch of bog to the riverside. Around noon the wind veered to the southeast and the morning's sleet turned to pouring rain. The group had made no more than a mile and a half all told, but the general state of fatigue and the soaking condition of their clothes and all their supplies led Buchan to call a halt to the day's travel. A camp was prepared beneath the studding sail which was strung in the trees as a tarp. By nine in the evening the rain had stopped and the men dried their clothes over the fires and turned in for the night.

As they started up the river the following day, the forest lining the river changed from poplar and birch to a dark corridor of black spruce, pine and larch. A fire had burned off the woods from the Bay of Exploits to the falls almost seventy years before and poplar and birch had replaced the old spruce forest across the burn-over. The change in the woods they travelled beside was abrupt and complete, as if a line had been drawn to separate two worlds.

The river above the falls was so rough and wild that it ran open in the centre and early that morning one of the sledges fell through the poor ice near the shoreline. It went down on a shoal and James Carey, who was hauling it, was swept back and beneath the ice by the force of the current. There was a moment of wild shouting as Buchan cleared the rest of the party onto the shore. Richmond threw himself flat on the ice and stretched shoulder-deep into the freezing water to reach for the man, rooting blindly with his face turned to the shore, as if he were searching for stockings lost beneath a bed. Carey was caught up in the heavy leather harness of the sledge and could not get himself free even after he latched onto Richmond's hand and was pulled into the open. His face bobbed to the surface and went under in the froth. Richmond yelled for help and Peyton crawled down as near as he dared.

"An axe," Richmond yelled over his shoulder, "a cutlass."

Buchan skittered a sword across the ice towards them and Peyton crawled with it to the ice edge.

"Cut him loose," Richmond shouted.

In the drive of the current Peyton could make out only shadowed movement beneath the surface and he stabbed wildly into the river's flow below the arm Richmond held. Water soaked through where his coatsleeve met his swan-skin cuff, so icy cold it felt like he was flaying his own skin with the blade. When Carey came free of the sledge the two men dragged him back to the shore where he lay shivering and spitting and bleeding like a gaffed seal.

They built a fire and stripped Carey free of his sodden clothes while a small group of marines used rope and grappling hooks to recover the sledge and its gear from the river. There were a number of gashes beneath Carey's arm that were staunched with raw turpentine from a fir tree. One cut had gone so deep in the flesh that it had to be cauterized with an iron heated in the fire to stop the bleeding. Afterwards Carey was covered in blankets. Peyton sat beside him and apologized for his injuries.

Carey shivered uncontrollably, his teeth hackering from the cold and shock. "A damn sight better than being drowned," he said.

Richmond had taken off his coat and hung the wet sleeve over the heat. He said, "You have to spill a little blood to keep body and soul together sometimes."

Two of the Blue Jackets had ruined their shoes in the previous day's rain and galled their feet almost clear to the bone and they'd found it difficult to keep pace with the rest of the company. Buchan decided to leave them with Carey while his clothes were drying and they were ordered from there to return to the *Adonis*. The rest of the party continued upriver, clinging close to the shoreline with ropes and poles at the ready.

Four miles above the falls, when the ice finally settled and lay smooth, they encountered the first of the Indian caribou fences. It was like walking into a darkened hallway without doors. On both sides of the Exploits, as far as they could see ahead, trees had been felled one across the last to form a wall eight to ten feet high. The youngest Blue Jackets balked like horses at a hedge. Buchan ordered them up off the ice, a fire was kindled to boil water for cocoa, and William Cull spoke to them about the herds of caribou that cross the river each fall, hundreds and thousands beyond counting, how the swimming animals were led by the fences into slaughtering yards where the Beothuk stood behind wooden gazes and took them down with arrows and spears.

After they had eaten their food and rinsed their metal cups and packed them away, Buchan sent the party back to the ice, shouting orders much louder than he needed to be heard, as if to instil in the men a sense that his authority extended far into the wilderness that appeared now to belong to someone other than themselves. The group was watchful and quiet as they continued upriver. Where the woods were too thin to support the construction of a fence, a line of sewels had been raised with clappers of birchbark suspended from salmon twine. The bark swung in each breath of wind and raised a racket that was intended to spook the caribou and keep them from leaving the river and escaping into the bush. The noise was irregular but steady, like scattered applause, and it spooked most of the men who were coming up the river for the first time as well. Each mile or so along the south side, narrow openings extended back into fenced clearings that served as slaughtering yards.

The pervasive sense of caution among them added an urgent energy to the party and they made good progress on the clear ice. They didn't stop until well after dark and covered twelve miles altogether, getting clear of the caribou fences around 3 p.m. The following day they managed a further nine miles beyond Rushy Pond Marsh. On the twentieth, another eight miles were covered, including two miles beyond the second waterfall. The rough ice above the overfalls took its toll on the sledges and two were so severely damaged they had to be abandoned and all the provisions and gear repacked. That evening they crossed the river above Badger Bay Brook to camp in a green wood on the south shore.

Signs of habitation were all around them by then — trees cut or marked with blades, dilapidated mamateeks standing on the larger islands, mooring poles erected in the river ice near Indian paths — but William Cull offered that the Indians probably moved further up the river to the lake after the caribou migration and guessed they would see none in the flesh before they got there.

With a full week of heavy toil behind them, most of the men were haggard and sluggish by nightfall and stayed awake in camp only long enough to eat. Richmond by comparison appeared to grow stronger each day, to the point that he hauled a sledge constantly while the rest of the group traded the others among them. The only noticeable change in him was a sour turn in his mood. He never spoke to Butler but in a mocking gibberish or to ask him to speak some more of his mother's Indian. Among the other furriers, he referred to Buchan as "sheepdog" or "shep." He baited Reilly whenever the opportunity arose, improvising elaborate Catholic oaths. "By the immaculate blood of the blessed Virgin, Holy Mary, Mother of God, it's a cold morning."

Cull had dropped back to walk with Peyton that afternoon and told him to keep a short leash on his man. "That one is getting right black," he said. "He might be up to something foolish if we're not careful."

Peyton nodded. It was a warm day with dead snow on the river that made the hauling heavy and he leaned into the drag of the harness. "I'll be watchful," he said.

At camp he sat up by the fire long after the food was eaten to wait for Richmond and Taylor to take to their bunks. Buchan was sitting beside Reilly.

Everyone else had already dropped into leaden dreamless sleep. Reilly stretched his bare hands out to the fire to warm them.

"I've been meaning to ask," the lieutenant said to him. "Those are quite the nasty scars you have."

Reilly looked at the back of his hand quickly as if he hadn't noticed the dark web there before. He rubbed the welts with the palm of the opposite hand. It seemed to Peyton as though Reilly was trying to erase them.

"A world ago, sir," Reilly said to the officer. He looked across the fire and caught Peyton's eye. "In the old country. And not something I'm fond of recounting. It involved a family of blacksmiths and a daughter of theirs, and to say more than that would be hurtful of the girl's honour and to the esteem in which I would hope you now hold me."

Richmond swore and kicked at a junk of wood at the base of the fire, sending up a small shower of flankers that settled and winked out in the snow. "How much could it hurt the honour of an Irishwoman?" he said. "Hey, Tom Taylor? Or the esteem in which an Irishman is held?"

Taylor gave a non-committal shrug, but did nothing more to discourage him.

"Carry on with your tale of woe, Paddy," Richmond continued. "You've got nothing to lose as far as we can see."

Peyton looked across at Reilly and Buchan. The lieutenant was smiling and had placed a hand on Reilly's forearm to keep him from responding. "I trust," Buchan said, and he spoke with as thick a brogue as he could muster, "you dinna think so poorly of all the Celtic peoples."

"In no way, sir," Richmond told him. "But this one in particular is bothersome, given as his loyalties are so clearly divided."

"Richmond," Reilly said, "shut your goddamn mouth."

The furrier ignored him. "As Mr. Mick Mac here is married to an Indian, it seems to me the height of folly to expect him to choose the life of Protestant Englishmen over one of his own."

Peyton was on his feet before Richmond finished speaking and he knelt to face him and Taylor, whispering for a few moments. Richmond said, "Out of respect for your father," and nodded at the fire with a look of furious exasperation. Peyton stood and addressed Reilly. "Richard would like to apologize, Joseph. We all know Annie is a good Christian woman. It was meant in fun and not to offend you or Annie."

Reilly stood up as well then. "I appreciate that, John Peyton," he said. "Although it would mean more to me had it come from the mouth of that one behind you." He turned to Buchan. "Good night, sir," he said.

Buchan nodded.

Peyton circled the fire and sat in the spot vacated by Reilly and the four men stayed there longer than anyone would have liked, until Richmond finally cursed under his breath and went to his blankets and Taylor followed him, more sheepishly, nodding to Peyton and Buchan as he went.

"Your man Richmond," Buchan said, shaking his head.

"The devilskin, he is, sir. But a long chafe up the river such as this is where you see the worth of him. If I go through the ice hauling a sledge, I'd like to have him somewhere handy."

Buchan nodded slowly and stared across at the younger man. Peyton's face was boyish, he thought, remarkably unscarred. He had a full head of dirty-blond hair, a ready look of astonishment that made him seem younger than his years.

"What is it, sir?" Peyton asked.

Buchan pointed directly at him. "I'm looking for your father there," he said. "And I can't see him."

"John Senior's quite a face, it's true." Peyton stared into the fire. "Perhaps I'll be lucky enough to keep clear of it."

Early on the twenty-second, they came upon another stretch of caribou fences and after travelling two miles found a large circular storehouse constructed of spruce wood and caribou skin near a slaughtering yard that Cull said was not present when he'd come by this way eighteen months ago.

Two mooring poles were stuck in the ice near the shoreline and the carcasses of several caribou lay butchered and strewn outside the store.

They stood for a few moments inside the building while their eyes adjusted to the light and the row of haunches and torsos hanging from the rafters came out of the shadows. Near the storage shelves at the back of the room they found a marten trap and Tom Taylor used his walking stick to press the bed. They found four other traps set around the store to keep scavengers from the meat. The name *Peyton* was inscribed in the beds of the traps. Richmond said they'd been stolen from his tilt in the fall.

Most of the frozen meat was stored in square boxes of spruce rind, large fatty blocks of flesh off the bone packed with a heart and kidney or a liver at the centre of the container. They found a number of lids from copper kettles that Cull said might have belonged to the Indian woman he had taken to St. John's. There were also a few furs hung about the room, beaver and marten and caribou, and Buchan ordered that these be taken along with two packs of meat. He and the ship's boy went to one of the sledges and came back with a pair of swan-skin trousers, a pair of yarn stockings, three cotton handkerchiefs, three clasped knives, two hatchets and some thread and twine, which they stacked neatly in the centre of the store in trade.

Richmond stood with the traps across his shoulder and asked what the lieutenant intended to pay the Indians for the return of his stolen goods.

They travelled ten miles more before they set up camp and roasted the caribou meat for their supper. Hughster complained of the condition of his feet and Buchan asked Peyton to accompany Cull and himself as they reconnoitered. On the horizon, the setting sun was refracted by evening mist, arms of shimmering red light reaching to the points of the compass. The sun-gall like a burning cross over the forest. Cull pointed towards it. "A real strife of wind tomorrow, make no mistake." They walked a further two miles up the river and returned well after dark. Cull guessed they'd be no more than a day's march from the lake if they were without sledges. Three watches were set and those on guard were under arms through the night.

By morning the weather had turned freezing with a wild westerly gale, just as Cull predicted. Peyton had taken the last watch and was at the fire when Buchan roused himself from his blankets. They nodded at one another but didn't attempt any conversation over the noise of the wind. A few minutes later, one of the marines nearby sat bolt upright in his blankets. "Private Butler!" Buchan shouted in greeting.

The marine turned slowly towards the fire. His face was a mask of haggard astonishment, like a man recently returned from a harrowing journey through the underworld.

"Welcome back to the land of the living," Buchan shouted.

During their breakfast, the men sat as near the fire as they dared, the flames whipping in one direction and then veering quickly in another like an agitated animal tethered with a short length of rope. They had to sing out to be heard above the howl and their voices cracked and streamed in clouds that were whipped away by the wind.

The river above them narrowed and shoaled and ran so rough it was clear of ice right to the banks. The group struggled forward four miles on the shoreline, using the axes and cutlasses to clear a path through the foliage when necessary, but by 10 a.m. it was obvious they would be unable to continue with the sleighs. Buchan decided to divide the party, leaving the four Blue Jackets and Cull's men to wait with the bulk of the provisions while the rest continued along the riverside with four days of food in their packs. He wanted to leave both Taylor and Richmond behind, but the men had presented such a volatile air of injured pride at the suggestion and most of the others in the party were so weakened by travel that Buchan felt forced to reconsider.

Above Badger Bay Brook the landmarks and features they passed were mostly nameless, and whenever the party came upon a river feeding into the Exploits or crossed a significant point of land, Buchan called the men into a huddle and they shouted suggestions over the wind. They dropped names behind themselves like stones set to mark the path out of wilderness — Cull's Knoll; Buchan's Island; Deep Woody Point; Surprise Brook for a stream that

Peyton had fallen into through the ice. Richmond made it known he wanted something named for himself and each time was disappointed to be overlooked.

"The day is young," Tom Taylor told him. "We're bound to set on a rock thick enough to suit the Richmond name before long."

Four miles along, Cull discovered a short portage on the south side where a canoe had recently been hauled through the snow to clear a rapid.

"Dick's Drag," Taylor christened it, and Richmond called him a miserable blood of a bitch and said he could go straight to hell for what he cared to know of him any longer.

A mile further on they rounded a long point of land and the lake appeared ahead of them, grander than anyone but Cull had expected it to be. The expanse of ice and snow looked to be at least a day's travel from end to end, a magnificent keel of silver running the length of the valley. It was after 3 o'clock and the wind had dropped enough to make the weather tolerable. The sun had fallen below the ceiling of grey cloud, illuminating the enormous stretch of ice, and the snow on the branches of spruce terraced on the valley's hills burned gold all around them. It was like walking into a cathedral lit with candles and the group stood there exhausted and breathing heavily, leaning on walking sticks and bent forward to balance the weight of their packs, all with the worn look of awe of a group of pilgrims.

Peyton was the first of them to speak. "There's someone out there," he said, pointing to the far shore where two pale shadows could be seen moving against the darker shadow of the trees. Buchan hurried the group out of sight into the woods where the men squinted and argued over what the figures might be.

Taylor said they had four legs and were most likely caribou. Richmond scoffed. "You're as blind as a goddamn sea urchin, Tom Taylor, and you haven't got half the sense," he said. "Those are two-legged creatures and if they're not Red Indians, then I'm a Papist."

Cull thought Richmond was most likely right and suggested they get a closer look but keep to the trees to avoid being detected. They removed their packs and scrambled through the bush as quickly as the scrabble of alders and spruce and underbrush allowed. After half an hour they seemed not much nearer the moving figures and Buchan was about to call a halt when Corporal Bouthland pointed out across the ice. "Is that last one hauling something, Lieutenant?"

The men shielded their eyes and peered against the last of the sunlight. "A sledge," Cull said. "Of some sort."

Several other men nodded their agreement. "That settles it then," Buchan said and he turned the party about to head back to the river. "The camp won't be much beyond this point if those two are out this near to dark. We'll come back this way at first light and try to catch them unawares while they sleep."

They crossed the point of land that hid the lake and set up camp, and as they guessed the Indian settlement would be more than two miles distant, Buchan allowed a small cooking fire to be lit. While they ate he advised the men on the level of conduct he expected from them the following day and especially so in the company of women. Then he announced that the party's rifles would be left with their packs in the morning.

Richmond stood up out of the spot where he'd been sitting and threw the scraps of food from his plate into the fire. "No," he said. "No goddamn way."

"Mr. Richmond," Buchan said calmly.

"John Peyton?" Richmond said, turning to the young man in appeal.

"We are here on a mission of peace on behalf of the governor of Newfoundland and His Majesty the King," the Lieutenant continued.

"The governor can kiss me arse, and the King besides," Richmond shouted.

"Mr. Richmond!" Buchan stood and motioned for the marines to stand as well. Everyone in the company came to their feet then and there was a moment of wild shouting, with Richmond backed by Taylor stabbing his finger in Buchan's direction and Reilly and Peyton standing between them and the marines. Peyton said, "There'll be no mission at all if you don't all shut up," and he repeated this until everyone had calmed down enough to take a step backwards.

Buchan told Richmond that it was only the extraordinary circumstances that prevented him from having the marines strip and flog him senseless and he insisted on an apology to the King and the governor before consenting to speak or listen to another word. Peyton prodded him gently in the back. Richmond looked off into the dark and offered his apologies in as insolent a manner as he was sure he could get away with. "But I will not go up the lake tomorrow without my firearm," he said.

"Then you will not go," Buchan told him.

"Me neither then," Taylor said and he sat by the fire, and Hughster with obvious reluctance added his name to the list.

"Lieutenant, sir," Cull said, "we got no notion of how many of them Indians we will come upon in the morning. There could be two hundred or more."

"We have little hope of inspiring them to trust us with rifles in our hands."

"That may be so," Cull acknowledged. "But we'll be a damn sight nearer to trusting them."

Buchan suppressed a sigh of exasperation. He turned to Peyton. There was a twist in the younger man's face, as if he had swallowed something sour. "Mr. Peyton?" he said.

Peyton was thinking of sitting across from Cassie at the table while she repeated John Senior's words to him. It was galling to see him proved right. "I have some sympathy for your sentiments, Lieutenant, but I'm sorry to say I'm more in line with Mr. Cull's assessment."

"Very well then." Buchan took his place near the fire and those still standing took this as an invitation to sit. "The marines will leave their rifles and carry their pistols only. The rest of you may carry whatever firearms you wish. But there will be no action of any sort without my express order. Am I understood?"

There was a general round of nods. A light snow started to fall and as they blew through the light of the fire the stray flakes flared and went out like sparks struck off a flint.

╫

Buchan roused the party at 4 a.m. They ate quickly and each man was portioned a dram of rum as fortification against the bitter cold. By the time they came upon the place where they'd last seen the two Red Indians there was enough grey light to follow the tracks they'd left in the snow. Several of the marines complained of the cold and the party occasionally sheltered in the lee of the forest to get a few minutes out of the wind. The path of the sledge rounded a point of land and crossed to the opposite shore. The party was entirely exposed on the open ice and everyone cursed the weather and marched as quickly as their swollen legs and blistered feet would allow.

On the western shore they found a small sheltered bay where two mamateeks stood close together and a third within a hundred yards. The sun was about to come up. Buchan stopped the party and examined the firearms of each man and charged them all to be prompt in executing any orders that might be given. They stole up the bank in complete silence and Buchan motioned them into positions to secure the shelters. When everyone nodded their readiness he straightened where he stood and squared himself to attention. "Hello friends," he called. "I bring greetings from His Majesty the King of England." There was no other sound but the low whine of wind in the trees.

He motioned Bouthland forward and the marine pulled the skins from the doorway of the largest structure. Peyton stood beside Buchan and Cull near the entrance and they stared into the gloom where a group of men, women and children lay still. Peyton counted quickly: seventeen, he concluded, and an infant or two. No one in the mamateek moved or spoke or even looked through the open entranceway to acknowledge the presence of the strangers.

Cull said, "What's wrong with them, do you think?"

Buchan suddenly remembered Butler and called him to his side. "Tell them they have nothing to be afraid of," he ordered.

The marine did so. After a moment he said, "They don't seem to understand, sir."

"Well, damn it, say something *else*. Try another language."

"Yes sir," Butler said and he stumbled through the same words in Swedish, Finnish and a ragged version of German without success.

"All right, all right," Buchan said finally and he forced himself to continue smiling at the frozen tableau of bodies in the dimly lit shelter. "We will have to make do."

Peyton said, "It might help if those of us in view put our firearms away." Buchan nodded agreement and Peyton and Cull set their rifles down and Buchan dropped his pistol and cutlass on the snow. He held his hands in the air and walked towards the mamateek and stood in the entranceway.

"I am Lieutenant David Buchan," he said cheerfully, "of the HMS *Adonis*."

The faces in the room turned slowly towards a man near the back of the mamateek who stood finally and approached the white man. He was fully six feet in height and dwarfed the lieutenant he stood before. His long black hair was coloured with red ochre, as were his face and hands and long leather cloak. Buchan extended his hand and the Indian accepted it and they exchanged words in their own languages. Buchan motioned Cull and Peyton forward and introduced them and the Indian returned their smiles and shook their hands. He turned and spoke to the people still lying about the fireplace and several of them stood and came forward to shake hands with the white men in their doorway.

Within minutes the entire camp was assembled — thirty-eight Peyton counted altogether — and greetings were exchanged among members of both parties. After an initial period of wariness, the women began examining the dress of the white men, touching the material and buttons, and talking loudly among themselves. All of Buchan's party but Richmond had set their rifles aside. Handkerchiefs and small knives and other articles of interest the party had among them were gathered and presented to the Indians and half a dozen marten furs were given to them in return.

After the exchange of presents a cooking fire was kindled, a girl kneeling to strike sparks into a ball of tinder. Peyton guessed her to be around twelve years old. She looked up to see him watching and he smiled at her and nodded. He knelt beside her and cupped his hands to encourage the flame as it caught. The tinder she used was a tuft of down from the breast of a blue jay. The girl blew gently and added small shavings of wood to the fire. Their heads were so close together he could smell the oil in her hair.

Large caribou steaks were roasted, and sausages made of seal fat and eggs were presented to the white men. They sat about the fireplace and ate and talked among themselves while smiling and making gestures to their hosts to indicate how much they enjoyed the food and how full they were. They drank fresh water out of birchbark cups sewn with spruce root.

Corporal Bouthland spoke up to say the Red Indians were not as large as he had been given to believe they would be, the tallest among them being the first man to approach Buchan that morning, who seemed to have some sway over the group.

"They look more like people of the Continent than Indians, I should say," Butler announced.

Richmond turned to the marine. "Do you get a word of what this lot are saying?"

"I'm afraid not, no."

Richmond grunted and shook his head, as if he had thought it a cocka-mamie idea from the start.

By 10 a.m., the party had spent all of three and a half hours in the company of the Red Indians. Buchan sat with the tall chief and drew a rough map in the dirt and used gestures to indicate his wish to return to the place where the gifts had been left and to carry these up to the lake. The white men stood and made ready to leave and the chief pointed to himself and two of his companions to indicate they would accompany the party. When this became clear, Corporal Bouthland requested permission to remain with the Indians as it would allow him to make repairs to his rackets. Private Butler volunteered to stay behind with him.

They reached their previous night's camp at the riverhead before noon, and seeing nothing in the nature of goods or gifts as had been intimated by Buchan, the tall chief left to return to the lake but sent the other two on with the white men. They found the river opened, which made for difficult going on the narrow fringe of ice that remained at the shoreline, and the group marched in single file to navigate their way. One of the Indians walked ahead of Buchan and the second followed behind the party. By mid-afternoon, they came within sight of the fire kept by the remainder of Buchan's expedition and the two Indians pointed and carried on a brief conversation and within minutes the man at the back of the group turned and fled towards the lake.

"He's running," Reilly shouted and the entire group stopped and turned upriver.

Taylor said he was still within half a musket shot, but Buchan ordered everyone to lower their rifles. He gestured to the last Indian to tell him he was free to join his companion but he did not and the party continued on to the sledge camp where he was presented with a pair of trousers and vamps and a flannel shirt. He changed out of his leather cassock and leggings and was so pleased with his new dress that he shook hands again with each man in the party. Buchan also showed him the store of blankets, woollen wrappers, shirts, beads, knives and other goods, and indicated they were all to be carried to the lake.

They sat to a meal of cocoa and salt fish and the white men carried on a conversation of worry and discontent while maintaining a cordial appearance towards their guest. Cull and Hughster were of the belief that the Indian who'd left them after sighting the fire may have come away with the impression that a party of men were secreted here to take them captive or kill them.

Buchan nodded. "I share your concerns," he said, "but the presence of this individual," and he gestured towards the Indian with his chin and smiled broadly when he met the man's gaze, "is insurance enough for the lives of Butler and Bouthland. The good treatment he continues to receive will speak against any rumours currently being spread by his companion." He stooped to the fire and lifted the kettle clear and poured more hot water for himself and for their Red Indian guest.

They woke next morning to a storm of sleet and blowing snow with wind out of the northeast. Buchan left eight men at the camp and the rest lowered their heads and pushed on into the bleak weather, walking single file up the river. Once they reached the lake the Indian ran ahead of the group at points and returned to walk with the lieutenant. Within half a mile of the mamateeks he pointed to an arrow sticking up out of the snow on the ice. There was a recent sledge track nearby.

They reached the Red Indian's camp at 2 p.m. and found it deserted. The shelters had been left in a state of disarray. Everything of any value or use was taken from them but for a few caribou hides and a row of long shank bones hanging from the rafters.

A fire was recovered from the coals of the firepit in the largest mamateek and the men set about drying their boots and stockings. They boiled the marrow out of one of the caribou shanks to make a broth. There was very little conversation. The Indian seemed not to understand what had happened in this place or why. While the others ate he moved about the mamateek to tidy and set it in order as if to say he expected his people to return shortly. Several times he pointed in the direction of the opposite shore, which the white men took to indicate where he thought they had gone. The gesture was accompanied by a strained, peculiar laughter.

"That bugger's a bit queer, I'd say," Richmond said.

Tom Taylor shrugged. "I'd be maze-headed meself if I was in his place."

The dirty weather worsened as night fell and the doorway was closed up with caribou skins. The noise of the wind in the trees and the hail and sleet against the sides of the mamateek made it conceivable that a party of any number could steal upon the shelter without being heard and Buchan divided the men into two watches to sit under arms through the night. Peyton was a member of the first watch and he and his group sat spaced around the circular floor with only the sullen light of the fire to see by. No one spoke.

The morning he started out from his father's winter house, Peyton had stuffed a small parcel tied up in a piece of muslin cloth into his knapsack and he took it out now, unwrapping a sheaf of papers written over by hand. It was too dark to read and he flipped through them blindly, running the tips of his fingers across the pages.

Reilly was sitting nearest him and leaned forward to peer. "What's that you got there?" he said.

Peyton shook his head.

"Cassie," Reilly whispered and Peyton nodded without looking up from the pages.

John Senior had left Peyton behind at the winter house during his first year in Newfoundland to watch over Cassie, though he'd begged to be taken trapping. Near midnight on Christmas Eve, Cassie had come to Peyton's room and shaken him awake. She was fully dressed and had already pulled on a heavy overcoat.

"What's wrong?" Peyton asked.

"Get up," she said. "It's nearly time."

When he came into the kitchen she was standing at the door with the musket his father had left them. She was tamping powder into the barrel.

"The time," she said.

"What are you doing?"

"The time, John Peyton."

He pulled out the new gold pocket watch given to him by his father before he left for the traplines and turned the face to the light of the candle on the table. "Three of twelve."

"Get your coat on now. Hurry."

She stepped out the door and he followed behind her as quickly as he could. They stood just outside the house, the clearing at the door banked on both sides by drifts of snow piled above their heads. There was no wind. She lifted the rifle to her shoulder and cocked her head to one side. They stood that way a few moments more. Her lips were moving and Peyton leaned forward to hear her slowly counting down under her breath.

He looked up at the stars and shook his head. Then he heard them. Gunshots, two, three, maybe more. The few inhabitants up and down the shore standing outside their tilts and firing into the night to mark the day's arrival. Cassie pulled the trigger, the roar of the rifle deafening, the flash of powder deepening the dark that followed.

Inside she poured them each a glass of rum. Then Cassie brought out the small package wrapped in muslin and tied with a length of twine. She placed it in his lap and went back to her seat. Peyton stared at the package without speaking. The rum shimmered in his belly like a sun-gall. He looked up at her.

"Open it," she said.

He smiled stupidly as he tried the knots and unwrapped the cloth. "What is it?" he asked. He lifted the sheaf of papers clear and laid it flat on his lap. "Cassie?"

She brought the candle from the table so he could see more clearly. The top sheet was printed over in a loose, sloping hand. He leaned closer to read it. "'The Tragedy of Othello, the Moor of Venice,'" he read aloud. He flipped through the pages, dozens of them, each written out in the same hand. Beneath *Othello* was a handwritten copy of *The Tempest*. Peyton was mystified. He had seen in her trunk all nine volumes of Nicholas Rowe's stage edition of Shakespeare's plays.

"It was a way to pass the time," Cassie said, "when my mother was ill. Near the end she slept most of the day and night and I was too tired to just read. I thought you might like to have them."

Peyton stared at her, his mouth opening and closing uselessly. He stood up and placed the papers in her lap. "I have something for you," he said. She heard his feet hammering the stairs, a scuffling noise from his room overhead. When he came back into the kitchen he held one hand behind his back. "Close your eyes," he told her. "Put out your hand." He placed a small leather pouch in her palm.

Cassie emptied the bag in her lap and held each item in turn in the light. The carved antler. The bird skulls. The fire stone. "Where did you get these?"

"Out on Swan Island. John Senior found the pouch in a cave along the shore."

"They're beautiful, John Peyton."

He nodded and blushed, embarrassed to be the object of her gratitude. Besides which, he had told her so little of the truth of the gift's origins that he felt he had somehow lied to her.

She had cajoled him into reading through *Othello* with her, and they took on parts as necessary to play off the lead characters, their heads leaning together over a candle. Peyton read tentatively and Cassie prompted him by touching a finger to his forearm, whispering the pronunciation of each word that brought him up short. She seemed to have the play memorized and sometimes recited lines with her eyes closed. He never imagined people could speak so nakedly from the heart. When Cassie said, *That I did love the Moor to live with him, my downright violence and storm of fortunes may trumpet to the world*, he could not find his place on the page. And that same lost feeling came to him in the Indian shelter now as he fingered the pages in the near dark.

The sleet and snow continued into the next morning. Buchan had his men divide the blankets and shirts and tin pots they had carried up from the sledge camp among the mamateeks and they set out across the ice in the direction the Indian had pointed the day before. He ran ahead of the group in a zigzag pattern as if tracing a path that no one else could see and sometimes looked behind to the white men to motion to the distant shoreline. Before they had travelled a mile onto the ice the Indian edged to his right a ways and stopped still for several moments. Without looking back then he fled across the lake. "Jesus, Jesus," William Cull said, and the party picked up its pace in the face of the gale until they reached the spot where the Indian had paused.

The bodies were about a hundred yards apart, stripped naked and laid on their bellies. The heads of both marines had been cut from the torsos and carried off. The flesh at their necks was flayed ragged as if a blunt blade had been used to behead them and loose scarves of blood draped the snow above the mutilation. Their backs were pierced by arrows. The group stood over the scene in a stunned silence until one of the Blue Jackets in the party turned away from the bodies and vomited. The sound of his retching unleashed a string of curses and several of the men, including Peyton, dropped to their knees and threw up into the snow as well.

They covered the bodies with spruce branches and secured the branches with stones dug from underneath the snow on the nearest point of land which they named Bloody Point. Buchan read from his prayer book and those that knew the words joined him in repeating the Twenty-third Psalm and the Lord's Prayer. Then the men turned away and began walking towards the head-waters of the river.

Richmond and Taylor had threatened biblical revenge over the mutilated corpses of their companions and in some measure had recruited the remaining marines and Matthew Hughster to their cause, but Buchan had insisted on an immediate retreat. Only three men had their rifles with them and there was likely to be larger numbers of Indians on the lake than they had seen in the single camp. It was possible that a party of them had already been dispatched to ambush the eight men left behind with the sledges and this thought alone made Buchan anxious to get back to them. At the headwaters of the river the men stopped to eat bread and refresh themselves with rum. A column was organized and those with rifles stood at the front and rear while those with only pistols or cutlasses travelled between. They walked single file back to the camp where the rest of the party waited for them.

The rapid thaw that followed the sleet storm made the trip down the river more treacherous than it had been coming up. The ice had come away from the banks below the sledge camp and the men packed their knapsacks with as much provision as they could carry and left the sleighs behind. They constantly fell through the jagged ice and soaked themselves and scraped their shins raw. Occasionally pans broke loose and carried men into open water and they had to be rescued with extended walking sticks or ropes thrown from the shore. In the stretches where the ice was still solid, the rush of water from the river above and a steady rain had covered it in several inches of water that numbed the men's feet and galled away the skin still clinging to their ankles and heels. They reached the camp they'd struck on the twenty-first well past dark, completing a journey of thirty-two miles in a single day.

Each of the next three days the party travelled eighteen miles or more, often walking knee-deep in freezing water or stumbling through rotten ice that sliced at their clothing and skin. There was near total silence among them but for the encouragement shouted by Buchan and they moved forward with the somnambulant expressions of sleepwalkers. Partway through each day's march Peyton lost all feeling in his legs and feet and watched them moving as if they belonged to another man's body. Even Richmond seemed to have exhausted his reserves and plodded stupidly ahead, sometimes falling to his hands and knees. At night most of the group complained of swollen legs and Buchan had them rub their calves with a mixture of rum and pork grease, which offered some relief. Each night one or more of the party started awake from a dream of Butler's perfectly blond head on a stake, of Bouthland's eyes as dead and sightless as the mole on his cheek. Some tried desperately to stay awake then for fear of where their dreams would take them, but exhaustion always pulled them under. In the morning Buchan roused each man personally and he worried at their heels throughout the day to keep them out of the river and moving towards the coast.

On the last leg of the trip, when they were in sight of Little Peter's Point and only a few hours' heavy slogging from the *Adonis*, a peculiar elation came over the group. The men shouted encouragement back and forth to one another and laughed when they stumbled and spoke incessantly of the food they would eat and the hours they would sleep when they gained the ship, as if all they had been through on the river was a nightmare they'd suddenly woken from together. Even the wrenching guilt of abandoning the marines naked and beheaded on the lake left them briefly.

Already the men had begun remembering the expedition as a series of distinct episodes, the words for the tales they wanted to tell beginning to form in their minds. It was knowing they would live to recount them to others that made them giddy and filled them with a strangely inarticulate hope those last hours on the River Exploits. Like everyone else around him, Peyton felt drained and perfectly clear, bleached of everything but the urge to speak. All the way across the Arm with the *Adonis* in sight, he thought only of seeing Cassie, of looking her in the face and saying, "Listen to me now. I have a story to tell you."

SEVEN

The governor leafed through the report as Buchan ate his meal. He had returned from wintering in England only days before and was still trying to digest the news that awaited him. He sipped distractedly at a glass of brandy but hadn't bothered to order food himself. He had no appetite.

"I blame myself for this," Duckworth said. He lifted the papers he was reading from and shook them gently.

Buchan set his fork and knife across the plate and placed his forearms on the table. He bowed his head slightly. "It was bad luck," he said. "Bad luck all around."

Duckworth nodded at the papers again.

"They were afraid, Your Worship. They acted out of fear."

The governor said, "I blame myself for this."

"I will not allow you —"

"Don't patronize me, Lieutenant." Duckworth lifted his brandy to his mouth and held the glass under his nose. "David," he said softly. "Marie is keeping well, I hope."

"Fine, yes."

"And the girl?"

"Couldn't be better, by the last correspondence I received. I hope to have them join me if I'm to be posted here longer than another year."

Duckworth set his glass back on the table. He drummed his fingers against the wood. He wondered how much longer he was likely to be here himself. "Would you like to stay?"

Buchan was wiping his mouth with a napkin. He looked at the governor. "What I would like," he said, "is to have the opportunity to return to the Red Indian's lake."

"Out of the question." Duckworth pressed a hand to his stomach as if he'd suffered a sudden stab of pain. "It is plainly too dangerous."

"Those men died in the course of duty."

"They died in the course of a reckless expedition undertaken to satisfy my own personal whims."

Buchan smiled across the table. "You do yourself a disservice, Governor. Which I understand completely, but will not condone."

"Lieutenant."

"We have always known that risk accompanies the righteous course."

"Goddamn it man," Duckworth shouted and then caught himself. "Goddamn it," he said again, barely above a whisper. He pointed a finger across the table. "You cannot have stood over those men lying headless on that lake — *headless*, Lieutenant — you cannot have witnessed that and be so sanguine."

"The most sensible way I can think to honour the memory of my marines, Governor, is to carry on in this endeavour until we are successful."

Duckworth shook his head and turned away, as if he was trying to avoid an unwanted kiss. "You are still a young man in these things, I see."

Buchan picked up his knife and fork. "Now it is you who patronize me."

"There will not be another expedition to the winter camps. It is too dangerous." Duckworth sighed. "My constitution will simply not survive it," he said.

"For now, I will accept that. But I want permission to return this summer, to try again to make contact with the smaller bands on the coast. I think it would be prudent to have a presence among the settlers besides. In case any among them are planning to exact their own measure of revenge."

The governor helped himself to a huge mouthful of brandy. "This job will be the death of me," he said.

Buchan nodded. "Thank you," he said.

"Don't thank me," Duckworth said. "Don't you dare." He raised his hand in the air. "More brandy," he shouted angrily.

The following summer, Buchan returned to the Bay of Exploits as a surrogate magistrate, and when not holding court or seeing to other duties, he carried out extensive searches of the mainland coast and the islands along the northeast shore. He visited occasionally with the Peytons on Burnt Island and shared a meal while gleaning all he could of their recent sightings of Beothuk. He took notes in his journal, drew free-hand maps to fix locations in his mind. Peyton had seen a recently abandoned camp at the mouth of this or that river. One of the hired men caught sight of a canoe rounding a point of land in one bay or another.

There was a quiet, almost elegiac tone to the discussions, as if they were discussing creatures who had all but disappeared from the earth, ghosts, spirits who drifted occasionally to this side of darkness.

Peyton offered all the information he had on hand and made suggestions for likely areas to search. John Senior sat by quietly, responding to direct questions but mostly keeping to himself. When the officer left he ridiculed the whole undertaking. "How he could leave two men dead on the lake and act like this is beyond me," he said. He spoke softly, with a note of pained surprise in his voice. "If it had been someone from the shore been killed, there'd be hell to pay and proper goddamn thing."

"I know what your ideas of the proper thing are," Peyton said. He found everything the man said these days disagreeable, and he made a point of making sure his father knew it.

John Senior shook his head. "Richmond and Taylor are all for going back down the river come the winter and I can't say I disagree with the sentiment." He spat into the idle fireplace. He said, "If it had been *you* was killed, John Peyton."

A picture of his father in Cassie's bed came to Peyton and he got up from his seat and went to the window to drive it out. It was infuriating how they carried on around him as if nothing was happening between them. He said, "Lieutenant Buchan knows well enough what's right."

"He'll wind up with his head ordained for an ornament in some wigwam on the lake. That's how much he knows of what's right."

John Senior's pessimism only served to goad his son into a state of blind enthusiasm for Buchan's attempts at reconciliation. He collected stories from other men on the shore to pass on during the officer's next visit, gathered artifacts from his own travel on the salmon rivers. On several occasions he abandoned his work to hired men in order to accompany Buchan to areas of the coast the officer was unfamiliar with.

"If I didn't know any better," John Senior said when he returned from one excursion, "I'd think you was after a Red bride."

They argued then, standing inches from one another and spraying each other's faces with spittle. Cassie came out to them, drawn by the shouting, and she put a hand to each of their shoulders. Both men took a step backward, embarrassed to have been seen in such a naked state of fury. Peyton walked off to the house and shut himself up in his room. He found it disturbing, Cassie's touch obliquely connecting him and his father that way, and he wondered if he was the only one of the three of them to be bothered by it.

+++

In late August, Peyton and Cassie rowed across to the mainland for the haying. Richmond and Taylor had already arrived and were on the beach with Reilly when they rowed up to the salmon weir.

Annie Boss came down the narrow path from their tilt to greet them all, carrying her child. It was their first sight of the baby for all of the visitors but Peyton who had come to Charles Brook twice that summer as he inspected the catch at John Senior's salmon rivers. There was a round of handshaking and best wishes for the new parents. Richmond pushed Reilly's shoulder roughly and said, "All this time we thought you was all powder fire and no shot."

"Don't pay no mind to the noggyhead," Tom Taylor said, shaking Reilly's hand. He and his wife had had their own difficulties and he couldn't bring himself to ridicule others, even a Paddy and his Indian wife. He said, "The best to you both. And Siobhan would say the same if she was here, I know."

They spent three solid days in the waist-high meadows. Fragments of the shorn grass worked into their shoes and collars and beneath shirts and the band of the haymakers' underwear and it stuck there in the sweat on their skin. At the end of the third day, they came down to the river and walked into the water to wash away the dark stain of chlorophyll on their necks and wrists and ankles. They bobbed their heads beneath the surface to wash the sweat from their hair. Back on shore the men removed their shirts to wring them dry. Reilly walked up the bank to lay a fire in the tilt. Cassie paddled out onto the river, turning there to float on her back, the white muslin of her dress moving on the water's surface like a leaf dropped from an overhanging tree.

Peyton waded in the shallows and watched her. Her hair floated loose in the river. Through the wet fabric of her dress he could see the dark aureole of her nipples and he looked down suddenly at his own soaked clothing, afraid the water might have revealed something of himself in the same way.

Richmond laughed on the beach behind him. "No way he'll get on the inside of a cold flinter like she," he said.

Peyton spun in the water to stare up the beach but Tom Taylor had already turned on his friend. "Richmond, you got no more nature than a picket." He stood with his hands on his hips and shouted, "You haven't got the shame God gives a louse."

"The devil haul you, Tom Taylor. I'll speak my mind when it suits me." And to prove his point Richmond slapped Taylor's stomach and said, "You've fallen into flesh, you have. All chuffed out like a cock with the mites."

Peyton climbed from the water and took off his shirt to wring it out, then pushed on his shoes and walked past Richmond and Taylor as their argument escalated into a shouting match. Reilly was sitting outside the tilt on a junk of wood, a pail of river water that served to cool several bottles of spruce beer beside him. He passed one to Peyton with his scarred hand. The beer was sharp and browsy as tree sap. Peyton drank off half the bottle before he pulled on his wet shirt and took a seat on the ground. He kicked at the dirt with the heel of his shoe.

"What are those two into it over now?"

Peyton shrugged, but didn't look up at the Irishman.

Reilly said, "Your face is dark as the depths of January, John Peyton."

He nodded, but said nothing and they sat in silence, listening to Richmond and Taylor carrying on down on the beach. Cassie was likely still in the river, drifting slowly downstream. Peyton closed his eyes against the late afternoon sunlight and leaned his forehead against a fist.

Peyton was eighteen the first time he and Cassie came across to Charles Brook for the haying without John Senior. The old man had insisted she go in his stead so she might have the chance of a little "female company." Cassie was still tutoring Peyton in the late afternoons in those days, though he was allowing work to keep him away more often as he became increasingly dissatisfied with the thought of being her student. In the week before they crossed over to Reilly's tilt, he sulked through several evenings of *Robinson Crusoe*, a book Cassie had thought he would find of particular interest, being cast upon the shores of a strange island himself.

"Are you missing England?" she asked him.

"No," he said curtly. He was taller than she was now, which served to make him more impatient with the notion of being taught by her.

She could see he wasn't willing to admit the specifics of his irritation and she carried on as if it was a general question she'd been asking, something related to the book. "Is there anything about England that you miss having here?"

He shrugged. "Orange marmalade," he said. "And I used to have honey in my tea on occasion."

She nodded slowly. She tapped the pages of the book. "Go on," she said.

As they were preparing for that first trip together to Charles Brook, she packed an odd assortment of materials into a knapsack — a compass, several sheets of clean paper, heavy leather gloves, a brass container, molasses, an empty glass jar. At the end of the haying, after the hired men took their leave of Reilly's river, Cassie told Peyton she wanted to spend a few hours more in the freshly mown meadows. They were on the beach with Joseph Reilly. He was adding wood to a well-burning fire. He said, "We'll have a bit of bread you can carry home to John Senior if you bide a while longer."

Cassie and Peyton walked half an hour into the meadows, stopping in one of the wide clearings of shorn grass and boulders. The day was warm though the northerly wind carried a nip when it gusted up and they settled in the lee of a large scaly rock that caught the heat of the sun. There were long white threads of cirrus cloud on the horizon. While Peyton gathered dead wood, Cassie laid out the contents of the bag she had packed.

She stood over the new fire with the container of molasses and poured a long string of it onto the flames, then sat back beside Peyton.

"What are you doing?"

"Just wait."

The smell of the molasses lifted on the heat of the fire into the air around them. She laid the paper flat on the ground and used stones to hold the corners down.

Within a few minutes the first scatter of bees arrived. Cassie said nothing, though she smiled at Peyton as if they had wagered a bet on something and she was certain now of winning. "Take out your watch," she said. She poured another dollop of molasses onto the paper and then opened the metal container, carefully shaking what looked to Peyton like some sort of red pepper or tiny metal filings onto the paper around the molasses.

Two fat bees landed on the paper and wandered about in skewed circles. When they lifted away, their bellies were red as a sunset. "Check the time," Cassie said. She stood to watch the bees hover into the woods, using the compass to note their direction. Then she sat back beside him without a word. Within four minutes the first reddened bee returned to the paper. The second was right behind it.

"Now," she said. She tilted her head and squinted into the sunlight as if making an intricate mathematical calculation. "That would be somewhere between two hundred and two hundred and fifty yards, is my guess." She stood and took the leather gloves and empty jar. They had carried a pouch of water from Charles Brook and Cassie told Peyton to put it on to boil for tea. "With any luck I'll be back in twenty minutes or so."

He was just beginning to realize what she was about. "You'll never find it in there, Cassie," he said.

She was sighting with the compass and didn't look back over her shoulder. She marched off through the field, her habitual limp exaggerated over the rough rolling ground, and she disappeared into the trees without another word. Peyton set the water to boil and stared into it as it began to bubble at the base of the pot. He fished out the bag of tea and as soon as he had a full rolling boil he dropped in a handful of the leaves, then took the pot off the flame and set it beside the fire. He looked off in the direction she had gone.

"That'll be froze over by the time she gets back," he said to himself. He checked his watch. Seventeen minutes. Nineteen.

There was a sheen of sweat on Cassie's face when she got back to the fire. She carried the heavy gloves under her arm and held the jar before her, filled nearly to the brim with honey and wax.

"I had to climb the tree a ways," she said. There were half a dozen startling bright welts swelling on her neck and face.

"You've been stung," Peyton said.

"Pour us a mug."

He strained tea into tin cups and Cassie heaped a spoonful of wild honey into each. She passed Peyton one and lifted the other in toast. They drank together and even through the scalding heat they could taste the clear, rich sweetness.

"Where did you learn to do this?"

"My father took me out when I was a girl," she said. "We spent Saturday afternoons tramping around the backcountry above St. John's. He taught me —" She looked shyly across at Peyton. She'd barely spoken of her family since coming north with John Senior and she seemed to regret it coming up. "He taught me to swim, to fire a rifle. He taught me this," she said, lifting the jar of honey. "It was this made my mother fall in love with him, my father told me. He took her off into the valley when she was not much above a girl and he'd mine honey from the woods this way." She shook her head. "Mother always said falling in love with my father was the biggest mistake of her life."

"How old are you, Cassie?" Peyton asked.

She watched him slyly from the corner of her eye, as if she was assessing him anew. "Why that is very forward of you, John Peyton. I am twenty-four years old."

He turned his face to the sky and squinted against the sun as she had, making several quick calculations in his head.

"Is that older or younger than you expected?"

"Why did your mother say falling in love with your father was a mistake?"
Cassie looked off towards the border of trees. "My father drank a great
deal. He squandered money, he refused to set foot in a church." For the first
time since coming to the northeast shore she spoke of the public house her
father owned, one of the dozens of grog shops near the harbour where fishermen and sailors drank away their season's earnings. She told Peyton the
tavern's motto: *Drunk for a Penny. Dead drunk for tuppence. Free Straw.* The
fishermen drank dark Jamaican rum as long as they could afford it, then calli-
bogus or king calli, a concoction of spruce beer mixed with rum or gin or a
locally stilled alcohol that was so harsh and potent it could be set alight and
burned like a candle. Men slept on the straw against the walls and urinated in
their clothes, arguments and fistfights spilled out the door into the streets. Two
or three impoverished prostitutes drifted from table to table in the poor light.

Cassie lived with her parents in a narrow two-storey house consisting of
a single room downstairs and two bedrooms up a steep, unrailed staircase. It
was built adjacent to the pub, though she might have grown up in London,
for all she knew of the tavern's interior as a child. Her mother forbade her to
step inside the establishment under any circumstances and she orbited the
building like a moon all her young life, never coming within a few yards of
the door. "My mother was a good woman, God rest her. She was ashamed to
be associated with the public house," Cassie told him. "And with my father
too, I suppose. She used to say that love was a fire to warm fools."

They fell into a long silence then, as if this idea embarrassed them both.
They finished their tea and then set out the food they had brought with them.
The day continued clear and mostly warm. Bees hovered over the sealed jar
of honey and the crumpled paper stained with molasses, their steady buzzing
like the hum of a planet in motion around the sun.

Peyton lifted his forehead from his fist and looked across at Reilly. He was
exhausted with the long days of work and the beer had gone straight to his
head. His stomach felt hollow.

Reilly said, "I thought you were asleep over there, John Peyton."

He shook his head. "I was thinking about the first year I came across for the haying with Cassie. The Red Indian," he said. "Do you remember?"

Reilly smiled. "Thought you were going to come out of your skin when you laid eyes on him," he said.

Peyton and Cassie had come out of the woods several hundred yards above Reilly's tilt on their way back from the honey meadow that afternoon and followed the shoreline downriver. Reilly was on the beach with his back to the water. Peyton was about to call to him when another voice sounded across the river. On the weir near the opposite shore, a Beothuk man was kneeling and staring into the swirl of water. He had hair down his back as black as peat, his face and neck and his hands were darkened with an ochre stain the colour of blood. He was dressed in caribou leather and hefted a long staff of spruce wood or boxy fir at his shoulder. He drove the spear into the river and lifted it clear, a late-season salmon impaled and writhing at the tip so that the entire length of the staff vibrated. He stood slowly and looked across at the Irishman on the beach with an expression that was somehow proprietary. "Joe Reilly," he shouted again.

Peyton ran ahead of Cassie to where Reilly was standing. He kept his eye on the spot where the Indian had disappeared back into the woods and stumbled several times. "What should we do?" he shouted as he ran. "What should we do?" Even standing beside Reilly he stutter-stepped and flailed towards the opposite side of the river with his arm. He stopped suddenly and looked at the Irishman. "He knew your name, Joseph."

Reilly turned his face down to stare at his boots. There was an uncharacteristic sheepishness about him. Cassie had come up to them, and Annie Boss was making her way down from the tilt. "This used to be their river," he said. "They come by once or twice a week and take off a fish. It doesn't cause any harm."

"They murdered Harry Miller."

"It's not my place to speak against the dead," Reilly said, "but Harry Miller was a hard, hard man."

"Red man not bad man," Annie said.

Peyton said, "They killed Harry Miller."

"Truth be told," Reilly said, "they could kill any one of us whenever they pleased and we'd never see them."

Annie Boss reached a hand to hold his forearm. "John Peyton," she said. She had never touched him before. He could see how her brown eyes were flecked with gold, like small stones starred with mica. "Red man not bad," she said again.

Reilly shook his head. "I don't suppose your Da will appreciate the fact I let Red Indians walk off with his fish."

Peyton looked at Cassie and then back at the hired man.

Annie Boss picked up the skirt of her apron to wipe her hands. "Bread ready," she said. "We got bread for John Senior."

She knelt on the sand near the spot where Reilly had been feeding the fire that morning and began digging with a trowel. Steam rose from the ground and she reached in with a bare hand to lift out a round loaf. She brushed away loose grains of sand from the snow-white crust before passing it to Cassie.

The heat scalded her fingers and she had to tip it back and forth from one hand to another. "I'm sure John Senior will appreciate your kindness," she said and she caught Peyton's eye and held it for a moment.

"Tell him we were asking," Reilly said, and there were nods all around.

The afternoon had turned surprisingly humid and warm. Reilly shaded his eyes and looked off into the points of the compass. "It's a broad day," he said. "Could be weather behind that."

As they rowed home to Burnt Island, Peyton sat facing Cassie in the stern, the bread resting in a fold of her skirt between her legs. To the south and west a large front of dark cloud had pushed up quickly over the horizon and the sun had passed behind it. They would be lucky to get in off the water before the rain started and there was likely lightning and wind coming as well. Peyton hauled at the oars. His skin felt tight around him, as if it was no longer large enough to accommodate everything that was going on inside it.

Cassie said, "What are you thinking about, John Peyton?"

He came back on the oars with everything he had. "Nothing," he said.

She smiled at him. "Was that your first sight of a Red Indian?"

"I saw one in Poole," Peyton said between strokes. "Before I come over. A little girl. She didn't look. A thing like that."

Cassie nodded but didn't say anything more. Peyton leaned hard on the oars again. Without discussing it they had agreed not to mention the Indian to John Senior. A shared secret, a space cleared just for them. It made him want to kiss her. He looked overhead at the oncoming weather. Where the black banks of cloud met and overlapped there were brilliant red and gold seams of light burning through, the colours as vivid as molten lava.

Years after that first trip to Reilly's for the haying, Peyton still thought of Cassie's mother making the mistake of her life. He could still smell the fresh baked bread in Cassie's lap, heat rising from its centre. Peyton took a slow mouthful of his beer which was piss-warm and tasted just as foul.

Reilly reached into the bucket of river water for another bottle. He said, "You never mentioned that Indian to John Senior, did you?"

The younger man shook his head. "Not a word," he said.

Reilly nodded. "Is your man Buchan still hunting the coastline for them?"

"He is." Peyton look up at the Irishman. "What do you give for his chances?"

Reilly said, "He'll not but lay eyes on them, is my guess. And after what happened the winter, that'll as likely as not be a blessing."

"Why did they kill those marines, Joseph?"

"There's no odds in guessing at what that crowd were thinking."

Peyton pointed with the tip of the bottle he held. "You know, don't you."

A look passed across Reilly's face, as if he'd stepped wrong on a gimpy ankle. They could hear the argument between Richmond and Taylor still going on near the water.

Peyton said, "It was them, wasn't it? Those two on the beach?"

Reilly sat up straight and put both hands on his thighs.

"And Cull and Hughster."

The Irishman let out a long breath of air. "They might have had suspicions about some of us. If they recognized anyone, I'd be willing to wager it wasn't from the most pleasant of circumstances."

Peyton pointed with the bottle again and was saying, "John Senior —" when Annie Boss came out of the tilt carrying the child and seated herself near the two men. He didn't finish the thought.

Annie pushed the dress away from her breast and settled her son at the nipple. When she raised her head from the baby, Peyton could see the gold flecks in each iris sparking in the sunlight. She smiled across at him, a close-lipped smile that seemed to him to be an apology of some kind, as if she was embarrassed to be sitting with him, nursing a child. It was an embarrassment they all felt and had no notion how to overcome.

Reilly said, "What do you figure to do, John Peyton?"

"Do with what exactly?"

He gave an elaborate shrug and then looked directly at the younger man. "It must be hard living in that house," he said. "With the two of them."

Peyton stared down at his feet and scuffed at the ground. "Where have I got to go?" he said.

The following year Buchan returned to the northeast shore, although he sensed the governor's will to continue the search fading as the summer progressed. He responded with an intense, desperate hope like a man attempting to save a failing marriage. He sent detailed reports to St. John's each month, including a list of all camps, trails and artifacts he'd come across and recounting the sightings reported to him by others. Each letter included assurances that the hoped for encounter was not only likely, but inevitable. *There is the greatest probability of attaining our goal if we follow up the operation without intermission until the end of August,* he wrote. *Our continued efforts to bring the natives into civil society,* he insisted later in the season, *should be considered a national object and our ultimate success will wipe away a certain degree of stigma brought on us by the former barbarity of our countrymen.* He wrote, *My dear Duckworth.*

John Thomas Duckworth's service as governor of Newfoundland ended in the fall of 1812. The discreet expeditions he had permitted to be undertaken in Red Indian country he considered to be abject failures and he returned to England complaining of headaches so severe he lost peripheral vision in his right eye for hours at a time.

Lieutenant Buchan's petition to the governor's successor to continue the work Duckworth initiated on the northeast shore was denied. It would be seven years before he returned to the Bay of Exploits.

Part 2

dwall n also **drool, dwoll** *MED* dwale n 'dazed or
unconscious condition' (c1400-1450); *EDD* dwal(l) sb 1
'light slumber'[...]
    28 Dwoll: a state between sleeping and waking....

— Dictionary of Newfoundland English

Other Losses

1817–1818

ONE

In the early evening of November 7, 1817, a fire broke out in a small house adjoining the shops and warehouses of Lower Path, known by this time as Water Street, in St. John's.

Almost the entire path had once been covered by high fish flakes, rough trellises of spruce logs where salted cod was spread to dry. Most of these were gone now, some victim of a Water Street fire the previous winter, others torn down to make way for buildings as St. John's became less a fishing village and more a centre of commerce and trade for the colony. But several stretches of the street still ran under the rows of loosely fitted lungers, which were themselves covered with a layer of tinder-dry spruce boughs.

On the harbour side of Water Street a row of large wooden stores warehoused dried cod for export in the late summer and, by early fall, much of the imported food and supplies that saw the inhabitants through the winter months. The north side was a mile-long strip of houses interspersed with retail shops selling food, hardware and clothing, patent cures such as Extract of Mustard, sarsaparilla, Balsam of Life, antibilious pills. There was a shoe repair shop, a millinery, a bakery, a blacksmith's, there were taverns such as the Royal Oak, Shoulder of Mutton, the Globe, the Jolly Fisherman.

The street itself was still unpaved, uneven and rocky at the best of times, in inclement weather a relentlessly muddy quagmire. Up to fifteen feet in width at its most generous, there were points where little more than six feet separated the shops on either side. The prevailing wind funnelled through this long, narrow tunnel of two-storey buildings, ripping hats from the heads of pedestrians, inverting the ribs of parasols, restlessly swinging the painted wooden signs of dogs, goats and fish that hung over merchants' stores.

On the night of the seventh, a steady wind lifted large flankers from the single burning building and showered them along the darkened street like sparks flailing off a pinwheel of fireworks. Within minutes the neighbouring houses and fish flakes were alight and the flames had jumped to the south side of the path. The fire bell was sounded and parties of marines and soldiers and volunteers from the town itself were dispatched with buckets, hatchets and hawsers to try to contain the blaze. Every establishment between King's Beach and the Governor's Wharf was raging by the time the firefighters assembled on the street, the fierce glow of the flames under a low cloud of smoke lighting the harbour's ring of hills like torches set around a stage. Ships docked at the wharves slipped their moorings to drift free of the fire's reach, the calm surface of the water roiling with reflected light beneath them. Wind carried flankers onto their decks and several caught fire, the vessels burning down to the waterline. Crowds of people from the shanties and tilts built higher above the harbour came down to Water Street and began looting from the buildings in the path of the flames. Some merchants guarded their wares with rifles until the fire forced them to abandon their posts, others threw open their doors to allow the looters to make off with whatever they could carry before the conflagration overtook their stores. There was an intermittent roar of roof timbers collapsing two storeys into the buildings they once covered. Burning walls foundered and fell into the street.

Within six hours of the first alarm the merchant houses along Water, Duckworth and Holloway streets had burnt to the ground, along with the courthouse, dozens of storehouses, sheds and wharves and 130 homes. On the eastern side of the town as far as Hill o'Chips nothing but a few scattered outbuildings remained standing.

━┼┼━

The first official residence of Newfoundland governors was established in 1781, inside the walls of Fort Townshend on the hills above the town of St. John's. It was intended to act only as a summer residence during the fishing season, but even in this limited role it was regarded by its inhabitants as less than adequate. It was built of fir with heavy slate roofs that damaged the structure to the extent that rain dripped steadily into offices and bedrooms. Drifts of snow driven by winter gales filtered through the same nooks and crannies to pool beside beds and desks as early as September and as late as May each year. Successive governors ordered additional rooms and offices attached to the core of the building for their servants, for secretaries and clerks, the residence spiralling outward from its dysfunctional core like a malignant tumour. There were complicated labyrinths of long windowless corridors and passageways illuminated with borrowed light that trapped dampness and cold inside. Each room was equipped with a fireplace but the constant draughts made it impossible to maintain a comfortable temperature anywhere in the building.

The first governor to be saddled with the responsibility of year-round habitation, Vice Admiral Francis Pickmore, had spent a long miserable November in the governor's house at the heel of the previous season. He wrote to His Majesty's government, begging for money to construct a home that would better suit someone of his station and the extreme conditions a winter-long stay was likely to bring. The earl of Bathurst in his response cited economic circumstances in England as a deterrent to such extravagance.

Two weeks after the fire and not yet a full month into his first St. John's winter, Pickmore sat in one of the relentlessly chilly offices trying to comprehend the enormity of the loss, the myriad implications. A second consecutive year of depressed markets for cod in Europe had left many of the island's residents in a condition of severe impoverishment and much of the store of food stockpiled for the winter was consumed in the fire. Temperatures in

November were already dipping twenty degrees below zero. At night, gangs of rowdies roamed the village, made reckless by hunger and the cold, beating and stealing from anyone they encountered on the streets.

Pickmore brought his handkerchief to his mouth. He said, "We're in for one hellish winter, I expect."

Buchan was standing across from the governor's desk, his hat beneath his arm. "Likely so, sir."

Pickmore looked up. His face was pale and bloated and somehow lifeless. Dank brown hair, large watery eyes. A drowned man, Buchan thought, a man too listless to be overwhelmed. "What are the estimates on the losses, Lieutenant?" the governor asked.

"A million pounds, at the least. A portion of that amount, perhaps a hundred thousand pounds, will be written off by insurance. Most of the fishermen have lost everything."

"How many homeless?"

"Perhaps a thousand or more."

Pickmore nodded. "How does that compare with those burned out in last year's fire?"

"About on a par, I would say."

"And these rals roaming the streets at night?" He waved his handkerchief.

"They seem as bold this winter as last. Public floggings tended to temper their mood somewhat. I've taken the liberty of setting up a small force of marines to patrol the town after dark."

"Most commendable," Pickmore said. There was a distracted quality to his voice that made his compliments sound like censure. "We are fortunate to have a man of your experience in these situations. I confess I would be at a loss where to begin with it all."

Buchan inclined his head slightly. The previous winter's fire, and the hardship and unrest among the inhabitants of St. John's that resulted from it, had been the sole reason for installing a governor year-round in the colony. But Pickmore, he could see, and by the man's own admission, was going to be of little help. "They are already starting to build shanties, Your Worship, along the same miserable paths. I think it might be best to discourage this until the spring when construction can be undertaken in a manner more carefully reasoned or we will find ourselves living in the same fire trap as always."

The governor pursed his lips and nodded. "Agreed," he said. He interrupted himself to cough a dark plug of phlegm into the white silk handkerchief he held in his left hand at all times. "It hardly seems creditable," he said, "that a house could be built to hold the cold as this one does." He got up from his seat and walked across to the fireplace where he placed two junks of wood onto the flames and reached for a third. He stood staring blankly at the flaring light.

Buchan said, "Is there anything further, sir?"

Pickmore turned with the junk of wood in his hand. He looked almost as if he was about to burst into tears. He said, "You don't hold a very high opinion of me, do you, Lieutenant."

Buchan disliked the man, it was true. He'd made attempts to interest the governor in the plight of the Red Indians without much success. "I have other things to worry about," Pickmore had said, shaking his handkerchief like a man engaged in an act of perpetual surrender. It seemed to Buchan he worried mostly about himself. Pickmore's endless complaints, his nagging sickliness, gave him the air of a spoiled child. He had said so to Marie on a number of occasions and considered saying something to that effect now. But in the end he said, "I have a position, Your Worship. Not opinions."

During what remained of the afternoon Buchan toured the burned-over area above the harbour. The jet-black of char still showing through the snow that had fallen in the days since the fire. Along Water Street, men picked through the ruins of the warehouses and stores with sticks, hoping to turn up bits of burnt fish or salt beef to feed their families. Three women in long skirts and kerchiefs sat in an alcove where the remains of two walls still formed a corner, their arms around a handful of children between the ages of two and ten. Towards the east end, along Hill o'Chips, a row of recently erected shanties stood shoulder to shoulder, tiny shacks of scavenged wood and canvas not high enough to allow even a man of his modest height to stand upright inside.

Somewhere an infant was crying inconsolably. The sun was falling behind the western hills and the piercing, disembodied wail of the child seemed to Buchan to be the sound of the sun's descent. Long winter shadows seeped across the harbour, dragging dusk in their wake. He turned away from the waterfront and started back up the steep hill towards the fort.

He found the navy patrol as they prepared for their evening's tour of duty and he repeated his orders to use any force necessary to protect the citizenry from the gangs roaming the streets. "You are permitted five minutes on the hour to shelter inside out of the cold, not a minute more," he told them. "Am I understood?"

He marched across to the mess where supper was just being served. He stood behind an empty chair and placed both hands on the wooden rungs until the room had fallen silent. Three hundred marines and Blue Jackets turned to watch him. A piece of cutlery clattered to the floor. Someone asked, "Are you joining us, Lieutenant?"

"Corporal Rowsell," Buchan said.

The man jumped to his feet, nearly knocking his chair over behind him. "Sir," he said.

"In the morning, you will take a patrol of eighty men to the Hill o'Chips and remove, by force if necessary, all men, women and children residing in temporary shelters built since the fire."

"Sir."

"The shelters will be torn down. The people will be moved to the church hall most amenable to their faith. If necessary, tents will be erected in the churchyards to accommodate the numbers."

"Yes sir."

Buchan took a breath. He had deliberately avoided raising his voice and he could feel the men in the room leaning towards him, straining to hear. He said, "As of this evening, all members of His Majesty's Service will be put on half rations."

Rowsell cleared his throat. "Yes sir," he said again.

Buchan turned his attention away from the corporal then and spoke into the centre of the room. "The extra rations will be distributed evenly through the churches to those people residing within their doors." He looked back to Rowsell. "Is that clear?"

"Perfectly clear, sir," Rowsell said.

He stood there a moment longer looking at the faces of the men, all of them staring straight ahead now or into their plates. "Thank you, Corporal," he said. He pulled the chair away from the table and took a seat. "I would be pleased to join you."

It was nearly eight o'clock by the time he made his way back to the apartment he shared with his wife and four-year-old daughter within the walls of the fort. The child was already asleep. Marie was sitting near the fire under a thick layer of blankets and shawls. She was pregnant a third time and expecting the birth within days or weeks. Her belly distended the flow of material around her and her exposed head looked comically tiny atop the mound in the chair. Yellow ringlets in her hair. A small delicate nose, a high red blush in her cheeks as if she'd spent hours running outside. It was still the face of the girl he'd met when she was fifteen and barely conversant in the English language.

"Your supper is ruined," she told him without turning from the fire.

"I ate with the men at the mess," he said. "I'm sorry."

"You are always sorry, yes?"

He pulled a chair next to hers and smiled across at her.

"Do not smile," she said. She shifted uncomfortably, unable to find a position where the baby did not press against her ribs or her spine. She took quick, delicate breaths to avoid the painful stitches that folded through her stomach, across her back. "You 'ave no idea what it is to live in this condition. I cook for you in this condition and you eat with the men in the mess."

"You have a perfectly capable servant to cook for you."

"She is useless, the Irish 'ave no ideas what is cooking. They are worse even than the English."

Buchan shifted his chair again and lifted her right foot into his lap, removing the heavy leather slipper and rubbing his thumb firmly along the length of the sole. Her head lolled backwards. He said, "*Pardonnez-moi, chéri. Tu es tout pour moi.*"

She sat up straight and pulled her foot from his hands. "I must share you with the men in the mess, this is your idea of marriage? I must share you? And your French is terrible," she said.

He smiled and reached for her left foot. His French was not good, it was true. But at times he went out of his way to speak it poorly, to tease her. He said, "*C'est vrai?*"

After the seventh month of her pregnancies, his wife endured constant discomfort and the petulance her discomfort provoked was astonishing. Buchan's resolutely good humour in the face of her anger occasionally needled her into a more furious state of mind, but on the whole it was one of the few things that made the last eight weeks of carrying a child bearable. She winced a smile back at him. "*Oui,*" she said. "*C'est vrai.*"

They sat without speaking while Buchan massaged her swollen feet, and before she dozed off in her chair, Marie said, "*Pardonnez-moi, chéri. Tu es tout pour moi.*" She spoke the words with a flawless imitation of her husband's Scots burr.

"Go to sleep now," he said.

"You love me, yes?"

"Yes."

"You love only me, *c'est vrai?*"

"*Oui,*" he said. "*C'est vrai.*"

Buchan watched her sleeping. She had left their oldest daughter at a boarding school in England the past three years in order to be with him in Newfoundland. And even here he was away for weeks, sometimes months at a time. If he added the absences together, they accounted for several years of their marriage.

With the exception of the last two months of her pregnancies, Marie never complained or asked for anything different from him. It still surprised him to see the strength of her will once she committed herself. Her face was the only childlike thing about her any more, that and her devotion to him which he felt less and less worthy of. He had to make a conscious effort not to respond to it with the cloying attention of a delinquent parent. He massaged his thumb the length of the tendon that stretched from her big toe almost to her heel. It was the only thing that gave her any relief now.

At the time Buchan and Marie first met, England and France were about to go to war after a brief cessation of hostilities. He made a half-hearted attempt to talk her out of marrying him. On the HMS *Nettby* he had seen men disembowelled by round shot, arms shattered by flying debris. The wounded were carted to the surgeon on the orlop deck where they were laid in a row and treated strictly in turn, regardless of rank or the severity of the injury. Many bled to death while they waited. Limbs were amputated with only a mouthful of rum for anaesthetic, a leather gag forced between the injured man's teeth. On the gun decks, the dead and those men wounded beyond hope were pitched through the gun ports to make way for replacements.

None of these things Buchan felt proper to tell a girl of Marie's age, but he did his best to imply what marriage to a navy man could mean. Through the years that followed, he thought of himself as an appendage his wife would have to make do without if necessary — a finger, an ear, a foot. He was a soldier after all, he'd managed to find something menacingly erotic in the risking of such things. And he comforted himself with the thought that she had made her decision to marry him in full knowledge of the possibility.

But the notion he might have to learn to live his life without Marie had never occurred to him before the last child.

The birth had been a harrowing, nearly fatal experience. Thirty-six hours of labour, a breech, their second daughter born feet first. For a while, the midwife thought she would lose them both. When she passed the afterbirth, Marie bled so much the bed sheets and towels, even the mattress, were beyond recovering and had to be burned. Buchan was cloistered away in another room while the women dealt with these things. He heard the story after the fact, knowing it had been abbreviated, censored in the interest of delicacy. Less than what it signified, he knew, not as horrific as the event itself.

Her constitution never quite recovered from the extremities of that labour and she had fallen into a more and more delicate state of health through this latest pregnancy. It was clear to them both, though it had never been spoken aloud, that the approaching birth could kill her. An increasingly familiar twinge of regret hammered at him, like the heel of a tiny foot kicking at his ribs from the inside.

He worked her slipper carefully over her foot and placed it gently on the floor. He stoked the fire and added more wood, then went to the bedroom where he pissed into the chamber pot. He lifted a hand-stitched quilt from the bed and carried it back to the hearth where he lay down beside his wife's chair and fell asleep.

At half past three that morning, the twenty-first of November, the watch on one of His Majesty's ships in St. John's harbour observed long curtains of flame billowing through the windows of a property owned by Messrs. Huie & Reed on Water Street, near Adelaide. The ship's cannon was fired to alert the town and in the early morning stillness the report echoed back and forth between the surrounding hills, throwing the entire village into a bleary state of confusion and panic, as if the settlement were suddenly under siege. Thousands of people rushed from their houses into the winter night, barefoot and wearing only their nightshirts, many of them carrying crying children and infants into the bitter cold.

There was no wind, but the fire travelled quickly through the closely packed rows of wooden buildings and stores of drygoods. By the time Buchan reached Water Street, everything east of Adelaide to the boundary of the previous fire was burning and beyond help. He marshalled a group of marines and fishermen and led them west beyond Huie & Reed's premises. The few remaining fish flakes over the path he ordered torn down. On the roofs of the buildings along the street men had climbed ladders to lay wet blankets or carpets on the shingles. They scrambled back and forth with brooms to sweep away the drifting flankers as they pitched on the roofs. They had no chance, Buchan could see, of saving their homes and businesses. What was needed was a firebreak, an open space the fire wouldn't be able to cross on a night without wind.

He ordered marines into two houses facing each other across the narrow street, telling them to clear the rooms of anyone still inside. Men with axes and saws severed the main wooden support beams of the building on the south side of the street and a Blue Jacket was sent up a ladder with a hawser, which he secured to the opposite eave. A crowd of several hundred had gathered by then and Buchan ordered as many men as could get a hand in to stand along the free end of the hawser. They lined diagonally down Water Street, almost a hundred strong. Buchan shouted against the roar of the approaching fire as the men came back on the rope. The two-storey structure creaked, tilted sideways like a drunk man trying to rise from a chair, then stumbled into the street, collapsing in a cloud of dust. There was a cheer from the men on the line and from the people watching along the street.

Before the dust had settled a woman came at Buchan, using both her fists to pummel his chest and slap at his face. She was still in her nightclothes, her head covered with a nightcap. A marine ran up behind her and grabbed at her arms. She was yelling incomprehensibly as she struck Buchan and it took several minutes to restrain her. She looked up at the officer from the ground where the marine sat beneath her, pinning her arms to her side. "That was my house, you bastard," she shouted. "That was my house."

"I tried to keep hold of her, sir," the marine explained. "She's strong as a mule."

"Get her out of here," Buchan said.

The hawser was already attached to the second residence and the men were lined along the rope, waiting for the order to heave. The heat of the fire was building in the street behind them, the noise too loud to be heard over. Buchan took a handkerchief from his pocket and held it in the air as if to signal the start of a race. Three times he raised and lowered it as the volunteers leaned back against the weight of the rope, but the house did not budge. More men came forward to grab the hawser after each failure.

"Take it down," Buchan shouted uselessly. "Take it down!"

The sound of voices reached him then, men on the line chanting a heave-up song from the docks, the words drifting beneath the fire's racket like smoke. *Haul on the bowline, the bugger must come this time, haul on the bowline, haul, boys, haul,* the refrain growing stronger as the spectators on the street joined in. When the building suddenly crumpled and fell, men tumbled backwards over each other along the hawser. Another cheer went up as they got back to their feet and slapped the shoulders of those beside them. Buchan moved among the men directing the marines to begin clearing the debris from the lots. It was several minutes before he reached a dark knot huddled over a figure still lying in the street. A large bearded man wearing a patch over his right eye was cradling the head of the fallen man in his lap. He looked up as Buchan pushed near.

"Get him out of the street," Buchan shouted.

The man with the eye patch shook his head. He said, "He's gone, sir."

The dead man still clutched his shirtfront in both hands, as if he was trying to tear it from his body.

╫

The firebreaks preserved the last 150 yards of buildings on the north and south sides of Water Street, but an additional 240 homes and businesses were lost in the second fire of the winter. One in three residents was left homeless and impoverished during one of the harshest winters ever recorded in the colony. Even those people with money had little or no access to food or other supplies, most of which had been burnt to cinders. During the course of the following months the most vulnerable starved or died of exposure in the pathetic temporary structures the governor could not prevent the homeless from cobbling together. The cemetery ground was hard as flint and the dead were salted with chopped ice in their coffins and kept in a storage room at the fort until graves could be dug in the spring.

Vice Admiral Francis Pickmore became the first governor of Newfoundland to die in office. He was already suffering long-standing and nagging illnesses when he took up residence at Fort Townshend in October. The severe conditions of the winter, the turmoil in the aftermath of the fires, the constant damp and cold of the governor's residence overtook him like a predator running down a wounded animal. He died on February 24 of complications arising from bronchial congestion.

The constant frost of that year had sealed the coast in a solid band of ice from the early days of December. In order to return the governor's body to England, Buchan pressed three hundred shoremen into service beside crewmen from the *Drake, Egeria* and the *Fly* to carve a passage clear of the harbour. Close to shore the ice was as much as five feet thick and the men used axes and ice-saws and simple stubbornness to make their way through it. Three weeks after the work began, the HMS *Fly* left St. John's with the earthly remains of Governor Pickmore preserved in a large puncheon of rum. Buchan was present when the body was lowered into the murky bath of alcohol. The face darkened under the sepia surface, the features bearing an expression of beatific indifference. A drowned man, Buchan thought as the cover was nailed into place.

The channel the workers had muscled through to open water on the

Atlantic was 2,856 yards in length. Within a week the relentlessly cold weather had closed it over again and the harbour remained inaccessible to shipping until May.

To everyone's amazement no lives were lost in the fires themselves. The man who died of what was assumed to be a heart attack while tearing down the firebreak houses on Water Street was the only fatality recorded during those two disastrous nights. The body was laid out for viewing before the burial in one of the few taverns not lost to the fire, a single-room affair owned and operated by the man with the eye patch. He introduced himself as Harrow when Buchan arrived to pay his respects.

"I was a navy man meself," he said. "Years ago this was. Till I lost the eye." He gestured at his head.

Buchan nodded.

The coffin was set up on the bar and there was a row of drunken fishermen standing beside it. It was built of plain board and the dead man inside it was dressed in a black suit several sizes too large for him and thirty years out of fashion.

"The suit was my own," Harrow told the officer. He wore a slop smock tied at his waist that draped almost to the floor. "Haven't put it on my back since my first year out of the navy. And he didn't have a proper fit-out for burying, poor bugger."

"Was he a relation of yours?"

"No sir, a business partner at one time. Before his wife died. He sold his share in the establishment afterwards and then drank away the works."

Several men near them at the bar toasted the corpse's legendary exploits as a drinker.

"When is the funeral?"

"Tomorrow noon." Harrow shook his head. "I'm surprised the Church would have him. He never set foot inside one in all the years I knew him."

"Is that a fact?"

"And so it is. He was a queer stick, I'll grant you. Had a daughter, a clever girl. He dressed her up in men's clothes one August and they traipsed off to Portugal Cove before there was a road. And I've heard stranger things that the presence of his remains prevent me from speaking of."

Another round of salutes from the mourners.

Buchan looked around the dimly lit room. "Where is his daughter now?"

"She left twenty-odd year ago. She was in the employ of a northern man, one Peyton, owns half the country up there. No saying where she is these days. Would you take a complimentary beverage, Lieutenant?" Harrow had gone around the bar and was out of sight behind the coffin.

"No," Buchan said. "Thank you. I just wanted to offer my condolences."

Harrow reappeared at the side of the bar and leaned a shoulder against the head of the coffin. "We thank you," he said. "On his behalf. Come back on a happier occasion, the complimentary will still be here."

It was weeks afterwards before Buchan could bring himself to take pen and paper to write a letter that would be sent on the first packet boat out of Portugal Cove after the spring breakup. He began, *Dear Ms. Cassandra Jure. It is with regret and the most heartfelt sympathy I write with news of your father's passing from this world in the early morning of November 21, 1817.*

TWO

Cassie was telling John Peyton about the first walking trip she took with her father as a girl, between St. John's harbour and Portugal Cove. She was sitting next to the fire at the summer house, wearing a thick wool sweater and flannels beneath the pale linen of her skirt against the chill of early May. The letter carrying news of her father's death was in her lap and she worried at the paper absently as she spoke.

"I was only twelve at the time," she said. She and her father were travelling an Indian path, an overland route through miles of what the books she read would have called *impenetrable forest, impassable bog-land*. It had been decades since the Beothuk Indians occupied this part of the island and the trail seemed to be little more than a rumour of their passing, barely marked, sometimes petering out halfway across a marsh, sometimes disappearing in a copse of spruce. They would spend half an hour or more then, zigzagging aimlessly to pick up some hint of the direction it continued in, her father walking bent at the waist as if he might be able to sniff out the path like a hound. He had thickly curled sideburns, a head of thinning hair showing pale scalp. He carried a nunny-bag packed with food and clean stockings, a costril of spruce beer tied at his waist. He squatted where depressions in the moss indicated the path might turn northward and pulled at the sideburns with both hands, considering.

He caught Cassie watching him and smiled across at her. "Yes," he said, as if her watching was the deciding factor. "This way then." He straightened and started off, and Cassie settled in behind him, her eyes at his feet, trotting every few steps to keep up. She was exhausted and near tears by this point, but refused to give in by naming it, by asking for relief. Her father was moving at the same pace he'd set when they began walking out of St. John's in the dark that morning and she was determined not to alter it, not to slow him down. At the time she aspired to his indiscriminate appetite for the world. Just as her mother once had.

Her mother was a girl of barely seventeen years when she met the man who would become her husband, moving away with him to Newfoundland to protect her parents from unacceptable public embarrassment.

Cassie looked at Peyton, to see if he understood what she was saying. He nodded for her to go on.

Her mother wanted to live a respectable life, and before the years and her father's increasingly dissolute behaviour exhausted her, she struggled to maintain some semblance of dignity. In her eyes, the pub operated by her husband was another humiliation she had to endure and she couldn't speak of the place without a tremor of distaste in her voice.

Peyton said, "You've told me how she felt."

Cassie nodded. Her father complained his wife had airs about her, but thought she had suffered enough at his hands to have a legitimate claim to some disappointment. He let her censure of the tavern stand without serious rebuttal. But the unresolved disagreement between the two spilled over into other areas of the family's life, particularly when it came to their daughter. Her mother was fastidious and demanding, attentive, solicitous, firm. Her father was reckless, delinquent, uninhibited by notions of what was proper for a girl her age, particularly if he was under the influence of drink. He allowed her to read the early poems of John Donne, took her lining for conners off the wharves in the harbour, taught her to swim at Quidi Vidi Lake. He taught her to load and shoot a rifle in the hills above St. John's.

"You're going to ruin that girl," her mother warned him.

"I'm through ruining girls, m'love," he told her.

She gave him a dark, disparaging look. "I wish I'd never clapped eyes on you."

Cassie sometimes worked the tension between her parents to angle for concessions from her mother that would otherwise have been out of the question. John Donne was a little beyond her comprehension, lining for tomcod was more or less a bore. But learning to swim, firing a rifle, these things were exhilarating and worth fighting for. When her father announced his plans for the walking tour to Portugal Cove, she began lobbying to accompany him.

"Don't be ridiculous," her mother told her.

"Leave the child be," her father said. But his tone suggested it would take some convincing to bring him around.

"What kind of a creature are you raising?" her mother wanted to know. "Dragging her down to the wharf. Stripping her half naked at the lake. What are people to think if they see you stealing her off through the country in her petticoat?"

"People? What people are you concerned with?"

"By all that is sacred, Garfield Izakiah Jure, I will not allow you to carry Cassandra off into the woods."

"You won't allow it?"

"No," she said. "I will not. That's no place for a girl."

Her father nodded thoughtfully. "Indeed," he said. He looked at his daughter who was sitting quietly while events took their course and then he looked back at his wife. "I quite agree," he said. And he left the house without a word.

Cassie stared down at her shoes, studying the polished buckles. Her mother paced the floor. It was as if they had come to an impasse in an argument they'd been carrying on with each other. It was clear there was more to come. They were both expectant, apprehensive.

Half an hour later Cassie's father came through the door carrying a pair of men's trousers, stockings, a hat and a short Spencer coat. "We shall need a name for you," he said to his daughter.

"Now, Izakiah," her mother said.

"Try these on," he said. "We'll have to make some adjustments."

"Where on earth did you get these clothes?"

"From the smallest gentleman I could find next door. Cost me a bottle and a half of Jamaican rum. Something regal would be in order, something with the ring of royalty about it. What do you think of Henry as a name, Cassie? Or Charles, I've always fancied Charles. That's what we'd have called you if you were a lad."

The stockings were full of holes and filthy and the rank smell of them filled the room. Her mother stood helplessly in the centre of the floor. There was so much wrong with what was happening that she couldn't focus on the order in which she should be objecting to things. Finally she said, "She will not wear an item of those clothes until they have been washed."

It was a small concession to make and conceded so much to them in its turn that Cassie and her father immediately agreed to it.

They set out an hour before light, a week later. Her mother watching from the open doorway, her silhouette in the dim light of a candle behind her, her shadow cast on the dirt path. "You bring her home in one piece," she shouted to her husband when they were almost out of earshot. Cassie turned and looked back down the hill as the door closed, cancelling out the square of light.

The first three miles beyond the town they walked a wide, well-travelled road to a place called Tilt House, making good time. The sun was well up by then. Cassie could feel the itch of new blisters already forming on the heels of her feet.

"It gets much worse from here, young Charles," her father said. He tipped the costril of spruce beer to his lips and then replaced the cork. He took out a small jar of pork fat. He used two fingers to scoop a dollop from the jar and offered it to Cassie as he began liberally applying the white grease to his forehead, face and neck. He nodded ahead to the broken path of tree stumps and shallow bog. "Nippers," he said.

Cassie nodded and began applying the grease in the same manner her father had.

They travelled another three miles to Twenty Mile Pond, following a trail used mostly in winter to reach the lake. It was rutted and studded with tree stumps and stones and crossed by running streams of water. The mosquitoes hung about their heads in shaggy halos so thick and active they had to cover their mouths with their hands when they spoke. There were stretches of marsh spotted with deep, black-water flashes. Where the trail was most sodden, rocks or logs were lain at intervals for travellers but even these had begun to disappear into the muck. Cassie's shoes were slightly too big for her feet and she lost them both on separate occasions, rescuing them from the dark sucking mud with her hands.

At Twenty Mile Pond they stopped to rinse their shoes and stockings in the water and to eat a meal of cheese and bread. There was a strong breeze in the clearing that kept the insects down and dried their clothes as they sat at the water's edge. She lay back on the stones with bread still in her hand and fell asleep.

Cassie paused there, as if telling the story was exhausting her as much as the actual trip had, years before. Peyton watched her stare into the fire.

Beyond the lake the Indian path knifed into the trees, becoming so narrow that they couldn't walk abreast of one another. Stones pushed up to block the trail, some as high as the axle tree of a wagon. Her father waded waist-deep rivers with Cassie on his back, both of them staring into the current, his foot shifting carefully ahead to feel out each step. They lost the path and found it and lost it again. They clung to tree branches, stepping across exposed roots to cross patches of thigh-deep mud. Their hands were cut and scraped and coated in spruce gum. Cassie's legs were numb with walking, the soles of her shoes caked with blood. It was nothing like she expected and everything she wanted it to be all the same. "Do you see what I mean?" she asked.

Peyton raised his shoulders. "I guess so," he said.

She said, "I wanted whatever he wanted is the thing."

Peyton only nodded.

It was dark by the time they reached Portugal Cove and her father approached the first tilt they came across to inquire after lodgings and food. The building consisted of a single room only and through the door they could see the light of a small fire laid against the evening chill. They were ushered in and introduced — Cassie as *Charles*. "A pretty young lad," the man who had come to the door said. His name was O'Brien, an old Irishman whose high forehead and remarkable jowls seemed too large for the rest of his face, for his body. His wife, Margaret, was the only other occupant of the hovel, a small spry woman who they would learn later was nearly blind. She walked about the room with the confidence of a cat.

Margaret warmed a pot of seal meat in a stew of potatoes and turnip for their supper while they went outside to wash their feet in a brook running a few yards from the tilt. Her father lifted Cassie's feet into his lap and dried them with his shirt-tail, then applied a little of the pork fat to the bald patches of blister.

Cassie had never tasted seal meat — her mother refused to buy or eat it where salt pork was available — and she was of two minds about the dark, oily flavour. But she was so hungry from the travel that she ate her bowlful and accepted an offer of seconds, using her index finger to clean every bit of gravy from the earthenware. Her father was telling their hosts a fictional story about his son's appetite, how insatiable it was, when she fell asleep against his arm. She woke up the next morning on a layer of spruce branches spread over the dirt floor near the fireplace. Her father's coat laid over her as a blanket.

Cassie turned her head towards Peyton. Her face was sickly pale, which made her eyes seem black and spent, like bits of char left behind by a fire. Peyton said, "Perhaps you would like a drop of rum."

She looked around the room suddenly and he realized she was thinking of John Senior. She'd never touched a drop in his father's presence that he could recall. The old man had gone down to the stage house to work on the nets or simply whittle wood as soon as she opened the letter and the news came out. He placed a rough hand to Cassie's shoulder for a moment — his only comment on the matter — then stepped out the door without a word. Peyton tried to imagine Cassie telling this story to his father and couldn't. The talking, at least, had always been left to them.

Down on the stagehead John Senior was staring out over the sea. No wind to speak of, but there was a heavy send in the water of the cove. The smooth slate-grey surface looked like a stone courtyard riding a swell of tectonic motion.

He had come down to meet the sloop when John Peyton hauled in from Fogo with a load of spring supplies. "There's a letter," Peyton said to him, jumping from the gunnel after they had collared the *Susan* to the stage. "From St. John's."

They'd walked up to the house then, the bearers of bad news, neither of them doubted that. After she opened the letter John Senior put his hand to Cassie's shoulder and thought he might say something, a word for comfort. But nothing he could think of seemed the leastways appropriate, given the circumstances under which he first encountered Cassie and her father.

During their visits to St. John's to market the catch of salmon in the old days, he and Harry Miller stayed in rooms let by public houses for as long as a week. They drank hard after the day's business was complete and each night Miller availed himself of the services that were at a man's disposal in the island's capital. At first John Senior had resisted the undertow of his own loneliness and lust, holding himself apart from the women who circled the tavern tables like gulls over a cutting room. "I was beginning to wonder," Harry Miller said, after finally goading his younger partner into bringing a woman back to his room, "what sort of oil you required to set a flame to your wick, if you follow my meaning."

John Senior never shared the obvious relish with which Miller engaged in his annual ritual of debauchery. Miller's drunken propositioning of every female he encountered, his howling orgasms that could be heard on all three floors of the public house, embarrassed him, pricked at his sense of propriety in the sober light of day. But for a time they became partners in this, as in all other things.

The two men had once spent part of an evening in St. John's at the tavern owned by Cassie's father and after joining their table for several rounds he'd brought them next door to his house. Miller shouted propositions to the two women who'd taken refuge upstairs and Cassie's father, far from being insulted, laughed and urged him on. He got up from his seat then and leaned low over Miller, as if he was crying on the man's shoulder. They nodded together and Cassie's father slapped Miller's shoulder several times and then went drunkenly up the stairs. Miller sat on the edge of his chair, paddling at his thighs with the palms of his hands. He was singing tunelessly, wordlessly, *de dee dee dee, de dee.* He fingered at his crotch, leaning back in the chair as he made adjustments.

John Senior stared across at his partner. He experienced a peculiar moment of heaviness, as if the strangeness and uncertainty of the world suddenly weighed in on him. If things had gone differently, he knew, his father would be sitting beside Miller now with the same look of drunken, predatory expectancy.

John Senior's mother had accused her husband of sleeping with prostitutes all their married life. When he was thirteen she moved into the room his sisters shared, in protest. It was a change that was never spoken of, the necessary accommodations and compromises within the family made silently, like sleepers shifting to make room for another body. But he felt the humiliation it was for both of them. It was like a sickness they passed back and forth, a virus surviving first in one host, then the other, and kept alive for years in this fashion.

Without setting out to, he had satisfied himself as to the truth of his father's habits through remarks from neighbours and friends, through a more explicit awareness of the man's routines and whereabouts. He said nothing to either of his parents but felt as if the knowledge made him complicit in the whole affair.

In the last weeks of his life, his father was bedridden, withdrawn and uncommunicative, babbling, incontinent. John Senior sat up with the dying man through the night while his mother and two sisters slept in the adjoining room. Morning and evening he changed the square cloth diapers, scraping the inevitable mess of feces into a chamber pot. It was a kind of penance for knowing, an indignity he was determined to spare his mother. She came into the sickroom early one morning as he squatted over the pot with the diaper. The smell beneath him was putrid, an undeniable proof of rot at the world's core. His mother said, "A man is all stomach where women are concerned, Johnny." She shook her head then with a wounded contempt that he had never thought might have included him in its dismissal.

Miller's endless racket was making him feel nauseous. He could hear voices from the upstairs rooms, a hushed argument. He stood up from his seat. "Miller," he said, starting towards him. His stomach roiled and lurched, like a salmon writhing at the end of a spear.

"Jesus Christ, Peyton!" Miller yelled.

John Senior had him by the hair, hauling him across the room. Cassie's father called from the top of the stairs, but they were already going through the door. John Senior pushed and kicked and slapped Miller ahead of him.

"Are you mad, man?" Miller screamed. "You Christly devilskin," he said.

They continued in this fashion down the tiny dirt alleyway, then along the entire length of Lower Path until they'd reached the public house where they were lodging.

John Senior went back the next afternoon and waited near the house until he saw Cassie's father come out the door and nip across to the tavern. He stood before the two women with no notion of what needed to be said or why exactly he had come. He rambled stupidly about the book Cassie held and offered an awkward apology for Miller as if he was a dog who had piddled on a good rug. The women clearly distrusted him and their distrust was heightened by what they could see of his own fear and uncertainty. They looked away and said nothing. And before he could settle on a proper way to take his leave of them Cassie's father returned.

John Senior made his hurried excuses then and left, relieved to be released from a duty he didn't fully comprehend. But before he went out the door, he'd looked into the man's eyes a long moment, searching the alcohol-dampened flicker of them, thinking he might be able to tell just from that. Which one had he gone upstairs for, his wife or his daughter?

John Senior watched the grey water of the cove billow towards the shore, fighting the same surge of nausea he'd felt sitting beside Miller in that room. Feeling the same peculiar heaviness come over him. He'd had no plan to offer Cassie a position in his house and did so on a murky whim, hearing about her mother's death on his way through St. John's years later. Soon after Cassie came north, it seemed likely to him that she and John Peyton would make a pair, so he let the question he'd been asking himself lie. It was sometimes better, he had learned, not to know. He left the two of them on their own when he could, sent them across to Reilly's for the haying alone. Matchmaker is how he saw himself. The good father.

He shook his head at the thought now. The good father. He'd been on a round of his salmon rivers a summer some years after Cassie's arrival, inspecting the cure, the state of the weirs. He was meant to stop in at Charles Brook, then go on to Richmond's river, but had foregone the last leg of the trip for an omen of weather. There was no one on the stagehead when he arrived, John Peyton and the hired men hand-lining for cod in shoal water at the backend of Burnt Island. He went up to the house and walked in on Cassie in the wooden tub in front of the fireplace. She was standing in water to her knees, a cloth in one hand, her hair pinned up at her neck. He stared a moment, stunned, as if someone had clapped the breath from his lungs. Sunlight slanting through the windows, dust motes moving in a slow waltz through the air.

It had never before that moment occurred to him he might have her himself. That he wanted her. She made no attempt to cover herself, just stared back at him with a fierce, knowing look. Her breath hard through her nostrils, her wet skin glowing like a pane of glass facing a sunset.

The memory of that look still made John Senior's chest clutch helplessly about his lungs. He turned away from the steady thrum of the water and walked in off the stage. He felt ashamed of himself and fearful, as if he'd just woken from his nightmare. *His wife or his daughter?* He set out towards the hills behind the summer house. The ground beneath his feet seemed hardly more solid than the ocean and he could sense the earth's dark, inevitable undertow. Eventually the earth opened up and swallowed a person, body and soul. Cassie's father gone now and they were all, every one of them, being pulled along in his wake.

Peyton came back from the pantry with glasses. He poured two small shots of rum and added a splash of water to both. He sat back in his seat. "You woke up beside the fireplace," he said.

"Two more things," Cassie said.

The old woman was already up and about the tilt, a fire burning to boil water. The smoke vented through a wooden barrel fashioned into a kind of chimney. Margaret squinted down at Cassie, at the blur of movement in the place where Cassie had been sleeping. Her eyes were nearly shut with peering. "Child," she said and she held a hand in Cassie's direction. Both men were still asleep on opposite sides of the room. Margaret took her hand at the wrist and smiled suddenly, staring off into the air as if there was something clandestine about physical contact between them.

"Now," she said. "I wonder would you ever do us a small favour?"

Cassie shifted where she stood, resisting the urge to pull her hand away. Her feet burned where the skin had been galled from the heels, the toes.

Margaret said, "Tell me your name for real."

"Miss?"

"You're no lad, even I can see that."

"Are you blind, miss?"

"Almost and nearly. Tell an old blind woman your name now."

She stepped nearer. She was almost the same height as Margaret and lifted herself on her toes to speak directly into her ear. She felt as if she was betraying a confidence, putting herself at risk somehow. "Cassie," she whispered. "Cassandra."

The Irishwoman was still smiling and patted her arm. "I won't tell a soul," she promised.

In the afternoon O'Brien took them out in a small skiff to hook lobsters for their supper. The water was dead calm and they drifted about the shallows near shore. O'Brien had a wooden staff fourteen feet in length that was tipped with a thin metal hook. He knelt in the bow, bracing his knees against the sides of the boat while Cassie lay across the gunnel to watch him at work. The water was so clear she could see the stones and dark fingers of seaweed on the mottled ocean floor. O'Brien held the staff near the bottom as they drifted, the shaft refracting under the water's skin like a bone broken and bent at an impossible angle. His arms dipped suddenly, gently, and he brought the staff up hand over hand then to lift a lobster from the sea, the prehensile tail curled into a ring to grip the hook. He shook the lobster into a wooden tub half-filled with water.

Cassie stared at her supper a while, at the eyes so densely black they seemed sightless, the long feelers waving like insect antennae. "Why did she come up like that now," she said, "with her tail wrapped on the hook?"

"You just have to slide the tip underneath, Charlie," O'Brien explained. "A little tickle and they ball up to protect themselves. The poor buggers can't help it, you see. Its in their nature."

The lobster's thick half-moon claws opened and closed, opened and closed. What she now remembered, she told Peyton, was the unexpected pinch of sympathy she felt for it. The sudden urge she had to shove a finger into its desperate, blind grasping.

Peyton thought she had come to the end of the telling there, though he could feel the story pointing towards some unspoken third thing. The heaviness of it weighed on him, like the loneliness he'd always sensed in her that she refused to surrender to scrutiny. He felt no less lost in her company for knowing so much about her. When she hadn't spoken for what he thought was a long time, he said, "Is that it, Cassie?"

She looked up from the letter in her lap. She was crying and there was a sad, serious smile on her face. She said, "That is never *it*, John Peyton."

THREE

At the end of that summer's work, John Peyton and his men loaded the *Susan* with three hundred tierces of dried salted salmon and were waiting for a fair wind to make way for the market in St. John's. It was colder than normal for the time of year and there was no sign of a favourable change in conditions. Peyton sent Reilly and Taylor up to the hired men's outbuilding to join Richmond and young Michael Sharpe who'd already gone to get some sleep. John Senior was aboard, dozing under a thin blanket in the weather house. Peyton stood beside him in the dark, trying to guess from his breathing if the old man was awake.

"Father," he said in a whisper.

"I'm all right."

"You'll catch your death of cold down here." He leaned down and pulled the blanket away from the bunk.

"Jesus, John Peyton."

"Go on up to the house."

The old man muttered as he sat up and began pawing in the dark for his hat, his gloves. "Where is that now?" he said to himself.

"What is it?"

"My watch is here somewhere."

"Leave it now, we'll be back down in a few hours' time and on our way. Go get some sleep."

All evening it had been pitch dark under cloud but a nearly full moon was beginning to come clear as the cover dispersed. The light was pale, phosphorescent, it seemed to emanate from the ground itself, from the walls of the summer house. Peyton watched John Senior make his way up from the dock. He was seventy years old and Peyton could see the discomfort of that age in his walk though he still handled the work of men half his age, hauling nets or cleaning fish or cutting a cord of birch billets. There was something almost unnatural about the man's capacities and it invested him with a peculiar authority that Peyton resented.

"Keep an eye," John Senior said over his shoulder.

"Don't mind me."

Peyton spent the next hour wandering the stretch of ground above the beach, walking out the dock and back, the clump of his boots on the dry lengths of spruce like waves flobbing the hull of a boat. A thin line of moon-light laddered across the harbour towards open sea. The horseshoe of forested hills behind the house and outbuildings was a black wedge shimmed into the speckled dark of the night sky. On the summit of the highest ridge there was a single tree that stood head and shoulders above those around it, as if it had been ordained to afford an unobstructed view into the cove. Peyton shivered as he looked up at it. There were still moments when some-thing in the country moved through him this way, a wind in the woods approximating the sound of footfall behind him, a cold current of watchful-ness on the shoreline when he sculled by to check the family's weirs. He promised himself he would climb up there this fall and cut the bastard tree down. He checked his pocket watch. It was nearing one in the morning and he took a final look around. The *Susan* nodded lazily at her moorings. There was no sound but the contrary wind and the motion of the sea, inhale, exhale, against the beach.

He made his way up the path to the house, turned at the door to overlook the dock and the boat again, and went inside to the warmth of the kitchen. John Senior was on the daybed with his face to the wall. Cassie was asleep in a chair beside him, her head slumped forward so that her chin rested on her shoulder. They looked like an old married couple.

He moved the kettle as quietly as possible to the full heat of the fire and slipped into the parlour. He lay in the cool air on the high-backed settle and closed his eyes a moment while he waited for the water to boil.

The Beothuk had watched the white men loading their boat for two days from a sentinel tree on a hill overlooking the cove on Burnt Island. On the second night of their vigil, when the ship was packed to the gunnels and ready for departure, seven men and a woman in two canoes paddled under the cover of darkness into the sheltered water of the cove. The voices of the fishermen on watch carried across to them as they mirrored the uneven curve of the shoreline, moving slowly towards the dock. Their paddles worked soundlessly through the lap of salt water, each stroke perfectly synchronized, perfectly silent. They slipped beneath the spruce timbers of the wharf and sat there while the sporadic talk and farting and laughter of the white men went on into the late hours of the evening. Each breath they took was as measured and subtle as the paddle strokes that had carried them into the harbour and they waited until only the footsteps of a single white man echoed on the wharf lungers overhead. And some time later they heard the sound of the door to the house opening and closing up the hill.

They hacked the vessel free of its moorings and then leaned into their paddles, the boat sheering around with the silent grace of the moon travelling through cloud overhead. A fever of euphoria crept through them as they made for open water but no word was spoken, all their energies poured into hauling the weight of the ship that followed behind them like a well-trained dog.

Peyton came to himself on the settle when he heard the eruption of garbled shouting in the kitchen. And Cassie's voice then trying to wake his father from his nightmare. He jumped to his feet and ran past them through the front door. He pulled out his watch and tried to read the time by the moonlight as he ran down the path towards the dock. He was halfway along the hill before he looked ahead to the water and stopped where he was. His breath came in shallow gasps and steamed in the night air. He looked around wildly, as if he expected to see the boat being carried up the hill on the backs of Indians. His father shouted after him from the door of the house. He looked down at his watch. It was one-thirty in the morning.

The occupants of the house straggled down to the dock behind him in unfastened boots and holding their trousers up with their hands. They stood together at the edge of the wharf and stared into the blackness of the water and off across the harbour where the vastness of the sea was just beginning to run away from them on the new tide. The *Susan*'s mooring ropes still noosed the stage timbers.

"Red Indians," Tom Taylor said.

"They can't have got far," Peyton offered.

"No bloody sense going after them in the dark," Richmond said. "We couldn't tell an Indian from our own arses in this."

John Senior said, "Father's watch was on that boat."

"As soon as there's a hint of light we'll get after them," Richmond promised.

The group turned and made their way back up to the house. Cassie set out tea and raisin cake for them all and they sat around the table to eat in silence.

John Senior emptied his cup and stood to go upstairs to his room. "They could have dragged her anywhere between Leading Tickles and Gander Bay. Let's try not to sleep through the morning." He looked across at his son, but said nothing more.

The next day was fair with a brisk wind. A perfect day to sail. Peyton shook his head. He and Taylor were sculling among dozens of islands that crowded the mainland like a flock of ducklings trying to keep close to their mother. The coastline offered enough coves, bays and tickles to hide a stolen sloop somewhere different every day of the year. "Needle in a haystack, Tom Taylor," Peyton said every thirty minutes or so, like a clock striking the half-hour.

Taylor said, "For all we know, the buggers might have dragged her out somewhere and scuttled her."

By early afternoon they had reached Chapel Island and stopped in at Boyd's Cove for a boil-up on the beach.

"Not much sense to go beyond here, I don't expect," Peyton said. "It would have taken the British navy to haul it much further than this."

Taylor nodded. "If we turn back now, we might get in before it's too far gone to dark."

"All right," Peyton said. He tossed the dregs of his tea into the sand and looked slowly around himself. Grey ocean, grey sand beach. Low cliffs up the shore behind them.

Taylor stood beside him and kicked sand over the embers of the fire they'd made. He said, "Maybe the others have had more luck than we."

Late in the afternoon Richmond and the green man, Michael Sharpe, came upon the *Susan* abandoned on shoals near Charles Brook and in trouble on the rising tide. The sails and some of the rigging had been cut away and there was damage to the hull from the beating that was underway. They could see there was a chance she might be taken into the rocks and lost altogether, but there was no way to get safely aboard of her in the meantime.

Richmond managed to throw ropes with grapples across the gunnels while Michael Sharpe handled the oars, slewing around in the ocean roil, coming as handy to the sloop as he dared. They fastened one of the ropes to a killick to anchor the boat oceanward and secured the other line ashore in hopes of keeping the boat from slamming helplessly against the cliffs or the low-lying skerries. By this time it was near six o'clock in the evening. Richmond left Michael Sharpe with a rifle to keep watch over the sloop and then headed back to Burnt Island in the falling darkness.

When Taylor and Peyton arrived, Richmond came down to the water to meet them.

"Found her out at Charles Brook," he said. "No surprise there, hey, Tom Taylor," he said as the two men clambered up onto the wharf. "On the doorstep of our very own half-breed and his brood of Jackietars." He laughed then, although there was no humour in his voice. The little civility that Richmond once showed the Irishman was long gone. Reilly had been Peyton's choice for head man when his father gave up the day-to-day concerns of the family enterprise. It was a decision John Senior hadn't disagreed with although the set of his head when Peyton told him, the slow thoughtful way he tamped his pipe full of tobacco, suggested there might be some trouble to accompany it. Taylor felt slighted, clear enough. But Richmond felt betrayed, as if his own flesh and blood had turned on him, and he seemed determined to wage a petty war of revenge. If Peyton could think of a way to sack him without John Senior taking his part, he would have done so long ago.

"The sails are gone," Richmond reported, "but from the way she's riding she still has a load of salmon aboard of her."

Peyton said, "We'll have to try to get on her at low tide tomorrow if she doesn't go down tonight."

John Senior and Reilly came in from their search an hour later and the men ate together in the kitchen, drinking cups of tea liberally laced with rum before wandering off to sleeping berths, leaving Peyton alone with Cassie as she cleared the table.

He said, "A year's work we could lose there. And the boat besides." He was doing the calculation in his head to try and figure the enormity of the loss.

"You should have woke me when you came in last night," she said without looking in his direction. "I would have gone down while you slept."

"I only intended to close my eyes a *second*," he said.

"Well you needn't get cross with me, John Peyton."

She said this so softly he could just make out her words and he was immediately ashamed of himself. Since the news of her father's death reached them in the spring there was a change in her that no one but Peyton took note of. Something beneath the hard surface she showed to the world had given way. She seemed hollow to him, brickly, fragile as the first layer of ice caught over a pond in the fall. He sighed and placed his face in his hands a minute and then looked to the rafters. He said, "*But day doth daily draw my sorrows longer, and night doth nightly make grief's strength seem stronger.*"

She stopped fussing about the table to look at him. "I thought you lost interest in all that," she said.

He shook his head and turned his face away from the light of the candle. "I never had the head for it is all," he said. He looked across at Cassie where she stood beside the table. She was smiling, surprised by the scrap of verse he had managed to carry with him from those sessions years ago. He felt an immense, infuriating rush of pleasure to have given her a moment of satisfaction.

"You should get some sleep," she said softly.

They found the vessel at first light next morning in much the same condition Richmond had left her. When Peyton got aboard he found the ship's cargo intact and largely undamaged although anything movable in the cabin and below had been stolen, along with the canvas sails and a good part of the rigging. The mast had been hacked at with rough blades, though it seemed solid enough when he leaned his weight into it. Michael Sharpe discovered the two rifles that had been aboard in the shallows of Charles Brook the previous evening. The barrels had been bent, the trigger works and flints were smashed and beyond repair.

On their way to the shoals that morning John Senior had stopped into Little Burnt Bay to request the help of several small boats and they arrived shortly after Peyton got aboard. He set about running lines across to them. The cord that was secured ashore the previous day was shifted to the top of the mast and half a dozen men stood holding the other end to try and rock her off the shoals on the rising tide.

By noon she was clear and in tow, on her way back to Burnt Island. There was at least a week of work to be done on the damage to the hull and mast, repairs to the rigging and fitting up new sails, before she would be ready for the trip to St. John's. But most of the year's work was salvaged.

FOUR

Something was following John Peyton through the bush.

He was moving down-country, tailing a line that meandered through rattling brooks and shallow reservoirs backed up by beaver dams before it vented into the Exploits within a few miles of Reilly's old tilt. All day the back of his neck prickled, as if his habits were being slyly scrutinized from the trees. He'd tried to ignore it a while, the way he refused to acknowledge the first symptoms of illness, hoping the headache or cough or slight fever would come to nothing. But the sense he had of being trailed and appraised would not leave him.

It wasn't yet quite gone to winter, which made travel in the woods difficult. The snow was spotty and what was down was often dead and heavy. None of the rivers were quite fast with ice and three feet off the shoreline it was too unpredictable to chance walking on. They were only two weeks back from taking the *Susan* to St. John's with the salvaged load of salmon. It was, as his father pointed out to him, a fortnight too soon to make a sensible start at furring.

John Senior had long since given up working his own traplines. For years he had been slowly divesting himself of responsibilities in the family enterprise and Peyton had taken them on with the same single-mindedness, the same myopic drive as his father. He pushed himself relentlessly, spending weeks alone on the water each summer inspecting the salmon weirs and the quality of the cure, working a trapline in the backcountry each winter. The immersion in work was a divestment of his own, a conscious withdrawal from his father, from Cassie. And this fall in particular he'd been chafing to get away from them as soon as he could manage it.

In the years since John Senior had passed the oversee of the fishery to his son there were half a dozen instances of pilfering and thievery by Red Indians he wanted to put right, but Peyton had refused any suggestion of sending a party up the river. It was an ongoing source of frustration to the old man. "I didn't realize when I passed off to you," he said, "that it was all to go to leeward to keep them cock Indians in gear."

It was the only dispute Peyton ever had with his father that hadn't ended in capitulation. He'd heard stories enough of raids on Beothuk camps in the old days to know what could come of it. When he played the possibilities out in his mind, it was the Indian child displayed on the table in Poole who was carried screaming into the woods while the guns went off and the shelters were set alight. It was the young girl he'd watched strike sparks into the down tinder that morning on the lake, her dark hair sheened with oil, who suffered the pawing attentions of Richmond or Taylor. When traps went missing from a tilt, when a fleet of new salmon seines were cut from their moorings, when John Senior ridiculed and browbeat him, he'd managed somehow to hold fast.

Until the *Susan*. The day after salvaging and bringing her into the cove at Burnt Island, they'd fought about the proper course of action to follow, circling and circling the question like two men rowing oars in opposite directions. There was a lull in the argument in the early afternoon and they turned away from each other, both thinking they had settled the issue in their favour. On the shore next the stage, John Senior was limbing and rinding a fir tree. Richmond, who was working on the deck of the *Susan*, shouted across to say, "We'll bring them Indians a proper weight of gifts this time around, won't we, Master John?"

"We'll get our own back, and then some," John Senior said without looking up from his work.

Peyton walked across to his father and squat down beside him. The fluid skimming motions of the axe-head took the bark off the white flesh of the log with a precision that made his stomach roll. John Senior was working with a reckless speed that reminded Peyton of a man running downhill and just managing to keep his feet. His thinning grey hair was raked across a liver-spotted scalp, twin wattles of flesh shook under his chin. *My father*, Peyton thought. But he couldn't make himself feel it.

John Senior lifted his head and stared, the warm axe-head raised in a temporary truce with the fir tree. Peyton could see in his father's appraisal of him the same moment of tormented puzzlement. The pale grey eyes looked washed out, depleted of colour.

John Senior said, "Don't lap back at me on this one, laddie boy." He wagged the axe-head in his son's direction.

The other men had stopped their work to watch, Richmond and Taylor, Reilly, the green man, Michael Sharpe.

"Father," Peyton said.

"You can come with us or stay back with the woman, that's your choice."

Peyton stood up and leaned towards his father. He gestured helplessly. "John Senior," he said.

The old man went back to skimming out the log, his arms repeating the same relentless and delicate motion along the length of the fir. Peyton watched the bark curl away in thin uniform strips. "You bastard," he whispered. But his father didn't look up from the stroke of the axe. The hired men turned back to their work. Ocean surf lapped blindly at the shore.

Trap season in the backcountry was usually the only time Peyton felt clear of all that tormented him. It was a less complicated place, to his mind. Or a place where the complications were balanced by compensations. The warmer weather might slow him down, but it also meant he was able to place simple drowning sets in open water near beaver slides and he took a fair number in dry sets on riverbanks.

Being out this early in the season also allowed him to scout the mounds of tender alder and birch that were carefully stacked in shallow pools to feed the beaver through the winter. Once the rivers froze over completely he would axe holes above them, slip the trap and chain rings over a long stake hammered firmly into the lake-bed, then lash a cross-stick above the ice in case the animal worked it free below. If the water was shallow enough, the carcass would sometimes be frozen into new ice by the time Peyton came back to the trap and he had to be careful not to damage the pelt by tearing it free. He worked bare-handed with a small axe and sometimes just the blade of a knife, chipping away chunks of ice attached to the fur before hauling the animal clear. It was cold, frustrating work. But it was a problem with a simple, concrete solution, something he could manage without confusion or embarrassment. He understood the backcountry, the habits of animals, the patterns of weather. And it was this knowledge that made him feel he was closest here to belonging, to loving something that might, in some unconscious way, love him in return.

But this year his anxiety followed him into the woods and would not leave him. Peyton couldn't countenance allowing John Senior to take his men after the Indians without being there himself to keep a leash on their anger, and he had agreed to mount an expedition to the lake in March. Reparation was what John Senior spoke of, but he could see it was revenge that animated his father. He was burnished with anticipation, like a blade freshened on a whetstone. Peyton could feel the appointed month grinding towards him, inexorable as a Labrador icefield chafing its way south, ruining the few weeks of peace he enjoyed each year.

There was also that sense he had just now of being watched. Not concrete at all, he admitted to himself. He trudged on, deliberately not looking over his shoulder, not flicking sidelong glances into the trees to the left or the right. He was at a loss, for the moment, as to how to shake it.

He decided to walk the extra two or three miles to Reilly's tilt on the River Exploits instead of kipping down in the lean-to at the end of the trapline. The sky was still grey with the day's last reflected light when he reached it, but along the river it was dark, the forest unremittingly black and without definition. The tilt had been abandoned by Reilly years before when the rapidly expanding size of his family made the trip from Charles Brook unwieldy and he decided to run traps nearer to home. A gloom of light filtered through the broken roof, through the door hanging on by a single hinge. Peyton felt his way to the fireplace where a pile of rotten wood was stacked on the stone. He set about making a fire and once it was well alight he stopped a minute to listen as the dark gathered outside, trees swaying in the wind. Whatever had been with him most of the day, he decided, he had left behind.

It was a long, restless night. His body felt swollen and dull with fatigue, but he slept only in troubled snatches, the tiredness on him like a weight of water. The spruce logs of the tilt ticked steadily in the wind — *the death clock*, his father called it, a foreboding of someone's dying. Several times he got up from his blanket to stoke the fire or to piss through the door into the snow and afterwards could not be sure whether he had actually done these things or simply dreamt them. He'd heard stories of men losing their minds in the backcountry. At some point through the night it occurred to him he might be suffering the first signs of that affliction.

In the morning he woke to several inches of fresh snow on the floor under the broken roof. A blue jay called from the woods outside. It was a fierce, lonely sound to Peyton's ears, as if the bird was warning comfort away from itself.

He looked around the dilapidated shelter. The glass was gone from all four panes of the single window. He stared at the corner of the room where he once sat beside Cassie, her face ashen, one eye dark with blood. The pregnancy aborted to preserve the rules of her clandestine relationship with John Senior, to spare him siring a moss child, a merry-begot, a moonlight child. A bastard. "You'll not say a word of this to your father," she'd said. She was afraid of losing her position, he thought, of being sent away like the fallen servants in her books.

In all the years since her visit to Annie Boss, Cassie had never spoken of it to him. If anything, she became more insular, settling further into what he thought of as an iron-willed surrender, an obstinate, opinionated state of abdication. She had her books, the daily litany of chores to complete. She had

John Senior's bullish silence, his habit of indifference, which she preferred to anything Peyton might have been able to offer.

When Peyton was a boy of six or seven, John Senior abandoned his marriage bed and began sleeping with his son when he wintered in Poole. His mother saw Newfoundland as a vortex into which some additional portion of her husband disappeared each year. The months he was away were a relief to them both, a time when the emotional and physical facts of their lives achieved a kind of equilibrium. The relationship between his father and Cassie was something else again, but it had the same peculiar, monastic balance. He couldn't imagine them as lovers now and he doubted there was ever much of a physical relationship between them. What Cassie chose was the old man's distance, Peyton thought. She wanted to marry it to her own detachment from the world.

Out of loyalty to her he had kept his mouth shut about the pregnancy and he spoke to Reilly to make sure the story didn't spread beyond their circle. But it galled him. He had no notion of what he wouldn't do for her if she asked. He felt owned in sections, as if parcels of himself were under Cassie's name, others under John Senior's. And the prickle at the back of his neck that dogged him yesterday was like the itch of a brand healing. As if the place itself was laying claim to its piece of him.

He looked around the room before getting up from his blankets. A sparse row of Annie's dried flowers and herbs still hung upside down over the hearth. They were grey with age and moved in each draught of wind like silent chimes.

The light fall of snow had blown in his tracks, the marks of his Indian rackets barely discernible where he'd passed through hours before. It looked like he had come this way years ago, almost in another life altogether. The wind soughed in the trees. Reilly's tilt was the end of the line and he had no choice but to go back the way he'd come, tempting the panic he'd kept down all the day before.

He stopped on a small vale over the last set he'd made and looked down. The oval dimples of his rackets under fresh snow like a delicate pattern of lace on a tablecloth. And something else. A line of small regular depressions, nearly buried. Tracks. He breathed a short, tight sigh of relief.

Every one of his sets had been visited by the same animal and it looked as if it had turned and backtracked down the line as Peyton was now doing. Two hours shy of his halfway tilt he found a beaver in one of his dry sets turned on its back. The soft underbelly was eaten into, the cod, the liver and gizzard and a large chunk of the intestine picked out like delicacies. The fall of snow made it impossible to identify the tracks but he guessed it was fox. A cat wouldn't have trailed him so brazenly. The animal was obviously used to the presence of men like himself and probably familiar with traps. He left the carcass as it was and went on his way. The snow was still coming down softly and it covered his head and shoulders in a thick spotless pelt of white.

The halfway tilt was a glorified lean-to facing a small red rock cliff used to reflect the heat of a fire into the open maw of the shelter. He woke early and left without bothering with a cookfire for breakfast, reaching his main tilt by noon. He packed the gear he needed there and started back down the same trail, hoping to make the halfway tilt again before it was too far gone to dark.

From the look of the beaver when he saw it again, the fox had come to the site at least once to feed since he'd been there. Peyton took what remained of the beaver's carcass from the trap and dragged it thirty yards along the riverbank to a nearly bare patch of ground under the branches of spruce trees and placed the dead animal in front of a large stone. He held his pack on his knees where he crouched near the ground and he removed tools and materials as he worked. He used a short trowel to half-bury the meat with snow and dirt and dry bris fallen from the spruce branches. He hammered an eighteen-inch stake deep into the ground and secured the rings of a trap and chain over it, then scraped a shallow depression in the earth about six inches in front of the bait. He laid the trap and covered the pan with a piece of cloth that had been boiled with spruce bark, then covered the works with a mix of gravel and snow.

Six inches behind the first set he dug another shallow hole. He removed his gloves to handle the trap this time, setting it as he had the first, but not bothering with the pan cover or a set stake. He buried it and gathered his materials and backed carefully away.

Back at the halfway tilt, he boiled a piece of salt pork for his supper and sat a while afterwards feeding the fire at the foot of the rock face. He lay back and stared at the thickly layered roof of spruce branches angled above him. He raised a hand into the glow, making shadow animals in the firelight.

After John Senior gave him his ultimatum about going to the lake — *laddie boy*, he'd called him, crouched low over the fir log, the axe poised in his fist — Peyton had stalked up to the house alone. He sat at the table in the kitchen and placed his face in his hands.

"Is it tea you're wanting, John Peyton?"

He folded his arms on the table.

"What is it?" Cassie asked him.

Peyton turned to look at her. "He's going to go after them the winter."

"What do you mean?"

"John Senior. He's going down the river with Richmond and Taylor to make amends. To the lake if necessary."

Cassie sat across from him. She was surprised by Peyton's reluctance. "You can hardly blame him for wanting to recover the losses."

He stared at her. He and his father had never argued in front of her about the Indians' thieving or talked much about the days on the shore when Harry Miller was alive. Still, he didn't think it was possible she could be so naive about his father after so many years in his house. In his bed. He kept staring.

She shrugged and made a face to say she thought he was being unfair. And in that wordless gesture he saw that it was true, that she knew next to nothing of the man, of what he had been party to in his day. What he was capable of.

He shook his head. He said, "It's Richmond and Taylor I worry about. They still carry a grudge from the last time down to the lake. And once someone gets killed the law comes into it and there's no saying where that will take us." He took his pipe from a coat pocket and cut himself a plug of tobacco.

"Perhaps it would do to bring the law into it beforehand," Cassie said.

"Meaning what exactly?" he asked angrily. He had no idea what she was talking about.

She spoke in a tone of mock officiousness. "His Majesty is still anxious to establish a friendly intercourse with the native population?"

Peyton pointed with the mouthpiece of his pipe at nothing in particular. "The reward still stands." He stared up at the rafters as her notion came clear to him. "We could ask for permission to go in. Make it an official party. That should temper the mood of anyone who might be inclined to cause trouble."

She tipped her head side to side. It was her way of allowing someone to claim an idea they would never have lit upon themselves.

"I'll need some paper," he said. He was already out of his seat after an inkwell and a pen.

After they finished their supper that evening, Peyton meticulously copied the final version of the letter he'd drafted on the back of bills and ledgers and then gave it to Cassie to read over.

September 26, 1818

Sir,

I beg leave to lay before Your Excellency the following statements by which it will appear to what extent I have been a sufferer of depredations committed against my property by the Native Indians, which have at last driven me to seek your leave to undertake an expedition to recover said losses.

In January 1815, Dick Richmond, a furrier of mine, came out from one of my tilts in the country on business to me, leaving in the tilt his provisions, some fur and his clothes. On his return he found that some persons had been there in his absence and carried away and destroyed the provisions and all the fur with many little things yet valuable to a furrier. The distance being twenty miles from the tilt to my residence, Richmond was obliged to sleep there that night, but came out next day to bring these matters to my attention. In the company of Richmond and a second furrier in my employ, Mr. Thos. Taylor, I visited the tilt and found all as has been described. Nearby we discovered part of an Indian's snow racket and a hatchet, which satisfied us the depredation had been carried out by Red Indians. We after this followed their tracks to Richmond's different beaver houses and found they had carried away seven of my traps. Damage and loss on this occasion cannot be estimated at less than fifteen pounds independent of losing much of the season for catching fur.

In June 1816, a new fleet of salmon nets consisting of two nets sixty fathoms long were cut from their moorings on Indian Arm Brook and nothing but a small part of the Head Rope left. From the manner the moorings were cut and hackled, and the marks of Red Ochre on the Buoys, we strongly suspected it had been done by the Indians, no other persons being near at the time. The following August, some of my people discovered the cork and part of the head rope at a camp once occupied by the Red Indians. The damage done me by the loss of the nets was twenty pounds independent of the fish that might have been caught that summer.

Other losses of nets, traps and provisions in separate incidents have set me back an additional fifteen pounds at the least.

At the beginning of the current month of September, the Indians came to my wharf at Exploits Burnt Island and cut adrift a large boat which I had just loaded with salmon, &ct., for St. John's market. On my missing her at half one in the morning, several small boats were readied for a search commencing at first light. About seven o'clock next evening, I discovered her ashore in a most dangerous situation. There was damage to her hull and the Indians had cut away her sails and part of her rigging and had plundered her of almost anything movable. Two rifles were later recovered from the bed of a nearby brook, but they had been deliberately broken by the Indians and were beyond repair. The damage done to the boat and some part of her cargo, and the property stolen, cannot be replaced under 140 or 150 pounds.

All previous losses I have borne without seeking redress in light of the cruelties inflicted on the Native Indians by His Majesty's subjects in times past. This latest, I fear, cannot be so ignored as it bodes of similar depredations ahead that would likely bankrupt myself and others. The frustrations that are sure to follow cannot but lead to bloodshed.

I offer this deposition in hopes that Your Excellency will grant permission for a small party of my men to follow my property into the country this winter and regain it if possible. It is also my most anxious desire to be able to take some of the Indians and thus through them open a friendly communication with the rest of the tribe.

All of these endeavours will be undertaken at my own risk and expense. From my acquaintance with the place of resort for the Indians over the winter, I am most confident of succeeding in the plan here laid down.

I have the honour to be,
Your Excellency's very humble
And obedient servant,
John Peyton Jr.

When she was done she passed the letter across the table. She held the lobe of her right ear between her thumb and forefinger. Peyton was folding the pages she had just read and pressing the creases flat with the palms of his hands.

She said, "I didn't realize there'd been so much thieving."

"A waste of time to bring the bloody St. John's crowd into our affairs," John Senior said. He was making a determined effort to muzzle his anger in front of Cassie. He said, "Permission be damned, we'll be going in come March. You make sure you tell the governor that."

Cassie smiled at Peyton. "It's fine," she said. "It'll do just fine."

When they brought the salmon to market in St. John's they met with the recently appointed governor, Charles Hamilton, and he confirmed that the reward for bringing out a Red Indian to the coast stood at one hundred pounds sterling. Given the extent of the Peytons' losses, he offered the blessing of his office to the proposed expedition. For a while this comforted Peyton. He even enjoyed a period of carefully concealed exhilaration, thinking he had outflanked John Senior for once, taken control of the situation. But that assurance left him soon enough. He saw again now how the expedition would take its own shape regardless of his wishes, gathering momentum until it was a careening downhill surge he would be helpless to direct or divert.

He sat up in the lean-to and stretched, pushing his arms out at the sides as if he wanted them to come free of their sockets. He placed more stunned wood on the fire, the flame licking up around the dry surface like a living thing feeding a hunger.

The fox was taken just above the right front foot and was lying as far from the set stake as the chain allowed when Peyton first came upon her. Fresh snow had blown in and covered the ground. He could see from the tracks around the stake that the animal had been there some time and had done a bit of wild dancing to pull herself clear. There were three or four bright circles of piss within the circumference of the trap chain.

The fox raised her head and looked at him when he came into view but she didn't get to her feet. The dummy trap in the set that he had deliberately handled with bare hands lay on top of the snow nearby. She had sniffed it out as soon as she arrived, dug it free of the ground and tripped the bed by using her paw or her nose to flip it upside down.

He stepped off the trail to cut a sturdy truncheon of birch wood and then walked to within twenty yards of the animal, crouching there, speaking quietly across the distance. "There you are now," he said. A medium size, maybe fifteen pounds, he guessed. A beautiful creature, the fine coat a mix of silver and red, the thick tail almost black. The perfectly symmetrical face like a sign of her craftiness, her intelligence. Bright yellow eyes sizing him up. There was no show of panic or fear, only the light of her calm stare of assessment. He recognized that stare, he thought, the sense of being observed by it. He could see a ring of raw skin above the clamp of the metal jaws where the fox had been trying to gnaw through her own leg to get free.

Without standing he removed his gloves and pack, then picked up his rifle. Shooting the animal would ruin the pelt, which he wanted to avoid if possible, but it was best to be careful. Either the stake or the animal's foot could have worked loose in her struggling and one last lunge might be all that was needed to finish the job.

He stood up and walked forward carrying the gun and the stick of birch. The fox stayed low on her haunches and tried to back further away, but managed only to move slightly from one side to the other at the end of the trap chain, jerking at the clamped foot. She gave a sharp bark and rolled onto her shoulder in the snow, baring her teeth at the man standing above her. Peyton struck the skull once with the truncheon, solidly but not hard enough to draw blood, and the fox flopped completely onto her side, her tongue lolling onto the snow, her eyes half closed.

Peyton lay the rifle aside and knelt beside the animal, placing a bare hand against the fur where he could feel the short panted breaths through the thick coat. He moved his other hand up to the neck and stroked under her ears.

"There you are now," he said again. He set his right knee just behind the fox's foreleg and used his weight to stove in the rib cage, forcing the broken bones into the internal organs. Peyton placed his hand back against the fur then, waiting as the blood pooled in the lungs and the light leeched from the animal's eyes.

He removed a knife from his belt and touched the tip to the gelatinous surface of the eye, testing the blink reflex to be sure it was dead. After he released the bloodied paw from the trap Peyton used his hatchet against the trunk of a deadfall to remove the front paws above the wrists. He used his knife to cut through the fur along both thighs, from the feet to the bared flesh of the anus, then skinned out the back legs and cut the pelt free from the ankles. He tied one naked back leg to the branches of a tree about chest-high and worked the thick chimney-sweep tail clear of the tailbone, then split it open along the underside. He used the weight of his body to inch the pelt down the length of the carcass and free of the pawless front legs, pulling them from the fur like a child's arms helped from a troublesome sweater. He clipped the ear cartilage from the skull, cut deftly around the eye sockets, then skinned out the black lips and the dark, still-wet nose.

Peyton reached a hand into the length of the animal's coat and pulled the fur right-side out. It was a few weeks shy of priming out, but the plush was thick and even, the colour bright as life. The heat of the body still clinging to the pelt, the fur warm against his bare hands.

The Lake

March month, 1819

FIVE

Conditions on the river were near perfect for travel: steady ice, fair weather. There were eight of them in the party all told, Peyton and John Senior, Richmond, Taylor and Reilly, Matthew Hughster and William Cull — who was nearly the age of John Senior — and the youngster, Michael Sharpe. They walked from sun-up till well past dark, and without the loaded sledges they'd hauled up the river with Buchan they made astonishingly good time, averaging more than twenty miles a day. By the fourth night they had nearly reached Badger Bay Brook and were within a day of the lake. Two men were put under arms through the night, Taylor and Michael Sharpe taking the early watch while the others settled about the fire. Peyton lay awake, listening to Taylor talk to young Michael who was new to the shore and still too green to burn. He was telling the story of the man who died of exhaustion in a whorehouse after drinking a glass of beaver pride.

Michael Sharpe said, "A man can't die from that."

There was no conviction in his voice and Taylor laughed at him. "What would a pup your age know about it?"

"I know a thing or two."

Taylor gave a long, dismissive groan. "I wasn't much above your age when I come this way," he said. "But not half as wet."

"You come up to work for Master Peyton?" Michael Sharpe asked.

Taylor shook his head. "Harry Miller was the one took us on, me and Richmond."

Three weeks after John Senior had carried them across to Miller's property from Fogo Island, Tom Taylor kissed his new bride goodbye on the steps of Miller's winter house. He and Richmond followed Miller into the woods for their first season of trapping, each man carrying packs that weighed in at eighty-five kilograms. There were two sledges hauled by dogs over the first snow of the season. The weight of the sledges and the thin snow made for heavy going and at times the men took it in turns to replace the dogs in the harness to haul over rough or exposed ground.

For the next three months the men bunked in together as winter came on in its full strength and snow filled the woods slowly like the bilge rising in a boat shipping water. They marked their lines through the bush, long crooked spokes extending from the hub of the log tilt. They were out for up to a week at a time and they took beaver, fox, marten and an occasional wolf. Miller tutored them on the skinning of the animals and how to separate the thin layer of fat from the hides without ruining the coat and how to mix the combination of wood ash and animal lard that cured the pelt.

Michael Sharpe said, "Did you see much of the Reds in there?"

Taylor shook his head. "No, not the winter. I didn't get my first look till the spring. Miller had us build a new weir on a salmon run beyond Charles Brook."

As soon as the thaw was well underway Richmond and Taylor began constructing a log-and-rock dam at a narrow, shallow bend in the river. For two weeks they worked waist-deep in frigid water, weighting a frame of spruce logs with stones to construct a wooden weir across the river. Each afternoon when he stripped out of his soaked clothing Taylor's feet were white and numb, the shrivelled skin of the soles embossed with patterns like frost on glass. His scrotum was as tight as a shell, the testicles drawn up into his torso, and he had to force them back into the sac with his fingers.

In the second week of June, a canoe carrying five Beothuk came up the brook. Siobhan was inside the tilt, Richmond had gone into the woods to cut logs to build a gallows for drying the salmon nets. Taylor was in the water, rooting around at the base of the weir and didn't see or hear them. He didn't know how long they had been watching when he finally took notice. They had pulled the canoe to the side of the river and stared at him in silence. They were close enough that he could count them where they sat and guess at their ages and relative physical strength.

All at once, as if by some signal he couldn't distinguish, the five men in the canoe began shouting and shaking paddles or bows. Taylor stumbled on the wet stones on the riverbed and once he'd regained his footing he pissed through his pants into the brook while the wild shouting and gesticulating went on and on. He bolted across the river finally and crawled on his hands and knees up the bank. He ran towards the tilt, sloshing water from his boots and the waistline of his trousers, screaming all the way. He shouted at his wife to keep inside and ran out with a single-shot rifle and a powder horn which sent the Beothuk into a retreat, though they continued yelling as they paddled downstream towards the ocean. Taylor dropped most of the shot intended for the barrel of the gun and was shaking so furiously he couldn't hold the powder horn still enough to pour. The Indians had disappeared around a bend in the river before he looked up from his sloppy loading and he threw the gun down in disgust. He swore at the trees as he paced. He kicked the powder horn into the river and had to wade in after it, swearing all the while.

Taylor looked across at the face of Michael Sharpe. He was shaking his head. "You pissed your pants, Tom Taylor," he said. He seemed profoundly disappointed.

Taylor nodded. "That I did," he said. "That was the summer they killed Harry Miller, not more than a month after I seen them." They found the body on the way to the clearing in the trees behind his tilt that he used as a toilet. There were half a dozen arrows piercing the flesh, in the back, arms and legs. The area around the corpse was trammelled with recent tracks of animals and the body had been picked over for days, the bloodied clothes torn and pulled away from the torso. Most of the flesh was eaten away from underneath. Grey lengths of bone showed through, the surfaces pocked with tooth marks. Richmond had said, "That's hardly worth burying."

Taylor leaned in close to the green man. "They cut off his head and left the rest of him to the scavengers, they did. Same as they did for those two marines the last time we came down to the lake."

Peyton sat up in his blankets. "Tom Taylor," he said. "Don't be poisoning the boy's mind."

"Better he knows what we'll be facing on the morrow." This was Richmond speaking. Everyone, it seemed, was still awake and listening. "There's no sense keeping the truth from the lad."

There was a giggle of laughter from the dark where Reilly lay in his blankets. "Well spoken, Dick Richmond," he said. "Why don't you tell young Michael Sharpe how you came to lay hands on the little Indian girl that wound up in Poole?"

"What little girl?" Michael Sharpe asked.

Richmond said, "Mind your goddamn business, Reilly."

The two men began arguing and Peyton yelled at them uselessly, until John Senior sat up in the light of the fire and raised his pistol. He held the gun there until everyone fell silent and then he said, "I will shoot the next man to speak a word before daylight." He looked around the circle of men watching him. "By Christ, so I will," he said.

Everyone settled back onto their beds of spruce. Peyton covered his head with his blanket. Several times through the night he considered getting up to stand in front of his father and say something, any word at all.

Richmond hadn't had a thought of the girl since the last time he'd come down the river with Buchan, when Peyton mentioned seeing her in Poole. He lay a while deliberately thinking of other things, but when he fell asleep he began dreaming of the summer morning he'd set out for one of the half-dozen bird islands off the coast. It was a clear day when the sun rose but there was a shroud of mist around the base of the nearest island as he pulled towards it. Thousands of birds circled the sheer cliffs and pitched and took flight again like blackflies tormenting the stoic face of a cow. He rowed into the mist and along the shore-line. The bottle-nosed divers and hagdens and skurwinks and turrs were so thick on the water around his boat it seemed possible to walk ashore on their backs.

There was one small beach in the face of the island where a boat could be hauled up onto the shore. The Beothuk had arrived ahead of him and were already off along the cliffs to gather eggs, their canoe lying against the grey stone. His first notion was to turn about and pull for the mainland, but he looked down at the twelve-bore long-barrelled duck gun he'd brought for birding and the musket he carried with him at all times. There couldn't be more than six people in the one canoe, he guessed.

He muffled his oars as he rowed into the shallows and stepped out into knee-deep water. He grabbed the painter at the bow and sloshed up onto the beach. Above the landwash was the only bit of woods on the island and Richmond flipped the skiff onto an edge and coopied underneath to heft it onto his back. He nestled the boat out of sight and sat as deeply in the droke as he could without losing his view of the canoe. He loaded both guns, humming tunelessly under his breath and stealing glances up towards the beach. He laid the shotgun near his feet and sat with the musket across his lap and waited as the day steadily burned off the mist.

Taylor startled him awake with the toe of his boot, kicking at his shoulder where he lay asleep. He looked up over the edge of his blanket at the figure standing above him. It took a moment to register where he was, to place himself on the banks of the River Exploits, on the way to the Red Indian's lake. "Your watch," Taylor said and then turned to wake John Peyton.

"Leave him," Richmond whispered. "Let him sleep."

He laid an armful of dry scrag onto the fire for the quick heat and put water on to boil for a mug of tea. He ran his fingers through the length of his beard as if the dream's greasy residue was tangled there and he was trying to ferret it clear.

His sister had been hanging out sheets on the line beside her house when he came up from the landwash at Tom Taylor's river, carrying the girl. There was a sharp, warm breeze of wind and the wet clothing tailed out and snapped behind her. She had clothespins in a pocket of her white apron and held three in her mouth. Her long dark hair was tied back into a ponytail but fine wisps had come free of the ribbon and blew around her head and into her face. She took the clothespins from her mouth and stood to watch him as he came up the low grassy hill. She used both hands to keep her hair clear of her eyes. Richmond carried the girl awkwardly against his shoulder, as if he was shielding her face from the weather. When he reached his sister he held the staring child out in his hands. "Here," he said.

She handled the girl but never took her eyes from his face.

"She haven't made a sound since I found her," he said. "Out on the bird islands." He motioned over his shoulder with his head. "She was left all alone out there."

Siobhan looked down at the girl.

"Where's Tom?"

She motioned to the forest behind them. "After a bit of wood."

"She's probably half starved to death," he said. "Find her something to eat, will you?"

By the time Richmond found Tom Taylor and the two made their way back to the house, the girl was sitting at the table with a fig tit, sucking at the flavour of raisins through a cloth. Her free hand held a wooden figure, a doll of some sort, to her chest.

"Well Jesus loves me," Taylor said.

"We got to get her into St. John's Tom."

Siobhan looked from Richmond to her husband and back several times. "And what do you think you'll be doing with her there?"

Richmond said, "She's worth fifty pounds if we can get her to the governor."

Taylor shook his head and looked at his feet, embarrassed to have it stated so plainly. Siobhan's face was pale as milk despite her years of working outside and her pulse pounded in the blue veins at her temples. "And you think the governor is going to believe you found this child wandering around on her own on the bird islands?"

Taylor said, "I knew it was a mistake to let her see the girl."

"I suppose you're in for it as much as he is," she said to her husband. "I never seen the likes of the two of you in all my born days."

The girl stared and sucked at the cloth in her hand.

"Well now, there she is, like it or not," Taylor said. He took his hat from his head and folded it between his hands. "We can't go put her back on the island and leave her there, can we?"

Siobhan had suffered two miscarriages early in her married life and had never managed to become pregnant again. The two men could see all the grief and anger she accumulated through those losses expressing itself now in her protectiveness of the child. Taylor turned to Richmond and said, "We'll never talk no sense into her."

"Well, we'll see what Master Peyton has to say about it all then," Richmond said.

They slept that night at the Taylors' house. Richmond lay on the daybed in the kitchen and the girl was given a tiny room opposite the one where Tom and Siobhan slept. Taylor tied a string to the doorknob of her room and, once in bed, tied the end of the string about his big toe to guard against her sneaking the door open and wandering off in the night.

Siobhan shook her head. "She's not five years old, Tom Taylor."

"Those are not normal creatures," he said. He leaned up on an elbow to blow out the candle.

The girl woke crying in the middle of the night and Siobhan went to her, nearly dragging her still-sleeping husband from the bed by his foot when she pushed the door open. She spent the early hours of the morning at the child's side, offering what little comfort she could in the dark.

By noon the next day the two men were on their way to Peyton's summer house on Burnt Island with the Beothuk girl in tow. After conferring with John Senior, it was decided she should spend the rest of the season with Siobhan and Tom Taylor. They would carry her into St. John's when they brought the cured salmon to market and hope to catch the governor before he'd scuttled back to England for the winter.

They requested a meeting as soon as they made St. John's harbour, but had to wait three days for an audience. John Senior spent much of that time attending to business, leaving Richmond and Taylor to occupy the girl in some fashion. They carried her around the stores on Upper and Lower Path and shop owners offered her cubes of sugar to suck on or small sour green apples. Respectable women who would have otherwise passed the men by without so much as a nod stopped and spoke in singsong voices to the child and asked her name and age. Richmond tried once or twice to say honestly who the girl was, but the confusion this created led him to fashion a story that would better suit the questioners, telling them the girl was his sister's child, that she was dumb and had not spoken a word since she was born. He became increasingly comfortable with the fiction the more he repeated it and he added details as he went, giving the child a name (Rowena, after her grand-mother), an elder sister who had been stillborn, a love of old Welsh songs. Tom Taylor watched in disbelief as the tale grew in length and complexity, but never contradicted his friend until Richmond explained to one inquirer that the child was a bit unknown and had an unusual predilection for eating grass as an infant, which some now blamed for her inability to speak.

"Dick Richmond, that is the biggest load of gurry," he said.

Richmond looked hurt. "It's not my opinion neither," he said, bristling. "I only said that some thought it so."

He began referring to himself in her presence as Uncle Richard and each day bought her a block of hard taffy to occupy her during the evening. The streets near the harbour were ground to mud by carts and animals and the hundreds of people who came to St. John's from across the island looking for

winter passage back to England. Richmond was afraid she would fall or that
he might lose sight of her in the crowds and eventually he sat the girl on his
shoulders and left her there much of the time.

In the eyes of the British Crown at the time, the island of Newfoundland
wasn't considered a proper colony, but a sort of floating fishing station and
training ground for naval recruits, a country that existed only during the
summer months. Most of the planters and fishermen returned to England for
the winter, as did the governor himself. According to the stories Richmond
and Taylor gathered while wandering the settlement, the current represen-
tative of the Crown was a minor functionary related distantly to royalty who
was offered the position as a kind of punishment for profligate living. In
England he had become so fearful of creditors that he awoke before dawn
and stayed away from his house until dark. He accepted the governorship of
Newfoundland first and foremost as a way to temporarily escape his debts.

The reward Richmond was seeking had been offered by a previous administration and before the arrival of the men who stood before him the governor had never heard of it. He listened to Richmond's story of finding the
child wandering alone on the bird islands without comment or even much in
the way of expression.

"What does she have in her hand there?" he asked afterwards.

"A doll, Your Honour," Richmond said. "It was all she had when I discovered her."

"She hardly looks like an Indian to my eye."

"We have done our best with the little we have to civilize the child," John
Senior said. "The paint was scrubbed off her face and we cut her hair and
provided some sensible clothes."

The girl stood between her captors and the sickly looking gentleman in
his chair who continually passed a palm across the thinning hair on his head.
Mud covered her shoes and her legs to her knees. She placed her chin on the
head of the doll and held it there.

"Have her speak something in her native tongue."

John Senior cleared his throat. "She haven't uttered a word since she's been with us, sir."

The governor gave a long, weary sigh. "Gentlemen," he said, "however you may have come into possession of this Indian, if indeed an Indian she is" — he looked at the men a moment to communicate his doubts on the matter — "she is of no use to the Crown whatsoever."

Richmond said, "We've come a long ways with this child here."

The governor was already on his feet. "And I wish you a pleasant return trip. Your petition for the Crown's reward is denied."

The three men went straight from their meeting to a public house. They felt foolish and unfairly used and it took them most of the evening to disguise those feelings with drink. The Indian girl stood beside them, her eyes just above the tabletop staring at the candle's flicker, a block of hard taffy in her hand. Eventually Richmond placed her in the straw along the wall and he took off his coat and tucked it around her where she lay clutching her doll.

John Senior left for Poole in the morning. Richmond and Taylor took the sloop back to the northeast shore. Without ever discussing the possibility, both men expected that Siobhan would take the girl in and raise her as her own when they returned to the Bay of Exploits. They carried her up there as soon as they shipped in from St. John's and they sat in the kitchen together, the girl fidgeting quietly with her doll in Siobhan's lap. A mix of snow and rain whipped around in a contrary wind outside and the gusts roared in the chimney.

Tom Taylor said, "Perhaps it was God's way of giving us a bairn, Siobhan."

Siobhan lifted the girl from her lap and stood her on the floor. She had cared for the child for months now and in a barely conscious way had come to cherish her. But something fragile in the woman came apart then and she refused what a day earlier she would have admitted to calling love. Her voice shook slightly when she spoke. "God never intended me to raise a dumb savage in place of my own child, Tom Taylor." She turned to her brother.

"You'll take her with you when you go." She left the room then, the girl pointing after her as she walked away.

An elderly couple from Poole who had been on the shore a decade and were about to retire back to England on a late crossing out of St. John's agreed to take the girl and raise her as a servant. To cover the cost of her passage and board in England, she was exhibited to crowds of curious onlookers in a warehouse on the waterfront in Poole. Admission at the door was two pence.

Richmond was staring blindly at the fire as these things came back to him, the brittle fingers of scrag flaring and then curling in the heat like creatures helplessly trying to protect themselves from the flame. By the time the kettle boiled he was too unsettled to make himself a mug of tea. He sat wrapped in a blanket while steam rose into the air over the fire. The same scalding commotion working in his belly.

Peyton and his men breached the head of the lake in the late afternoon of the following day, March 6, after walking without rest since dawn and they crouched out of sight among a thick blind of spruce trees on the shoreline. Several miles across the ice a cluster of winter shelters stood in a clearing, loose braids of smoke rising into the glare of the day's end. They backtracked along the River Exploits as the sun fell behind a dark blind of trees at the crest of the valley, and circled into a gully where a small rattling brook met the river. They tramped a piece of ground firm before unlacing the Indian rackets from their boots and standing them up in the thigh-deep snow. They cut spruce limbs from the near trees and set the largest against crosslogs for a windbreak and settled the rest over the places where they intended to sleep. By then it was night with a fair breeze of wind brought up but Peyton refused to allow a fire to be kindled for fear it might give them away. He set three watches and the group settled to wait out the stars. No one managed to so much as doze off in the bitter cold, but the night was edgeless and surreal as a dream and each of the men felt lost in it.

Before first light they roused themselves and packed up the camp. They gnawed on cakes of hard tack to quiet their bellies and then shook out the old priming of their muskets, pricked the touch holes and fresh primed. Most of the party's ammunition consisted of slugs or quarter shot or drop shot, but Tom Taylor and Richmond and John Senior loaded their pieces with balls. After they'd laced on their rackets Peyton reminded them that no one was to fire on any account without his permission. Richmond allowed he was just a hired man, but thought it an awful thing to be ordering your father about in such a fashion. John Senior said, "He knows my mind well enough," and Peyton repeated his order to wait on his word. They tramped single file out of the gully, turning south on the bank of the river towards the point of land that intersected the lake.

The forest along the shoreline was dense with underbrush and they were forced to skirt the edge, but stayed as close to the trees as they could. Loose snow had drifted heavy against the shore and they struggled forward two and a half hours before stopping a hundred yards shy of the clearing where the shelters stood. They hunkered among a stand of trees on a small finger of land pushed out into the lake. John Senior was breathing in short laboured whiffs beside Peyton. He shook his head. "Panking like the devil," he said. "Haven't got neither bit of wind like I used to."

Peyton glanced across at his father. His own feet were galled, his knees and ankles were swollen and stiff with the cold and exertion, and it was painful just to crouch there. He'd been worried about his father's stamina before they set out, but John Senior had been the first from his blankets each morning and urged the men on past dark. Peyton shook his head and turned back to the clearing.

Two of the mamateeks were shingled with sheaves of birchbark stitched together with spruce root or sinews. The third was wrapped with a canvas sail that had been stained with a mixture of red ochre and grease. Richmond lifted his bearded chin towards it and said, "She'd be ours, I imagine."

John Senior nodded. "Won't be more than fifteen or so to a wigwam," he said, "so fifty at the outside." He looked across at Peyton who had pulled out his pocket Dollard and was squinting through it to study the clearing. "Well?" he said.

He closed the glass and shook his head. "Nothing doing." He could feel the intensity of anticipation around him, the hum of it in the air like the noisy heat of green wood laid on a fire. Joseph Reilly touched his shoulder then and pointed where a figure had just stood clear of one of the shelters. He lifted the glass back to his eye.

Richmond offered they should get a move on before any more of the Indians started the day and there was a general mutter of agreement that Peyton ignored. He stood up and walked out of the trees towards the clearing. Several of the party followed up behind him and he waved them back into the woods. There was still only the one figure moving outside the mamateeks, and there was such an immense quiet in the valley and across the frozen surface of the lake that Peyton imagined for a moment the woman was alone in this place but for him. Through the telescope he had seen the well-kept sheen of her black hair, her face darkened with the same red stain they had used to mark the stolen sail.

He lifted his arm. "Halloo," he shouted.

His voice echoed back to him from the trees as the Indian woman turned to stare across at the point where he stood. Before the sound of her first alarm reached his ears he could hear John Senior cursing behind him and his party burst out of the woods at a trot.

By the time they'd snowshoed halfway across the cove the camp of Beothuk was in flight, most of them clearing the mamateeks and taking to the bush while a smaller group set off south across the frozen lake. Some of them were only half-dressed and they carried nothing away in their hands but infants. Peyton shouted at his men to hold their fire as he ran. The large Indian rackets they wore were awkward and nearly useless on the hard-packed snow and ice on the cove and they slipped and slid towards the shoreline beneath the camp.

"What's in the bush is gone," Richmond shouted when they stopped there.

Across the ice the smaller party was still in sight, a cluster of bodies in the lead and one straggler losing ground. Peyton tore his feet free of the rackets and set off in their direction, shrugging off his pack and powder horn and the bulk of his greatcoat as he went. He ran with a panicked, superstitious urgency, as if he felt disaster could only be averted if he was the first of his party to touch a Red Indian, to speak his name aloud to their ears.

It was well into morning by this time and the snow and ice shimmered in the sunlight like a mirage, the figures ahead of him distorted in the brightness so that it sometimes seemed they were hovering several feet above the surface and sometimes as if they had no legs at all. The straggler was the woman he had called out to and as she fell further behind he could make out the flap of her caribou cassock and its thickly furred collar. One of the lead group came back to her and gathered up a package from her arms, but she continued to struggle and Peyton quickly closed the distance between them. "Haloo," he shouted after her. He was close enough to see that her leggings were stitched with spruce root, bald white thread against the red-ochre stain. There were bone pendants and a bright red bird claw attached to the outside seams that rattled as she ran. "Halloo," he shouted again.

Ten yards in front of him, unable to run any further, she dropped heavily to her knees and Peyton came to a stop behind her to keep the distance. Her breath was ragged and uneven and she choked and coughed as the rest of her party disappeared around the point of land in the distance. She turned where she knelt to face the stranger, loosening the belt and lifting her cassock over her head to reveal her breasts in an appeal for mercy, the nipples barely visible beneath the red paint that covered her torso. Peyton looked away from her, breathing heavily to stop his body from shaking. The frost in the air had galled his throat and lungs and the dark peaty taste of blood flooded his mouth.

He set his flintlock rifle on the ground and kicked it away, then he removed his pistol from its harness and threw it to the side so that it skittered over the ice for twenty feet, the metal barrel flaring in the sunlight. "All right," he said, looking across at her. He held his hands out at his sides. The first of his party were making their way towards them and the woman on the ice looked past him to the approaching men. "All right now," he said and stepped towards her.

She looked over her shoulder to the point where she had last seen her companions, then covered herself with the leather cassock and stood to meet him. He nodded his head and smiled towards her, "John Peyton," he said, thumping his chest with the open palm of his hand, "John Peyton." She was still crying but nodded her head and smiled helplessly as she came up to this man with her hands extended and Peyton was struck by the evenness and uncorrupted white of her teeth.

Michael Sharpe was the first to reach them. He stood and stared at the Indian woman with the same look of wonder and mistrust he would have turned on a tree that had uprooted itself from the shore and walked towards him across the ice. Peyton held her arm gently above the elbow and named the man for her and she took his hand and nodded and spoke her words to him as she had to Peyton. When the rest of his party arrived carrying Peyton's greatcoat and other supplies, she greeted them as well. John Senior walked off to collect Peyton's guns.

Peyton explained how the other Indians had disappeared around the point of land ahead and when they turned to look in that direction they saw three figures standing at the shoreline to watch them. One of the distant figures gesticulated as if to gain their attention.

"All right," John Senior said then, and he removed a heavy leather mitten to reach inside his coat, taking out a long linen handkerchief that he shook free in the sunlight. The cloth snapped in the cold air. "Here," the old man said, and he handed the handkerchief to his son.

Peyton nodded and took the handkerchief and turning towards the three figures on the point of land ahead he waved the white cloth over his head.

"Her hands!" John Senior snapped at him. "What a goddamn fool," he said. The old man retrieved his handkerchief and grabbed the woman's arm to turn her back towards him. She looked to John Peyton as her hands were knotted behind her back and he nodded and did his best to indicate everything would be all right.

Across the ice two of the figures stepped down from the bank of the shore. The man in the lead carried a branch of white spruce and held it before him as they walked towards the party on the ice. Peyton spoke to the group without taking his eyes from the men approaching them. "No one fires," he said, "without my say-so."

S I X

After they gathered spruce branches and stones from the near point to fashion a crude burial mound and kicked snow over the blood stains on the ice, the white men retraced their steps across the lake to the Indian camp. The largest of the three shelters was big enough to sleep nearly twenty people, a circle of shallow sleeping hollows radiating around the firepit at the centre. There was a wall of horizontal logs three feet in height at the base of the structure, the chinks stodged with moss and dirt banked up on the outside. A cone of longer logs raised above it served as rafters for the thickly layered birchbark covering. The walls inside were hung with bows, hatchets, iron axes, clubs and spears, all of them covered in red ochre and all laid out in the neatest order.

A bewildered sense of calm had settled among the men and they expressed a reverent appreciation for the objects that surrounded them. They found a birchbark container of arrows and John Senior took out a couple of samples, sighting down the perfectly straight pine shafts before passing them among the group. The ends of the arrows were fletched with two strips of grey goose feathers, the points were all of reworked iron. John Senior said most of the arrowheads were fashioned from the beds of stolen traps or square spikes flattened and moulded with a stone, and that he'd interrupted an old Indian working a trap-bed to that purpose on the river more than thirty years ago.

A fire was revived from the coals in the centre pit as the party sniffed about the shelter. At the back of the mamateek William Cull came upon a roughly carved wooden figure and around its neck was hung the silver case of a watch. The case had been pried open and emptied and the inner workings were discovered nearby, knotted into leather thongs of various lengths, the gears polished and strung beside stolen coins and periwinkle shells on necklaces and bracelets.

"You lose a watch on that boat?" William Cull asked, holding up the wooden figure.

"My father's," John Senior said. "Brought it over from Poole my first year across with Miller."

Cull removed the watch case from the figure's neck and threw the wooden carving to the floor. The Indian woman, who had settled near the fire, took offence to this and gabbled at the man in a tone John Senior found unacceptable. He picked up the figure and stood holding it over the fire with his thumb and forefinger. He tipped it gently back and forth like a pendulum, threatening to let it fall. The woman went on scolding and several of the men urged him to drop the head into the fire to see if she would be willing to pick it out with her teeth.

"That's enough now," Peyton said curtly and John Senior said he supposed it was so enough. Peyton took the figure from his father and set it up where William Cull had found it and the woman turned back to staring at the fire.

"I expect she was angry with you, John Senior," Richmond said. He crouched across from her. "At least her face is some red."

They roasted caribou steaks found in a storage pit lined with birch rind beside the shelters and they boiled water for tea. The woman refused to eat the meat and Peyton offered her a cake of hard tack instead, biting off a mouthful to show her it was edible, and she gnawed at the bread until her saliva had softened one end almost to paste.

After their meal, Peyton left Michael Sharpe to watch the woman and took the rest of the men to look through the camp. There was a small smokehouse where the Beothuk jerked meat and a storage shed where they kept their dried pelts, most of them caribou. Half a dozen furs were still stretched on racks for curing.

Inside the other mamateeks they discovered items pilfered from the *Susan*: two copper kettles, a splitting knife, a fishing reel, line and lead. The stolen nets had already been unknitted and the strands of twine plaited to make rope. All but the ruined nets were gathered and carried back to the larger mamateek where the men packed the items among their gear.

By this time it was near dark and the kettle was boiled again for tea. It was warm enough inside that the men took off their coats and some removed their boots to stretch their stocking feet to the fire. Peyton sat beside the woman and made signs with his hands and drew figures on the dirt floor to indicate they would be leaving in the morning and that she would accompany them. She watched him carefully but didn't nod to indicate she understood or shake her head to disagree.

About eight o'clock, John Senior gathered the men outside the shelter, leaving Peyton to sit alone with the woman. The party fired three powder shots into the air and gave three rousing cheers to warn any Indians close by away from the camp. The woman's body started with each report of the guns and she looked intently at Peyton as if for reassurance. He did his best to offer it with gestures and his useless English words. She was not much more than a girl, he decided, twenty or thereabout. He counted the years back to the trip to the lake he'd made with Buchan's expedition. She was probably the same age as the girl who lit the fire that morning, leaning over the ball of tinder and striking sparks into it with the fire stones. Same age as the child in Poole — that sad little figure staring up at him through the gauzy layer of years, like a drowned face under ice.

The men sauntered back into the mamateek and Peyton assigned Richmond to the first watch at the entrance. There was some talk among them once they settled in but it was subdued and sporadic. Peyton slept fitfully and in his dreams was unable to move or speak. He often woke himself with the stunted effort of raising his hand or shouting and each time he sat upright and stared in the poor light to be sure of the woman beside him.

In the morning they breakfasted on tea and cold strips of the roasted meat. They went to the storehouse and hauled out the pelts, eighty caribou hides in all and the skins of several dozen other animals, which they divided up into equal parcels and loaded onto sealskins that were outfitted with plaited leather thongs for handles. There was talk of stripping the sail from the third mamateek, but it had been cut and stitched with sinews and ruined with the Indian concoction of grease and ochre, so it was left behind. Tom Taylor and Richmond both advocated setting fire to the shelters. Peyton told them there'd be no burning of anything but the bows and arrows and spears and when they turned to John Senior the old man simply shrugged.

Peyton assigned Taylor and Richmond and Michael Sharpe to collecting the wooden weapons into a pyre and then went inside with his father. Joseph Reilly was sitting with the woman, mending the thongs of his Indian rackets. Peyton settled beside the fire and opened his coat, then fished in the greatcoat pocket for his pipe and tobacco.

He said, "I don't know about taking the woman out with us."

John Senior grimaced in his severe old man's way. There was dried blood still on his upper lip, his nose was swollen and slightly askew and was most likely broken. "Those skins outside is not worth fifty pound all told," he said. "That woman, now the governor believes she's worth a hundred by herself. That would just about cover our losses."

Peyton nodded uncertainly. "Reilly?" he asked.

The Irishman raised his head from his work and stared up at the spruce rafters. He said, "The ones in the woods won't ever lay off your materials now unless you can recruit her to talk them out of it."

"And what would you guess are my chances of that after what happened yesterday?"

"Every way's likely," Reilly said, but there was no conviction in his voice.

"Well given the circumstances, I'm not sure it's wise to have her learning how to talk regardless." Peyton motioned outside towards the lake with his chin.

John Senior shook his head. "There's not a soul going to listen to a Red Indian over the word of eight of us, John Peyton." He looked at his son and shook his head again and spat into the fire. "Am I right?" he asked.

Peyton didn't answer him so he turned his attention to Reilly. "Am I right?"

Reilly stared into the fire where the old man's spittle hissed dry on the back of a junk of wood.

An hour later the party was ready to start north towards the river, each man dragging a sealskin sledge loaded with furs. Most of them had come away with trophies, bows and a raft of arrows or thigh-high moccasins stitched from the shanks of caribou. After a few minutes of hauling, Michael Sharpe dropped the halter of his sledge and ran to the edge of the woods where he vomited into the snow.

"Well Jesus," Richmond said in disgust.

Peyton walked over to the boy. "You all right then?" he asked.

He was leaning forward on his thighs and spitting repeatedly. "I never seen a man killed before, is all," he said. "All that blood," he said, and shook his head and then urged again.

It was another fifteen minutes before they got properly underway. The Beothuk woman walked in the middle of the file, next to Peyton. Before she left the shelter she had carefully combed her hair with a carved bone comb and oiled it with seal fat, but carried nothing with her except the clothes on her back. Behind the party the small bonfire of carved spruce and pine and boxy fir went on burning late into the morning.

A week after the altercation on the lake they made it back to the winter house and brought the Indian woman into the kitchen. The two men sat in chairs on opposite sides of the room, still wearing all their gear. Their clothes smelled of woodsmoke and frost. The woman sat on the floor near Peyton.

John Senior held the empty silver case of his father's watch by the chain and swung it slowly back and forth as though he was trying to mesmerize himself. "You see what they did to my watch," he said to Cassie, opening the cover to show her the hollow inside. "Now what is that going to be good for?"

Peyton seemed not to hear his father speaking or even register where he was. Cassie thought he seemed exhausted by grief or desperation more than simple exertion. She said, "You look gallied, John Peyton." He made a dismissive gesture with his hand but didn't offer anything more in response.

John Senior said the Indian woman was brazen and not to be trusted, that she had twice tried to sneak away from the party while they slept. The second time she was bound hand and foot and had crawled into the bush on her knees. She'd worked the leather cassock over her head and used it as a muffle beneath her, crawling away from the guttering fire and the circle of sleeping men a foot at a time, the leather obscuring the marks of her passage behind her as she went. She was three hundred yards into the bush when they caught up to her.

She could not be convinced to take a chair.

Cassie said, "What's to be done with her?" She was boiling kettles of water to fill a wooden tub in front of the fire.

"I'll ask that of the governor, I suppose," Peyton said. He rubbed at his eyes with a thumb and forefinger. "There was some shooting on the lake. Some bloodshed that'll have to be explained."

Cassie turned to them from the fireplace. "What happened?"

"We had to deal with the savages is what happened," John Senior said.

"Mind now," Peyton said to his father and he looked across at Cassie. "I'll tell you by and by." He gestured towards the Indian woman with his chin. He said, "Is that water hot enough yet to wash this one up?"

Investigations

1819

SEVEN

The courtroom was high-ceilinged and cold, despite the fair weather and the forty spectators crammed into the tiny public gallery near the entrance. There was a simple table at the front that the presiding judge sat behind and a row of chairs along one wall for the jurors, a long polished rail in front of them. Most everyone in the room wore their dark coats during the proceedings, and when the jury left to begin its deliberations, people wandered outside to smoke and walk in the watery sunlight of late May.

Peyton had come alone to St. John's on a packet boat, refusing his father's offer to accompany him. He alone had been subpoenaed to appear before the grand jury and there was no need, he said, to complicate matters by having his father or anyone else from the expedition there to testify as well. On his second night in town, the governor met him at the London Tavern which had risen from the ashes of the 1817 fires. "An unfortunate business, all this," Hamilton said. "But mostly a formality." He had a full head of silver hair, a highly formal manner that came naturally to him and that most people found appealing as a result. He talked with his hands folded beneath his chin. "You understand I had no choice but to take this route."

Peyton nodded. "Did you bring the letter I sent Your Worship?"

The governor reached into a pocket to retrieve it. He smiled across at the younger man. "I think this should be sufficient for the court's inquiries. Now as to the Indian woman in your care."

"We are at your disposal in that regard." Peyton scanned the pages briefly, as if trying to identify the handwriting. "Our housekeeper has been teaching her to speak and she should be a serviceable translator by the next freeze-up if you choose to send an expedition inland to the lake."

Hamilton frowned briefly. "Would the matter at hand be of any concern in such an undertaking?"

"I'm not sure I follow you, sir."

"A man was killed," Hamilton said. "Perhaps returning with the woman would simply make matters worse."

Peyton said, "We'll have our treatment of the woman in hand to speak for us by then."

"Fair enough," Hamilton said smiling. "A discussion for another day perhaps. What about the meantime?"

"We would maintain her at our place on Burnt Island if that meets with your approval."

"Of course," Hamilton said. "Now on to other business. My predecessor, Governor Pickmore, was intending you should become a Justice of the Peace on the northeast shore."

"I'd been made aware of some such possibility."

Hamilton said, "As soon as this matter is cleared up, we will make it official." He raised his glass from the table. "Shall we drink to that?"

When he was called to the witness stand the following morning, Peyton asked the court's permission to read into evidence the letter he'd sent to Governor Hamilton the first week of April. "'I beg leave to lay before Your Excellency,'" he began. He coughed into his fist. "'I beg leave to lay before Your Excellency the circumstances surrounding a recent expedition undertaken by my father and myself and six of our men into the heart of Red Indian country, after obtaining Your Excellency's permission to follow property lost to thievery. We left from our house on March 1, 1819, with a most anxious desire, as stated to Your Excellency, to lay hold of some of the Red Indians and through them open a friendly communication with the rest of the tribe. In this spirit, everyone was ordered by me not on any account to commence hostilities without my positive orders.

"'On the sixth of March, having made the Indian's lake and cresting a point of land, I discovered one Indian coming towards us and three more walking in the opposite direction. I could not as yet determine whether the Indian approaching was male or female. I showed myself on the point openly and when the Indian discovered me she screamed out and ran off. I immediately pursued her but did not gain on her until I removed my rackets and jacket when I came up with her fast, she kept looking back at me over her shoulder. I then dropped my gun on the snow and held up my hands to show I had no gun, and on my pointing to my gun, which was then some distance behind me, she stopped. I did the same and endeavoured to convince her I would not hurt her. I then advanced and gave her my hand, she gave hers to me and to all my party as they came up.

"'Shortly afterwards, the three Indians I had seen moving in the opposite direction appeared, and two of these men advanced upon us. Having observed something concealed under the cassock of one of these, I ordered one of my men to investigate and he found there a hatchet which he took from the Indian. The two Indians came and took hold of me by the arms, endeavouring to force me away. I cleared myself as well as I could, still having the woman in my hand. The Indian from whom the hatchet was taken attempted to lay hold of three different guns, but without effect. He at last succeeded in laying hold of my father's gun and tried to wrest it from him. He grabbed my father by the throat, at which point I called for one of my men to strike him. He relented briefly and my father extricated himself and retreated, the Indian still forcing upon him with a savage grin. With no other option I ordered a defence of my father, and several shots followed so close together that I did not know until some time afterwards that more than one gun was fired. The other Indians fled immediately on the fall of the unfortunate one. Could we have intimidated or persuaded him to leave us, we would have been most happy to have spared using violence. Nor should I have held to the original plan, as it was laid out before and granted Your Excellency's permission, to carry the Indian woman into our midst if we had wantonly put an end to the unfortunate man's existence.

"'My object was and still is to endeavour to be on good terms with the Indians for the protection of my property and the rescuing of that tribe of our fellow creatures from the misery and persecution they are exposed to in the interior from the Micmac and on the exterior by Whites.'" He looked up then at the audience assembled at the back of the courtroom. Light slanted into his eyes through the windows and hid their faces. He couldn't begin to guess what their expressions might be. "'I have the honour to be,'" he said without looking down at the paper, "'Your Excellency's very obedient and humble servant.'"

Hamilton took Peyton across to the governor's house at Fort Townshend to join him for lunch while the jury deliberated. They ate bread and cold meats and tea in the dining room while Lady Hamilton outlined her plans for establishing a school in St. John's, as Hamilton warned him she would. The lack of any formal education for the children of the fishermen was abhorrent to her, she said. It was negligent, almost criminal. She hardly touched her food, which helped to disguise how little Peyton himself was able to stomach. "You must eat something, dear," Hamilton told her. She said the language spoken by the lower orders was nearly incomprehensible, that without education their state was little above that of savages. Hamilton turned to Peyton. He said, "I should have known better than to marry a reformer."

She was much younger than the governor and not what Peyton would call a plain woman but she was clearly most remarkable for her energy and enthusiasms. He could see that her gestures were carefully corseted, muffled by a cultivated restraint. "Now you, Mr. Peyton, would understand my argument. You have obviously benefited from an education. This was in Poole, was it?"

"Partly," he told her. "For a number of years I was also under the instruction of a woman employed by my father. She was raised here in St. John's, a Miss Cassie Jure."

A brief flicker crossed Lady Hamilton's face.

Her husband said, "Yes, her father died fighting one of those dreadful fires last year."

There was a pause. "I'm aware he was a drunkard," Peyton said then. "It's not a secret."

"Of course," Hamilton said. He and his wife briefly stared into their plates. "A bad business that was," he said.

"Which, sir?"

He looked up. "The fires, Mr. Peyton."

A marine entered the room and stood at attention at the end of the table. "The jury is returning," he said.

In the days after John Peyton left to testify at the courthouse in St. John's, Mary stayed as close to Cassie as she could. Mary had looked to the younger Peyton as her protector and advocate in the house since her arrival and she refused to take direction from or spend time alone in the company of anyone but him. He did his best to explain before he left that he would return from St. John's as quickly as possible, but no one was sure how much of this she understood. She greeted Cassie each morning with the same question. "John Peyton?"

"John Peyton will come home soon," Cassie told her.

She nodded her head although it was clear from her expression that the word "soon" meant little to her and did nothing to alleviate her anxiety.

For the first time, Mary took on a share of household chores as a way of keeping near to Cassie. It seemed to Cassie she wanted to avoid being alone with John Senior. She left the room when he entered or, if this wasn't possible, moved off as far as the limits of the room allowed. They repelled one another like the negative poles of two magnets.

As they went about their work together, Cassie made efforts to improve the Indian woman's grasp of the English language. She would point to objects Mary was unfamiliar with or for which she had yet to learn the English word and repeat the syllables until Mary had mastered them. *Boat. Stagehead. Chamber pot. Needle, thread, cloth. Brook. Stars. Moon. Sun. Plate. Tinder. Pillow.* Mary was naturally curious and retained the names of everything after the first hearing and she understood simple instructions. But she seemed uninterested or unable to progress much beyond the noun in her own speech, managing only the simplest declarations. "Mary hungry," she would say. "Mary thirsty." "Mary tired." Cassie thought of this as a limitation of the Red Indian mind and language. But there were moments when it seemed a deliberate strategy, a protest of some sort. A refusal to enter their world any further than was necessary for her survival.

Mary had been given her own room in the winter house after she arrived, with John Peyton sleeping in the hired men's quarters. As far as Cassie could tell, the Indian woman had never used the bed, preferring to lie with a blanket on the wooden floor. She slept late each morning and Cassie would find her curled in a corner when she went in to wake her. Mary wore an old muslin dress given to her by Cassie, but she kept the leather clothes she'd been wearing when she was taken from the lake with her at all times, carrying them around in a cloth bundle, tying it across her back while she worked or sitting it on her lap.

John Senior found this habit of Mary's particularly trying and he never ceased to complain about it, as if Mary was persisting in it simply to annoy him. On the day of the trial in St. John's he came up to the house from the shore where he and Richmond and Taylor and Michael Sharpe had spent the morning resurrecting the stagehead and cutting room for the coming season. It was a surprisingly muggy day with the threat of rain in the air. Before he and the hired men had taken their places at the table for their dinner he said, "I can't stand the smell of that dirty leather she carts around."

"It would make a fine bit of burning," Richmond said.

Cassie gave him a look and he seated himself without another word. Mary took herself off into the pantry where she would stay until the men made their way back down to their work.

"The stink of it is enough to ruin my appetite," John Senior said.

Cassie smiled at him. "In all the years I've known you," she said, "I've yet to come across anything that could ruin your appetite."

The old man stared at her a moment and then shook his head. He turned to Tom Taylor. "The lip on her," he said. "Why do I put up with it?"

Taylor smiled stupidly, as if to say he could guess why, but modesty wouldn't permit him to speak it aloud.

"Eat your dinner," Cassie said.

John Senior said, "I guess they're all but done in St. John's by now."

The three hired men nodded soberly and bent their heads to their plates.

After she had set out all they would need, Cassie left the men to sit with Mary in the pantry. They did not speak or even acknowledge one another at first. Mary's breathing was short and ragged, as if she had just come in from a long sprint. Sitting this close, Cassie could make out the smoke and old sweat smell of Mary's clothes that John Senior complained about. It was something she would forever afterwards associate with fear. When the rain began a few minutes later, striking at the single pane of glass, Cassie pointed out the tiny window. "Rain," she said.

Mary nodded but said nothing. A long, low rumble of thunder carried across the bay.

"Thunder," Cassie said.

Mary looked at her. She had a tortured expression on her face and seemed to want to ask a question of Cassie. She said, "*Baroodisick.*"

Cassie cocked her head to one side.

Mary pointed at the ceiling with her finger, thunder clapping overhead again, closer this time. "*Baroodisick*," she said.

"Ba-rude ..."

"*Baroodisick.*"

"*Baroodisick*. Thunder?"

Mary nodded. "Thunder. *Baroodisick*."

Cassie raised her hand, hesitating a moment. She could feel a flush rising through her cheeks. She reached to touch a button at the front of Mary's dress. "What is this, Mary?" she whispered.

"*Agamet*."

"*Agamet*," Cassie repeated. "Button?"

The Indian woman nodded. Then she said, "Mary go." She turned and stared directly into Cassie's face. "Mary go home," she said. Her first English sentence.

The jury foreman was a man named Newman Hoyles, a short, portly St. John's merchant. He was nearly bald, his forehead permanently creased by the band of his hat. He stood from his chair and pulled at the cuffs of his jacket to bring the sleeves down to his wrists. He held a single sheet of paper. There was an obvious tremor in his hands that shook the paper as he read and Peyton could not tell if it was habitual or a result of the task he was undertaking. He felt the tremor all the way across the room. That slight unsettling motion in his gut.

Hoyles said, "'The Grand Jury beg leave to state to the Court that they have as far as possible investigated the unfortunate circumstances which occasioned the loss of life to one of the Red Indian Tribe near the River of Exploits, in a late rencontre which took place between the deceased and John Peyton Senior and John Peyton Junior; in the presence of a party of their own men to the number of eight in all and in sight of several of the Indians of the same tribe. The Grand Jury are of opinion that no malice preceded the transaction, and that there was no intention on the part of the Peyton party to get possession of any of the Red Indians by such violence as would occasion bloodshed. And, further, that the obstinance of the deceased warranted the Peytons acting on the defensive.'"

There was a glass of water on the rail of the jury box and Hoyles paused to wet his lips. He looked quickly across the room at Peyton and then again at the paper he held. "'At the same time as the Grand Jury declare these opinions arising from the only testimony brought before them, they cannot but regret the want of other evidence to corroborate the foregoing, viewing it as they do a matter of the first importance, and which calls for the most complete establishment of innocence on the part of the Peytons and their men. The Grand Jury therefore recommend that four of the party be brought round at the end of the fishing season for that purpose, or that a magistrate within His Majesty's Royal Navy be assigned to travel to the Bay of Exploits to collect what evidence may bring a more satisfactory resolution to these circumstances.'"

As Hoyles took his seat a murmur buckled through the public gallery and the presiding judge knocked his gavel, calling for order. Peyton crossed and uncrossed his legs. He didn't hear anything that followed of the judge's comments and didn't move from his seat even after everyone else in the room rose and began shuffling towards the exit. Governor Hamilton came across to him and laid a hand on his arm. There was a pained, conciliatory expression on his face. "I suppose," he said, "we shall have to delay your appointment a while longer."

He ate by himself at the London Tavern that evening and spent several hours after his meal drinking alone. The governor had apologized repeatedly for the jury's odd request that afternoon. "Completely unforeseen," he said quietly. There was an air of uncertain concern about him, as if he wasn't sure any longer where it was safest to place his sympathies. He said, "I don't believe there's anything binding in such a verdict. My guess is it will simply languish and we'll hear no more of it."

Peyton refused his invitation to dinner. In the morning he would take a coach to Portugal Cove and from there a packet boat to the northeast shore. In the meantime, he made a determined effort to drink himself into a stupor that might lead to something resembling sleep. By half past eleven, that possibility seemed as unlikely as it had at the start of the evening. He settled his bill and went out the door into the dark. There was a new softness in the air, the first unequivocally warm night of spring, no hint of frost in the wind. Lanterns bobbed along the length of Water Street as pedestrians walked from one tavern to another or made their way home.

He headed west, drunk and stumbling often on the rough path in the blackness. He stopped men carrying lanterns and made inquiries and continued along the street until he was directed a little ways north up a dead-end laneway. The door of the tavern was propped open and the noise of it spilled out into the night. A narrow two-storey building stood beside it, the windows unlit. Inside the pub he sat at the only table with a free chair, beside a man who had fallen asleep on his folded arms. Three men stood together singing near the front of the room. Only one of them seemed to know the words of the song and the other two filled out the fragments they could recall with nonsense, half-words, syllables emptied of consonants.

There was something illicit to his being there, to have come through a door forbidden to Cassie. Peyton lifted a hand to signal the bartender, an old man wearing an eye patch. He paid for an entire bottle and sat slowly filling and emptying his tumbler until the singers had all passed out in the straw laid against the wall.

The two or three girls of the class Cassie spoke of walked from table to table, trying to engage the patrons in conversation. They left in the company of a man periodically, sometimes ushered out in a drunken rush, sometimes lugging the weight of a companion to keep him on his feet. Fifteen minutes later, an hour later, they came back alone and began their rounds again. He watched the movement of their hips under their skirts, appalled and aroused by the thought of what he vaguely knew they'd been engaged in only moments before.

Women like these often worked the taverns he and John Senior frequented when they brought the season's catch into St. John's, and his father always turned away from them with a seriousness that Peyton at first thought was disgust. But there was something closer to embarrassment in the dismissal, he decided, an old shame. The same embarrassment that made him keep his relationship to Cassie a secret all these years. The thought of John Senior made Peyton furious. *The maggoty fucker*, he thought. Then he said it aloud to himself.

Each of the women had come to his table through the course of the night and he had turned them away each time. He was so drunk now that he couldn't distinguish one from the other. They smelled of lavender. For some unknown reason they called him Jimmy. "D'you like some company, Jimmy?" "Want a little time alone with a girl, Jimmy?"

He had his arm across her shoulder and she was keeping him on his feet as they went through the door. He was trying to ask her name but the words would not come out right, they seemed to have no bones or cartilage to them and they flopped around uselessly. The girl led him down an alley between the tavern and the two-storey house beside it, already working at the spair of his trousers with her free hand. "That's lovely, Jimmy," the girl said. "That's lovely." Everything solid in him seemed to have dissolved but for what was concentrated where she touched him. He didn't want it and didn't want it and she pulled him to her where she leaned against the wall, wrapping a bare leg about his waist, his face awash in the sickening smell of lavender. He pumped his cock inside her with furious little motions, grunting into her hair, until his body shook with spasms and then there was nothing at all to hold him up. She let him fall back onto the ground and stood a moment straightening her skirt. In the pitch dark he couldn't see her, only heard the motion of clothes rustling into place. He tried again to ask her name as she knelt beside him.

"You got something for me, Jimmy?" she asked softly.

She helped him raise his pants around his hips after he slipped several coins into her palm and she left him lying there with the slick oil of her and the soggy mess of his semen turning rank in the tight curls of his pubic hair. He rolled onto his side on the rough ground and held himself until the night finally overtook him and he passed out in the dark.

EIGHT

The officer seated himself at the plain board table and flipped through his notebook until he'd opened it to a blank page. He was impeccably dressed and his manner was creased and pressed in the same fashion as his uniform. His hair was carefully oiled and combed back from his forehead. Peyton thought it had thinned considerably, and there was a leaner, more severe look about the man than he remembered. He had been promoted since anyone in the household had last seen him. It was only the Indian woman, who had never met the man and whose English consisted of a few words and pidgin phrases, who didn't find the change awkward and somehow foreboding. *Captain* David Buchan.

Buchan dipped his pen and tapped it primly at the edge of the inkwell. He stared across the table, as if he was about to sketch them all — John Peyton in the chair opposite, John Senior behind him on the daybed and looking away out the window, Cassie and the Indian woman sitting side by side near the pantry. Mary wore one of Cassie's muslin dresses and an apron and she held a tied bundle in her lap.

Buchan cleared his throat. He said, "You and your party undertook the unfortunate expedition to Red Indian Lake in March of this year. Is that correct?"

"As I testified in St. John's, yes, that is correct."

"There were eight men in your party."

Peyton nodded a moment and turned to look to his father who was lying back on an elbow. John Senior spoke to Cassie then about starting supper and she and Mary rose from their seats and disappeared into the pantry.

Buchan sat back in his chair and set the pen in the inkwell. He pulled at the hem of his jacket. "I am speaking to you now," he said, "as a gentleman and a friend."

Peyton smiled severely. "You are welcome on this floor as always, Captain," he said. "And if you and your man Rowsell" — he nodded to the corporal who stood handy to Buchan's chair — "wish to stay to a bit of supper and spend the night, there's food and a bed for you. But there's nothing you can write in your little book that will change what happened on that lake, sir. It was told the way I felt it ought to be told when I testified before the grand jury in St. John's."

Buchan sighed and templed his fingertips, considering. He reached for the notebook and buttoned it away in a pocket. "Supper," he said, "would be welcome." And he motioned Rowsell to take a seat with them at the table.

The men sat to a meal of salt pork with boiled spuds, cabbage, turnip and greens. Their plates were spooned with food and then ladled with the salty liquor from the pot that the meat and vegetables had been boiled in. John Senior took up a mugful of the liquor and sipped at it through his supper. Cassie fussed about the table as they ate and carried empty platters away into the pantry. The Beothuk woman sat at the back of the room, working a square of leather with an awl fashioned from an iron fishing hook. Cassie had tried to teach her to use a needle and thread when she'd first been brought to the house in March, but she'd pushed the materials away impatiently and Peyton had to tell Cassie to leave her be. Her bundle of belongings sat beside her on the floor.

"She's being employed as a servant," Buchan said.

Peyton shrugged. "We made an effort to give her a few regular duties in the household, which she did not take kindly to. As long as she isn't ordered about she seems happy enough to help out."

"She don't mind minding our business is what I find," John Senior said. "And don't think she's not listening to us over there. Or that she don't know we're talking about her."

Buchan and the marine peered over the shoulders of their hosts. Mary stared at her work with the blank expression of someone hypnotized by the fluid motion of a fire. There was a clotted undertone to her breathing they could all hear, as if each lungful of air was being filtered through a wet cloth. In the months since the trial, she had begun showing unmistakable signs of a congestive illness.

"She's into everything not her own besides, and I would keep close account of my materials if I was you," John Senior went on. "She could sneak a schooner's anchor off in that bundle she carts around."

Buchan looked to Peyton who was tapping his fork impatiently against the table. "Has she been stealing from the household?"

"There was the one occasion, yes."

Cassie interrupted. "It was not thieving as commonly understood, Captain."

"Uncommon thievery," the officer said lightly. "I'm intrigued."

"I missed a bolt of cloth from the cupboard and turned the house upside down looking for it. In the course of these investigations I asked Mary if she had seen it." Cassie smiled across at the Indian woman. "She is a poor liar." Mary didn't look up from the work in her lap. "I went to her room and began looking through her drawers. She followed me up there and was none too pleased with my presumption, but she didn't try to stop me, only sat on her trunk in the corner and complained."

"And of course the trunk was the location of the missing material," Buchan said.

"I had to remove her forcibly from her seat and at that point she began trying to convince me that John Peyton had given her the material, so I called him up to join us, which ended that line of argument. She ran off before we opened the trunk. When we did we found, well, not the bolt of cloth exactly."

"Miss Jure, I am in the greatest suspense," Buchan said in mock anguish. "Please."

"It has always been her custom to go up to her bed early. But she was sleeping less than we believed. We found sixteen pairs of blue moccasins, all of different sizes and with the finest needlework."

Peyton said, "The wigwam where we stayed that night on the lake. There were, as best we can recall, seventeen or eighteen sleeping pits around the fire."

There was a pause around the table.

"She will of course be returned to her people," Buchan said.

Peyton nodded. "I'm not averse to the idea."

"We've yet to see any of the governor's reward for our trouble," John Senior said.

Buchan said, "In the event that Mary's return to the Red Indians leads to improved relations, the money will be forthcoming." He sounded as if he was reading a public proclamation he found personally distasteful.

Cassie brought a full jug of water to the table and refilled glasses all around.

"There's a few weeks yet we might hope to find some of the Indians around the bay," Peyton offered. "Otherwise we'll have to wait till the freeze-up and carry her to the lake."

"We, Mr. Peyton?"

"I feel some responsibility for her well-being given the circumstances under which she came to us. I'm at your disposal if you'll have me."

John Senior forked into his plate of food and chewed fiercely, but said nothing.

Buchan nodded. "You would be welcome."

After the meal was cleared away and the dishes done, Mary was brought to the table and sat in a chair beside Buchan. He used a blank page in his journal to trace a rough map of the Bay of Exploits. He drew a boat manned by marines and a figure he pointed to with the tip of the pencil and then touched Mary's chest with his finger. On a point of land, Buchan roughed in triangular shelters and a fire to indicate their being inhabited. Mary leant over the table, the weight of her breasts pressed into the tied kerchief of clothing in her lap. She looked from the paper to the face of the artist and back again, as if she might be able to somehow influence what he would draw there. Buchan drew the boat along a dotted line to the point of land and placed Mary on the shore. Then he showed the boat travelling away without her.

"No, no," she said. She waved her hands before her face. "No good for Mary."

Buchan looked around the table at the others, but no one offered assistance. "Why not, Mary? What is no good for Mary?"

She continued shaking her head.

"I don't understand," Buchan said. Finally he relented and placed the abandoned figure back among the crew of the boat.

"Yes, yes," she said. The relief she felt was obvious but listless, enervated.

Peyton said there was no telling who they would happen upon in the bay, if they managed to find anyone at all. It was possible she wanted to be returned only to the group she was found with at the lake.

"Very well," Buchan said. He roughed in a sketch of the river and the northernmost section of the lake and the boat appeared there as if by magic.

John Senior protested. "There's no way on God's green earth to get a boat from the bay past the falls on that river."

Buchan looked up at him. "It's just a symbol," he said. "A mode of transportation. This isn't meant to be literal."

"And you see her following your meaning in all this?"

Buchan stared at the old man for a moment, but turned back to the map before he said anything. Mary continued to stare at the paper. "Mary?" he said. "Good for Mary?"

She nodded.

He placed her figure on the shore, watching furtively for signs of how she would react to this. She placed her hand to her mouth. Buchan began drawing a dotted line to indicate the boat leaving the lake and Mary immediately sat back in her chair.

"No," she said. "No no no no no." Her expression was pained, helpless. She covered her mouth with her hands.

"We are meant to bring you back to your people," Buchan said, but she continued offering her one word repudiation through her cupped hands.

John Senior made a noise somewhere between disgust and satisfaction.

Cassie said, "Let her do it."

"I'm sorry?" Buchan said, looking up quickly.

"Let her draw what she would like."

"Can she draw?"

Cassie leaned forward to examine the crude figures Buchan had sketched on the paper. "I'd say she would be able to meet the rigorous standard set by His Majesty's Royal Navy."

Buchan felt himself beginning to flush. It was such an unusual sensation that his visible embarrassment compounded itself, until he had turned nearly the colour of his tunic. He held the pencil towards the Indian woman without taking his eyes from Cassie. The men around the table were doing a half-hearted job of suppressing their amusement. Mary looked back and forth between Cassie and the officer and would not touch the pencil for fear of seeming to take sides.

"It's all right, Mary," Cassie prodded.

Buchan smiled at her finally. "Please," he said.

She nodded and accepted the pencil. She turned the journal on the table several ways until it was arranged as she wished and she began fixing the drawing of the River Exploits. Her picture was minute and detailed, with a cluster of small concave strokes indicating prominent rapids on the river and a billow of vapour where each of the waterfalls was located. She dotted portage paths around each of these obstructions. She added a third mama-teek to the two figures drawn by Buchan at the lake. She paused a moment and raised her head to the group of faces around her.

"Go ahead," Buchan said quietly.

She drew something near the figure of herself on the shore, something the figure was holding at the level of her waist.

"What's that?" John Senior asked. "Is that the bundle of clothes she drags around?"

"A child," Cassie said. "A baby, Mary?"

"Yes, yes. Baby."

"She has a child?" Buchan asked. He looked up at the men across the table.

"That seems to be the gist of what she's suggesting," Peyton said flatly.

"Did you know this?"

"There wasn't what you would call a proper round of introductions made at the time," John Senior told him.

"Mary's baby," Mary said.

"You would like to go home to your child," Buchan said, but she didn't understand him and simply stared. He took the pencil from her and again indicated the boat leaving the lake. Again she protested. "All right," he said, "all right." He returned the pencil to her and pointed to the page. "Show me what you want," he told her.

Mary moved the figure with the child in her arms from the shoreline beside the mamateeks back into the waiting boat. Then she drew a line up the river, across the portages at both waterfalls and around rapids into the Bay of Exploits. She drew Burnt Island and then a square house on the stretch of beach where they were sitting around the table and placed herself and her child beside it. "Good," she said obstinately, though her stubbornness seemed somehow infected with her illness, drained of energy and confidence. She placed the pencil beside the journal. "Good for Mary."

Mary went to her room shortly after drawing her map. Cassie finished clearing up the supper dishes and then took a seat with the men who had settled into a bottle of rum. For six months in 1818 Buchan had been part of an expedition to the Arctic, attempting to reach the Pole by ship, and he was giving an account of his travels. He was in command of the *Dorothea*, accompanied by Lieutenant John Frankland in the *Trent*. They sailed out of Spitzbergen on June 7 and passed easily beyond the northwest boundary of the island. Near Red Bay they were icebound for thirteen days and then took shelter in Fair Haven. On July 6, they again headed out, reaching 80° 34' North before they were forced to turn back due to the ice conditions. The weather was so cold and inclement at times that the ship's canvas and rigging was encased in ice. Cauldrons of water were boiled and the steam used to free knots sufficiently to allow sails to be set. Men chopped the bows and decks free of thick galls of ice with axes and cutlasses.

Cassie watched him from her chair across the room. His face seemed to be lit from within as he talked, like a man recounting an encounter with God. He used his hands to indicate the position of ships, the angle of rafted ice, the distance from ship to land. Their constant motion added to the distractedly busy air that rarely left him in the company of other men. The Peytons and Corporal Rowsell leaned forward on their thighs to get as close to the story as they could manage, as if they were drawing heat from a fire.

Returning along the edge of the icepack towards Greenland, the two ships sailed into a gale. Buchan was tipped out of his bunk by the extreme pitch and roll. He dressed and clawed his way onto the bridge. The storm was so furious they had no choice but to run before it into the Arctic ice. "The impact," Buchan said. He slapped a fist into the open palm of the opposite hand. "Every man was taken off his feet, the timbers roaring. I don't know what kept the masts from snapping at the base." He used his forearm to demonstrate the severe angle they had somehow recovered from. "The ship's bell tolling in the wind after we'd been brought up solid." He shook his head. "I made my peace with God," he said. "Rather quickly," he added.

Before the laughter died away Cassie rose and took her leave of the men and went to her bed. She lay awake listening to the murmur of surf drifting in through the open window and the louder tide of talk from the kitchen. She waited until she heard the scrape of chairs and the men dispersing to their rooms, John Senior going out the door with Rowsell to a bed in the hired men's quarters, insisting Buchan sleep in his room. She waited longer still, until the tide had almost turned and the sound of one furtive set of footsteps descended the stairs above her. They sounded, she thought, like the steps of a man come to steal away valuables, to lift jewellery, silverware, hidden caches of sterling coins.

She found him sitting on the daybed beside the fireplace. He'd lit a single candle and the acrid smell of the wick hung in the air.

"No need for a fire tonight, I suppose," she said.

"I wasn't sure you would join me."

"Nor was I, truth be told."

Buchan nodded and took a breath. "To be honest, I would have felt some relief if you had not."

She watched him a moment and then turned to go back to her room.

"No, please," he said and he rose to get a chair and set it in front of himself, motioning for her to sit.

They stared a while. Cassie was forty-one years old and Buchan had seen that age in her face earlier in the day — crow's feet fanning at the corners of her eyes, a tautness gone from the skin of her neck. In the near dark of the single candle those changes were imperceptible, but there was a more fundamental difference he could sense, something in her manner that had altered. The subtle disregard for station that could be mistaken for arrogance was still with her, but the ease of it was gone. There had always been an air of caution about her, though when he first met Cassie it was furtive, subterranean. It had come to the surface now, as if she was too exhausted to camouflage it any longer. The woman sitting before him had the intense, diffuse look of a person in the midst of a lengthy fast.

Cassie crossed her legs and shifted her nightdress on her thighs. "It's been a long time," she said. "Don't you think we ought to have something to say to one another?"

For the second time that evening Buchan felt himself blush.

The first time the sound of the officer's movement on the stairs had broken Cassie's sleep was in October of 1810. The front door pushed roughly open and closed, the house giving a brief audible sigh as the plug of wind rushed in. She'd looked through the frosted pane of her window, but there was no sign of morning in the sky. She wondered if Buchan had for some reason gone to look in on his marines who were sleeping in makeshift bunks in an outbuilding used by hired men. Under the flapping sheets of wind there was the tortured barking sound of someone vomiting into the snow outside her window. She got out of bed and went to the kitchen to stoke up a fire to make tea to settle his stomach. "I was lying awake anyway," she told him.

The harsh weather continued into the next day and kept Buchan at the winter house a second day and night. That morning, he'd sat across from her with his hands in his lap, listening as if he expected her to tell her life story. As if he'd paid to be entertained. She didn't fully understand what came over her to have leaned forward and lifted her dress, to show him the scar on her leg. He was a stranger to everyone on the northeast shore. He was a stranger to her and his transience meant he would remain so, whatever she told him of herself. "There's no sense in standing on ceremony from here," he had said. She chattered away to him like wind in the chimney.

And he went to the kitchen again that night, having crept down the stairs an hour after he and John Senior went to their beds. She pulled the shawl around her shoulders and walked out into the hall, standing in the doorway to the kitchen. He was sitting on the daybed, a fire already burning. He was dressed a little more formally than he'd been the night before.

"Are you feeling all right, Lieutenant?"

He smiled up at her. "Perfectly all right, thank you," he said. "I poured."

"Is it tea you're wanting, Mr. Buchan?" she asked him.

"If that's what's on offer," he said softly.

Cassie looked at him a long moment and then went to the fireplace, lifting the kettle onto the crane over the heat. "You mustn't think much of me, Lieutenant, is all's I can say."

"On the contrary," he said. But he didn't say anything more.

She pulled a chair from the table across the floor to her spot beside the fireplace, determined this time to keep her mouth shut. He could sense this or something like it about her, and after they both settled with mugs of tea

Buchan talked to her about his childhood in Scotland. He told her about his father who was a navy officer himself and had died of a simple cut to the hand when it turned black with infection and the subsequent fever brought him down. His mother had remarried within the year and he could see now it was a practical decision and he had forgiven her for what at the time he thought of as callousness or indiscretion. He had joined the navy as a cabin boy then, to punish her, and she was unable to refuse permission having so recently disappointed him by taking a new husband. She'd wept for days before he left. He said he had yet to forgive himself for that selfishness.

"You were a child," Cassie said.

"It was cruelty, nonetheless. I knew what I was about, and make no mistake, I wanted to cause her the same pain she'd caused me. Simple revenge. And it was something I quickly came to regret."

He was employed as a servant for the Warrant Officer, a James Richardson, who was quartered in a canvas-sided cabin along the wall of the lower deck with his wife. The rest of the low-ceilinged room was occupied by two hundred men and boys who slept in hammocks strung above the cast-iron cannon. The only light entered through the gun ports, which were sealed in rough weather. The sailors rarely bathed. Their clothes were washed every other month in a bucket of sea water after being bleached in urine collected in a barrel. The stench of dry rot and bilge and human waste fogged the air.

Buchan and the other ship's boys were quartered with the midshipmen in the cockpit of the orlop deck below the waterline. Many of these officers-in-training were not much above Buchan's age, eleven and twelve years old, and they tormented and bullied one another and the other boys aboard ship. Because Buchan was Scots and among the youngest in service, he was a favourite object of their attention. They cut his hammock down while he slept, stole his clothes and his food, set upon him in groups of two and three and roughed him up. Buchan was beside himself with frustration and rage. He had bargained away his half rations of beer and grog in return for some peace, but to little effect.

It was Mrs. Richardson, who had been going to sea with her husband for years, who set him straight on the steps he needed to take. She procured a starter for him, a length of knotted rope used to rouse men from their bunks in the morning. Together they decided on a midshipman named Marryat, not the worst of his tormentors but a boy about his size who was rumoured to suck his thumb in his sleep. Buchan made his way to the orlop deck just before dinner when most of the midshipmen were at table. He walked directly to Marryat and pulled him backwards onto the floor, then proceeded to beat him with the starter. The other midshipmen gathered around them, shouting wildly, but they offered their companion no assistance. When it became clear Marryat was incapable of defending himself, they shifted their allegiance to Buchan and cheered him on. The rope raised welts on the boy's face and forearms and Buchan pulled his shirt over his head to mark his back and chest, the knots drawing blood where they struck. Only when two of the older midshipmen decided Marryat was in danger of permanent injury did they pull him clear. Buchan was caned and then mastheaded for the attack, lashed to the cross-trees of the topmast for the better part of a day, but the worst of the persecution he suffered came to an end.

"How old were you, Lieutenant?" Cassie asked him.

"I was ten. And I doubt I would ever have gone back to sea if not for Mrs. Richardson," Buchan said.

"I find it difficult to imagine that a mother with any feeling for her child would have allowed you to return to such disgraceful conditions."

He smiled at the strength of the emotion in her voice. She seemed genuinely affronted. He said, "Of course my mother heard nothing of this."

"I see," Cassie said. "Of course." After a moment she looked up from her lap. She asked if his mother ever forgave him for leaving the way he did.

Buchan shook his head. "We never spoke of it before she died," he said. "I feel sometimes as if I'm father to the memory of my mother as I now hold it, a woman abandoned first by her husband and then by her son. The thought of her clings to me like an unhappy child." He looked up at the ceiling.

"When the dead have been wronged they never leave you quite, even if you might eventually wish it."

Cassie turned her head away and then stared into her mug.

"I'm sorry," Buchan said. "I didn't intend to upset you."

She shook her head, her mouth set into a thin, furious line. "A fine story, Lieutenant. A story to move an audience to tears. I'm sure it's a particularly fine tale to tell," she said, "if you're looking to weasel your way into a woman's bed."

The officer tapped a finger thoughtfully against the bridge of his nose. "It seems to be you who doesn't think much of me, Miss Jure."

She looked across at the man with a sorry expression. She said, "Perhaps we are alike in many ways."

"And perhaps it would be best if I take to my bed." He stood up from his seat. "I thank you for your company. And the tea."

After he left she sat in the kitchen for a long time while the fire embered to coals and the gale endlessly tried the windows and the latch of the door. She drank the last cold mouthful of her tea and then carried her shawl out to her room in the dark.

Two weeks later Buchan returned to John Senior's house to discuss plans for the expedition to the Red Indian's lake. At some early hour of the morning she heard him make his way downstairs and pass by her room. She lay in her bed for a time and tried to talk herself into staying there.

He asked if she would care to join him in a drink rather than tea. She turned to fetch glasses and the bottle, and they sipped at the liquor in silence a while.

Buchan said, "You never did answer my first question to you."

She creased her brow.

"Weeks ago," he said, "I asked your view on this matter of the Red Indians."

"Ah," she said. There was the tiniest note of disappointment in her voice. "It's a province of the menfolk more than myself."

"It seems to me that would hardly prevent you from holding an opinion."

She smiled. "To be honest I know next to nothing of them. They used to make quite a nuisance of themselves around here from the stories I've heard. But mostly they just seem lost."

"Exactly," Buchan said, pointing with the glass in his hand. "Exactly how they seem to me. They're like children who've been abandoned by their parents."

She shook her head. "No," she said. "No. They just seem lost. As if they don't recognize the country they live in any more."

He stared, not understanding what she had said. He placed his glass on the floor between his feet and folded his arms across his chest. "Have you ever been in love, Miss Jure?"

Her eyebrows pursed, the lazy eye drawing down suspiciously. "It's not something I've chosen for myself, no."

Buchan offered a troubled look. "And you believe this is a matter in which we have a choice?"

"I do," she said. "Yes. How long have you been married?" she asked him.

"Some years now." He looked to the rafters, counting. "Nine years June past."

"And how long have you been unhappily married?" Cassie asked him.

He said, "I am very much in love with Marie."

"You confuse me, sir, I must say. Perhaps you need a little more practice pouring."

Buchan sat forward and stared at the floor. He said, "Perhaps I too believe this is a matter in which we have some choice. Cassie." He paused over her name. "Cassie, I promise I will never speak to you about love." He looked up at her. "I will never talk about taking you away from this place."

She turned her face away from him. "I have no reason to trust you."

"Nor I you," he said. "And yet here we are."

She thought it was laughable how cautiously they approached one other. Like children testing the water on an unfamiliar shore. As if they both suspected a trap, the fatal rip of an undertow beneath the calm surface. It was a sad truth about the world, Cassie decided, that only a sense of mutual vulnerability promised any shelter at all.

Buchan and Cassie slept together on three separate occasions during his visits to John Senior's household, without once being completely naked in each other's presence. Her first orgasm was so unexpected and intense that she broke out into embarrassed laughter even as it shook through her. At all other times they fucked in a silence so complete and so charged with the effort of suppressing the sound of pleasure that they seemed to be moving under water. Cassie straddled Buchan's naked thighs, gripping the fabric of his shirt. Her hair fell loose around her face, so that even her expression was hidden from him. She pressed the bone of her pubis into him and rocked until she fell across his body, breathing as if she had just surfaced for air.

When he rolled from beneath her, Cassie lay on her belly and he pushed slowly into her from behind. She could barely feel him inside her after she came, but she liked the weight of him across her back, the blind heat of his body drawn to her like a plant pitched towards sunlight. She liked not being able to see his face when he finally went rigid and pressed his open mouth into her neck. It made their connection seem both more impersonal and more intimate somehow.

He fell asleep there while his cock went flaccid and slipped from her almost imperceptibly. She reached a hand behind herself, touching his face with the tips of her fingers until the sensation woke him and they shifted their bodies to lay side by side. They allowed themselves to kiss then, with the shyness of a fugitive affection they couldn't acknowledge or entirely expel from their time together.

Before he left her bed, Cassie would ask Buchan to tell her something about Marie, where she had grown up, how she wore her hair the first time he saw her, if she read or attended concerts. She could see his resistance to talking about her. His answers were hesitant, defensive, apologetic. But Cassie insisted on hearing the details of their courtship, the wedding, the first years of their marriage, and he wasn't able to refuse, seeing that she took some strange comfort from it. He told her about Marie's habit of scenting her letters with rosewater, the colours she chose for their apartment (light green damask in the parlour, distemper fine blue for the bedchamber), her oddly accented pronunciation of his name which the years in England hadn't changed, *Daveed*. Cassie kept her forehead against his chest, nodding at each new detail, as if she was making a list in her head. He spoke of Marie's shyness about her body, how even after years of marriage she wouldn't allow herself to be naked in his presence except in darkness. He had never spoken so intimately about her to anyone.

"How did you propose to her?" Cassie asked him.

"Not very romantic, I'm afraid. I met her by chance to begin with. She and her aunt were on a French vessel forced into Portsmouth by the Royal Navy and they spent a year waiting for an opportunity to return to France. She was just fifteen years old at the time. Marie and her aunt were invited to social events held by officers of the navy, as a show of hospitality. She didn't like England much, the weather or the food or the people. The first time we spoke, she had just learned that among the vulgar classes some men auction their wives at market like chattel if they wish to be rid of them. With a halter about their necks. I've not seen her so furious since. She said, 'Explain please, this, this *English* way.'"

"And how did you explain it?"

"I told her, 'I am not English.' Perhaps that is what endeared me to her."

Cassie shifted against him. "And the proposal?"

"Yes. That was during the Peace of Lunéville, in 1801. It was the first opportunity for the two women to return to France. By then Marie and I had spent some time in each other's company. She made it clear to me that she did not wish to leave."

"So she proposed to you."

"A proposal was implied. There was nothing else about England she would have been sorry to leave behind."

"Her parents allowed this?"

"The aunt returned without her. The peace lasted only a few months, which meant her parents couldn't leave the continent to retrieve her even if they objected."

"There was no dowry."

"No," he said. "There was not. After we married Marie renounced her allegiance to France."

Cassie said, "She gave up everything for you."

"A great deal," Buchan allowed. "I suppose so, yes. Why do you want to know these things?" he asked her.

She raised her head to look at him. She said, "It's time you should go to your room, Lieutenant."

After each encounter with Buchan, a shifting current of emotion coursed through Cassie as she lay alone in her bed, the force of it like a winter river capped under ice. She turned on her side with a hand pressed firmly between her thighs until she came a second time, a muted, nebulous climax that somehow made it possible for her to cry. Only then was she able to begin a slow descent into sleep.

In the morning she cooked breakfast for John Senior and his guest. She called him Lieutenant. He referred to her as Miss Jure. The old man slathered his gandies with molasses and recounted the pleasure of yet another night of uninterrupted slumber.

The last time they slept together was in January of 1811, just weeks after her trip to see Annie on the River Exploits when the child had been bled from her belly like a lanced boil, three days before Buchan's expedition was due to leave Ship Cove for the Red Indian's lake.

She was still weak and unsettled at the time, and her ability to stomach food and spirits was unpredictable. She fell into an exhausted sleep as soon as she left the men at the table and looked in on John Senior a last time for the night. Peyton had given his room to the lieutenant and slept in the hired men's quarters with the surgeon. She would have missed Buchan's trip to the kitchen altogether if the nausea hadn't forced her awake. She climbed from her bed and knelt over the acidic stench of the honey bucket and heaved her supper into it.

Buchan knocked gently at her door and let himself in. He stood over her with a hand to her back. "This is a bit of a turnabout," he said.

He helped her up and walked her into the kitchen where she sat on the daybed.

"I feel much better," she told him.

He went back into her room to fetch her shawl and set about making tea. They sat side by side as she sipped at the sweet dark drink, Buchan with his arm across her back, rocking her gently side to side. He pushed her hair back across her ear and kissed the side of her face.

"Much better," Cassie said. She placed her hand on his leg and squeezed.

They sat for a long time in that position. Buchan spoke to her about preparations for the expedition and the gear they would pack along, the inventory of presents for the Red Indians, the trials they could expect on the journey. There was something of the ten-year-old still in him, Cassie thought, in his perverse single-mindedness, in his fixation on lists as if enough of them could contain all that was important in the world, in his naked enthusiasm for peril. She was unsure why some men seemed never to outgrow these things or why in some it was so unaccountably attractive. She saw then that in this way he was just like her father. She rested her head on his shoulder as he spoke, regretting ever having sat alone with him in this room.

"Cassie," he said. "Are you listening?"

She looked up at him and allowed his name to pass her lips for the first and last time. "David," she said.

He was about to smile at her, but her expression spoke against it. "What is it?" he asked. "Cassie?"

She knelt on the cold of the wood floor in front of him. She reached for the waist of his breeches to open the spair and work them down his thighs.

"You're in no condition," Buchan said quietly, taking her arms and trying to lift her to her feet, but she pushed his hands away and set him back on the daybed, his head angled awkwardly against the wall. The legs of his pants turned inside out as she pulled them free of his feet and she leaned her face into him, kissing the bare skin of his thighs. She took the head of his cock into her mouth until it was wet with her saliva and then stroked him slowly, her fingers circled around the corona. She watched his face as she touched him, every movement of her hand causing muscles in his cheeks to twitch slightly, his head jerking from side to side. It looked to her as if she was rhythmically pricking him with a needle. His breath caught and caught again like a piece of cloth pulled through thorns. He was beautiful and ridiculous and watching his face filled her with a sadness that welled like the pleasure she'd discovered with him, and she had to bear down in the same way to hold in the roiling wail of it.

Buchan brought his hand to her shoulder. She dipped her head to catch the small flail of cum in her mouth and when he lay still she stood up from the floor to pass it into his. She kissed him hard and went on kissing him until there was nothing in their mouths but the sharp, stinging taste of him.

She held his head in both her hands. "We can never do this again," she said.

He looked at her, waiting, as if he expected more than this simple declaration. Finally he said, "I understand."

She smiled at him. "No," Cassie said. "You do not."

The taste of his cum was potent, medicinal, it made her tongue tingle like a numb hand coming to life and the sensation didn't leave her before she fell asleep, alone in her bed, the stars through her window winking sharply in the moonless dark of the sky.

"How have they treated her?" Buchan asked.

"Captain?"

That tiny note of disappointment in her voice. Perhaps she thought it unfair of him to suggest the Peytons might have mistreated Mary. Maybe she was hurt that the first thing he said to her was so distant and impersonal. The light of the candle bowed and righted itself in the breeze through the open windows of the kitchen.

"Is she a servant here?"

"Your tone implies you think it demeaning to be a servant in this household."

"Not at all," he said. The flush hadn't left his face and it deepened now, and he was glad for the near dark. "I am simply curious as to her circumstances —"

"John Peyton has already given you an account of her circumstances."

"Yes," he said. "Yes, I just — I was hoping. I thought I would be able to trust your word over his, if that were necessary."

"She has all she needs or wants. She sleeps twelve hours a night if she pleases and she often does. John Peyton dotes on her as he would a child and gives her little gifts of jewellery and whatnot. She is a help when it suits her, and if it suits her to sit and pout all day long, she is welcome to pout. She has visitors from all over the northeast shore, people coming to take a view of her, and I'd say she is partial to the attention."

"You make it sound as if she wants to stay here."

"You saw what she drew tonight."

Buchan said, "I cannot accept that she prefers to forsake her people to remain on Burnt Island."

"I doubt it's as simple as what she would *prefer*, Captain. It's rarely that simple for any of us, wouldn't you agree?"

"In the main," he said quietly, "I would agree."

"Her only use of the English language at first was to talk of returning. But in the last weeks she seems to have lost her fire for the Indian way of life." They stared at one another. Cassie said, "She's afraid of going back there is what it seems to me."

"And why do you think that might be the case?"

"She has been with us a long time now. Maybe she's afraid they'll think she left of her own accord."

"A man was *killed*," Buchan said.

"Some might think that all the more reason not to have walked out with the killers. And stayed with them this long."

Buchan bowed his head to stare at his feet. He had come down without shoes or stockings and it now seemed a ridiculous intimacy, as if he was interrogating a stranger in his small clothes. "What happened out there, Cassie?"

She smiled at him. "Do you ever think of me?" she asked.

He looked up, startled. "I beg your pardon?"

"When you were icebound in the Arctic and you lay alone in your bunk in the dark, did I ever come to your mind?"

"Cassie," he said. He felt a swell of panic rising. "It's been years since we've spoken."

"Of course."

"I think of our time fondly —"

"No, forgive me. Please don't," Cassie said. Her voice had the urgent, soothing inflection of an adult comforting a child afraid of the dark. "It's just I go months without seeing a soul that doesn't belong to this household, Captain. Do you see what I mean?"

He cleared his throat. "If I hadn't fallen in love with Marie before I met you," he said.

"Oh," Cassie said. She placed her hand over her mouth. "Oh no. No, you misunderstand," she said. And she started to laugh, using her hand to muffle the sound as best she could.

"What is it," Buchan asked, smiling. He was enormously relieved by her laughter and the relief fuelled a peculiar giddiness of his own. She waved her free hand to quiet him but couldn't manage to quiet herself. Moments later John Peyton appeared in the doorway in his nightshirt.

"I heard voices," he said. He looked them over as they tried to compose themselves. He felt as if he had caught them kissing. The officer's feet, he noticed, were bare.

"My apologies," Buchan said and he coughed out a last stupid giggle. He wiped at his eyes with the back of his hand. The bristle of hair at the wrist made a brief rasping sound that seemed inappropriate and somehow distasteful and immediately sobered their mood. He said, "I wasn't able to sleep and came down to sit in the kitchen. I seem to have awoken Miss Jure in my wanderings."

"I've always been a light sleeper," she said.

"Yes, well," Peyton said. "I didn't mean to interrupt."

"Not at all," Buchan told him. "It would seem more to the point that we have interrupted you. My apologies, again. However, now that you're up and about you would be welcome to join us."

John Peyton was staring at the back of Cassie's head. She hadn't turned to look in his direction since he first appeared in the doorway. "Thank you, Captain, no. I'd be best to go back to bed, I'm sure."

"As would we all, no doubt," Buchan said.

After he'd gone Cassie said, "I believe I'll do the same," and she rose from her chair and placed it at the table. She paused with her hands still on the back of the chair. "I wanted to thank you," she said. "For the letter."

The thought of her father in his coffin wearing his ill-fitting suit surrounded by drunken mourners embarrassed Buchan, on Cassie's behalf, and he simply nodded.

As she was on her way to her room he said, "Miss Jure," and then corrected himself. "Cassie," he said.

She turned to look at him over her shoulder.

"Would you help me speak to her?" he asked. "She seems to trust you. You seem to understand her better than I am able."

"If you like," she said. "I will talk to her."

NINE

The following morning Cassie took Mary down to the brook to fetch water. They balanced on stones over dark shallow pools and before they dipped the buckets Mary pointed to her likeness on the surface. She smiled across at Cassie. "Mary," she said, still pointing. Every time they came for water she repeated this ritual of recognition and naming, as if to reassure herself of her identity in the Peyton household. It had been months since it had given Cassie a moment's pause. She looked at the woman beside her. *Mary has a child,* she thought.

They pushed the rim of each bucket into their reflected faces and lifted them clear when they dragged full. They carried two buckets apiece by rough hemp-rope handles and they walked in the centre of chime hoops salvaged from pickling barrels, the buckets resting against the circumference of birch to keep the slop of water clear of their dresses. Mary's bundle of leather clothing was tied to her back in a sling of linen. The last mosquitoes of the summer swarmed their defenceless heads and the Indian woman chanted a song that seemed to Cassie to be as tuneless as the lilt of the insects. She'd asked once what the song was about and Mary had set the buckets down to mime tipping a glass to her mouth. "Wa-ter," she said.

When Mary first arrived at the winter house with the Peytons in March, Cassie looked at her as she might have if John Peyton had carted in a half-wild animal — as something that might be tamed, taught a few manners. She boiled kettles of water on the crane and filled the tiny wooden tub while the two men sat about the kitchen in their winter gear. Mary was sitting on the floor near John Peyton and as John Senior talked she looked surreptitiously about the room. "I don't suggest you being alone in her company," John

Senior said, but Cassie sent the men outside into the cold to cut and split wood and look to the animals and then she stood Mary up and stripped her naked on the kitchen floor. Mary averted her head as if she was avoiding the sight of an ugly wound.

There was a stench beneath her clothes, Cassie remembered, something sour. She didn't know then that Mary had been nursing a child, that her milk would have leaked and stained her cassock and spoiled. She'd assumed it was simply the smell of an Indian and something that might be scalded away in time. The leggings were tied at the waist with a string of leather that Cassie couldn't unknot and Mary reached to do it for her, her head still turned sharply to the side. Her entire torso was oiled with red ochre and when Cassie sat her in the tub the water curdled the colour of blood. There was a bar of lye soap and a brush used to scrub the wood floors and Cassie scoured with the same resolute thoroughness, paying particular attention to the corners and crevices where the ochre was most resistant — in the hollows above the clavicles, the line beneath the slight sag of her breasts. She worked until the water went cold and Mary began shivering. She poured more hot water into the filthy tub and went back to scrubbing.

The Indian woman spoke then, a single guttural syllable, and Cassie looked at her, their eyes meeting for the first time. She was kneeling beside the tub, her dress soaked in the water and suds and red oil that had spilled on the floor. Their faces only inches apart. Cassie could smell her breath, surprisingly sweet, untainted, with an undertone of something sharp and clear, like spruce gum.

"What is it?" she said, speaking softly because their faces were so close together.

Mary repeated the sound and tipped her cupped hand to her mouth.

"Water," Cassie said.

Mary nodded.

"Wa-ter," Cassie said again, in distinct syllables, and Mary repeated them back to her. After she had given her the cup, Cassie considered she should have taught her to say "please," as well.

Cassie set the empty cup aside and pointed to herself with a wet index finger. "Cassandra," she said. A tiny circular stain of water marking her dress at the breastbone. "Cassie," she said. "Ca-ssie." After they had worked on the pronunciation a moment, she pointed to the woman in the tub. "What is your name?" she asked. "Your. Name."

Without hesitation the Indian woman said, "Mary."

"We had to call her something," John Peyton explained later. "We couldn't make head nor tail of whatever she called herself." In all her time in the Peyton household, she would never refer to herself as anything but Mary, the English name like a protective talisman she carried close to her skin.

Cassie had Mary kneel up so she could scrub at her back and buttocks and thighs. She soaped a cloth and reached to wash between her legs but Mary grabbed her wrist and sat quickly back into the water. "All right Mary," Cassie said, "all right." She could feel the blood pulsing in her hand from the force of Mary's grip. She took the cloth in her free hand and held it in front of the Indian woman, offering it with tiny motions, as if it were a morsel of food. When Mary took the cloth Cassie stood and went into her room off the kitchen. She collected a white dress from the back of her door and dug stockings from her trunk and after she felt she'd allowed Mary enough privacy, carried them into the kitchen. She laid the clothes on the daybed and knelt at the tub. She reached into the cloudy water and extracted one tiny foot after the other, scouring the thickly callused soles, the heels and ankles. Her knees were still bruised where she had fallen to the ice nearly a week beforehand.

After she was towelled dry and dressed, Cassie went back into her room and brought out a small hand mirror. At the sight of herself Mary screamed and turned away. She grabbed the glass from Cassie's hands and held it at arm's length in front of herself and screamed a second time, then fell into ringing peals of laughter that brought the men running in from outside.

"Everything all right?" John Senior said.

Cassie sat in a chair at the table, surprised to find herself tired. The skirt of her dress was sopping wet and cold against her skin.

"She looks like a proper lady in that getup," Peyton said, and he nodded and smiled at Mary in a tired way, as if she needed to be encouraged, appeased.

Cassie looked at her then as if that was actually possible, in fact, just a matter of time. She had no idea if Mary was intended to stay with them or be sent to St. John's or if she would live at the parson's house in Twillingate, but she already had vague plans for teaching her to cook and sew, to speak English, perhaps even to read.

John Senior had said, "You can't dress that kind up on the inside."

Cassie saw that as the truth now, though not in the way the old man had intended. She watched Mary's bare feet on the dirt path in front of her as they hauled the water up to the house, their steps in time to the sound of Mary's singing. For the first time since she'd bathed her in front of the stove, Cassie wondered what her name might be.

Peyton and John Senior had risen early to hand-line for late-season cod and by early afternoon had pitched a decent day of fish up on the stagehead. They had a quick lunch and then went back down to the cutting room.

Shortly after they left, the two women sat together in the parlour with Buchan. Corporal Rowsell had been posted at the front door with instructions that they not be disturbed. There was an oval hook rug on the bare wood floor of the parlour and doilies on the polished side tables. Mary reached a hand to finger the intricate design of the one nearest her as Cassie fixed tea for herself and the officer. He was dressed in his red uniform coat.

"Now Mary," he said.

Cassie watched her face, the customary expression of eager uncertainty. It was her first line of defence, this willingness to please, this fretting after some notion of what was wanted. Every day Mary retreated further and further behind their expectations of her to the point that it was impossible any more to know who she might have been before the Peytons carried her down the river.

Buchan sat in a rigid posture in his high-backed chair and his voice took on the tone of someone presiding at a trial. "We wish to speak to you about the incident at the lake of this past March."

She looked quickly from Buchan to Cassie seated directly to her left. "John Peyton?"

"The Misters Peyton," Buchan said, "are nowhere nearby. You have nothing to fear from them, I assure you."

Mary regarded him with a mix of confusion and coolness, what Cassie thought might almost be contempt. "I don't believe," she said to Buchan, "that Mary is expressing fear."

"John Peyton," Mary said again.

"It's all right," Cassie said to her. "If there are things you have forgotten or are unsure of, we will ask John Peyton when he returns. Just tell us what you remember. All right?"

She nodded.

Cassie smiled across at the officer. "I think you may proceed."

Buchan cleared his throat and flipped through the notebook on his thigh. "Yes," he said, "very well then. Mary, according to John Peyton, you were taken by a party of Englishmen on March 6 of this year."

She looked to Cassie and then stared blankly at the officer.

"Were you forced to come away with them?"

She still didn't respond.

Cassie held her wrists together in front of herself. "Did they tie your hands, Mary?" she said. "Like this?"

She shook her head no. After a moment she sat forward in her chair and moved her hands behind her. She twisted so they could see the hands clasped at the small of her back.

"I see," Buchan said. He scribbled notes in his book. "Behind the back," he murmured and then raised his voice. "Did they strike you?"

She sat back in her chair, startled.

He raised his palms in apology and spoke more softly. "Did any of the

Englishmen hit you?" He showed her his fist and brandished it over his head.

Mary shook her head, slowly at first, and then more forcibly, as she seemed to piece together what was being asked of her.

"Did they —" he said. He shifted in his chair. "Did anyone *touch* you?"

"Captain, please," Cassie said.

"These are necessary questions, Miss Jure. I apologize if you feel they are an affront to your employers. Mary," he said.

The two women exchanged a look and Cassie nodded finally to encourage her. Mary shook her head no, although she was clearly uncertain what the exact nature of the question was.

The officer bent to his notebook. When he looked up from the page he said, "The man who was killed, Mary, who was he?"

She hesitated and turned to Cassie.

"Dead man," Cassie said softly. "Dead man on the ice, on the lake."

Mary nodded.

Cassie pointed to the Indian woman. "Your father?"

"No," she said. "No father."

Buchan broke in. "Brother, Mary? Husband? Uncle?"

Mary nodded. "Yes," she said.

Buchan sat forward. "Which one," he said. "Husband?"

"Yes," Mary said again.

He nodded and looked down to write the word *husband* in his notebook. "Captain."

He looked up to see Cassie staring at Mary. The Indian woman's face was tortured and expectant. She was waiting for something more.

"What is it?" he asked.

Cassie felt a cold trickle at the back of her neck. She leaned forward. "Dead man on the ice," she said. "Your brother, Mary?"

"Yes," she said.

Buchan slumped back in his chair. He made small disgusted motions across the face of the page with his pen. "I have a feeling this will be of very little use, I'm afraid," he said.

The two women were watching one another. Cassie could hear the wet labour of Mary's breathing. Her hands were folded over her bundle of clothing. Cassie said, "Captain, how many Red Indian men came down to meet John Peyton's party on the lake."

"Two," he said. "The man who was killed and the second man who ran off once the struggle ensued —"

"Husband *and* brother," Cassie said to Mary, raising her fingers in a *V*. "Two men. Two men dead."

Mary saw the growing expressions of consternation on their faces and she opened her mouth without speaking.

"Both shot," Buchan said, and he mimed holding a rifle to his shoulder. "Bang," he said. "Bang." He was sitting on the edge of his seat, incredulous. The notebook had fallen from his lap and lay face down on the floor like a wounded bird.

Mary had begun to cry and lifted her bundle of clothing to hide her face.

After Cassie settled Mary in her room she came back down the stairs and leaned in the doorway to the kitchen. Buchan had retrieved the fallen notebook from the floor and was sitting at the kitchen table, making notes and nodding furiously as he wrote.

"Why would they hide that?" she said. "Why admit killing one man and not another?"

"Obviously they felt the one reported could be justified before the courts. The second, quite clearly, could not."

"Perhaps she is lying."

"I have it on good authority our witness is a poor liar. And there is no profit to her in telling such a story."

Cassie shook her head. "Poor John Peyton."

He slapped the pen on the table. "I'm not convinced your sympathies are properly placed in this instance, Miss Jure."

She regarded Buchan with a puzzled expression. He had been clipped and professional in questioning Mary, cold, even obtuse. Not the same man to whom she'd confessed her father was a feckless drunk. "Do you think Mary is pretty?" she asked him.

He looked at Cassie and then quickly around the kitchen, as if the question had come from some invisible source.

"Do you find her attractive? As a woman?"

"Of course not," he said. "No, I retract that statement. What could it possibly have to do with anything of consequence?"

"I was simply curious." She shrugged. "What do you hope to see come out of all this, Captain?"

"Two men have been killed. Lies have been presented as fact. I want justice done."

Cassie looked behind her and up the stairway and then directly at the man across the room.

He said, "It perplexes me, Cassie, why you see fit to protect these men, seeing what they've been party to."

"It has never been my business," she said quietly, "to see what they have been party to."

Buchan shook his head. "Don't tell me you don't know the truth of what these men have done in their day."

Cassie bowed her head and whispered something he was unable to make out.

"What? What are you saying?"

"You are such a simpleton about the truth," she said. "You think there is never anything to fear from it."

The officer worked his jaw silently a moment.

"Tell me, does your wife deserve to know the truth, Captain Buchan?"

"I love my wife," he said.

"But that's only part of the story, isn't it?"

He stood from his chair. "I must ask you not to report the substance of our conversation with Mary to anyone. It would be best for the investigation if those involved believe their subterfuge remains intact. May I count on you in this regard?"

She shook her head slowly. "I will not promise that, no."

"So help me, I will use every means at my disposal to ensure that anyone undermining this investigation receives due attention."

She looked at her hands and raked absently beneath the fingernails. Buchan's belief in justice was so evangelical that at times it seemed completely irrational. Stories of the "Winter of the Rals" after the 1817 fires in St. John's had come to them on the northeast shore. Dozens of desperate men were arrested for stealing, for muggings, for disorderly conduct. The sentence for a first offence was thirty-six lashes, offenders stripped to the waist in the courtyard of Fort Townshend and tied on their knees to a four-foot post. Buchan was always present, overseeing the administration of punishment.

One Irishman in particular they'd been told of, a frosty-haired, pug-nosed father of seven, went straight back to robbing on the streets of St. John's after his release. The wounds of his first whipping were still open and raw when his shirt was stripped away from him in the courtyard. At the fifteenth lash, Buchan ordered a bucket of water thrown across the swollen, pulpy mess of his back. When the punishment resumed the frozen flesh came away in long raw strips and the Irishman eventually fainted, then fell into convulsions. The attending surgeon had to order the punishment stopped at the twenty-third stroke. John Senior related these details to Cassie with a kind of satisfied contempt. "Mr. Christian charity himself," he'd said.

Cassie looked up from her hands at Buchan. She saw his face as it had been when she knelt before him years before, the pale vulnerability of it, as if he was suffering through a fever of hallucination. The head tossing from side to side, the lips dry and parted slightly. She couldn't reconcile the conflicting pictures of him in her head.

"I am perfectly aware," she said, "of how seriously you take your office, Captain."

He took a step across the room. "There is a certain latitude I will allow you, Miss Jure, in light of the circumstances that briefly existed between us —"

"But?" Cassie said.

He couldn't bring himself to complete the threat and turned away from her, pulling the front door open roughly.

Through the window Cassie saw him walk away towards the landwash, past Corporal Rowsell who had been sitting on a hump of rock until the door opened and now stood at attention, his hands held at the small of his back. The officer's journal sat beside an inkwell on the table. She moved across the room and touched the pale calfskin cover. She opened it and flipped back and forth through the pages of closely written script without reading. From upstairs she could hear Mary coughing — long ripping convulsions like someone tearing sheets. She turned away suddenly and walked across the kitchen to her room, closing the door behind her.

Thirty seconds later she was back at the table. She dipped the pen in the inkwell, turned the journal sideways and began writing in the margin on a page chosen at random. *There was a child*, she wrote. *Before I ended it, David. I was pregnant.*

She set the pen down and looked up from the journal where the ink was slowly drying. John Peyton stood outside the window, watching her. She slapped the book shut and went immediately through the door. She walked up to Rowsell who was still standing at attention, his hands behind his back. "Captain Buchan forgot his journal," she said. Behind her she could hear the door open and close as Peyton went inside.

"Thank you, miss," Rowsell said. "I'll see he gets it."

Over the next three weeks John Peyton accompanied Buchan and a crew of marines in a cutter and gig, travelling through the Bay of Exploits with Mary in hopes of locating and surprising a camp of Beothuk they might safely leave her with. The weather was fair and seasonable, but Mary wore flannel underclothes beneath her dress and a heavy cloak as well. Peyton and Buchan consulted her on likely locations of Indian encampments, but her ill health and lethargy dampened everyone's hope for a successful outcome. They rowed forty miles west of Fortune Harbour to Badger Bay and a constant watch was kept to the shoreline for signs of fresh-cut paths that would indicate recent habitation by the Beothuk. On the evening of September 8, as they made way through a heavy thunder squall, a canoe was spotted a mile to the windward. The cutter gave chase, rounding a point of land beyond which the canoe had disappeared but there was no further sign of it. Buchan gave the order to come ashore where he guessed the Indians must have landed. He and Peyton and several marines spent more than an hour in pursuit through the bush. The marines grew increasingly sullen and uncomfortable the further they travelled inland from the cutter and Buchan finally relented and turned back. When they reached the shoreline they found Mary seated under a piece of canvas rigged up against the weather and showing no interest in the outcome of the chase.

The cutter was next taken up the River Exploits, rowed with muffled oars on a night guard almost twenty-five miles into the interior. Buchan and Peyton went into the woods with three marines, spending a full day in search of Indians. The only habitations they encountered had been abandoned since the previous summer. Mary remained at the camp and again gave no sign of wishing to join the search. They left the river that evening, rowing night guard all the way to the coast.

They camped near the mouth of Charles Brook and Buchan sat with Peyton after they had eaten. "That leaves us the area around Boyd's Cove to look into," he said.

"My guess is they've all begun moving up the river for the caribou hunt by this time."

"Another winter trek up the Exploits then," Buchan said brightly, as if he looked forward to the opportunity.

Peyton looked across to where Mary was bundled in a blanket on the opposite side of the fire. "If our girl lasts through to the freeze-up."

Both men sat quietly for a few minutes. "This is one of your rivers," Buchan said then.

Peyton nodded.

"Who's on this one?"

"Joseph Reilly."

"Anyone else near here?"

Peyton spat between his boots and kicked at the ground. The nights were coming on cold suddenly and he had his hands pushed deep into the pockets of his coat. "Richmond has a weir a little ways west of here on Little Rattle River. He has a green man up there with him, Michael Sharpe. Everyone else is a day's travel at least."

Buchan nodded. As far as he knew, Cassie had said nothing to Peyton about their conversation with Mary, but he couldn't be certain. "I wouldn't mind taking a side trip to look in on Mr. Richmond while we're about. Perhaps we could impose on Mr. Reilly and give the marines a day's rest here tomorrow."

"Burnt Island is no more than a couple hours' haul from here. We could give your men a roof over their heads for the night at our place."

Buchan shook his head. "The change of scenery would be good for the men," he said.

Peyton chuckled. He was about to say the scenery on Charles Brook was no different from the country they'd been picking through the last two weeks. But instead he said, "As you like, sir."

On the shoreline of Little Rattle River, Richmond and young Michael Sharpe were preparing the kit for winter trapping when the cutter first rounded a bend in the brook, making for the weir.

"Hello now," Richmond said.

Michael Sharpe looked up at Richmond and followed his gaze downriver. The colour went out of his face.

Richmond gave him an angry look. He pointed a finger. "Not a word to him, you hear me? I'm going up to the tilt. You send him on up when he gets here. Not a word or I'll cut your throat myself."

Michael Sharpe nodded and as Richmond snuck away up the bank he made an effort to look engrossed in the work lying about him.

When the cutter made the weir, Buchan stepped ashore and walked across to the young man. There were half a dozen traps on the ground, a large cauldron of water was boiling over a fire. The traps had been left out in weather to accumulate an even coat of rust and Michael Sharpe was using a wire brush to scrape down to the bare metal. Several freshly scraped traps were immersed in the kettle to boil clean.

"Michael Sharpe?" Buchan said to him.

The boy looked up at the officer. His face was reddened and raw across the cheeks, as if he had only recently begun shaving. He was sitting cross-legged on the ground with a trap in his lap. "Yes sir," he answered.

"I am Captain David Buchan of the HMS *Grasshopper*."

"I know who you are, sir."

Buchan crouched beside him. "And you know why I am here as well, I imagine."

The youngster nodded.

"I wonder could I ask you a few questions —"

"You'd best go on up to talk to Mr. Richmond, sir."

Buchan smiled at him. "You realize you could hang for your part in all this."

Michael Sharpe nodded again and burnished furiously at the trap. His hands were stained with a mixture of rust and sweat. He said, "Mr. Richmond is up at the tilt, sir."

Buchan waited a few moments longer, staring at the boy. Then he got to his feet and walked up the path to the tilt. He left the four marines outside the door to avoid offering any hint of fear or uncertainty on his part and stepped alone into the near dark. He could make out a rough table and chair in the foreground, a wood box piled high with junks of split spruce. A fire muttered to itself in the stone fireplace. There was a single window in the back wall that glowed with light. A voice from underneath it said, "You'll be closing the door behind you, if you don't mind."

"Of course," Buchan said. The voice had startled him and he moved quickly to pull the door closed. He turned back and squinted into the darkness. There was a rustle of movement and Richmond's silhouette passed across the square of light in the window. He came forward rubbing his eyes and combing his beard roughly with his fingers as if he had just woken from a nap. He nodded to the visitor. He was wearing a large, closely knit gansey that hung halfway to his knees. "You've only just caught me," Richmond said. "I was on my way down to the water. Did you see young Michael?"

"He directed me up from the river."

Richmond nodded and clanked a heavy kettle onto the crane over the fire. "Tea?" he said.

"May I have a seat?" Buchan asked, pointing at a chair beside the table.

"Wouldn't force you to drink a cup of tea by the door. What did Michael Sharpe have to say for himself?"

Buchan smiled. "Only that I would best talk to you."

Richmond nodded his head. "He's a quiet lad, young Michael."

They sat across from each other and Buchan looked around the tiny room as his eyes adjusted to the poor light. The packed dirt floor opposite the stove was stacked with Indian rackets of various sizes and shapes, traps, poles, coils of hemp rope, drag-twine, plain board, tools, netting, rolls of canvas, a bag of nails. The walls themselves were papered with what on closer inspection turned out to be the pages of a Methodist missionary magazine. Buchan leaned in to read a paragraph next to his head. "Regular subscriber?" he asked, nodding towards the walls.

"Can't read meself," Richmond said. "Bloody great armfuls of those things up at the church on Twillingate Island though." He reached out and slapped the wall with the palm of his hand. "Keeps the draught down a bit."

Buchan watched him a moment, the face almost masked — his beard covering the cheekbones nearly as high as his eyes, bushy mare-brows above them. "Were you born in Newfoundland, Mr. Richmond?"

"No sir. But I came here young enough to wish I had been, when I was a boy of eight or thereabouts." His family, he explained, settled on the west coast of Newfoundland, sharing a small sheltered bay with Tom Taylor's family, building a stagehead and splitting room and several tilts framed with saplings handy to the foot of the harbour. The latest in the endlessly recurring conflicts between Britain and France was underway and the French Shore, as that part of the island was known, had been abandoned by French fishermen.

At that age he and Tom Taylor worked on shore with his grandfather and mother and Mrs. Taylor and several of the other older children, carrying mounds of wet fish in handbarrows from the press piles to wash them in the shoals, spreading the clean cod to dry on the flakes and constantly turning them to keep the sun from scorching the flesh. Richmond's father and Mr. Taylor were on the water each day with two hired men, hand-lining for cod. They skiffed out to the grounds before the wick of first light was lit and worked there until they'd brought up the full of the boat or until the onset of darkness forced them ashore. They worked with thirty-fathom lines, their hooks baited in the first weeks of May with mussels dug from sandy beaches, then with seine-hauled herring, and by mid-June with the capelin that came ashore to spawn in such unbelievable numbers a boy could stand knee-deep in the landwash and dip them from the water in nets or baskets.

Richmond shook his head, as if that harvest still amazed him, the lavish roil of silver bodies about his shins, hundreds of the capelin shovelled onto a small patch of garden for fertilizer, thousands more simply rotting on the beach after the gulls had their fill.

The kettle, which was still warm when it was set over the fire, came to a full rolling boil and Richmond got up to see to the tea. He had the permanent hunch of large men used to stooping under doors and low ceilings. It made him seem coiled, Buchan thought, unpredictable. Richmond picked up two cups from a sideboard and stared into them for a moment. He blew into them in turn, held them upside down and shook them and stared into them again. He poured without straining the leaves.

"How did you come to this part of the country?" Buchan asked.

Richmond looked across at him with a queer grin that made Buchan's stomach turn. "The war ended is what happened," he said cheerfully. He passed the officer his tea.

Four years after they arrived on the west coast, the Treaty of Versailles returned the entire French Shore to France, extending the territory south of Pointe Riche to Cape Ray. In the months that followed, the French drove English settlers from Sop's Arm, Holm Point, Noddy Bay, Hawkes Bay, River of Ponds and Port Saunders. News of these expulsions reached all the English on the French Shore as fishermen abandoned their homes further up the coast.

Richmond's grandfather had died of pneumonia their second winter in the harbour and they'd wrapped his body in a sheet of canvas and buried him in a tiny clearing among the trees above the cove. It was like planting a flag. The hired men left as soon as they could secure a berth to St. John's, but Richmond's father vowed not to surrender his home and Mr. Taylor promised to stand beside him.

That fall Richmond and his father dragged three cords of spruce logs out of the woods with their dog and had set to splitting and stacking the junks behind their tilt. "I was just a little bedlamer in them days," Richmond said. The handle of the axe stood as high as his chin and he arced the heavy blade awkwardly overhead, coming off his feet to add his weight to each strike.

His father wiped the sweat from his face with a ratty handkerchief and looked away across the harbour. He stopped and stared, shading his eyes with his hand.

The vessel brought in its sails as it floated partway into the bay and anchored offshore. Three boats rowed up to the Richmond fishing room and the entire population of the harbour came down to greet the English marines. They stood at the edge of the wharf and shouted to the men in the boats and applauded. The Royal Navy had come to them. It was as unexpected and miraculous as a visitation of angels.

On the stagehead, a young officer with a face as sharp as a mole's and a white powdered wig unscrolled a parchment to read a proclamation from John Campbell, governor of Newfoundland. He quoted King George's promise to prevent his subjects from interrupting the French fishery by their competition and ended with the governor's direct order to remove all fixed English settlements on the French Shore.

Richmond's mother, pregnant with her eighth child and nearing her time, put a hand to her mouth and began crying silently. The officer escorted the men into the buildings and allowed them to gather any valuables that could be easily transported, then returned with them to the stagehead. He turned to the marines and nodded and they marched up to the shelters where they carried the split firewood inside the largest building and set it alight, then set fire to the tilt beside it and to the few outbuildings nearby. Everything of use was left inside and two armed soldiers prevented the families from attempting any rescue. The marines removed the settlers under guard to the vessel waiting in the harbour and then they burned the stage house and the wharf as well.

Richmond recounted these events impassively, as if he was reading them from a text, but Buchan could feel the weight behind the words, their intent. The noise of the fire beside them like an echo of that earlier fire passed down through the years. He stared at Richmond with the same counterfeit impassiveness, refusing to give him the satisfaction of any visible response. He set his feet flat on the packed earth floor. He said, "Where is your family now, Mr. Richmond?"

"My father is dead some years now. My mother, I believe, is in London."

"Is that where her people are from?"

Richmond drank from his cup and winced at the scalding heat. He turned his head to spit fragments of tea leaf from his mouth. "My mother is Welsh."

Buchan nodded into his mug. It smelled of salt pork.

"You'll be wanting to talk about what happened at the lake, I s'pose," Richmond said then, to indicate he was through gaming about.

"I have a few questions, yes." Buchan pulled out his notebook and rummaged in a pocket until he located a lead. He said, "You were one of the shooters, Mr. Richmond?"

Richmond raised his eyes above the rim of his mug.

"You were one of the men who shot the Red Indian," Buchan repeated.

"He had Master Peyton on the ice by the throat."

"John Senior."

Richmond nodded angrily. "Yes, John Senior. By the throat, as I said. And he would've strangled him unless some action got taken."

"An unarmed Indian man approached a party of eight settlers brandishing rifles and, unprovoked, he accosted one of the party. Is that correct?"

"That is how I feature it, as far as I can remember. He come down off the shore carrying a sprig of white spruce. He walked straight up to the lot of us and started in to talking. He went on with his arms flicing about and no sense to be made of a single word. We just looked at one another. He kept pointing to the woman and striking his chest" — Richmond used his own fist to demonstrate — "and waving at the wigwams on the shore. Then he stepped in and shook John Peyton's hand and the hands of several others. It seemed we might come out of it without bloodshed at that point."

"But you did not."

"He took the woman by the arm then as if to walk off with her, you see. And John Senior made it clear he would do no such thing."

"Even though he was simply attempting to protect his wife."

Richmond gave a little laugh. "Whether she was wife or no, as I said, we couldn't understand a sound the savage made. And our party was attempting to bring out a Red Indian with the blessing of Your Lordship, the governor." Buchan suppressed a grunt of dissatisfaction and Richmond said, "They got all in a roke then, both of them shouting, John Senior rhyming off the oaths. And the Indian grabbed him by the throat and commenced to choking him."

"That's when you and Mr. Taylor stepped in?"

Richmond nodded his head.

"Was there no other course of action open to you? There were eight of you to face a single Indian."

Richmond said, "The facts are the facts and I regret your disliking them, sir. But dislike is not enough to alter the past. He was nearly as large as myself, an awful length of a brute. He had hold of a seventy-year-old man and was not about to give him up. Tom Taylor and I laid onto him with the butts of our rifles and we battered him about the head, but he would not relent." He paused and considered the officer observing him. "A curious thing it is to me, sir, that you are more concerned with the death of this Indian than the murder of your own men on that selfsame lake."

"Your curiosity," Buchan said slowly, "is irrelevant."

"And is the curiosity of those men you've got standing outside the door irrelevant?"

More than likely then, Buchan guessed, he had not been sleeping when they arrived.

Richmond said, "Odds of fifty years now, John Senior and his like have been fighting for this shore. You know yourself there's been deaths on both sides. And you thought going up the river to hand out a few blankets would take the savage out of that lot."

"I had hopes we might change their view of us."

"You hoped to have the governor kiss your heroic little arse."

"Mr. Richmond —"

"I know your kind."

"Mr. Richmond —"

"You'd fuck your own mother if the King gave the order."

"Mr. Richmond!"

He sat up at mock attention. "Sir," he shouted.

Buchan gripped his tunic at the waist and pulled it straight. He wanted to take the pistol from his belt and shoot from inches away, to blow the man's nose through the back of his head.

Corporal Rowsell stuck his head in the doorway. "Captain, sir," he said.

Buchan raised his hand without turning his head. He waved the corporal back outside. He said, "You shot the Indian, Mr. Richmond, is that correct?"

"John Peyton ordered us to get the Indian off his father, yes. I stepped away and used my rifle. I shot him once in the back at close range and even then we had to pry his hands free of John Senior's neck."

"After the Indian had been shot, what did you do?"

"Sir, we collected spruce branches and covered the corpse on the ice, sir."

"The second Indian. What became of him?"

"He run off, to the best of my knowledge."

"No additional shots were fired?"

Richmond turned his head to look at the officer. "Not that I recall, sir, no."

"And then what?"

"We spent the night in one of the Indian wigwams, sir. We collected our belongings what had been stole from John Peyton's boat. We carried the Indian woman down the river to the Peyton house along with a quantity of furs we felt we had some claim to by way of compensation for losses."

"Was there any contact with other Indians on the way down the river?"

"Not of the Red persuasion, no."

"Of which persuasion then?"

Richmond rapped the knuckles of one hand against the tabletop. "A Micmac trapper is all."

"Does this trapper have a name?"

"Noel Young."

"You knew this man?"

"Everyone on the shore knows Noel Young. He kipped down with us for the night and we went our separate ways in the morning."

Buchan nodded and made a note in the journal. "Did the woman come down the river willingly?"

"She did not say, that I recall, one way or the other."

"In your opinion," Buchan said. "Based on your observations."

Richmond settled back into his habitual slump. "She had little choice in the matter, now, did she?"

"She tried twice to escape, is that right?"

"Twice she took a stroll into the woods at an hour that might lead one to see it as an attempt to run off. Perhaps she meant to take care of some delicate business and lost her way."

Buchan tapped his pencil against the page.

"We had the governor's blessing to take a Red Indian back from the lake," Richmond said again.

"But not, I believe, to murder two men in the process."

Richmond leaned back from the table as far as his chair allowed.

"The second Indian on the ice. I don't believe you were the shooter, Mr. Richmond, there would hardly have been time to reload."

"He run off," Richmond said.

"He may have run, yes. But he was shot and killed as he did so. Without provocation. In cold blood. And I promise you, Mr. Richmond, someone will pay for that."

Richmond stood from his seat.

"You have an opportunity now to save yourself from the gallows."

"I have a fair bit of work to do before dark," Richmond said. "I trust you enjoyed your tea." He took the still half-full mug from where it sat in front of the officer and emptied the contents onto the floor, then made his way out the door into the piercing afternoon light.

Richmond strode past the marines outside the tilt and made his way to the shoreline where Michael Sharpe was lifting traps from the cauldron with a metal hook. He was in a fury and cursed at his green man and pulled the hook from his hands. "You'll only make a shag of this," he muttered. "Watch out now." There was a large wooden bucket of water with a layer of beeswax floating on the surface beside the kettle. Richmond plunged the steaming trap into the bucket and waited a moment for it to cool, then lifted it slowly through the wax so it would take on an even coat.

Buchan and the marines came down to the cutter and pushed off into the water and they left without a word to the men on the beach. Michael Sharpe looked across at Richmond for some sign of what had gone on behind the tilt's closed door, but the older man refused to catch his eye as he went about his work. Richmond hung the freshly coated trap from a nail in the seine-gallows and went to the kettle for another.

He had never talked much of his time on the French Shore, of being burnt out by the navy, not even to Tom Taylor. He'd told the story to Buchan intending to get under the officer's skin, and was surprised to find how savagely it burred at him as well. When they were released from the navy vessel in St. John's, the two families booked passage on a ship bound for London. Mrs. Taylor attended Richmond's mother when she delivered a still-born child halfway across the Atlantic. Richmond hadn't seen England in years and the filth and the noise he had taken no notice of at the time were terrifying. The families shared two small rooms near the Thames. All night an unruly tide of traffic and shouting roared in the streets below their windows. The crowds of people and animals roaming free and the slop in the street made his skin crawl. Even the Thames was slubby and clouded and stank like a bog pond.

In the mornings, Richmond and Taylor accompanied their fathers to the dockyards where the men sometimes took a day's wages unloading a vessel arriving from Africa or the Caribbean. When there was no work the men took their sons to the skittles grounds where they gambled away bits of the precious little money they had, or sat with them in alehouses and drank it away instead.

In late November, Richmond's mother secured a position as a wet nurse and housekeeper for a well-to-do family and he rarely saw her in the months that followed. Her youngest was still breast-feeding and the infant was nursed by Mrs. Taylor. Even if Richmond was awake when she arrived home, she barely acknowledged him or her husband, stripping down to her small clothes in the dark and falling immediately to sleep. In the morning she was gone before he woke.

She used to sing her children to sleep at night — old Welsh songs of a beauty that made his toes curl — but that winter the songs he'd grown up with disappeared for good, though the change went practically unnoticed in the flood of changes that overcame them in England. Once it was decided they would head back to Newfoundland in the spring, Richmond expected things to return to normal and much about their lives did. But the Welsh songs that his mother had carried from her own childhood seemed to have died inside her like the daughter delivered on the Atlantic and buried now at sea. Richmond had never learned to speak but a few words of her native tongue and could bring to mind only the thinnest scraps of the melody or lyrics, though the sensation of hearing them never left him. And like the dead child, those songs came to occupy a hollow place in Richmond's life, faceless and nameless and lost as they were.

T E N

John Senior came to himself in the dark, shaken awake by his own shouting, by the stifled thrashing of his arms. He stared into the blackness, his body roked in sweat, breath ragging in his throat like a branch of thorns. He could hear his heart's panic, like the manic barking of a dog behind a closed door.

The rasp of the ocean's surf through the open window. It always surprised him how dry a sound it was, like someone kicking through dead leaves in the fall. He turned to the window, hoping for the barest glim of light that might justify his getting out of bed.

He heard footsteps underneath his bedroom, muffled activity in the kitchen. Cassie up and starting the fire. He dressed in the dark, then felt his way downstairs to the kitchen where Cassie was kneeling at the hearth, nursing the new fire.

"I woke you," he said.

She turned from the frail light to look up at him in the doorway. "I was already up," she told him. It was an old lie between them, one he never questioned. She poured the kettle full with water and set it on the crane. "Tea now the once," she said.

He nodded at her and took the bucket she had just emptied and a second wooden container to go down to the brook for water. The stars were still bright. There was silver thaw on the ground from a spell of freezing rain some time through the night. The chill in the air made his skin feel tight across the shoulders. The freshwater brook ran fifty yards off the side of the house and rattled into the ocean at the foot of the cove. He walked towards the steady murmur of it, the dirt path under his feet trodden hard as rock. At the riverbank he balanced over stones as the buckets dipped and dragged full with darkness. Before he turned to start up the path he looked out across the water to the crooked arm of land that sheltered the cove.

He was a boy of seventeen the first time he arrived on the northeast shore, coming across from Poole with Harry Miller in April of 1766. They disembarked on Fogo Island and took Miller's sloop into the Bay of Exploits, a spill of rough country almost uninhabited by Europeans at the time, the coastline shadowed by a ragtag fleet of smaller islands. Humpbacked granite, dark pelts of spruce. Barely submerged skerries breaking white water. Most of the winter's snow was still on the ground, which suggested there was no colour to the land but white and the wet black of the forest and grey shades of ocean and fog and stone. Just sailing through the raw country set John Senior's heart on edge. It made him feel he was capable of anything.

Among the islands there wasn't enough drift to allow the sloop to travel any direction in a straight line. Miller cut and tucked through the tangle of ragged rocks and sunkers as if he was making up the route as he went. They came to anchor in the same small cove where John Senior now stood, below what was nothing more than a single-storey spruce tilt with boarded windows at the time. Two boats were hauled high up on the beach and overturned, covered by canvas and a layer of spruce branches. An uneven ring of hills rose into a thickening shawl of fog behind the shelter.

Miller stood at the gunnel of the sloop and opened the spair of his trousers to piss into the harbour. "How does she strike you, Mr. Peyton?" he asked.

John Senior didn't know if he was referring to the cove or the miserable-looking little tilt or to the country in general. "Well enough, I guess," he said carefully.

Miller grunted. He fastened his trousers and spat into the water. "She's a whore is what she is," he said. The country he was talking about, the place itself. "She'll spread her legs for you, but you'll have to pay for the privilege, don't forget it." He smiled across at John Senior. He was obviously content with such arrangements. He was happy to be back. The fog capped in the cove, the backdrop of hills disappearing behind it.

There was something in John Senior's memory of that first arrival that brought the tidal bore terror of the dream back to him. He had carried it with him across the Atlantic from the old country, he knew. There was a long period of years when it lay dormant and he thought he had outgrown or simply outlasted it somehow and for a while he forgot it entirely. But it came back to him before John Peyton moved over from Poole and it was becoming more persistent as he grew older. The dream had changed only in the sense that it became murkier with time, less articulate. Like a cloth dyed with the colours of fifty years, it grew ever darker, the stain deeper and more sinister. Always he was flailing his arms, hands balled into fists or holding something cold and hard, and he was beating something helpless beneath him, something utterly defenceless. Each time he woke from the nightmare yelling, begging himself to stop.

He started up the hill from the brook, moving as quickly as his burden allowed, slopping water from both buckets as he went.

It was the first time in months that Cassie and John Senior spent time alone in one another's company. They ate in silence but for the clatter and scrape of cutlery and the regular clicking of John Senior's jaw as he chewed, the sound like a clockwork sprocket marking time. He had seemed unconcerned about Buchan's prying while the officer was in the house and hadn't mentioned him since he left with John Peyton and Mary, but his churlish manner seemed heavier than she remembered. He refused to talk even about the course of the day's work, the weather. Most nights the Old Hag dragged him out of sleep and he woke Cassie with his yelling.

She had always maintained a rigid lack of curiosity about what the old man was thinking, about his personal life or his past. Her affection for John Senior was clean and uncomplicated, a limited thing but genuine, and it had endured unchanged for years. She had overheard enough scraps of conversation in her days to know he had been party to rough dealings on the shore, but more detail than that she was willing to forego. Insisted on foregoing, in fact. She navigated her way around John Senior like a blinkered horse on a well-worn path, looking neither right nor left. It was enough for her that he was forthright and fair in his dealings with her, that his taste for drink never led to crying jags or fits of wild pacing and stammering. That he never laid a hand on her.

But she watched him now with a question in her head and nothing she did to distract herself from it was any help. She knew it was impossible to come at it directly and one evening after she brought him his tea she said, "Why did the Reds kill Harry Miller?"

John Senior shifted in his seat. "No saying why that crowd does what it does." He looked at her steadily then as if something about her had changed, her hair or the colour of her eyes, and he was at a loss to say exactly what it was.

"Joe Reilly said he was a hard man."

He nodded. "As hard a man as ever I seen. There's any number of stories could account for the Reds disliking him. Not one of them is fit for a woman's ears, Cassie."

"I know hard things have been done on the shore."

John Senior shook his head. "What you know," he said softly, "amounts to a piece of dun fish."

"I'll let you know when I've had enough."

He said, "I think I would prefer a drop of rum to this tea."

In the fall of 1781, a group of Beothuk delayed their trip down the River Exploits to the winter camp until after Harry Miller left his house on Burnt Island. He was on his way into St. John's with the season's catch and from there was travelling to Poole. He rarely made the trip to England any more, but was making an exception to attend the wedding of his business partner.

On a clear night at the end of September, after they'd watched Miller and his hired men nail boards over the windows and set the sails of a sloop packed with barrels of dried salmon, they struck up a fire near the front step and lit long torches of dry reeds wrapped at the top of sticks and circled the building to set it alight. They shouted into the flames and sang as the wood popped and the windows cracked and melted behind their temporary shutters. Smoke poured from the chimney and then the roof began leaking smoke through its thatch. The fire climbed the lengthening vines of the song the Beothuk chanted into the night until it had lifted a second storey of red light above the building. When the walls collapsed, the Indians dragged up two boats that had been overturned and sheltered above the beach and added them to the fire.

By the next evening the square of char and ash had cooled enough to be picked through and the Beothuk used the ends of their torch sticks to turn the ruined wood and sharded panes of glass and cracked porcelain and pieces of leather. The long, square-headed nails they were hunting for were black with soot and still too hot to touch with a bare hand. They were flicked into piles and left another night to cool. Other bits and scraps of metal — blackened pots and cutlery, brass buttons and several buckles, the cast-iron crane from the fireplace — were gathered as well. All of this salvage was packed and carried up the river and at the winter camp hammered and worked to some use among the Red Indians or thonged into jewellery or simply displayed as trophy.

Miller and John Senior were at the rail of their sloop which had wintered in St. John's. Miller was singing a bawdy song about a wedding night, a song he'd returned to repeatedly and sung at length during the trip back from England. There was no malice apparent in his rendition and it seemed almost a mindless occupation. Occasionally he would come to himself and the song he was singing aloud and the recently altered status of the man in his company would make contact in his mind. "Oh me," he'd say and he'd slap John Senior's back.

He was singing *Her arse was white as a chamber pot* as they rounded the point of land behind which his house once stood. The last of the season's snow still covered the blackened ruins so that it seemed the building had simply vanished. For a moment Miller considered that he had mistaken Cox's Cove for his own and that he still had half a day's travel to reach his station. "Oh me," he said.

John Senior braced for a slap across the shoulders. He looked up when it didn't come and then into the harbour where Miller was staring. "Those bloods-a-bitches," he said.

All summer Miller brooded over his losses in his misleadingly cheerful manner. He whistled and hummed as he worked and composed ditties to old tunes in his head, singing them with such regularity that they came to him unbidden and almost unnoticed. Once a month John Senior rowed in to Burnt Island to spend several days helping to finish Miller's new home and the two sat up through most of the night drinking. Late into the bottle, Miller would sing all the new songs he'd come up with since their last visit. "This one, this one," he said to John Senior, his index finger pointed at the ceiling.

Pray, you Indians, what burned me house
you're bound to die like vermin louse.
I've loaded me gun with powder and ball
I'll hunt you down and kill you all. Hey!

John Senior fixed him with a drunken look of disgust for his childish rhymes, which Miller misinterpreted.

"Don't pretend you've got religion on me, John Peyton. If it had been your house, you wouldn't have waited till the fall to light into the bastards."

In late September of 1782, when the summer's business had concluded and before trapping began, Miller, John Senior and William Cull, who had stopped through on his way to St. John's, rowed into Ship Cove and then took a jaunt up the River Exploits. There hadn't yet been a significant fall of snow and the heart of the caribou migration was still several weeks off, so they expected to come upon Red Indians somewhere well short of the lake. Each man carried a musket, bayonet and hatchet, and a pack weighted with eight pounds of hard tack, a piece of salt pork, ammunition and a quart of rum. The weather was poor with rain and wind, and they made slow progress through the dense bush along the riverside. After three days' travel they came within hearing of a group of Indians in the landwash of a small cove. They crept close enough to make out four mamateeks in a clearing and half a dozen Indians crouched among canoes near the water, the hides of several caribou stretched on the shoreline. Each of the white men removed his pack and loaded his musket. John Senior poured thirty-six balls into the barrel of his gun. Miller smiled his gap-toothed smile across at him. He tamped ten fingers of powder into his own weapon. "No sense saving fire," he said quietly.

As soon as they broke into the clearing the Indians began shouting and dispersing into the woods. Miller and Cull shot at the running figures but John Senior fired directly into the mamateeks, the fan of musket balls ripping through the bark coverings. As he reloaded, men and women ran or limped from the entrances into the trees, some of them carrying children.

Within minutes the sudden confusion of noise and motion in the cove had swirled into a quiet broken only by the muffled sounds of weeping and moans from within the mamateeks. The three white men approached cautiously, two entering each shelter in turn while the third stood guard outside. In one shelter they found an old man who had taken a musket ball in the gut and was unable to stand. He held a trap-bed in his lap that he had been working against a stone. He was bleeding through the fingers of the hand that cupped his belly, and the lap of his leather cassock and the trap-bed were red with it. He stared at the two strangers standing before him and sucked air in gasps through clenched teeth. He wept and repeated a single grunted syllable between breaths.

"What do you figure he's saying, Miller?"

"Couldn't begin to guess. I'll bet you two good oars that's one of our traps though."

John Senior stepped forward and bent to pick up the trap-bed. The Indian swung it then with a small fierce motion that caught the side of the white man's face and sliced into his ear. Miller stepped back and levelled his musket, but John Senior had already pulled the bed from the Indian's hand and was beating him about the head with it. The old man bent to the ground and raised a single arm uselessly against the blows until he lost consciousness, and John Senior continued striking with the sharp edge of the metal until he was too exhausted to lift it any longer. He stood catching his breath over the dead man. The battered skull showed through the long shearing wounds and tiny yellow flecks of bone had landed on John Senior's boots. His trousers were sprayed with blood.

Miller stood in silence a few moments and then said, "That old fucker had all his teeth." He tongued the array of spaces in his mouth. They were like palings gone from a fence. "Did you see that, John? That seems an unfair thing to my mind."

"Shut up, Miller," he said. He lifted his hand to his ear and then examined his fingers, but couldn't tell if the blood he found there was his own or that of the old Indian man lying dead at his feet.

They found a quantity of meat in the nearby shelters and two women huddled together in the last mamateek. The older woman was crippled by shot, which made it impossible for her to hobble away into the woods, and the younger had stayed behind with her. The white men stoked the fire there and cooked a large meal of caribou which John Senior found himself unable to stomach. He sat off to one side while Miller and Cull licked and sucked at the fresh caribou and wiped the juice that dribbled down their chins with their sleeves. He had never particularly liked his partner, but the strength of the disgust he felt watching the man eat surprised and perplexed him. He felt suddenly nauseous and made his way out into the open air.

Miller watched him go with a shrug. "There's food enough for all in that case," he said to the two women. The younger of the two would not make eye contact with the white men or look anywhere but directly into her lap, but the older woman was vocal and defiant. Miller held a morsel of caribou on a stick towards her and she spit on it and laid into him with a stream of incomprehensible invective. Her face was darkened with red ochre and the accumulated soot of a hundred cooking fires.

"Now Old Smut," Miller said, "that's a fine piece of meat you ruined."

He offered it instead to the younger woman. She would not look up from her lap and he touched it to her chin, leaving a dark stain there.

"Fancy a bit of dessert?" Miller said to Cull.

John Senior was folding the caribou skins into bundles and tying them to his pack. The bodies of the dead lay around and just beyond the camp. He kept his mind on the task at hand, refusing to estimate the number they'd killed, to guess at their ages. He dragged the birchbark canoes up from the shoreline, pushing them into the doorways of the abandoned mamateeks. There were odd rustlings and grunts and the sound of a woman crying from the occupied dwelling. When Miller came outside he was buttoning his trousers and singing the wedding song he'd tormented John Senior with all the way across the Atlantic. He walked to meet his partner across the clearing. "Mr. Cull has chosen," he said grandly and with a note of derision, "to abstain." He gave a little bow and pointed towards the mamateek with a flourish. "She is all yours, Mr. Peyton, sir."

John Senior could smell it off the man, the juice of seared meat, the marshy odour of semen, the sharp palpable fear of the Indian women. He gave Miller a look and then turned away to busy himself with his pack.

"Which just goes to show," Miller said angrily, "that marriage sucks all pleasure out of a man's life. And don't say I didn't tell you so."

They set each mamateek afire before they left. The two women had been brought out into the clearing and there was some talk of carrying them up to the coast but John Senior would have none of it. They left them sitting in each other's arms in the savage light, their backs turned to the white men's sullen but leisurely retreat.

Cassie had poured a drink for herself as John Senior told his story. He'd never seen her touch a drop in all her time in the house and it seemed a clear sign that everything he knew was about to change for good. He topped up his glass and refilled hers as well. They sat drinking in silence a while. He felt light-headed and reckless. All the time he was speaking he'd waited for Cassie to stop him, to say she'd heard enough. But she had let him go until he finished. He'd never told this story to anyone, although different versions of it had been told by others in his presence. It surprised him how complete his rendition was, how little he'd censored it in Cassie's presence, as if he'd composed it in his head years ago and was merely waiting for this opportunity to recount it.

Cassie turned the glass of rum in her hand. She had several times stopped herself from speaking for fear of her voice breaking. She took a quick slug and through the grimace she said, "I had no idea."

He made a dismissive motion with his hand and a moment later he reached to touch her forearm. Cassie sat back in the chair, pulling away from him, shaking her head.

"Mary told him about the other Red Indian being killed on the lake," she said. "He knows."

"Who knows?"

"Captain Buchan."

John Senior said, "That little man."

Cassie set her jaw. "Was it you who killed him, John Senior?" She was whispering through her teeth.

The old man looked across at her quickly and then covered his face with his hands.

She nodded. She got up and began stacking dishes to take them from the table.

John Senior pressed his eyes so hard he saw the white of stars behind the lids. There was a sullen insolence to the clatter she made, he thought, to the rough way she handled the plates and cutlery. Cassie reached across the table to take the plate sitting between his elbows. He crossed his arms in front of himself and they stared at each other a moment. He saw in her face something of the same misery and derision that twisted his mother's expression the morning she walked in on him cleaning the diaper in his father's sickroom, her neck and cheek marked by the deep indentations of sleeping on a rough straw pillow. He wanted to tell Cassie how it was his mother's hurt still alive in him that led to the invitation that brought her to the Bay of Exploits. He said, "You know why I come for you in St. John's."

Cassie shook her head angrily. "You don't know anything about why I left. Why I've stayed here."

John Senior stared. "What's that now?" he said. He pictured Cassie as the young woman who stood before him in the house beside the tavern when he offered her a position on the northeast shore. That old unanswered question hanging in the air again: *His wife or his daughter?*

He had never known what to make of the fact that Cassie and John Peyton hadn't managed to hook, or who was to blame for it, though it was clear after enough time passed that it wasn't to happen. And his own wanting had been kindled then, seeing her stand naked before him in a wash of sunlight in the kitchen of the summer house. He could still picture the stare she'd given him, bald and unequivocal, but he wasn't able to settle whether it was meant as invitation or challenge. His uncertainty made him turn away from her and he never afterwards took it further than lying awake nights, having her in his mind. Even that he felt unaccountably ashamed of, wiping his thighs and belly clean with his shirt in the dark of his room, and he was unable to hold Cassie's eye in the light of morning. *Daughter or wife?* Daughter. Wife.

The air went out of his lungs. He felt as if he had fallen from a height onto his back and was too stunned to move. "My gentle Jesus," he whispered. "Your father didn't, Cassie."

"Of course he did," she said. "Of course."

It was contempt he heard in her voice. As if she was insulted to have to state something so obvious. She lifted the stack of dishes in her hands and walked away towards the pantry. Already making up her mind to leave, he could see.

"I been good to you," he shouted after her.

ELEVEN

At Reilly's salmon weir the marines were lying about the sand beach which caught and held the surprising afternoon heat of the sun. Most of them had removed shoes and stockings and covered their faces with handkerchiefs. A cast-iron pot on an improvised crane steamed over a fire.

Buchan found Mary and Peyton in the company of Joseph Reilly and Annie Boss and their three youngest children outside the tilt. Peyton and Reilly were sitting on stumps, leaning forward on their knees and talking until they caught sight of the officer. Reilly stood as he came up to them. The two Indian women were seated on the ground with the children. Mary was more animated than Buchan had ever seen her. She coddled and teased and clicked her tongue as the boy and two girls crawled across her lap.

Peyton said, "How was your visit with Mr. Richmond?"

"About what I expected."

Peyton nodded and the men fell into talk about Reilly's luck with the salmon this season and what the winter might have in store. Mary wandered off momentarily and returned with long strips of dry birchbark from wood cut and stacked near the tilt. As the white men talked she peeled the thin inner layer of bark from the sheet and folded it in half, then four, then eight. She spoke to the children in her native tongue, which they couldn't understand, and she threw out an occasional phrase of English. "You wait," she said as she pressed the bark between her teeth, turned and bit the bark, unfolded once and bit again. When she was done she held the bark at arm's-length and lifted each fold slowly before the children who were completely still and silent. The men stopped speaking as well and turned to watch her. The opened sheet of bark showed the impression of a clearly detailed flower.

The children held their hands to their faces, the adults applauded. Mary folded another piece of bark and produced an image of a mamateek in the same fashion. Then a canoe, then a paddle. She seemed to have briefly forgotten her situation, lost in a child's game she had practised a thousand times in her young life. A man wearing Indian rackets. A copse of trees.

Peyton said, "We've asked Annie to do what she can for the rattle on Mary's stomach."

The Mi'kmaq woman looked across at the officer. She rubbed her hands along the length of her thighs. "Got something on to boil, keep it close to the skin when she sleep tonight."

If it was consumption, as everyone suspected, there was nothing to be done for her. But no one said as much.

Buchan said, "I wish my surgeon had accompanied us, he would have been interested to know what you are preparing."

"No secret," Annie Boss said and she laughed. She pushed herself to her feet. "Come up and see."

They walked in together with one of Annie's children. The tilt smelled of spruce gum and brine and potash. There was a mewling from the back of the room where a slut with a litter of new puppies lay beneath a wooden bunk. Buchan crouched to look in on them. The eyes of the pups were still closed and they nestled into the dog's belly, fighting for the teats. The mother growled at his boots.

"She contrary today," Annie said. She was standing next to the fireplace and looked down at her daughter who was clinging to her dress. "Know how she feels sometimes." She laughed and covered the girl's face for a moment with her hand. She spoke a few words in Mi'kmaq and her daughter skipped out the door.

Buchan stood and walked across the room. The pot on the crane was filled with a mixture of leaves and roots boiling in water. Annie stirred the concoction and lifted some of the lank green into the air.

"Wrap in a cloth," she said. "Put it here." She touched her breastbone with the flat of her hand.

"A poultice," Buchan said, nodding. "What else do you use it for?"

"Bad head, broken bone. Burn." Annie smiled. "Use it on Joe Jep's hand, fix it right up."

"Your husband?" Buchan said. His look shifted, his curiosity suddenly sharpened and focused. "How long ago was that, Annie?"

"When we meet, years now. John Senior bring him out to White Bay, his hand gone black then, bad, bad smell, whew," she said, waving her free hand before her face.

"What did he say had happened to his hand?"

Annie's smile flickered like a candle crossed by a breeze. She looked back to the pot of boiling leaves. "Willow leaf and Indian Cup," she said pointing with the spoon, "bark of boxy fir."

"Annie," he said.

She looked back at the white man. She was still smiling, and pointed the spoon at him. "Joe Jep a good man," she said.

Joseph Reilly cooked up a feed that evening of pan-fried salmon in pork scruncheons with boiled potatoes. The spuds had just been dug out of the ground and were served under spoonfuls of the pork fat and fried onions. There was fresh dark bread to wipe the plates clean. A large pot of black tea was kept hot over the fire. Down on the beach the marines made do with a stew of salmon tails.

Mary had no appetite and sat with the youngest children on the floor. They held blind puppies in their laps while the mother shifted on her haunches and whined beside them. She leaned her long snout into the laps of each person in turn to sniff and lick at her young and then lifted her nose as if testing the air. Mary began talking to the dog in the same way she spoke to the children, in a singsong mix of Beothuk and English, and the animal cocked her head to listen, then stood and began barking in response.

The people at the table turned to the noise for a moment before going back to their conversation.

Annie Boss was saying she'd grown up in Red Indian country, but they kept clear of the Mi'kmaq same as they did the whites. She never saw one in the flesh before she was a girl of ten, travelling with her mother and father and her brother on a river near Grand Lake. Her father had been hunting and they had killed and quartered a caribou, the dressed meat packed between them in their canoe. Before dusk they sighted the light of a fire through the woods ahead and landed their canoe nearby. They walked through alder bush and spruce trees towards the fire and came upon a Red Indian shelter. Her father went to the entrance and pulled back the leather doorway. An old man and woman sat there, a boy almost a man, a young girl about Annie's age. They were roasting three tiny jays on sticks over the fire and they all looked to be — Annie paused and spoke a few words to Reilly in Mi'kmaq.

"Starved," he said. "Starving."

Annie nodded. They all looked to be starving, she said. They made no sign at first, no movement or sound, as if they thought the visitors might simply remove themselves if they remained motionless long enough. Her father smiled at them and made calming gestures, and after several minutes of miming back and forth, the young man followed Annie's family back to their canoe where they gathered several portions of the meat and carried it to the shelter. They roasted the venison and ate together and in the course of their interactions they gathered that the family had had little luck hunting caribou and were afraid to venture too much into the open to do so.

In the morning her father left much of the rest of the meat with the Red Indian family. He brought a rifle to the mamateek that he intended to leave with them as well. He tried to show them how to load and fire the weapon, but they refused to touch it and seemed somehow afraid of its very presence. Her father was exasperated by this and continued his demonstration and encouragement until Annie's mother finally took the rifle from his hands and carried it back down to the canoe herself. They left the family later that morning in much the same condition they'd found them.

There was a long moment of silence around the table.

Reilly said, "They'd come down here on occasion." He motioned with his head towards the river. "Looking for a few salmon."

"Red Indians?" Buchan asked.

Reilly nodded. "They never caused no harm."

"The Reds were on fairly friendly terms with this one, Captain," Peyton said. "They'd walk out on his weir and take their pick of the fish. They called him by his Christian name."

Buchan sat back in his chair. "Why hadn't I been told of this before?"

Reilly laughed. "Let's say it wouldn't do much for my standing on the shore if it was general knowledge."

"Do they still come through here?"

"You know yourself," Reilly said. "They aren't around in numbers like the old days. And the ones left are on terms with no one but themselves."

"Yes, well," Buchan said. There was just a trace of a smile on the officer's face. He seemed perplexed by something. "It is hard to know who to trust, isn't it?" he said.

Early in the evening Mary took herself off into a corner of the room and lay down with a blanket of caribou hide. Annie Boss went to her then and pressed the poultice she'd prepared in the afternoon to the woman's chest, using a long length of muslin around her torso to hold it in place. The men walked down to the beach where they joined the marines around a bonfire.

"When I was speaking with Mr. Richmond," Buchan said, "he mentioned a Micmac furrier you encountered on your way from the lake in March."

Peyton and Reilly hesitated, as if they were each waiting for the other to speak. "Noel Young," Peyton said finally and he nodded his head. "He come upon us on the river and spent the night in camp."

"He has worked in this area for some time?"

"As long as my father has been here at least. Runs traplines through the winter near New Bay Pond. Spends his summers off of Tommy's Arm River, out past Sop's Arm." He paused for a moment. "He's a hard man, Captain, and not much to be trusted. By his own count he's killed ninety-nine Red Indians in his day and wouldn't pass up the chance to make it an even hundred."

"Is that a fact?"

"There's no love lost between the Micmac and the Reds as a rule," Peyton said.

Buchan rubbed the bridge of his nose. "Mr. Reilly, this is obviously not the case with your wife."

"It's the Irish and the English, sir," he said. "There's some look upon us with Christian civility and more wish us dead and buried because we speak a different language and visit a different kirk."

"A preposterous oversimplification, Mr. Reilly."

The Irishman nodded. His face glowed a bright copper colour in the firelight. He said, "It's sometimes the simplest explanation is closest to the truth."

In the morning as the marines prepared the cutter and gig for departure, Buchan requested a private interview with Reilly. "Just a few moments really," he said, "to confirm testimony given to the grand jury in the spring."

"All right," Reilly said. He looked around the room. There were children scattered about the corners like furniture pushed aside to accommodate dancing. Annie Boss was clearing up from breakfast with some assistance from Mary. "We might find a bit of peace and quiet at the river."

On their way to the shoreline Buchan said, "Her breathing does seem a little less laboured this morning." Reilly was walking ahead on the path and seemed not to hear him. "Mary's breathing," he repeated. "It seems to have improved somewhat."

"Perhaps," Reilly said without turning his head. "I didn't take notice."

"From what I understand from your wife, that poultice is quite the miracle potion." They had reached the wide sand beach and were walking side by side. The marines milled about the two boats that had been dragged partway up out of the water. Buchan said, "She tells me it did wonders for the injury to your hand."

Reilly turned to look at the officer for only a moment. They had reached the point where the weir curved out onto the river and Reilly went ahead of Buchan and sat on the dam, facing upstream away from the marines. "You wanted to talk to me about what happened on the lake," he said.

"I am interested in hearing the rest of your story first," Buchan said. "The family of blacksmiths. In the old country."

Reilly shook his head. "There was no family of blacksmiths."

Buchan made a noise in his throat. He leaned out over the water far enough to see his own reflection on the surface of the river. He said, "I am aware that a second Indian was killed on the lake last March, Mr. Reilly."

"Is this what Mary is telling you?"

"The source of my information is irrelevant. The point is that with regards to that murder, you are lying to protect John Senior."

"We were speaking about my hand, Captain."

Buchan unbuttoned a pocket in his tunic and removed the journal and fished for a lead. "As you wish," he said.

Reilly held his right hand over the pages of the notebook to give him a clear view. There was nothing of sense there that Buchan could see at first, a criss-cross of black lines that began at the base of the thumb and climbed across the back of the hand nearly to the other side.

"It's still possible to see the truth of it, if you know it's there to begin with," Reilly said. He pointed with the index finger of the opposite hand, circling the triangular area of flesh between the tendons cabling the thumb and forefinger to the wrist.

It took a moment for the letter *T* to surface, for Buchan to register what it meant. He looked up at the Irishman. "There's worse that could have come to you," he said.

"And nearly did. Commuted to branding and deportation to the colonies out of regard for my age and the fact it was my first offence."

"The first offence you were convicted of," Buchan said.

"A fine distinction, sir. Well noted. You're a credit to the office of magistrate. I had quite the career behind me by that time."

"How old were you?"

"Fourteen, sir. No age to be riding a horse foaled by an acorn, I can tell you."

Buchan tapped his lead against the pages of the notebook. "What was the charge?"

"Lifting a watch from a gentleman among the crowd gathered at Tyburn to see the hangings. I was a poor pickpocket, I'm afraid. I came to it late, after a long apprenticeship as a river thief."

"You speak of it as if it were an honourable profession, Mr. Reilly."

Reilly shrugged. "Every honourable profession on the Thames had their hand in. A revenue officer could make thirty guineas a night to turn a blind eye to all the activity. There were rat catchers on the Thames would carry the same two dozen rats from ship to ship and get paid ten times over for clearing vessels of vermin. And all the while they'd be making note of all that was aboard. It was how we knew which ships were worth stealing from." Reilly shook his head. "We never cleaned out a vessel, just skimmed from the barrels and then tapped the heads closed again. There was some were more brazen about it. They'd cut the hawsers at night and let the barges drift on the tide to some spot out of the way and then strip it clean like crows picking a corpse."

Buchan said, "You'll forgive me if I see no reason to take notes."

"It wasn't my intention to sound nostalgic, Captain."

"Perhaps you could tell me how all of this is connected to John Senior."

The Irishman leaned over his knees and spat into the clear water. "I never chose to be a thief," he said. "I'd rather have been selling milk about the streets of St. Giles. It was my father's calling. He saw me off in London and he expected me back on the first ship out of St. John's, which was the route taken by most sentenced to the colonies. I made up my mind to stay if I could scavenge a bit of work. Which proved more difficult than I would have liked." Reilly raised his hand. "Not many men will hire a convicted thief. An Irish one at that."

"So you concealed it by scarring your hand."

"It never occurred to me is the God's honest truth. It was John Senior's idea."

Buchan nodded as if this confirmed something he'd suspected about the elder Peyton for years.

"He told me I'd not be allowed to live an honest life if I appeared otherwise."

"I would say he took the job rather too seriously."

"I was just a lad still. He walked me out to Quidi Vidi Lake and got me drunk while we laid a fire to heat a poker. He gave me a rolled-up handkerchief to chew on and sat across my back and held my arm to the ground. When I came to myself, my hand was wrapped in strips he'd torn away from the shirt on his back. I didn't look at it until the smell came through. Had to be brought across to White Bay to have Annie's mother clean it up, John Senior lost a full week's work carrying me there and back."

Buchan stared upriver where the spruce grew to the shore and leaned out over their slurred reflections in the slow current. He felt unsure of himself suddenly. He turned to Reilly. "Was all this enough to warrant lying about a murder?"

Reilly looked away to the opposite shore. "For argument's sake, Captain. If what you say is true, what would you suggest I do?"

"Provide me now with a deposition regarding the facts of the incident." Reilly threw his head back with a roar of laughter and Buchan was forced to raise his voice. "And when the time comes testify before the grand jury in St. John's."

"You've not heard a word of my story this morning now, have you?" Reilly got to his feet and looked down at the officer. "You could write the deposition yourself and have me sign it and I could repeat it word for word at the courthouse. What would you have, d'you think? The oaths of an Irish thief and a Red Indian with little more English in her head than a cow. You might as well ask a jury to take the oath of the devil himself." He took a long breath and looked back towards the boats on the shoreline. "They look about ready to leave, Captain."

Buchan nodded distractedly and pushed his notebook into a tunic pocket. Reilly leaned down to offer a hand and helped him to his feet.

Peyton and Mary had already boarded the cutter and Buchan climbed in to join them. Annie Boss and several of the children were on the beach to wave the party off and they stood there until both boats had disappeared around the first bend in the river.

"Up there a long time," Annie Boss said, still looking out across the water. "What you tell that man?"

"Except for one small detail," Reilly said, "I told him the truth."

Annie turned to look at her husband. From the band of his trousers beneath his shirt he removed a small calfskin-bound journal. He looked drained, despondent.

"I told him I was a poor pickpocket," he said.

The journal was perfect-bound, the signatures sewn firmly into the spine. Six inches by four or so, Peyton guessed, about 150 pages. The pale calfskin cover was smooth and cool to the touch.

Buchan had gotten himself into a small frenzy searching for it the night they'd put into Boyd's Cove. He patted the pockets of his coat, rooted through a leather satchel. He spoke in a fierce whisper to several of his marines who went off to search the boats. When they came back empty-handed he sent them off to look a second time. He stood before the fire, face blank with attention as he walked back through the events of the day, trying to locate it in his mind. There was his interview with Reilly on the weir that morning when he had it in his hands. After that he could not place it.

Peyton said, "Is there anything I can help you with, Captain?"

Buchan turned to him suddenly. He looked like a sleepwalker startled awake on a street outside his house. "No. No," he said slowly, as if he was just beginning to recognize his surroundings, to place himself. "I don't believe you can." He said this as if it was an accusation. He gave up the search then and took a seat beside Peyton in front of the fire. They both smoked their pipes slowly, tamping the bowls with their thumbs.

Buchan said, "I admire your father, Mr. Peyton. I admire the loyalty he inspires."

"He is what he is, sir. There's no puzzle to what John Senior thinks of this or that. Every man on the shore knows where he stands in my father's eyes."

"He'd have made a fine officer."

"He wouldn't have been much for taking orders from superiors."

Buchan made a noise to say he could see his point.

Peyton said, "You have a boy of your own now, Captain, have I heard right?"

"You have. Born in St. John's two winters past."

There was a rush of laughter from a group of Blue Jackets huddled on the other side of the fire. Mary lay asleep under a blanket beside Peyton and he looked down to see if the noise had disturbed her, but she didn't stir.

"And you, Mr. Peyton," Buchan said. "It's about time for a wife and family?"

Peyton relit his pipe. "It was something I once considered. I seem to have lost the fire for it. John Senior was my age and then some when he married. Perhaps I'll bide my time the same."

"Turning after a father in all things," Buchan said. His voice had a sad, mildly scolding tone.

Peyton looked down at the sleeping woman again. "She's sound to the world," he said.

Three days later the party returned to the house on Burnt Island. They'd had no luck sighting any recent campsites near Boyd's Cove and abandoned any hope of contacting the Beothuk on the coast. They settled on a winter expedition to the lake as soon as the weather allowed it. The following morning Buchan and the marines left for Ship Cove. He'd made no further mention of his missing journal and seemed to have given it up for lost.

John Senior passed it to Peyton that afternoon, when they were down in the cutting room away from the women. "Joseph Reilly brought that across Wednesday past. Said you had asked for it."

Peyton took the small book and turned it over in his hands. Then he said, "Buchan was across and spoke to Richmond and Michael Sharpe."

"Reilly told me as much." He shook his head. "Richmond isn't feared of the man. And young Michael will tell the clock to whatever hour you gave him." John Senior paused for so long then that Peyton asked what the matter was. "Buchan knows about the other one was killed," he said. "That one up to the house give it away to him."

Peyton forced out a breath of air. "Well," he said, "she never saw nothing more that could hurt anyone. As long as we all keep our mouths shut." He looked down at the journal, then held it up for the old man to see. "Not a word to Cassie. No sense dragging anyone else into all this."

John Senior looked away from his son. "She was there."

"Where?"

"With Buchan and that one, when she went on about it all."

Peyton picked up a thin knife from the cutting table and stabbed lethargically at the wood. "Well Christ," he said.

He sat alone in the kitchen now, the rest of the house asleep, the journal sitting on the table in front of him. He turned the book sideways and lifted the front cover slowly, then set it down again. The motion like a mouth talking, the jaws of a skull working open and closed. Something close to a death-wish weighted his shoulders, a desire to be free of all that surrounded him regardless of the cost. It was an urge that was no less appealing to him for being obviously irrational and illusory.

The afternoon he and John Senior had uncovered the skeleton of the dead Indian together on the beach on Swan Island, his father opened the tiny medicine bag and laid its contents on the ground, then handed his sixteen-year-old son one of the bird skulls to hold. The bone was dry and as light as the air and it seemed to Peyton to belong to a world beyond the one he knew. His father collected the materials together and retied the bag, then offered it to Peyton. *A keepsake*, he'd called it. Peyton looked at the stained pouch and then at his father. He refused to take it.

John Senior set the bag on the ground between his feet. There was an amused look of surprise on his face. He reached a huge gnarled hand and closed it around the skull of the Indian man. He lifted it clear of the frame and then gathered up the jawbone as well, holding the two together at the joint. All the teeth but one were still in place. He flapped them back and forth and spoke under this mime in a low-pitched voice. "Just a dead Indian," the skull said. "Nothing to bother your head about."

Peyton stared. He could feel the violation in that act, putting words so carelessly and callously in the mouth of the dead.

"Harry Miller used to play around with them like that," John Senior said. He seemed embarrassed, apologetic. He flapped the jaws several times more and then turned the skull to stare into the empty eye sockets, the full, baleful grin of those teeth. "Poor bugger," he said then and Peyton couldn't tell if he was talking of Miller or the Indian whose remains he held in his hand as he spoke. He replaced the skull and offered his son the leather pouch again.

Peyton turned the journal in circles on the table. He'd told Reilly he wanted some notion of how much Buchan knew, to be able to anticipate, to plot a defence. But he was afraid to open it now, after asking the Irishman to risk his life stealing it away from the officer. He would find himself in there, and his father and Mary, and all the men who made up the party to the lake, but not, he was sure, in the fashion they had conspired to present themselves. The start of their undoing, that little book, now or some time beyond their time. There were things he'd seen and heard in his days he vowed to take to his grave, as if that was a safe place for the truth. But two hundred years from now, he knew, some stranger could raise his bones from the earth and put whatever words they liked in his mouth. It was a broken, helpless feeling.

There was also the fugitive scrawl Cassie made somewhere in these pages, his real reason for wanting to get his hands on the journal. When he saw Buchan storm by towards the beach he'd gone up to the house to see what had happened and he caught sight of Cassie at the table then, the pen in her hand. The expression on her face when she looked up to see him there had sparked a long slow fuse of dread that was still burning in him, settling towards the charge. He moved the candle closer and opened the pages to the last entry and began reading his way backward through the journal.

⊹

A mile beyond Burnt Island, Buchan sent the gig on to Ship Cove and turned the cutter about. He had his marines row north past Fortune Harbour and then on to Seal Bay where they put up for the night. The next morning they continued on through Sop's Arm to Tommy's Arm River where they turned inland. The river narrowed as they travelled and at points was barely deep enough to admit the cutter's passage. A Blue Jacket lay across the bow to watch for sandbars and sunkers and deadheads, and Buchan kept an eye to the shoreline for some sign of habitation. It was late afternoon and coming on to dark when he spotted the smoke of a fire, and then a birchbark tilt hidden back among trees and tuckamore. There was no beach to speak of, only a narrow trail cut into the bush blocked by a canoe, and the cutter was hauled up into a tangle of alder. Buchan shouted up towards the shelter as he started along the path and Noel Young was in the doorway when he reached the clearing.

The Mi'kmaq looked down on the officer and the small entourage of Blue Jackets behind him. "Got some rabbit inside," he said.

The smell of stewing meat carried out to the white men. Buchan said, "*Nous avons de peu de pain et de rhum.*"

Noel Young stared at the officer a moment.

"*Ma femme,*" Buchan explained. "*Elle est française.*"

Noel Young nodded. He was wearing a frock of coarse blue cloth, a scarlet sash tied about his waist. A silver brooch the size of a large watch held the shirt closed at his neck. His hair was done up in long plaits of grey. "*Le repas est prêt,*" he said, then turned and went inside. Buchan sent Rowsell back to the boat for the bread and rum and he took the rest of the marines into the tilt.

Inside they sat on junks of wood or on the dirt floor itself. The smell of food cooking emanated from a large bark bowl of water set beside a fire in the shelter's centre. Noel Young used tongs to move heated rocks from the fire into the container to keep the water boiling.

Through the meal the Blue Jackets ate in silence while Buchan spoke to Young in French, asking where the Mi'kmaq fished on the north shore and where they ran traplines in the winter months, and how many of them there were on the island all told. He refilled Young's glass with rum at every opportunity. He said he had been told by the English on the northeast shore that Noel Young was a great Red killer.

The Indian man washed down a mouthful of bread. He told Buchan that you couldn't trust half what an Englishman was of a mind to tell you, and he smiled to say he meant no offence to the company present.

Buchan asked if he could speak the Red Indian language and Noel Young shook his head. He said, "They all talk the same dog, bow-wow-wow." He shifted back again to French. The Reds are a jealous people, he said, although it hadn't always been so. There was a time when the Mi'kmaq shared the land with the Reds and there was peace between them. But years ago the French had placed a bounty on the Reds in retaliation for the thieving and other depredations suffered on the west coast. In that same year a small party of Mi'kmaq had come upon two Red Indians alone on a river and they killed these men and took their heads to claim the bounty. On their way back to the coast they encountered a great camp of Red Indians who hailed the Mi'kmaq party as was the custom at the time and invited them to join in a meal. The Mi'kmaq consented for fear of raising suspicion and a number of Red Indians came to the waterline to help them bring the canoe ashore. The heads of their murdered people were discovered there, hidden under a piece of caribou hide in the bow.

Noel Young paused to wipe his plate clean with bread. No word was spoken, he said, the Reds gave the Mi'kmaq no indication of the discovery they had made. Instead they welcomed them in the camp as friends and seated them around a fire while the food was prepared, with a Red Indian seated at the right hand of each Mi'kmaq. There was laughter and stories and the food was served and eaten. And after darkness had fallen fully, at a signal unknown to the visitors, each Red Indian turned to the Mi'kmaq beside him and plunged a knife into his breast.

Young put the bread into his mouth and chewed slowly, staring absently into the air. He said that since that time, which was before the time of his father and the time of his grandfather besides, the two peoples had been enemies and not a civil word had passed between them. And he himself had killed Red Indians, as they would no doubt have killed him given the opportunity. He said it was sometimes necessary to spill a little blood to keep body and soul together.

Buchan nodded a while. It seemed to him, from the way the story had been told, that it was the Mi'kmaq who were mostly to blame for the enmity between the two peoples and for the bloodshed that followed, and he said as much to Young, as diplomatically as he was able in his stilted French.

Young shrugged. He pulled the cloak of caribou hide across his shoulders higher around his neck. He said he would have expected an officer in the British navy to lay the blame on the French who posted the bounty in the first place. But given the nationality of his wife, he supposed it was understandable that Buchan proved to be an exception.

It was night by this time and the only light in the shelter was cast by the fire. Noel Young pushed himself to his feet and announced he was about to go down to the river to fish and he invited the officer to come along.

Buchan looked at him. "*Vous allez pêcher maintenant?*" he said. "*Dans le noir?*" He'd seen no sign of it to this point, but he thought the man must be drunk to the point of senselessness.

"*Venez avec moi,*" Young said, and he went out the door and headed down towards the river.

Buchan got to his feet. "Rowsell," he whispered to the corporal. "Take a couple of men down to the shoreline in a few minutes. I'm not sure what this one has in mind. He says we're going *fishing.*"

"In the dark, sir?"

"Apparently, yes."

He found Young kneeling beside the canoe. A long torch lay on the ground beside him, the head wrapped with tightly woven dried reeds. The Mi'kmaq struck sparks into a ball of tinder and blew gently on the fragile ripple of flame, then held the torch above it, turning the head slowly until it was well alight. He stood and used a hand to invite Buchan into the canoe, then handed him the torch. He pushed the length of the canoe into the shallow water and stepped in himself, paddling out into the current and drifting slowly downstream.

"*Où allons-nous?*" Buchan asked.

They rounded a point of land and Young turned the canoe into a broad steady where the water ran twice the depth of the river. "*Ici,*" he said. He set the paddle down and took up a spear, its wooden shaft about five feet in length. The tip was barbed iron. There was a length of cord tied at the bottom and Young fastened the loose end to his wrist. He moved to the middle of the canoe and pushed his knees as wide as the sides allowed for balance. Buchan turned to face him, still unsure what was happening, or what might be expected of him. In the light of the torch he could see only the man kneeling across from him, the gunnels of the canoe, a six-foot circumference of river water. The shoreline, the forest, even the stars overhead were lost to him.

"You think Noel Young crazy, hey?"

"Not at all."

The Mi'kmaq smiled at him. "You think Noel Young drunk?"

"No," he lied.

Young told him to hold the torch out over the water, about two feet above the surface. He lifted the spear to his shoulder and stared past the torchlight down into the river. Buchan watched his face, the hairless upper lip, the motion of muscles in the jaw as he clenched and unclenched his teeth. His ears were pierced and hung with pendants of birds and fish carved from bone or shells. "You were on the River Exploits last March," he said, "when the Peytons carried the Red Indian woman down from the lake."

Young lifted a finger to his lips without taking his eyes from the water, then pointed. Buchan looked down to see one of the last salmon of the season rise to the light and turn from the surface, the pale length of its belly flashing in the glow of the torch before the spearhead drove through the water.

Noel Young lifted the spear from the water and the writhing fish came out of the river with it. He looked across at Buchan.

"Dick Richmond said that you spent a night with them."

"After they got the woman, heading down to the coast." Young released the salmon from the barbed head of the spear and it slapped its torn body helplessly against the bark of the canoe.

"They killed two Red Indian men. Did they tell you that?"

He motioned for Buchan to hold the torch back out over the water and lifted the spear to his shoulder again.

"Richmond shot one of the Reds, yes?"

Young nodded.

"And the old man, John Senior. He killed the other?"

The Mi'kmaq turned his face from the river to stare at Buchan. "Richmond say it was Irishman." He looked back to the water. "His wife Micmac."

"Reilly?"

"Reilly. Joe Jep. He put the rifle behind the ear." Young used his free hand to point to a spot above and behind his own ear. "Bang."

A second salmon rose staring into the light and torqued away too late. The canoe rocked and settled.

Buchan was stunned. "*Richmond vous a dit ceci?*"

Young nodded. He said that later in the evening after the party had turned in, he and Richmond tended the fire and kept watch. Richmond talked, talked, talked, he was a big man, Young said, but it was his mouth that made him dangerous. He told Young about the trip to the lake and the struggle on the ice when Richmond subdued the Red Indian who was the size of a bear and so drunk on rage that there was no choice but to kill him. Reilly sat up from his blankets and told Richmond he'd best keep his counsel, which Richmond took exception to. "Now Mr. Reilly here," Richmond said then, "never would have guessed he had it in him. Just walked up to the other poor bastard and shot him." Young again used his free hand to indicate the placement of the muzzle. "Bang," he said again.

"Reilly," Buchan whispered.

They were hammer and tiss about it then, Young said, and he laughed and shook his head. The two men rolled about in the snow like women and roused the rest of the camp with their cursing. They had a time of it trying to separate them and it was fifteen minutes or more of pushing and shouting before anyone realized the woman had made off into the trees.

"Reilly," Buchan said again.

There was a commotion upriver, the sound of oars in the water. Rowsell was calling across the water. "Captain Buchan! Is everything all right? Captain Buchan!"

The cutter rounded the point of land and Buchan stood slowly, holding the torch aloft. He swore under his breath. "I'm all right," he shouted back. "Everything's fine." He looked down at the Mi'kmaq man who was shaking his head slightly and smiling into the river. Buchan said, "Everything's fine, Corporal. We're fishing."

T W E L V E

Notes from Buchan's interview with Richmond were the most recent entries in the journal. Peyton guessed the officer had made them in the cutter, as they rowed back to Reilly's tilt or alone by the fire on the beach after all others had turned in for the night. Buchan had written *Micmac furrier on return trip* and underlined the first two words twice. Richmond was subtler and more cunning than anyone gave him credit for. "Bastard," Peyton said aloud.

There were a number of pages then referring to the fruitless days of searching the coastline, observations on the weather, Mary's delicate state of health, John Peyton's solicitousness where the Indian woman's comfort and well-being were concerned. There was a long entry written just after the conversation with Mary and Cassie in the parlour.

> *Two Red Indian men murdered during expedition, not one as reported by P. Jr. Second murder excluded from account of expedition during Grand Jury testimony. Clearly no justification for second killing. P only witness to travel to St. John's to testify, would have expected nothing further in the way of investigation. Obviously an attempt to protect murderer from prosecution. Most certainly J. Peyton Sr.*

Previous to this, a scatter of notes from the interview itself, *Two men* underlined and outlined in a box, the word *Husband* underlined and then crossed out. There were two pages of the naive maps of the River Exploits and the lake, of the coastline around Burnt Island, sketched and detailed by Buchan and Mary on the very table at which he now sat. An entry written following Buchan's first unsatisfactory attempt to examine Peyton's testimony directly: *Refuses to answer any questions, defensive and dismissive. Definitely hiding <u>something</u>. Under the influence of J. Peyton Sr. in this, as in all other things.*

Then pages of references to duties aboard the *Grasshopper* during the trip up the coast; meetings in St. John's prior to departure; a summary of Peyton's grand jury testimony; a list of the men who accompanied the Peytons on their March expedition.

He stopped there and hid his face in his hands. He rubbed his eyes fiercely and shook his head.

"John Peyton."

He jumped back in his chair and quickly closed the journal, covering as much of it as he could with his arm. "Cassie," he said.

She came into the kitchen behind him and sat in a chair across the table.

"How long were you standing there watching me," he said as lightly as he could. Her face was as drawn and gaunt as the winter he carried her down from Reilly's tilt on the river. "You scared me half to death," he told her. Peyton reached out to push the candle back to the middle of the table. He crossed his arms over the journal and stared at the light.

"Did you know about the trip your father took with Harry Miller and William Cull down the river? After Miller's house was burnt down?" She didn't look at him as she spoke, staring across at the fire, and Peyton slipped the book underneath his seat.

"Where did you hear talk of that?"

"John Senior told me, just now. Before you came home with Mary."

"I heard some of it from Cull. Richmond and Taylor used to talk of it now and then. John Senior never said a word to me about it himself." Cassie was shaking her head and he thought she was on the verge of tears. He said, "John Senior's a hard, hard man, Cassie."

She looked across at him. "I want to know what happened on the lake," she said.

The two Beothuk men came down off the shoreline and walked across the ice to where the Peytons and their men stood waiting. They stopped at a distance of about ten yards from the white men, and the larger of the two, the man holding the branch of white spruce, began to speak. His voice was clear and even and he went on for a long time while his audience alternately stared at him and one another. He beat his chest with the fist of his free hand. He held both hands in front of him in appeal. The cold of the ice stole up through the feet of the white men and they shifted and stamped where they stood and still the Beothuk went on. He made his argument in careful detail and with all the rhetorical flourish he could muster as if he believed simply the appearance of reason and civility would be enough to alter what his own experience told him was inevitable in the unfolding event. One of the Englishmen said, "Does anyone know what the hell he's going on about?" But no one answered. When the Beothuk reached the end of his plea he surveyed the group before him, each man in turn. He stepped towards them with his right hand extended, first to John Peyton who stood beside his wife. They shook hands and he turned to those men standing nearby and took their hands as well.

The Beothuk man turned to the woman then and spoke several words to her, and he took her gently by the elbow to lead her away from the white men on the ice.

John Senior said, "You keep that savage off the girl, John Peyton."

The younger Peyton began speaking to the Beothuk then while continuing to hold the woman's other arm. He motioned and pointed with his free hand to indicate the Beothuk man would be welcome to accompany the party back to the coast as well, and as it became clear he would not be permitted to remove his wife to the shoreline, the Beothuk raised his voice in response and held more tightly to her elbow. The woman's hands were tied behind her back, the loop of her arms mapping the shape of a heart as the two men pulled from opposite directions.

John Senior stepped up then and tried to loosen the Indian's grip, shouting against the words of the Beothuk, and their senseless argument spiralled like loose snow in a gale until it seemed that both men were blinded by it. When his hand was pried loose from the woman's arm the Beothuk turned on the old man, grabbing him about the throat and wrestling him to the ground, screaming into his face all the while, wetting the white man's face with spit.

Peyton backed away from the fight, still holding the woman. "Get him off," he shouted. "Jesus, get him off."

Richmond and Taylor both reached for the Indian and grabbed him uselessly by the hair and the thick cloak of caribou hide. Richmond took up his rifle then and began slamming the heavy wooden butt against the back of the Beothuk's head, succeeding only in silencing the man who clenched his teeth and refused to relinquish his hold on the old man's throat. John Senior could be heard then, an intermittent tortured grunting like a fading heartbeat, and there was the dull thunk of the rifle butt striking bone.

The woman was shouting and pulling towards her husband. Peyton turned her around and pressed her face against his shoulder. "Shoot him if you have to," he shouted.

Richmond turned to stare, the rifle held aloft in his hands like a spear.

Reilly said, "John Peyton."

"Shoot the bastard," Peyton yelled again.

Richmond turned the rifle around in his hands and held the barrel flush to the man's back, the report of the rifle shot muffled by the thick caribou-hide clothing. The woman screamed into the collar of Peyton's coat. The Beothuk man slumped forward and choked on a spurt of blood in his throat, though he held fiercely to John Senior's neck a few moments longer like an animal dragging its useless hind legs after its spine has been broken. Richmond and Taylor leaned in and finally pulled him free of the old man, pushing him onto his back on the ice where he stared into the pale blue of the sky and worked his mouth around a word that would never escape his lips.

John Senior turned and pushed himself to his hands and knees, his face mottled scarlet and purple. His hat was off his head and sweaty strands of grey hair hung away from the pale scalp, as dank and listless as seaweed. Everyone else stood about in the very spots where they had been when the Beothuk man began speaking, as still as the trees on the shore.

John Senior coughed and pounded the ice with his fist as the cold air galled his throat. When he looked up from where he knelt he saw the second Beothuk man, still frozen in place like the white men around him. They stared at one another a moment, and without coming to his feet John Senior scravelled towards his rifle. He sat and aimed as the Beothuk man finally turned to run but the gun missed fire. He recocked and missed fire again. He threw down the rifle and rushed to Tom Taylor to haul his musket from his hands. The Beothuk had made barely twenty-five yards when the shot took him in the back and he crumpled forward onto the ice. He tried to stand but was unable and he began crawling awkwardly and inefficiently towards the shoreline on his hands and knees.

John Senior had fired hurriedly, before he had pulled the rifle clear of Taylor's arms, and it had recoiled into his face, smashing his nose and knocking him onto his backside, and he sat there in a daze. Peyton continued to hold the Beothuk woman's face against his chest as she sobbed and tried to struggle free of him. No one else moved but the wounded man, still inching away from the party on the ice.

It was Joseph Reilly finally who walked out away from the cluster of dark-coated white men, past the body whose failing heat rose into the still air, across the span of clear ice. Up close he could see that the Beothuk struggling to remain upright on his hands and knees was no older than himself when he was a thief among the crowds at Tyburn. He crouched beside him. Dark plugs of blood showed through the back of his cassock, blood poured from his mouth like water from a spigot. The Irishman stood and placed the muzzle of his rifle against the boy's skull. He turned to look back at the silent group staring across at him like an audience in a theatre and then he pulled the trigger.

Cassie stood with her back to the fire while Peyton spoke. She placed a hand against her abdomen, clutching the fabric of her blouse, then releasing it, as if there was a thread of pain woven into her belly that she was trying to work free.

She said, "All along you've been lying."

Peyton covered his eyes. "A story is never told for its own sake," he said. "True or false."

"You bastard, John Peyton."

"I blame myself," he said. "They wouldn't have come down off the shore to meet us if I hadn't waved that handkerchief."

Cassie watched him, shaking her head. She said, "I wouldn't have guessed John Senior to be such a coward to ask you to lie for him."

He nodded. "Father wouldn't have suggested such a thing, you're right."

Cassie strode across the room and leaned with both hands on the back of a chair. "Tell me then. What am I not seeing?"

"Sit down a minute."

He took out his pipe and lit it with a coal from the fire as she settled at the table. He puffed slowly, drawing the smoke into his lungs, trying to calm his breathing. There was a threat implicit in her questions, a willingness to switch allegiances that he wouldn't have guessed at.

"I'm waiting," she said.

He nodded. "We never spoke much of it coming down the river, what to do about it all. There was going to have to be some sort of report, Governor Hamilton would want an account of what went on. A grand jury, I figured, just as it happened. We could argue self-defence in Richmond's case clear enough, and even though it looked dark for John Senior, there was some chance he could plead his condition, given the beating he'd taken. The young one had an axe tucked into his belt besides. He might have got off as it was and he'd have taken his chances if that was all there was to it. But there was Reilly to think about."

"What about him?"

"When he was a lad in London he was a thief. Caught picking pockets and sentenced to hang. You've seen those scars on his hand."

Cassie nodded.

"They branded him a thief, you see, sent him across to Newfoundland."

"I don't follow what you're telling me."

"He killed the Indian."

"That was an act of mercy."

"A fine distinction, and not one our Captain Buchan and those like him would be interested in making. He was sentenced to hang once already, Cassie. He altered the mark on his hand. Not Jesus Christ himself could have saved the man from the noose a second time."

Cassie leaned forward on the table. Her lazy eye drew down nearly closed, as if she was sighting down a rifle barrel. "You couldn't have told it as it happened and left Joseph Reilly out of it?"

He opened his mouth to speak and hesitated a moment. "He's my father, Cassie. And you —"

"What?" she said. "And I what?"

He lifted his hand, a dismissive gesture, an admission of helplessness.

She got up from her seat and walked three steps away before turning back to face him, shaking her head furiously, as if it was suddenly clear to her. "It was *me* you were protecting," she said.

He shifted in his chair so she couldn't see his face. "I wanted to spare you knowing if I could."

She covered her mouth with her hand and walked to the doorway. She turned then and was on him, knocking his chair over backwards to the floor. He grabbed for her arms as she beat him about the head and face. She cuffed an ear and set his head ringing. "Cassie," he said. She struck him across the bridge of the nose and he was nearly blinded by the shock of it, his eyes watering. Blood ran onto his lips and into his mouth.

Cassie was crying as she swung her arms, and when he finally corralled them and pinned them to her sides, he held onto her until the jag of broken sobs subsided. Her strength was a surprise to him. He hadn't had occasion to take note of it since their first year on the shore, when she took to the ice to gaff seals. He thought if she'd had a poker or a stick of wood in her hands, she would have killed him there on the kitchen floor. When he let her go she stood up and walked across to the door. She stopped there but kept her back turned to the room. She said, "I'll stay here until Mary is brought back up the river."

Peyton was on his knees on the floor. He wiped the blood away from his upper lip with the sleeve of his shirt. "You know she might die before the freeze-up."

"Then I'll stay until she dies."

Peyton picked his chair up from where it lay on its side and moved it along the table, still trying to catch his breath. He sat sideways to hold his hands in the light of the candle so their shadows moved on the near wall. He brought the two together to form the outline of a rabbit's head, then a dog. The shadow-dog's mouth opened and closed on the wall and Peyton made a low barking sound in time to the motion, then howled quietly.

When he was eleven years old, he stole two pence from the pocket of his father's short-cut spencer where it lay across a chair in the room they shared during the winter months. After school he ran straight to the waterfront and stood in line, the coins clutched so tightly in his palm that the outline was scored into the flesh long after he paid at the door. The room held close to one hundred men and boys and the girl was stood upon a tabletop at one end. People craned their necks and hollered for a better view, for the Indian to speak or dance. There was a gauzy drift of light through opaque windows, the room smelled of rain and tobacco. Someone had tied a feather in her hair and put three stripes of white on each cheek. Her dress was made of rough calico. There was a wooden doll in her hand that she gripped against her chest and she seemed to have no idea why she was there or what interest the assembly of white men might have in her. After five minutes of the crowd's restless shouting and surging towards the table where she stood, the girl turned her head up and howled with all the force of helplessness a child her age could manage. She was the loneliest-looking creature he ever laid eyes on.

Peyton leaned to the floor and picked up the journal, placing it on the table. He used a finger to turn it in slow circles, flipped it end over end between his hands. He riffled the pages back to front and back again, until he found the blur of words at the edge of a page, the only place in the journal anything had been scribbled outside the careful margins. The words were smudged where the book had been closed before the ink was fully dry, but he recognized the expansive slant of the hand, the tilted looping letters of her handwriting.

There was a child. Before I ended it, David. I was pregnant.

Peyton lifted a hand to his forehead. His first thought was that Cassie had cheated on his father somehow. He left the journal open on the table and walked out of the kitchen, across the hall to the door of Cassie's room, raised a fist to hammer at it. Held his hand motionless in the air then as it became clear to him finally. Blood still trickled at the back of his throat.

He placed his palm flat against the door, moving it back and forth across the rough grain. He waited there until he thought he might fall with shaking and then ran from the house, down the worn path towards the stage. He stumbled across the stone beach of the cove and sloshed into the frigid ocean water, until the cold stopped his breath, and he stared blindly out across the dark as the chill knifed into his skin. He could feel his intestines quivering. She had never been his father's lover, though she let him go on believing it. All these years it was her who held him away. Cassandra.

THIRTEEN

"I have to admit," Buchan said, "I came to this investigation with a number of preconceptions."

He was sitting in the Peytons' kitchen, a long ways beyond three parts drunk. He had arrived in the cutter that morning, coming straight across from his interview with Noel Young on Tommy's Arm River, and no one seemed that much surprised to see him. The day was passed in distant pleasantries and Buchan had the marines assist in taking down the cutting room and salt house to protect them from the ice that would rake the coast come spring. The supper was a staid event with little conversation and both Mary and Cassie excused themselves as soon as they had eaten. Rowsell had been with them for the meal as well but left to lie in with the other marines just before nine. Peyton and his father stayed at the table with the officer as the dark settled and a harsh autumn frost reached for them where they sat. Peyton laid more wood in the fire than any sober person would consider sensible and he kept it roaring through the evening. None of them had seen the bottom of their glass in a while.

"Blindness," Buchan went on, "to refuse to see what's before your eyes because you have already decided on the truth of a matter. I have been half-asleep this whole time."

Peyton raised his glass. "Welcome back to the land of the living, sir." He felt giddy with misery.

Buchan slammed the table with the open palm of his hand. "I feel a little as if someone has pulled the rug from beneath my feet."

John Senior said, "That's just the rum."

"I admire you, sir," Buchan said to the older man. "I have said so on a number of occasions to a number of people, your son being one of them."

John Senior drank off half his glass. "I could give a good Goddamn what you think of me," he said. "Sir," he added.

They all three burst into laughter and they went on longer than the thin joke warranted, until their guts ached from the effort and tears streamed down their faces.

Buchan cleared his throat, trying to stifle a last giggle. "I will be taking Mr. Reilly into St. John's to be tried when the *Grasshopper* returns," he said. He was still wiping away the moisture from his cheeks.

John Senior looked across at his son and then at the officer. "The hell you will," he said.

He raised his hands in a gesture of helplessness. "Fidelity to the law, Mr. Peyton. I have no choice."

"You promised a good word if ever it was needed."

"Concerning past offences, yes. This is another case altogether. Mr. Reilly will hang, I'm afraid."

John Senior said, "T'was me what killed him. I was the shooter."

"Shut up now," Peyton told him.

Buchan looked at the old man and then at his son. A squib of drunken uncertainty crossed his face. "An honourable gesture, sir. I expected nothing less from you."

Peyton held up a hand to keep his father in his seat. "Mind," he said. He refilled the round of glasses and sipped at the rum. "You have concluded your investigation, Captain Buchan."

He gave a non-committal shrug. "I believe I have," he answered.

"We are pleased and relieved to hear it," Peyton said. He turned to his father. "I'll need a few moments alone with the Captain."

The old man looked to his son quickly, about to argue with him, but said nothing. In the few months since they'd gone down to the lake John Senior seemed to have lost his place in the world, everything around him had shifted, breaking up like ice rotten with spring heat. The nightmares he suffered off and on for years had become increasingly frequent and violent. He seemed sure of nothing any more. "I was just on my way to bed," he said furiously. He got up from the table and he took his full glass with him up the stairs.

Peyton watched Buchan from across the table. He imagined the small room where they sat suddenly in motion, the two of them in an open boat with a heavy sea running. The sickening rise on a wave's crest, the sudden plunging descent. He got up from his seat and walking unsteadily to the daybed, bending to reach into the chill underneath. Back at the table he placed the journal between them. "I understand you misplaced this a number of days ago."

Buchan reached for the book. He held it in his hand and hefted it, as if guessing its weight. "I could have you flogged for this," he said. He shook the journal at his host. "I could have you *hanged*." He tried to sound more sure of himself than he felt. He let out a long breath of air. "But I suspect there was nothing much of use to you among the contents. And if I'm not mistaken, the actual thief is halfway to the gallows already."

"There are a number of things," Peyton said, "which I had preconceptions about myself when all of this got started."

He still had not taken his seat and he reached a hand across the table and held it there until Buchan reluctantly passed the journal back to him. He felt a tight corkscrew of disgust spiral through his stomach but couldn't identify the exact source of it, his father or Buchan, Cassie. Himself. He felt the bow of the tiny craft crest a whitecap and come down hard, the force of the impact shuddering through the entire vessel like a spasm of nausea.

He flipped through the pages until he found what he was looking for and he laid the book sideways before the officer. He pulled the candle closer. "You didn't know about the child," he said. "Did you, Captain."

Buchan looked up from Cassie's words in the journal and Peyton could see reflected in the officer's face a moment of sickening recognition, of bottomless panic. Dark sea pouring over the gunnels. Every seam leaking water.

Part 3

Bootzhawet *sleep* (verb?) K; ... **Isedoweet** *to sleep;*

— from a vocabulary compiled in
Howley's *The Beothuks or Red Indians*

The Losing of the Moon

1819–1820

losing vbl n Phrase *losing of the moon*: the period of waning.

— *Dictionary of Newfoundland English*

ONE

There had been an early fall of snow in St. John's by the time Buchan returned from the Bay of Exploits. Near the chimneys of the governor's house meltwater pooled and drained and dripped into strategically placed pots in the upstairs rooms throughout their meal.

Marie Buchan was feeling unwell before she arrived and was forced to retire to the parlour before the meal was completed, apologizing repeatedly in her formal English. The governor's wife, Lady Hamilton, excused herself to attend to her. The two men finished their food and then moved into the living room where they sat with snifters of brandy. It was mid-September. Buchan had already presented his report to the governor and the Supreme Court. He swirled his glass of alcohol distractedly. His head ached. The persistent damp smell of the house made it seem older and colder than it actually was.

"I've read your report," Hamilton said and then stopped. "You look peaked, old man. Are you coming down with something?"

"A little tired is the extent of it, I believe."

"Quite unlike you," Hamilton said. The governor's head of thick, carefully kempt silver hair was the envy of many men in positions of authority. He looked at once serious and solicitous, benevolent but stern. "Perhaps," he offered, "Marie has been overenthusiastic in her welcome?" Even his peculiarly adolescent sense of humour maintained something like an air of dignity in the shadow of his magnificent coiffure.

Buchan managed a smile, but couldn't sustain it. "She has not been well enough to offer the ... that kind of welcome."

"Yes, well," Hamilton said. "I see," he said. "I've read your report, Captain Buchan." He cleared his throat. "I must admit to feeling some relief."

Buchan had lobbied Hamilton for weeks to be permitted to conduct the investigation the grand jury requested. Left to himself, the governor, as he suggested to Peyton, would simply have allowed the jury's verdict to stand and the questions surrounding it to decay a little further each season, until they had disappeared altogether. Sending a naval magistrate to interrogate other members of Peyton's party would likely be seen in some quarters as a provocation. And if convictions resulted — Hamilton shook his head. It all added up to the kind of political trouble he preferred to live without in his first year as governor.

Buchan won him over with his typical talk of justice and integrity, and in a calculated political move he made his impassioned speeches in the presence of the reformer, Lady Hamilton, whenever an opportunity presented itself. He shamed the governor into taking his side. "It's what makes you so damned infuriating," Hamilton told the officer. "And, I suppose I must add, so invaluable. Go, investigate." He waved his hand towards the door. "Bring justice to the Indians or whatever it is you intend. Bring down the whole bloody Empire if you must."

"History will remember you kindly for this," Buchan had said.

It was that kind of fervour Hamilton associated with him: the belief that even in this unremarkable and casually overlooked corner of the Empire he was acting at the centre of the world's events. The man he sat beside now was a different person, although the change was too subtle for him to place. Water dripped relentlessly into the containers laid out upstairs. For years there had been attempts to locate and fix the leaks in the slate roof, all without any significant degree of success. Buchan seemed to be struggling with the same kind of fundamental, insidiously irreparable damage.

"There is no shame," Hamilton said softly, "in proving the innocence of your countrymen. However much you might have believed it would turn out otherwise."

Buchan stood and walked across to the fireplace. He lifted the snifter to his mouth and emptied it.

"Forgive me for so bold a question," Hamilton said, "but is everything all right between you and Mrs. Buchan?"

He made a motion with the hand holding the glass.

"She seems delighted to have you back before the onset of winter."

"She isn't well, Governor. Has not been, as you know, for a number of years. And I'll likely be gone again within a fortnight." He paused. "I once promised her, as all husbands do, no doubt, that nothing would ever come between us. I have not always been as faithful to that promise as I might wish."

"The life of a navy man, Captain Buchan. Unlike a governor, you cannot carry her to your every port of call."

Buchan turned towards him. "May I have another glass of brandy?"

Hamilton motioned towards the decanter. "By all means." When Buchan returned with a full glass he said, "Now what of our charge? This Indian woman?"

"Mary."

"Quite, Mary, yes. You will be in charge of the expedition to take her up the River Exploits?"

Buchan nodded. "I'm not at all convinced it is something she wants, but I can think of no better course of action. I'll have to return before the freeze-up, as early as mid-October depending on the weather. The Peytons have offered what assistance they can afford in terms of mounting the expedition and acting as guides and whatnot."

"Good of them, I suppose, given the nature of recent interactions."

Buchan nodded carefully. He stared into his brandy. "I tried to ascertain from Mary the state of the tribe at this time, an estimate of numbers, the general level of health among her people, locations of their camps, that sort of thing. The little she had to say was not encouraging. Only a fool would wager on there being a hundred left alive."

"A *hundred*? In total?"

"I would guess that to be ridiculously optimistic."

"Dear me," Hamilton whispered.

The two men sat in silence a moment, listening to the steady tick of water dripping into the half-filled containers above them.

"I suppose it would now be safe," Hamilton said, "to send a letter of appointment with you for young Mister Peyton to take up the duties of Justice of the Peace."

Buchan got up from his seat and walked across to the decanter of brandy.

"I don't remember you having such a fondness for drink, David."

There was a barely discernible note of reproach in Hamilton's voice that Buchan would have ignored if he'd registered it. "In my time on the northeast shore," he said, "I seem to have acquired a taste for it."

The HMS *Grasshopper* arrived back in Ship Cove on October 18 and Buchan immediately set about preparing the vessel for wintering over in the Bay of Exploits. The sails were dried and taken in and then folded and stored below. Chains fastened the ship securely to the shore. Marines were sent into the woods to cut trees for lumber and for fuel.

News of his arrival meandered among the residents of the islands and bays, although he made no effort to visit anyone outside Ship Cove. The few people who travelled in to call on him found a man less gregarious and energetic than they remembered him being only weeks previously, though he was as professional and courteous as ever. He attended his duties and supervised those of others with a meticulous and curiously distant attention to detail. He spent each evening alone in his cabin without company. In mid-November he sent Corporal Rowsell to the Peytons' winter home to request they send Mary down to the *Grasshopper* in preparation for the trek inland to the lake.

After the exertions of travelling along the coast in the last weeks of August, Mary had enjoyed a brief period of relatively good health on Burnt Island. But by the time the move had been made to the winter house her illness worsened to the point that she spent most of each day in her bed and could not make her way to the outdoor privy or even use her chamber pot without assistance. Cassie fed her weak broths and tea and sat at her bedside when her work allowed it, as she'd sat for months beside her dying mother, a book open in her lap.

When the order from Buchan arrived, Cassie argued with Corporal Rowsell and with John Senior about the wisdom or necessity of moving the sick woman to Ship Cove while she was in such a condition. "She'll not be making a trip up any river," she said.

Rowsell nodded. "No miss," he admitted, "that's true enough. But there is a surgeon aboard the *Grasshopper* might offer her some relief."

Cassie looked at the marine. He had been present or in the wings during all the events of recent months and she had taken no notice of him. A head of dark frizzy hair, deep-set eyes under a large brow that disguised their clear blue colour. He stood with his hands clasped behind him and she had never seen him stand in any other posture. He had a look of resigned dignity about him, as if the hands were actually tied behind his back and he was perpetually making the best of circumstances beyond his control. She said, "Promise me she'll be properly looked after."

He nodded again. "I promise to do what I can to ensure it."

John Senior accompanied Rowsell and the two other marines to Ship Cove. From there he would head inland to bring John Peyton down from his trapline for the expedition to the lake. The men outfitted a sledge with fur blankets to carry Mary across to Buchan's vessel and they waited outside then while Cassie prepared the Beothuk woman for the trip.

Mary was so exhausted by her illness that she was unable to comprehend why she had to get up out of bed and where exactly she was going. Cassie helped her into a sitting position, lifting her legs over the side of the bed, and even this effort brought on a fit of wet hacking that ripped at her like an oiled blade ragging through lumber. Cassie sat beside her with an arm across her shoulders and held a cloth filthy with dried and drying blood to her mouth. She could feel the woman's bones through her skin, their effort to hold together under the barrage of convulsive coughing. Cassie recalled the grip of Mary's hand on her wrist that first afternoon in the Peytons' kitchen, the fierceness of it and the wild look in her eye that Cassie had thought of as *Indianness*, when it had been nothing more or less than terror, the desperate kernel of a will to live when it seemed certain she would not. All that energy was bled from her now. The fear. The resolution.

In the kitchen Cassie helped Mary into her coat and boots and handed her the cloth package of leather clothes she had been wearing when Peyton and his party tracked her down on the lake-ice the previous March. She had folded the sixteen pairs of blue moccasins among the clothes before tying the package shut. John Senior came to the door to help her down the path and she reached for his arm. When she saw the white men waiting with the sledge she turned to Cassie. She said, "Mary go home."

Cassie nodded. "Goodbye Mary," she said.

There was a week's interval between John Senior leaving Mary in the hands of Buchan at the *Grasshopper* and bringing his son down from the trapline to Ship Cove. By the time they returned, Mary had been set up in a large room aboard ship with a buzaglo stove for heat. To Buchan's eye, she was genuinely delighted to see Peyton when he was shown into her room and the two talked quietly together. Her English was stunted but surprisingly effective, pared to its blunt essentials — subject-verb-object, the relentlessly present tense. Buchan set about boiling water for tea and exchanging occasional words with John Senior, whose English, he thought unkindly, was stunted in a much less obvious fashion. Mary fell asleep as he passed mugs to the men and they carried their chairs to the furthest corner of the room to avoid disturbing her.

The weather, which earlier in the season promised a harsh fall, had turned surprisingly temperate. Peyton told Buchan that the River Exploits was open almost the entire distance they had just come down, with only the thinnest runners of ice at the banks that would be treacherous for sledges.

"We'll have to wait until the frost comes on," Buchan said.

John Senior shook his head. "That one is thin as the rames of mercy." He nodded towards the bed where the Beothuk woman lay. "No way she'll make it through to the lake alive."

Buchan said, "You say that almost as if you cared one way or another."

John Senior gave his curious half-choked bark of laughter, placed his mug on the floor and then walked across to the door. His huge stooped figure disappeared in the rush of light as he opened it and walked outside.

Peyton cleared his throat and tipped his chair onto its back legs, rocking gently there for a moment. "What does the surgeon give for her chances, Captain?"

"He thinks a goodly number of people would have long ago been carried off by a consumption such as hers." He stopped what he was saying and stared at the man beside him. They listened a while to the wet seethe of Mary's breathing. Buchan shook his head and raised his mug to his chin to blow onto the steaming liquid. "We have taken the tragedy of an entire race of people, Mr. Peyton, and cheapened it with our own sordid little melodrama."

Peyton had to stifle an astonished grin. There was something pathetic in the officer's earnestness, he thought, and it surprised him to see this. He nodded slowly. He said, "I think perhaps that is the English way."

"I," Buchan whispered, "am not English." He sipped at his tea and made a face. After a minute of silence he said, "That girl you saw in Poole, the little Red Indian, do you remember?"

Peyton nodded.

"Do you know how she wound up there?"

"Richmond was the one got hold to her, I believe. Says he found her wandering alone out on one of the bird islands."

Buchan shook his head. "He found her. A child. Thirteen leagues out on the Atlantic."

"So he says."

"He must have killed the rest of her family to get her, I expect."

Peyton raised his shoulders. No one had ever said as much before, though everyone believed it to be true. "I expect he must have," he said.

Buchan nodded slowly and then looked across at Peyton. "Whatever became of her, I wonder?"

He cleared his throat again. "She died, sir. There was a write-up in the paper within the year. Scarlet fever, if I recall."

The following week continued unusually warm, and it was decided that even if weather conditions became immediately more favourable, they couldn't hope to leave in less than a fortnight. Peyton and his father made preparations to head back to their winter house and Buchan said he would send for them as soon as it looked likely the expedition could set out. Peyton stopped in to see Mary the morning they left and she held his hand and made him promise to return, even though he had never suggested he would do otherwise.

"You get well now," he said to her and she nodded emphatically, and they contented themselves with these small fictions they offered one another like a ritual exchange of gifts.

The two men walked slowly in the lee of the woods towards the winter house, along wide stretches of beach and through poorly marked forest trails where sheer cliffs or sharply rafted pans of ballycatter made shore travel impossible. Twice through the day they stopped to boil a kettle of water and smoke pipes while gulls skirled overhead.

John Senior said, "When do you think we'll be heading back there?"

"You say that," Peyton answered in a Scottish brogue, "as if you cared one way or another."

"The little prick."

Peyton shrugged. "He left us alone."

John Senior said, "So he did." He had never asked his son what arrangement had been made, what leverage used, what information dangled as bait or blackmail to make Buchan return to St. John's and state publicly that their party was fully justified under all circumstances in acting as they did. That no charges or additional investigation into the incident were warranted. He seemed to prefer not knowing.

Snow came down as they started out on the final leg of the journey. "The old woman is picking her goose now," John Senior said. The thick windless fall muffled the sound of the ocean to one side and the forest to the other. They strapped on the Indian rackets they carried with them and trudged into the near silence. By dusk they were within sight of the house. The animals in the closed shed whimpered to them as they walked by.

They pushed through the door into the bone-cold chill and Peyton called, as if Cassie might simply be napping in another room. He walked to the foot of the stairs and sang out to her again. Her trunk in the parlour was carefully packed full of her books and clothes, waiting, Peyton assumed, to be sent for. A rifle had been taken and a pair of Indian rackets, along with a pack and old winter clothing belonging to John Senior. The old man started the makings of a fire and Peyton sat on the daybed in his boots and coat. "She's gone," he said.

"I can see that," John Senior said. He knelt at the fireplace. He said, "There's no telling what all else she made off with or how long she's been gone. Perhaps you should go look in on the animals."

They spent the next weeks wandering around the house and property with the aimlessness of icebergs adrift among the islands. They propped up a length of fence at the back of the property, cleaned out the stalls in the animal's shed, went into the woods for lumber that could be planed to barrel staves, but there was no narrative to their days. The house fit them awkwardly, like familiar clothes put on after a long wasting illness. John Senior started drinking earlier each day until he'd begun having a shot of rum as soon as he came downstairs from his bed in the mornings. Every night he woke in the grip of his nightmare, yelling *Stop it, would you, for the love of Christ, stop it.*

Peyton took to reading through half the afternoon and in the evenings by candlelight as well, a habit he hadn't indulged in since he was a teenager. He dug through Cassie's trunk to look for books she'd treasured, Gray's *Poems*, Johnson's *Lives of the Poets*. He realized early on there was no comfort to be found in the exercise, but he persisted in it as a kind of penance.

Near the bottom of the trunk he discovered the handwritten copies of *Othello* and *The Tempest* she had given him. He lifted the sheaf of papers onto his lap. They were stored in his room the last time he'd laid eyes on them. Cassie obviously intended to take them away with her.

He carried the plays to the table and began leafing through the pages, studying the handwriting rather than the words themselves, the lines sloping slightly across the unlined paper. On the back of the title page of *The Tempest* he found a rough sketch of the Bay of Exploits, the winter and summer houses pencilled in. It reminded him of the map Mary had drawn for Buchan. As in that map, a stick figure stood beside the summer house on Burnt Island. There was a line of strange words in Cassie's handwriting down one side of the page. *Adenishit. Baroodisick. Gidyeathuk. Mamasheek. Messiliget-hook.* John Senior glanced at it briefly when Peyton asked about it, but claimed never to have seen it before or to know why it was drawn or what the words might mean.

He came back to it often, studying the particular features. Was that a fence of some sort drawn in at Charles Brook? Did Cassie ask Mary to draw this?

Had she done it herself? The map and its details were clues, he thought, but the story they hinted at evaded him.

One night John Senior, from his chair next to the fire, broke a fathom's length of silence by saying, "Maybe it's about time you found yourself a wife, John Peyton."

Peyton looked up from the circumference of candlelight on the table, his hands on the edges of the map. "Perhaps you're right about that," he said.

On December 14, Joseph Reilly arrived at Salmon Arm from Charles Brook. "Hello the house!" he shouted as he came up from the landwash.

Peyton and his father came outside in their shirtsleeves to greet him. The pinover across his face was wreathed with ice where the steam of his breath had frozen in the open air. He seemed surprised to see them. "God bless the mark," he said, shaking their hands. They got him inside and out of his coat at the fire and they plied him with rum and a plate of salt fish and brewis drenched in pork fat.

"How is your house now," John Senior asked. "How is Annie Boss?"

"Expecting again is how she is. We can't keep clear of it long enough to catch a breath."

They gave him another full plate of food. When he was satisfied and sat back in his chair he said, "I heard you had gone down the river with Mary. I come to look in on Cassie, help her clean the byre."

Peyton said, "The Exploits is open seven miles into the country. We'll need a good spurt of cold before anyone gets to the lake this year. Buchan is going to send for us when the weather turns."

The mention of the officer had them both nodding into their laps.

"Your man now," Reilly said. "Has he had much to say about it all?"

"Not a word, Joseph."

"I owe you a debt then."

Peyton turned to look at his father who was dropping off in his chair, a glass of rum tipping in his lap. "I would say we've more or less straightened our accounts at this point."

After he got John Senior up to his bed, Peyton stoked the fire and refilled Reilly's glass, then his own. They sat in silence a while. The house timbers ticked and creaked in the wind.

"You haven't asked after her," Peyton said finally.

He looked up, startled. "After who?"

There was no one Reilly could have heard news of the expedition from besides Cassie. He said, "She sent you to look in on the animals, Joseph."

Reilly looked down at his hands in his lap. The scars hidden under the palm of the opposite hand. "No," he said. "No, she came by." He nodded. "A fortnight past or nearly, I was on the line. She stayed two nights with Annie. We haven't heard talk of her since. I thought she might have come back to the house here."

"She carried off a sledge, a full kit of materials."

"I don't know more than what I'm saying. She was always one to keep her counsel." He stared across at Peyton. "You know how she is."

He nodded slowly. "You won't be lying to me now, Joseph."

Reilly turned his face to the fire. He said, "Leave her go, John Peyton."

"Is she at your place?"

Reilly shot him a wide-eyed stare and just as quickly looked away, shaking his head.

"You maggoty little mick," Peyton said.

The Irishman stood up from his chair. He touched his hips and belly briefly, as if he was expecting to find pockets he could shove his hands into. "My oldest is near big enough to take a share of work these days," he said. "I've been thinking to go on the plant for myself next season, have Annie and the boy do the shore work."

Peyton refused to look at him.

"You'll need to be finding another head man is what I'm telling you, John Peyton." He tapped his palm three times against his thigh. He cast aimlessly around the room a moment and then settled on Peyton in his chair. "I'll be off for home first thing," he said. "You tell Mary that Annie and me were asking."

At two minutes to midnight on Christmas Eve, Peyton stepped outside the doorway with a rifle. He raised the musket to his shoulder and counted calmly backwards from one hundred, firing into the night sky as if he was shooting at the stars and then stood waiting for the replies along the coast. Sharp pops followed by a softer chorus of echoes. He closed his eyes as if trying to discern a particular voice among a crowd of voices.

By Christmas morning the temperature had plummeted to twenty-five degrees below zero. Peyton woke to a beard of frost on the blankets near his mouth. The water in his wash basin, even the piss in the honey bucket under his bed, had frozen solid. He shook the stiffness out of his pants and shivered into a shirt and thick sweater. Downstairs a fire was already laid and spitting in the fireplace, a kettle of water on to boil above it. Peyton called to his father and then went to the windows to look for him.

John Senior was walking up from the animal shed, an axe in one hand, a goose held by its webbed feet hanging from the other. A steady spray of blood from the bird's neck unspooled like a thread being left to mark the path up to the house. Outside the door the old man placed the axe upright against the house and then knelt to pluck the down free of the warm carcass. He didn't see his son at the window. His hands were bare and red with the cold.

Fifteen minutes later he came into the house with the naked goose. He blew snot into the palm of his hand and wiped it across his pantleg. "A week of this," he said, "and we'll be getting word from Ship Cove."

Peyton could smell rum on his breath, a sharp sour twist in the cold air of the kitchen. He said, "You'll have to stay behind to watch the animals when I go."

The dead goose hung limply from John Senior's hand. The last drops of blood from the neck spattered the wooden floor. He looked slowly about the kitchen, as if the thought of an extended period alone in this place had never occurred to him before. "I suppose you're right," he said.

The weather continued clear and very cold into the new year and near dusk on January 8 Corporal Rowsell arrived with two Blue Jackets to inform them the expedition would be departing from Ship Cove on or about the twelfth if all went well.

"How is Mary?" Peyton asked.

Rowsell was still standing near the doorway, his hands clasped at the small of his back. He shrugged. "Some days worse than others. She seemed fair to middling when last I spoke with Captain Buchan."

John Senior said, "Let them in out of the door at least, John Peyton."

"Of course, of course." He ushered them closer to the fire and they removed gloves and hats and slapped the frost from the sleeves of their coats. John Senior had already moved off into the pantry for more glasses.

Rowsell said, "We would do well to get off early tomorrow if that's convenient. In case of weather."

"Of course," Peyton said again.

The corporal nodded and looked around. "I would be happy to offer a report on Mary's health to Miss Jure if she's about."

"She is no longer with us," Peyton said as he passed a glass of rum.

They left before light the following morning. John Senior came outside to help them pack the single sledge and see them off. He shuffled around the tight circle of men without speaking.

"Well," Peyton said when they were ready.

John Senior walked up close to his son. He fumbled off a glove and began rooting in the pocket of his greatcoat. "Give this to her," he said, passing over the empty case of the watch they'd retrieved from the Indian camp on the lake.

Peyton looked at the gleam of silver in his hand, surprised. "To who?" he asked.

John Senior grimaced and turned his face away. He seemed in a foul mood altogether. "I got no more use for it," he said.

TWO

It was well on the way to dark and Mary's room was lit with candles when they arrived. The fire in the stove had been extinguished that afternoon so the chill would slow the process of putrefaction. The coffin was constructed of neat deal and covered in a handsome red cloth decorated with copper fittings and breastplate.

"She was taken with a kind of suffocation about 2 p.m. yesterday afternoon and I was called to see her," Buchan said. "I sat with her while the surgeon attended. Within half an hour she had recovered to all appearances."

Rowsell said, "Poor creature."

"She was dead by the time I came to her the second time. According to the marine attending, she was asking for you before she expired."

Peyton was still wearing his hat and coat. He said, "May I see her, Captain?"

The officer motioned to a marine standing at attention against the wall and he walked across to remove the cover and the coffin's lid. Peyton stepped forward then, taking his hat from his head and folding it between his hands. The light in the room was dim and undulated like a web of shadow in dark weather. Mary's arms had been folded on her chest, two bright coppers covered her eyes. But the details of her features, whether her expression was serene or troubled or indifferent, Peyton could not say. He reached to touch her face: the skin was already cold as candle wax and had the same peculiarly oily feel. It made him want to wipe the fingers clean on his sleeve. He said, "What does this mean for the expedition, Captain?"

"I was to return her to her people." Buchan raised himself slightly on the balls of his feet. "I see no reason to alter that plan."

"I would still like to accompany you, if I may."

Buchan nodded. He said, "We did everything we could."

"I understand," Peyton said. His voice broke slightly and he cleared his throat. He felt embarrassed to be standing there suffering his mild fever of grief. For the first time it seemed true to him that what happened to this woman touched something larger than his life, the fate of the few people he cared for. Without turning to the officer, Peyton said, "I feel I owe you an apology, Captain."

"At this juncture," Buchan said, "apologies would seem to be beside the point." He motioned again to the marine to come forward and the coffin lid was closed, then covered with the finely decorated red cloth.

A warm shift in the weather delayed their departure another ten days and conditions on the river were still less than favourable when the decision was finally taken to set out. On January 21, a party of fifty marines, hauling twelve sledges of provisions sufficient for forty days' travel, a neat-deal coffin and a number of gifts meant for any Red Indians they might encounter, turned their faces to a cold easterly wind and crossed the harbour towards Little Peter's Point. They were accompanied by an auxiliary party of ten Blue Jackets and an officer who were to assist in the initial twenty-five miles of the journey, as far as the first great waterfall, and then return to Ship Cove.

Much of the River Exploits continued to run open and the ice along its banks was broken and unpredictable and the party was able to cover no more than four miles on the first day of the journey. The second day they managed only three more, with damage to a number of the sledges and several members of the expedition soaking their feet through to the skin. By early afternoon it was apparent to Buchan that they would soon have to make a stop for the night.

Peyton said, "We're not an hour from Reilly's old trapping tilt. It's been abandoned years now, but it might serve for the ones that have gotten themselves wet."

Buchan nodded. "Take Rowsell ahead and see if you can make something of the place, get a fire started. We'll be along directly."

The two men set out at a near trot and made good time along the shoreline. They both smelled the woodsmoke before they came within sight of the tilt and remarked upon it. Rowsell worried it might be a group of Red Indians, but Peyton assured him they were too near the coastline for that to be the case. He thought it was probably one of his furriers making use of the camp for the night.

As they came up towards the tilt from the riverbank Peyton shouted a greeting. The snow around the building was trampled and well used, a fine stack of split wood was laid against an outside wall. When he called again she came to the door and stood under the lintel, staring down at them where they had stopped.

"Good afternoon, miss," Rowsell said.

After Rowsell and the other marines had come to the winter house for Mary in November, Cassie was overcome with an uncharacteristic winter enervation, as if she was suffering the onset of a serious illness. But nothing more came of it. She sat listlessly at the kitchen window, looking down across the banks of snow rolling to the expanse of sea ice or watching dark rags of cloud skirr the air, the blue that emerged beneath them so bright and clear it made her eyes ache to stare at it. She managed to keep a fire running, but she ignored the chores that normally occupied her days. She couldn't even bring herself to read. When she ate her meals, she ran the flat of her hand across the surface of the table where Mary had drawn her map in Buchan's journal, insisting she didn't want to return to the lake except to retrieve her child. Cassie was still perplexed by that and puzzled over it for hours at a time.

Her second day alone in the house she began packing books into the trunk, without stating clearly to herself what she was about. She had a detailed list in her head of her entire library and checked each item as it was put away.

When she'd finished setting all her books inside she stood a few moments with her hands on her hips, then went up to Peyton's room and rummaged through his few belongings until she found the hand-copied plays of Shakespeare. She carried them downstairs to the table and leafed slowly through the pages. It had been a mistake to give the plays to John Peyton, to expect the boy to fall in love with them and not with her.

On the back of the title page of *The Tempest* she began making a list of the words Mary had taught her: the stars, the wind, thunder, islands. More than that she had largely forgotten. She sketched her own rough map of the Bay of Exploits: a scattered jigsaw of islands, hummocks of stone like obstacles strewn against the approach of the outside world. The crooked finger of salt water pushing inland to the mouth of the River Exploits. She drew a tiny box at Salmon Arm, the winter house snugged at the edge of the woods. At Charles Brook she used a series of strokes to indicate the hayfields above Reilly's tilt, the green grass she had cut and stooked to dry to straw. Another larger square on Burnt Island, a squiggle running to the shoreline where the freshwater brook rilled into the cove.

She stared at the map. Her refuge, is how she used to think of the place. Shelter. She had bunkered in on the northeast shore all these years, turning her back on anyone she thought might make a claim to her, deflecting, misdirecting, fighting to keep herself free and clear. And in the end she had failed.

She sketched in a stick figure beside the summer house on the map, as Mary had done in her own drawing. And just as Mary had, she placed a tiny figure at the level of her waist.

"A baby, Mary?"

"Yes, yes. Baby."

Messiliget-hook.

The child Cassie drew at her own waist was smaller than Mary's, a smudge on the paper that anyone else would have mistaken for an accident, a slip of the pen. Unseen shame. Crest wounding, private scar. She bowed her head until her face was resting on the table. Each time she thought she'd lost everything that mattered in her life, she discovered there was always a little more to lose.

The next morning she dressed again in John Senior's old clothing, starting out towards Charles Brook with a following wind that threatened to tumble her face-first onto the ice when it gusted up. At Reilly's tilt, Isaac, their oldest boy, was outside chopping wood. He stood and shaded his eyes as she came up the riverbank towards him, then turned to run inside for Annie Boss.

She spent two nights with them. The house was a cauldron of heat and activity and the clamour of the four children. Reilly was away on his trapline. Annie was pregnant again but hardly showing. The two women spoke little to one another during the days, Cassie settling into the morass of feeding and cleaning and comforting as if she had been hired on as a maid. In the evenings after the children had fallen asleep they sat together with cups of sharp spruce tea.

Cassie smiled across at Annie. "It's good to be here," she said.

Annie said, "You welcome to stay. Stay as long as you like."

She shook her head. "I'm going to follow Mary to the lake."

Annie Boss nodded. "Going to take some talk. Men not going to want to take a woman up the river."

"I'll go on through the woods to your old place. Wait for them there. They'll have no choice."

Annie gave her a troubled look and brushed her hands along the length of her thighs. "Hard chafe to the river," she said.

Cassie said, "I know the way." Then she said, "Someone will need to look in on the animals at Salmon Arm."

"Joe Jep go over when he come in. No worries." She nodded emphatically then and placed both hands to her belly. She said, "We going to miss you up here, Missa Jure."

Cassie looked beyond the two men to the river. Her face was grim, expectant. "I'd almost given up on you," she said.

Peyton said, "Mary's gone, Cassie."

She nodded.

"Captain Buchan did everything in his power that could be done for her," Rowsell said.

She nodded again. "Thank you, Mr. Rowsell." She turned and went inside, leaving the door open behind her.

Cassie had repaired the roof sufficiently to keep out the snow and boarded up the broken window and rehinged the door. An improvised crane served for boiling water and cooking in the fireplace. The floor was carefully swept, the bedding was tattered and insufficient to the weather but neatly made up. The wood outside she had cut and split herself. She had no candles or any oil to burn a wick of cloth and with the door closed the only light came from the fire. Her eyes, the hollows of her cheeks, were deepened and blackened by shadow.

"What have you got here for food?" he asked her.

"Partridge, beaver. I had flour for bread until the new year came in."

"We have men behind us that are wet and frozen," Rowsell said.

She nodded. "They're welcome."

"I'll take the news back to Captain Buchan," he said.

Peyton and Cassie shaded their eyes against the glare of sunlight reflected off snow that flooded in as Rowsell stepped outside. He pulled the door to behind him, shuttering the room into blackness.

"How many will need a place inside tonight?" Cassie asked.

"There's three men have got their feet in a bad way already."

She got up and began shifting her few pieces of furniture in the dark. Peyton cleared his throat. He wasn't surprised to see her, he realized. He had an urge to touch her, to place a hand to her shoulder, to hold the sleeve of her clothes between his thumb and forefinger. But she held herself off, as she always had, maintaining an old, familiar distance, and he found himself suddenly furious with her.

"It was Buchan you were with," he said then. "Buchan was the father."

Cassie gave a sad laugh. "That little man," she said.

"All along I thought —"

"I know what you thought, John Peyton."

He'd known the truth for weeks now and still it cut him to hear it, to have her state it so plainly. He sat still, regretting having flushed it into the open, wishing it back into the dark of his own head. Across the room Cassie's figure emerged slowly from the shadows as his eyes adjusted to the absence of light and he noticed her limp as she moved, how the lack of detail emphasized it, made it seem almost a new thing to him. He gestured at her and said as lightly as he could, "You never once told me about your leg, Cassie."

She stood with her hands on her hips a moment, staring at him, a furious crease to her mouth. Peyton put his hands to his knees and looked down at the packed dirt floor. "I was just asking," he said.

Cassie nodded. "My father," she said, but she stopped herself. He could hear the sound of her breathing from the other side of the room, the ocean rhythm of it, the jagged edges where it reefed and broke. She said, "I've never told anyone the truth of this."

"All right."

"My mother threw me down a flight of stairs when I was a girl. When I was twelve years old."

Peyton stared at her.

"I told her a story about my father. About the walking trip we took to Portugal Cove. We stopped by a lake to eat on the way back to St. John's and he took out his compass and his little brass container. He showed me why my mother fell in love with him." She paused there and they could hear the stiff needles of spruce branches scraping against the walls of the tilt. She said, "I thought my mother would protect me."

Peyton nodded in the near dark and he went on nodding for a long time.

"You wanted to know," she said finally.

There was a silence between them as Cassie carried on aimlessly shifting chairs. She straightened suddenly and turned to him. "I have stopped bleeding," she said. "My monthly," she clarified. "I haven't bled in years."

╅╤

Peyton, the two officers and those men most in danger of frostbite spent that night inside the tilt. It was the first time Peyton had ever slept in the same room as Cassie and he lay awake through hours of darkness, trying to disentangle the delicate skein of her breathing from the sounds of the others, the raw snoring, the discontented sighs as they shifted positions. In the morning Cassie dressed in the winter clothes she had taken from the Peyton house and walked down to the river with the men.

Buchan had tried to reason with her, but stopped short of refusing her permission to join them. "You understand," he said, "that we do not have the resources to offer assistance even should you require it."

Peyton said, "I'll watch out for her."

"I'll be fine," Cassie said.

It took four more days to reach the waterfall and convey the sledges and their contents up the Indian path, then across the marsh to the riverbank. Four men carried the coffin, which had been carefully wrapped in canvas to prevent damage during the trip. Each man stepped upward individually to find footing among the loose stone and ice, like a cat gingerly picking a way through fresh snow.

The following morning the auxiliary party left to return to the coast, along with one man suffering from frostbitten feet. The rest of the expedition made camp on the spot for two days while the sledges, which had been severely damaged, were repaired. Several had to be abandoned and three catamarans were fashioned out of green spruce and alders to replace them. At night the noise of ice cracking under the force of running water further up the river shook and echoed like artillery fire.

On January 31, five men including Buchan went through the ice and were soaked to the waist in the freezing current. A camp was struck and the men stripped off their clothes beside a fire while Peyton and Rowsell went forward to reconnoitre for the following day's travel. They crossed the river a mile above the camp and Peyton was climbing a tree to observe conditions beyond a point of land when the ice began to seethe like the skin of an animal infested with lice. It lifted and settled and seemed then to move in several directions at once.

Rowsell said, "Mr. Peyton, sir."

The ice was moving quickly in a honeycomb of large pans. They had to recross the river or risk being cut off from the party and its supplies. Several inches of water ran overtop from the river above and they soaked their feet as they ran. The pans gathered and separated in an unpredictable rush and the two men who had started out one behind the other were soon several hundred feet apart. They shouted to one another as they continued picking a way towards the far shore, the sound of their voices running between them like a cable they clung to until they'd gained solid ground.

By the time Peyton crawled up off the ice, Rowsell was out of sight around a slight bend in the river and he moved in that direction as quickly as he could in his wet boots. He found the corporal sitting on the riverbank, staring across at the opposite shore.

"Are you all right, Rowsell?"

The man looked up at him, his eyes hooded by the large brow of his forehead. "You'll pardon me for speaking freely," he said.

Peyton nodded.

Rowsell shook his head. "What a bastard country you live in, sir."

The ice had moved them more than half a mile down the river while they crossed and left them only several hundred yards to walk to reach the camp where they sat wrapped in blankets beside the fire while their pants and boots dried over the heat. The force of pent-up water bursting through the ice had flooded the shore on both sides of the river, and the sledges which had been pulled up onto a bed of alders close to the bank were nearly washed away before the marines hauled them to safety further in the woods. Some of the expedition's bread was ruined with wet in the process. The catamarans they had built were by this time battered to the point of uselessness and it became clear that not enough supplies could be hauled into the lake for the entire party. Buchan decided that a midshipman and thirteen marines, including two men who had developed badly frostbitten feet, would turn back to the coast the following day with packs of supplies to get them there.

Late that evening he found Cassie sitting apart beside one of the fires built up in the camp. She had wrapped her back and her head in a blanket and had thrown open her coat at the front to let the heat of the fire reach her body. He stood over her.

"I'm sending a small party back to Ship Cove in the morning. I think it would be best if you joined them."

Cassie motioned to indicate he could sit with her if he wished. "I prefer to stay with Mary."

"These are not conditions for a woman —"

"Have I slowed you down, Captain?"

Buchan said, "There is likely to be worse than this ahead of us."

Cassie nodded slowly and stared into the fire. "I have endured worse than this," she said.

Buchan felt a heavy turning inside him, as if his heart was shifting, settling into an unfamiliar position. He said, "I had no idea about the child, Cassie."

"I wasn't speaking about the child," she told him. And then she said, "I will stay with Mary."

He nodded a moment and then sat still. He said, "You were not the only woman."

She looked at him.

"Since I've been married," he said. He stared directly into the fire. "There have been others."

"A navy man, Captain. Surely your wife could have expected as much."

"Perhaps," he said. There was a harsh note of ridicule in Cassie's voice, but he ignored it and went on. "Early on, perhaps she might have. But it seems I am very convincing. Over the years she has learned to think better of me." Buchan looked up into the darkness over the fire. "I've almost lost her twice now. In childbirth. Her constitution has become very delicate. I'm not sure how well she would survive knowing me for who I am."

Cassie said, "Men should be what they seem."

Buchan nodded and smiled briefly. He said, "I lost two marines on the Red Indian's lake, I'm sure you know."

"I've heard the story." She shrugged. She seemed too tired to maintain her animosity.

"I've started to dream about them recently. About their bodies on the ice." Buchan shook his head. "A friend warned me at the time that regret would find me eventually. I didn't believe him." He turned and waited until Cassie was looking directly at him. "I wanted to say —"

Cassie stopped him with a hand to his arm. "I can't give you what you want."

He pulled his head back slightly, surprised. "What is it you think I'm looking for?"

Cassie turned back to the fire. She shook her head. "I don't know. Absolution."

"A very Catholic sentiment, Miss Jure," Buchan said. He hoped she would smile, but she did not.

They sat without speaking a few moments and then she said, "I would ask one favour of you, Captain. When this is over."

"Of course."

"I would like to come to St. John's in the spring when you leave."

"As you wish," he said.

"There's a trunk of mine at the Peytons' winter house."

"I will send the cutter to retrieve it." Buchan pushed himself slowly to his feet and turned away from the fire, then stopped. He lingered a moment with his back to her, waiting. Even two steps out of the circle of light the air was cutting, relentlessly cold.

Cassie said, "I didn't intend anyone to know of what passed between us."

A crow spoke in the trees, a harsh ratcheting sound like the dark turning a notch closer around them.

"I never expected less of you," he said.

⧾⧾

In the morning a portion of the remaining bread, pork and rum was buried for use on the return journey and the expedition continued upriver with only four of the original twelve sledges. Members of the party carried what couldn't be loaded onto the sleighs in knapsacks.

The ice conditions improved with the cold weather over the next four days and they made good progress up the river. On February 6, Buchan and Peyton came upon the tracks of Indian rackets during a late afternoon reconnoitre, but soon lost them on hard ice. Two days later they reached a storehouse constructed near three mamateeks, all of which gave the appearance of recent use and a hasty departure. One of the firepits, they guessed, had been used within the previous two or three days. Nearly everything of use or value had been stripped from the dwellings and from the storehouse as well. The tracks of the sledges used to cart away the food and furs were still evident. They found several paunches, liver and a quantity of caribou skins concealed in the snow. A raft of asp logs that was thirty feet in length and nearly five feet broad was abandoned beside the storehouse.

"What do you make of it, Mr. Peyton?"

"I'd say they know we're coming."

Buchan pawed at the snow with the toe of his boot. "Clearly they do not expect we are bringing good news."

The marines milled about the site. Cassie sat at one end of the raft, her head bowed almost to her knees.

"Do you think she'll make it to the lake?"

Peyton turned his head in the direction Buchan indicated with his chin. "Yes," he said.

At the base of the second waterfall additional stores were put away for the return trip, and two miles short of Badger Bay River everything but food for two weeks' travel, the neat-deal coffin and the gifts intended for the Beothuk were left behind. Above Badger Bay River water flowed freely over the ice and obscured all sign of the Beothuk retreat towards the lake, although there was no indication they had left the river for the forest at any point short of it.

On February 11, they reached the head of the lake, twenty-two miles distant from the second waterfall. They stopped there to refresh themselves with food and tea and then set out across the lake. At three o'clock in the afternoon they reached the camp the Peytons had surprised on a bright March morning the previous spring. There was no sign that anyone was on the lake but the party of white men themselves.

The naked frames of two of the mamateeks still stood. The third had been taken down and its materials used to construct a smaller shelter nearby. Buchan was the first to go inside, along with Peyton and Cassie. It was a tomb of sorts, a body on a raised dais wrapped in a shroud of canvas rubbed with red ochre and surrounded by spears, a bow and quiver of arrows, pyrite stones. There was a piece of linen that Cassie picked up and unfolded. The name *Peyton* was sewn into the cloth. The corpse was that of a large man by all appearances, easily six feet in height.

"This is your man, Mr. Peyton," Buchan said.

"I imagine so."

"I wonder what they've done with the other body?"

Peyton shrugged. He looked at Cassie as she carefully folded the linen and placed it back as she'd found it. "I couldn't say, sir."

Outside Buchan had two marines unpack a canvas tent from the sledges, and while it was erected next to the burial site of the Beothuk man, he had the coffin unpacked as well. The canvas and red-cloth covers were removed and Buchan inspected it carefully for signs of damage. The lid, which had been nailed shut, was pried free and they stood silently about the body of the woman. Twine had been used to secure the corpse in its place and the freezing temperatures had preserved her features throughout the trip up the river. There were a number of trinkets placed about the body, two wooden dolls that Mary had been fond of, gifts of jewellery and other things given to her by visitors who had come from across the northeast shore to see her.

Buchan motioned to have the lid replaced, but Cassie touched his arm.

"I have something I would like to leave with her," she said. She unbuttoned the outer coat she wore to get at the pockets of a lighter coat underneath. Peyton watched as she leaned over the body. When she stepped away he could see it was the medicine bag his father had stolen from the grave of a dead Beothuk on Swan Island — the gift he had tried weakly to refuse and then passed on to Cassie. He could name the contents still: carved antler pendants, a pyrite fire stone, two delicately fluted bird skulls.

If he'd thought of it at that moment, he would have placed John Senior's silver watch case beside the corpse as well, but it hadn't entered his head since finding Mary dead in Ship Cove. Two marines stepped forward to nail the coffin shut. The watch case was carried back to the coast and he discovered it sitting in a coat pocket months later. Turned it over in his hands then. Held it to his ear, listened a while to the endless nothing of it.

The casket was draped in a brown pall and raised six feet off the ground from a tripod of spruce sticks to keep the body out of the reach of scavenging animals. The cassock and leggings Mary had been wearing when she was taken were laid beneath it along with the materials that had been carried up as gifts for the Indians: blankets, knives, linen, several iron pots. The sixteen blue moccasins Mary had sewn of stolen cloth in her bedroom were placed in a row just inside the entrance.

The entire expedition stood about the tent after these gifts had been arranged and the flaps pulled closed and tied. There was a silence among them born of awkwardness, of an awareness they stood together in a moment they were at a loss to articulate, that even the importance of the moment was somehow beyond their understanding. Someone coughed. Snow complained under the shifting of feet as the silence crept on.

Buchan stepped away finally and orders were given to lay a fire and to cover the frames of the two shelters still standing. Peyton stood beside Cassie in the loud clap of movement that followed and he turned to stare out across the lake where he had chased Mary down and taken her hand in his own less than a year before. The sun was falling into the trees on the opposite shore and the pale moon was already visible above the horizon.

"I was thinking," Peyton said. "I thought it might be time I got married." After a few moments of her silence he nodded to himself. He wanted to ask if she would have had him if things were different, if she had come to the northeast shore from another life. But he was afraid of what her answer might be. He gestured towards the far hills, to the forest so green under the sun that it was nearly black. He shaded his eyes against the light, the white of snow on the lake. He said, "All my life I've loved what didn't belong to me."

He turned to face her then but Cassie was already moving away from him towards the trees.

The red ochre used by the Beothuk to cover their bodies, to decorate their tools and shelters and their dead, is a mudstone with the wet texture of clay. It occurs most frequently in tertiary deposits that are not common on the island of Newfoundland. The Red Indians gathered it from Ochre Pit Cove in Placentia Bay and Ochre Pit Island in the Bay of Exploits. There is a deposit between Barasway River and Flat Bay, close to St. George's Bay, which may have been used as a source. The ochre was mixed with oil or grease to make a stain that was applied directly to the skin and hair, to birchbark, to leather and wood, to stolen ironwork and canvas. When the ochre was unavailable in sufficient quantities, the Beothuk substituted a paste made of soil with a high iron content or a reddish dye extracted from alder bark.

Each spring before they dispersed into small bands on the coast, the Beothuk held an ochring ceremony on Red Indian Lake. Infants were initiated into the band with the sign of fire on their bodies, the dark light of blood. And at the day's end there was a time set aside for food and for singing.

There is no indication the Beothuk used drums in their ceremonies. They sang nakedly into the darkness from a deep well of songs that each man and woman had learned as a child and knew by heart. They celebrated what was simplest in their lives, the plain things that lived beyond them, the sun, the moon and stars, beads, buttons, hatchets, the rivers, the sea. They sang creatures through the forest around them, the caribou and bear, the crow, the beaver, the silver flicker of fox.

There is no record of the lyrics of these songs or the music to which the words were set. What remains of them now is the property of brooks and ponds and *marshes, of caribou and fox moving through the interior as they were sung two hundred years ago. Of each black spruce and fir offering up its single note to the air where not a soul is left to hear it.*

Acknowledgements

Anyone familiar with the history of interactions between European settlers and the Beothuk will see the debt owed to James P. Howley's *The Beothuks or Red Indians* and Ingeborg Marshall's *A History and Ethnography of the Beothuk*. Events as recorded in these two seminal sources had a huge influence on the physical and emotional geography of *River Thieves*. However, the novel makes no claim to factual or literal truth. Historical events have been shifted, conflated or otherwise altered and they stand side by side with events that are wholly invented. The names of many of the novel's principal characters can be found in Howley and Marshall, but the lives and motivations of each as presented here are fictions. *River Thieves* is a work of imagination.

There were other sources that helped shape the story as it developed, far too many to list. But I want to acknowledge in particular *The Dictionary of Newfoundland English*, which was an indispensable resource, and *The Newfoundland Journal of Aaron Thomas, 1794*, which I pilfered from freely.

Many people commented on earlier versions of *River Thieves* and I can't think of one who didn't contribute something that now feels essential to the book.

My agent, Anne McDermid, has been a tireless source of support, encouragement and advice, from first vague notions to final draft. Other friends read the book at varying stages and I'd like to thank (in chronological order) Helen Humphreys, Janice McAlpine, Marney McDiarmid and Mary Lewis.

I'm also grateful for the insight and editorial acumen of John Pearce at

Doubleday and Anton Mueller at Houghton Mifflin. The novel would have been something different, and lesser, without their suggestions and questions.

Martha Kanya-Forstner has been both editor and, for lack of a better phrase, guardian angel of the novel at Doubleday. It's her reading of *River Thieves*, more than any other but my own, that I've trusted in most.

Thanks to the Canada Council for the Arts and the Ontario Arts Council for being there.

A Note on the Beothuk

The aboriginal inhabitants of Newfoundland, a race of hunter/gatherers we know as the Beothuk, occupied or made use of most of the island's coast before the arrival of Europeans in the 1500s. While there is no way to place it with any certainty, anthropologists using a variety of measures now estimate the pre-contact population at somewhere between 500 and 5,000 people.

Before the second half of the 17th century, European settlement was concentrated on the Avalon Peninsula. Contact between the Beothuk and Europeans was consequently limited, although records suggest relations were precarious and often involved mistrust, pilfering and violence. With the spread of British and French communities throughout the island's coastline, the Beothuk lost access to much of their traditional territory. A combination of violence, exposure to diseases such as tuberculosis, and loss of coastal resources essential to their survival, decimated the Indian population. By the last half of the 18th century, the surviving Beothuk were confined to Red Indian Lake, the River Exploits and its watershed, and parts of the coast and islands of Notre Dame Bay on the northeast shore of Newfoundland.

The last known Beothuk died in St. John's in 1829. As Ingeborg Marshall writes, "Some individuals may have continued to lead a sequestered existence [afterwards], but as a cultural group the Beothuk had vanished."

About the Author

Michael Crummey is the author of three books of poetry: *Arguments with Gravity* (1996), *Hard Light* (1998), *Emergency Roadside Assistance* (2001). He published a collection of short stories, *Flesh and Blood,* in 1998. He has won the Bronwen Wallace Award and was nominated for the 1998 Journey Prize. Born in Buchans, Newfoundland, growing up there and in Wabush, Labrador, Michael Crummey now lives in St. John's.